CHIEF O'NEILL

A NOVEL

Ronan O'Driscoll

SOMERVILLE PRESS

SOMERVILLE PRESS

Dromore,

Bantry,

County Cork, Ireland

www.somervillepress.com

ISBN: 978 1 8382544 07

Cover design: Maurice Sweeney

For Lisa

This old anvil laughs at many broken hammers.
There are men who can't be bought.
The fireborn are at home in fire.

The People, Yes Carl Sandburg

About the author

Originally from Kerry, Ronan O'Driscoll moved to Chicago as a teenager in the 1980s. He returned to Ireland to study at University College Dublin where he graduated with a Masters in English literature. Ronan currently lives with his wife and children in Nova Scotia, Canada. Like O'Neill, Ronan found Irish music an important way to keep connected with his roots. It was through learning ¬fiddle tunes that he came to know of Francis O'Neill's compelling story. *Chief O'Neill* is his -first novel.

PROLOGUE

Chief O'Neill's Favorite

Chicago, Illinois, February 1902

"I've killed your chief."

The voice was muffled and high-pitched for a male.

Eileen Flannery, the police switchboard operator, frowned into the tangled mess of wires before her.

"I'm sorry, could you repeat please? Is it a message for the Chief you have?"

Eileen heard distorted cursing.

"You damn Irish. I could've killed you all once. I nearly did, you know. I cleared out this wonderful city and now look at it! Infested with you and..."

"Excuse me. Do you have a real crime to report? I'll ask you to stop wasting valuable police time."

Silence. As she went to disconnect, the voice snapped back at her.

"Chief Francis O'Neill is murdered. I killed him."

The line went dead.

★★★

Captain O'Brien had been looking forward to going home for supper when the call came through.

"It's Eileen, at headquarters."

Eileen's voice had a note of hysteria to it. O'Brien knew her as not normally given to panic. Many times, she'd dispatched officers to gruesome scenes with terse instructions.

"Is it true about the chief's murder? Have ye had any word from the chief?"

"Now, now, Eileen. What are you saying at all?"

"The chief!" she said. "A call came in saying they murdered him. Have ye heard from him?"

Standing at the telephone mounted to the wall, O'Brien looked around the busy station. The polished receiver to his ear, he covered the mouthpiece.

"Anyone seen the chief? Eileen says someone's killed him."

1

A murmur went through the room. James Markham, the chief's secretary, stood up in alarm.

"He went out around three," said Markham. "For some fresh air. Took his carriage. Didn't say exactly where. It was a quiet day so..."

O'Brien turned back to the telephone.

"He went out. Maybe he's gone over to you at Central. We think he left after three. Where did you hear that he was killed?"

Eileen erupted into tears.

"Poor Anna. Oh, the poor dear. Their youngest must be only fourteen."

O'Brien shifted his weight from foot to foot, unsure of what to say.

"Now, now Eileen," he said. "We'll find him sure enough. Did you call the house?"

"I did," she sobbed. "Of course, I did. There's no one home."

"Well. I'll get the word out and we'll find him. You can be sure of it."

★★★

Word spread through Chicago with the speed of the great fire of thirty years ago. At evening roll call, captains sent men out with instructions to be on the lookout for their missing commander. The chief's buggy was spotted in the barn at Fiftieth Street station. His driver, Henry Schmidt, was nowhere to be found. When his housekeeper reported that he was last seen leaving for the station early that morning, the alarm deepened.

★★★

McKenzie hugged himself in his thin navy-blue uniform, always tight on his big frame but never warm. He tugged on his helmet strap. In the chill Chicago winter, the thin metal provided scant warmth. He had to look twice in his notebook for the address.

"One Hundred North," he muttered, spotting a small house at the intersection.

He grunted and walked across the street. A cable car bell rang nearby. Its headlamp illuminated the deepening twilight. He noticed a little sign on the gate advertising musical education.

McKenzie pounded on the door.

"Police! Open up!"

His impatience grew as he waited in the cold. Eventually, the door opened a crack. A small wry man, his large head an incongruous match for his frame, peered back at him.

"Edward Cronin?" the policeman growled.

"Yes, officer? Sorry to have kept you waiting. I told the landlord that the rent would be covered in another few days. I've generally paid in full and I don't know why he can't spare…"

"Not my concern," barked McKenzie, halting the little man's fast-paced speech. "The chief. Superintendent O'Neill. Do you know his whereabouts?"

Cronin retreated into the darkness of his hallway.

"Francis? I ah…"

McKenzie pushed his way into the narrow hallway.

"Where is he?"

Cronin hid behind the glow of a lantern on a side table. There was something in his hand, behind his back. By reflex, McKenzie reached for his truncheon.

"What have you got there?"

McKenzie advanced, raising his cudgel.

Cronin lifted his hands. He was holding a battered violin.

"Please! Please, officer. You mistake me. Come inside, please. Come inside to the parlor. I haven't seen Francis, ah, the chief, in over a week or so. He's been busy gathering some Northern tunes, he said."

Cursing under his breath, McKenzie returned the weapon to his belt.

"Put that thing down," he commanded.

Cronin put the instrument on the table, the bridge was white with rosin.

"Why did you shrink away like that?"

"I wasn't sure if you, I mean, the members of the force, were aware of his, um, musical activities."

McKenzie grunted. "Everyone knows. That's why they sent me out here. He's gone missing. A call came in to say he's been murdered."

"What! How terrible. Come in. Come in. I'll make you a cup of tea."

McKenzie considered. He was supposed to be hunting for the murdered chief.

"No," he said. "Can you think of anyone that might want him dead?"

"To be honest, Francis and I had a minor altercation recently over the phrasing of a certain hornpipe."

There was an acerbic note to his voice.

"I'm sure that is neither here nor there."

McKenzie just looked at the odd little man, took a deep breath and warned him to stay home tonight. Walking away, he settled his helmet once more, ignoring Cronin's protestations.

★★★

As James Markham entered the ornate portico of City Hall, he paid little attention to the monstrosity of the building. Above the green glow of street gaslights, Doric columns bore down on the late evening stragglers on Clark Street. Markham looked with worry at the large lobby clock. Eight o'clock. His boss wasn't at Cronin's or McMahon's farm out in Palos—two favorite haunts. The young man scratched the back of his head in frustration. There had been no further report of an attack, just a single call to Mrs. Flaherty. James wondered where else could he be? It was his responsibility as O'Neill's secretary to always know his whereabouts. Now here he was reporting to an emergency session of the police board that their leader had disappeared. Markham sighed. The press hounded him with wild questions when he had made the first announcement on the missing chief. It might even make the front pages tomorrow– *The Tribune* for certain.

The long corridor was littered with wooden boxes of files and shelves. He opened the heavy mahogany door and entered the chamber. Various aldermen and officials were already seated. Tobacco smoke obscured the proceedings.

"There you are, Markham. You took your time. You can debrief us in a minute."

The chairman had preposterous sideburns. He directed the secretary to read some document or other.

Markham's anxious thoughts wandered in the tedium. He stared at the heavy wood paneling of the room. It reminded him of the chief's last words.

"A headache from the varnish they applied in the hall, James. Think I will go home early. Get some fresh air."

Markham hadn't paid a lot of attention. In truth he was also thinking of skipping out early to avoid the fumes. Where else would O'Neill go, if not home? His meticulous superior didn't often miss details. Capable and generous, the worst Markham could say about him was "occasional bouts of gloominess". Also, perhaps he was too stringent in his application of the law. In Chicago that meant enemies. Enemies who could well be lurking in this building. Just the other day, a sergeant had mentioned an alderman who had called about an appointment for some crony. The chief had loudly informed the politician when the next police exams were to be held.

"Mr. Markham, do you have any further information of the whereabouts of the head of the Chicago police force?"

The imperious tone broke him from his reverie.

"Jim!" exclaimed Markham. The other men in the large boardroom regarded him as if he had lost his mind.

"Who are you talking to, Mr. Markham?"

"Jim O'Neill! How could I have forgotten?"

He rushed from the room and out of the gloomy City Hall.

★★★

A rivulet of clear notes flowed from the flute. Then the same phrase played slow. Francis put down the wooden flute and raised his eyebrows at the younger man seated across from him.

"Did you get it, Jim?"

The large man nodded, scratching down musical notation quickly on lined foolscap.

"Know it at all?"

"It's not a Northern reel," replied Jim in the stronger accent of Northern Ireland. "My guess would be Sligo."

Francis clapped his knee and laughed.

"Not bad! Sligo is close. Eddie Cronin thinks it's a Galway tune. He should know as he's from around Limerick. Closer than either of us."

"Is it a reel or a march?"

"Not sure what it is. Might even pass as one of your strathspeys."

Jim looked back from under his brows at his superior.

"I honestly don't know where to put it," continued Francis with a chuckle. "We are grouping tunes by genre so this will have to go at the end."

"What's it called?"

Francis shook his head.

"No idea."

"Another one of those then..."

"How about 'All the Way to Galway'?"

Jim smiled, dipped his nib in the little jar of ink and inscribed the title on the page. Their table was littered with hand-written copybooks and music sheets, Jim's fiddle sprawled on top of them.

Francis stretched back in his chair and rubbed his eyes as he yawned.

"Better that than no name at all, I suppose. The main thing is the tune itself. I wonder how many we have for the book now, Jim?"

"More than a thousand, I should think."

"I really wonder if there will be much interest in our little collection?"

"Your name on the cover should help: the renowned Chief of the Chicago Police."

Francis snorted.

"You'll be on there too, Sergeant James O'Neill. Anyway, these tunes aren't about me or you or Chicago. We're saving them from being forgotten."

Kate Doyle bustled into the room.

"That last one sounded lovely," she remarked.

"Thank you, Mrs. Doyle," said Francis. "Do you know it at all?"

"Ah no," she said, "I just love hearing you men play. Reminds me of when I was small. I should bring Carter's children over some time to hear it."

"We can't have the mayor of Chicago's bairns in my dump of a house!"

"Not at all, Jimmy," she admonished him. "They'd love it. Besides, I reared them on Irish rebel songs. They know them all."

The two men laughed at this. She beamed back at them.

"Well, that's the best yet," said Francis.

Jim grunted and stood up. "D'ye want some tea, chief?"

"Don't you even think of it," she said. "I'll be back with some in a minute."

"Ah you're a treasure, Kate. I'm forever in your debt. The hospitality is always good at the Mecca."

"I'll give her a hand," said Jim with a smile. Mecca was the Chief's nickname for their narrow Brighton Park house. Many musicians had gathered to play here since their friendship began years ago. They retreated to the kitchen.

"Today's *Inter Ocean's* on the mantel if you want a gander at it," called back Jim.

Francis shook out the paper as he sat down. He chewed unconsciously on his bushy mustache while reading.

The door was thrown open and Markham ran in. He raced down the long hall to the kitchen.

"They're saying the chief's been assassinated! It is all over town. We can't locate him."

Jim laughed and pointed back to the front room.

"The chief's in there now. See for yourself."

Markham looked back to the parlor. Kate Doyle burst out laughing. Francis was halfway out of his chair.

"Sounds to me like that could be a rumor, James," he replied deadpan, straightening up.

"Chief! You've been here the whole time. But you said you were going home."

"Ah well. Jimmy and Mrs. Doyle are always good enough to have supper for me. I thought we'd have a bit of music after."

"You won't believe this, sir, but half of the force is out looking for you."

"What?"

"We had to make a release to press. The *Tribune* reporter said it will likely be on tomorrow's front page."

Francis groaned and sat back in his chair.

"Bring out that tea, Kate. Hope you made enough. Now. Tell me exactly what's happened."

PART I

SEA

CHAPTER 1

The Humors of Tralibane

The Convent of Mercy, Bantry, County Cork, Ireland, 1865

Hands sooty with charcoal, Daniel Francis O'Neill sketched the scene before him: the convent overlooking the town with the bay to its back. He hummed tunelessly to himself as he drew.

"What are you doing there, Daniel?"

The priest, a big enthusiastic man with youthful features, appeared from behind the bush Daniel was using for shade.

"Father Sheehan! I didn't see you coming."

"No, no. Don't stop on my account." The priest sat down on the bench next to the teenager. "Let's see."

Flustered, Daniel made to hide his drawing. It was on the flyleaf of one of his schoolbooks.

"Oh, come now. It is no secret you are quite the best artist we have. Well, this is very good. Very accurate."

The imposing building was drawn at a dramatic angle.

"You have captured the main features nicely. The Italianate style of the windows. The limestone bands near the base. Very good."

"Thank you, Father. I would love to know more about these things. I've read a bit about architecture."

"You have!" Excitement bubbled into Sheehan's voice. "I had a chance to study it myself in Maynooth. Ah, it's great stuff. Wish I could have gone further with it."

The Canon pointed across the bay.

"Don't say this too loud now but I think our convent is a much finer specimen architecturally than even Bantry House."

Daniel laughed.

"Well now," he turned over the tattered book Daniel had been drawing on, "Good and all as this picture is I don't think Sister Finbarr would be too pleased if she saw you drawing on one of her catechisms."

"I'm sorry, Father. I..."

Daniel hesitated. He didn't want to make up an excuse to his favorite teacher.

"It's alright, Daniel, I won't tell her. Lord knows we encourage precious little art with you lads."

"I don't need it anymore. I'm finished studies now and didn't have anything to draw on."

"Yes. I heard you were finished. What do you intend to do next?"

"I'm not sure. My father wants me to help out at home but I would like to be a teacher. Any further study is expensive though."

"How did you do at the exams for the higher diploma?"

"I did well, Father." Daniel looked away shyly. "I'm good at exams."

The Canon closed the book and handed it back to the youth. He looked Daniel over.

"Well, I have a proposal for you. You are easily the most talented boy I have seen in years. What would you think about furthering your studies in art?"

"It would be wonderful, Father," Daniel replied with a broad smile.

"Good. I happen to know the president of the School of Design in Cork. I'll put your name forward."

Daniel's eyes widened.

"You will?"

"Yes." He handed the catechism back to Daniel. "This drawing is proof of your talent. I can vouch for your academic skill. You'll have to get your father's support, of course."

A cloud rolled in across the bay. Daniel noted the timing of it. He thought of his six siblings at home and their father's grousing about "having to pay for them all".

"I know that mightn't be easy," added Sheehan.

Daniel's smile faded.

"If it helps, have him come visit me. I would be happy to put his mind at ease."

Daniel gave the priest a serious look, as if he were the one evaluating an over-eager student.

"I should be getting home now. They'll be waiting for me."

He got up from the bench and started down the hill.

"Thank you again, Father," said Daniel as he departed, voice full of false cheer.

★★★

Daniel basked in the warmth of the afternoon sun as he took his time walking the road home to Tralibane. The higher he went, the farther away the patched quilt of fields stretched to the west and County Kerry, but he paid little attention to the view. Cutting through a few fields to gain some time he eventually stopped to rest in an abandoned cottage. The roof was tumbled and gorse grew in the small front room. A family of badgers had made their set in the broken hearth. He was in no hurry to leave and started to sketch on another blank part of his book: a boat he saw in the harbor once. Despite himself, his thoughts kept returning to the words of the priest.

"The School of Design," he announced to no one in particular.

The moldy corners of the cottage took on a more sinister edge as the shadows lengthened. His empty belly got the better of his delaying and he snapped the book closed, scrambled through the broken window and back onto the dusty road—hedges full of fuschia pendants, flame-orange montbretia and red unripened blackberries.

As he traveled higher, cultivated fields became dotted with ash and sedge or overtaken by rocky copses of fir. The road switched back and forth. Occasionally, there was a view down to the town and the sea beyond. Daniel ignored the large world spread out like a map below him. Ahead of him, a barefoot child zig-zagged across the road.

"Seamus," called Daniel, catching up to the boy.

"*Dia duit,*" he greeted Daniel.

Daniel clicked his tongue in disapproval.

"In English, Seamus."

The younger boy bowed his head in assent and mumbled a greeting.

"Why are you walking like that?" asked Daniel.

"The other lads say it's how the cowboys in America walk up the mountains."

"That makes no sense."

"I don't know. Feels like I'm going faster."

Daniel laughed. They walked together up the hill. The younger boy kept up his zigzagging.

"Seamus, have you studied your Latin?"

"*Mun-say, Mun-saw, Mun-see.*"

Daniel raised an eyebrow.

"Ahh, why does anyone in Tralibane have to learn Latin?"

"To curse at the cows properly." Daniel snorted softly at his own joke. "Listen, if you ever want to be a real cowboy, you'd better study more. Come back to my class and I'll help you."

"Huh. Don't think cowboys have to learn much."

"Of course they do. Come on. The others miss you anyway. Why aren't you coming?"

"My father says it costs too much."

The boy hung his head.

"It's alright. You don't have to pay. Don't tell the others though."

"Really?" He brightened instantly.

"Yes. But you have to practice properly. The sums as well."

"I will," the boy promised.

Daniel chuckled.

"Alright then. See you at the shed in our haggard tomorrow. We might re-enact The Battle of Clontarf too."

"Oh that would be mighty. I like playing with those pikes and bayonets ye have."

"We got those off of my grandfather, Donald Mór O'Mahoney. The last chieftain in Munster!"

Seamus seemed unimpressed.

"They say he was a giant of a man," said Daniel. "I hardly remember him."

A cow regarded them from over a gap in the hedge, black muzzle sniffing.

"Who taught you all that stuff?" Seamus asked.

"Oh, books and going to school in town. But I'm done now. Timmy Downing is the only teacher I have left."

PART ONE: SEA

"You still have a teacher? But you're a man. You can do anything you want now."

"How old do you think I am?"

"25?"

"I'm only 16, Seamus. Anyway, there are always more things to learn."

"What can auld Timmy teach you anyway?"

"The flute and the right way to play it. We haven't even got to reading music yet."

"You can *read* music?"

"Of course."

Daniel laughed at his young student's open-mouthed shock.

★★★

The brook gurgled quietly beneath them as Seamus and Daniel parted at Tralibane bridge. A crow made a mocking sound as Daniel reached the family home, a large white-washed building with three chimneys irregularly placed, some distance from the bridge. Daniel recalled his excitement as a boy when his father and uncles knocked off one side of the house to add an extension. The yard, surrounded by outhouses, was off to one side. In the deepening gloom, a single downstairs window cast a light across the grass. Through the window, Daniel could make out a group of men around a table, backs bent as if wrestling a fractious animal. Strains of music made their way down to him as the front door opened. Polkas. His mother laughed back at the men from the open door. She threw scraps from a bucket out beyond the steps. A clutch of hens warily approached the offering. She hummed the tune to herself as she watched them.

"Mam!"

Daniel loped up the lawn to her. At the back porch, Daniel kissed his mother on the cheek. She shooed him away in embarrassment.

"There you are at last. The men have already had their supper."

"I can hear that," he said.

"I don't know what I'll do with you, Daniel Francis."

She put down the bucket and rested her hand on her hip.

"Now be sure and eat something before you get stuck into playing."

15

"Mam, wait 'til you hear my news," he enthused.

He pulled her fully outside.

"The Canon Sheehan. He says he'll put forward my name for the School of Design."

Her eyes narrowed.

"Where in the name of God is that?"

"It's in Cork. Near the Protestant cathedral. I can study art there. Canon says he'll try and talk Dad into it too."

She looked up at her son and took a deep breath.

"Fair play to you son." Her expression softened. "You've always been the smartest in this house. Come on inside now. We'll talk to your father about it later. After."

"Will you... Will you help me convince him?"

"I'll try. Go on now into the kitchen and first get a bite to eat."

★★★

The kitchen was plain with a stone floor. His older brother Johnny sat at the table with the *Cork Examiner* open. He did not look up from the paper as Daniel entered.

"I'm starved. What's left?"

"Don't know. There's a pot on the stove."

Daniel looked into it half-heartedly.

"How old is the paper?"

"Only a day. I was at the mart today."

Wondering why his brother was even more taciturn than usual, Daniel changed the topic.

"Are you not playing?"

"Ah, maybe later. They're going too fast for me anyway."

The music rhythm changed from jigs to slides.

"'Going to the Well for Water'," Daniel said, almost to himself.

"What?" Johnny asked, giving him a sharp look.

"The tune."

He did not reply. Daniel shrugged.

"Can you give me my teaching money back?" asked Daniel. "I have some big news. I'll be going to study in Cork soon and I'll need it."

"You are in your arse," Johnny muttered from behind his paper.

Daniel made a face at him and with his plate of cold porridge sat down at the table so he could see across the narrow hall to the parlor where the musicians were working to a frenzy. His mother had a distant smile on her face as she pumped the concertina in her lap, its drone gentle enough for the other players to follow her lead. His father sat across from her, a fiddle in his large farmer's hands so big and coarse they looked almost swollen. Daniel always thought it impossible such sweet and intricate playing could be produced by them. The set of tunes came to a finish. A surprised silence followed and the musicians looked away, suddenly shy.

★★★

Daniel missed the turn of the tune. His father darted a glance at him from under his bushy eyebrows. Looking away, Daniel took a deep breath and caught up on his wooden flute. He was impatient with playing music tonight. Usually, he was first to start and last to leave the table. Musicians made apologies one by one and left as the night wore on. Eventually, Timmy, the last remaining guest, put his flute down and stood up slowly.

"Won't you stay for a while longer, Timmy?" Daniel's mother asked.

"Sure I'd love to, Catherine. But we've to be up in the morning early. I promised the O'Donovans I'd give them a bit of a hand."

A general nod of understanding was made by the O'Neill family members still remaining.

"'Twas a great night though. Mighty playing."

"Thank you, Timmy," said Catherine. "Daniel, can you show your teacher out?"

"Ah, leave the lad," Timmy said, tucking his flute under his arm. He looked up at the ceiling and addressed them all.

"God! I don't know what I would do without the music in your house. That hoor of a parish priest is after banning the pattern dances below at the bridge and we have nowhere to play."

Daniel's eyes widened at the blasphemy.

"Don't worry, Timmy," said John. "'Tis only short-term. He'll be gone soon enough and we'll be back to old times again."

"I wouldn't be surprised if he tried to ban music entirely."

He was shaking with fury.

"Don't be worrying now, Timmy," said Daniel's mother. "Come on, you've an early start in the morning."

Catherine lead out the older musician.

"I don't know what kind of use he'll be to the O'Donovans tomorrow," John said with a laugh.

Yawns and stretches echoed around the table. John surveyed his family.

"Where's Johnny tonight?"

"Gone to bed," Daniel's sister replied. "I'm off myself."

"Dad. I have some great news," Daniel blurted out once his sister departed. He had been holding it in all night.

"Oh yes?" His father's voice was thick with whiskey.

"The Canon Sheehan. You know the one who helped me before? Well, he says he'll put me forward for the College of Design. In Cork."

Blank amazement around the table. His father blinked once or twice.

"What?"

"It's where you study art."

"Isn't it enough you waste time on Greek and Latin. What do you want to study art for?"

They looked at each other, Daniel's eyes wide.

"It's what I want."

"Want? Another month or two will be the threshing and everyone will have to help. Design? What in the name of God is that? I don't mind you teaching them children for a bit of extra money. But you're done with school now and have to pull your weight around here. Someday I'll leave you a piece of the land but you have to earn it. I'll not hand it out to some so-and-so who doesn't work for it."

"I always work hard," Daniel said, a catch in his voice.

"That's true enough. But you're always dreaming of something else. Or somewhere else. Even when you're playing. Why can't you be like Johnny and fix yourself on the land? Or at least go to the seminary and be a priest.

Johnny bought two fine yearlings today while you were off gallivanting. He warned me earlier you had some cracked notion about leaving for a school."

"John," Catherine warned, returning from the front door. "What if we met with the Canon and…"

"What if we what?" he interrupted. "Does he think we are made of money to be supporting these kinds of notions?"

Daniel worked his jaw in fury. A thousand replies wanted to blurt out at once. Anger got the better of him.

"You can keep your precious land," he spat at his father. He pushed past his mother and into the hall leaving shocked silence in the parlor.

★★★

In his room, Daniel threw a few clothes and books into a satchel. His little five-foot-wide wooden shelf normally stuffed with books looked like a smile with missing teeth.

Johnny stirred in his bed.

"What's all the commotion?" he asked. His voice was not sleepy, he had been awake and listening.

"I'm leaving. I'm sick of him."

"Are you now?"

"Not that you care. You've always been his favorite. And you told him I was going!"

Johnny looked at his shadowy form across the room.

"Look. Go out for a bit and cool down. In the morning…"

"No! I need my money now. You said you'd keep it safe for me."

Johnny was silent.

"Where is it?"

"I spent it today on those cattle," he replied. "What are you going to do about it?"

"I've been years earning that money," said Daniel in shock. "I'll tell them."

"Should have thought of that before burning your bridges with Daddy."

"You bastard!"

Daniel threw himself on his brother. They tussled clumsily in the darkness. In the midst of the shouting and pummeling, Daniel realized that his

19

fury was giving him the advantage. A part of him observed this coolly and didn't flinch from the violence. He landed a punch on his older brother who retreated with a shriek, knocking over their ancient dresser. Daniel went in for another blow.

"Get off him!" His father pulled him back and out onto the landing. The big man faced his son.

"Leave this house now," he shouted. The smell of drink was as hard as his words.

Daniel wiped a little trickle of blood from his nose.

"I don't care to stay," he replied. "You've always favored him anyway."

The big man raised his fist but Catherine cried out. She ran into the room and grabbed Daniel's bag.

"Go son," she said, her voice cracking with emotion. "Come back to us when things have calmed down. But go now."

Daniel took the bag from his mother and walked stiffly past his father.

The Little House Under The Hill

Daniel awoke to the badger's snuffling. It was not yet dawn but he could just make out the beast's form in the abandoned fireplace. He stirred himself from his uncomfortable bed of hard earth. A few remaining stars were still visible from the roofless dwelling.

Daniel groaned.

The enormity of what happened hit him again. Did he really say that to his father? Only hours before they were sitting around the kitchen table and then the impossible happened. They had always been wary of each other but at least they could play tunes together. Should he go back? He could imagine Johnny's sneering if he did. He cursed his brother aloud. The badger retreated, growling his annoyance.

Daniel stood and picked up the satchel he had been using as a pillow and felt around inside it. He rejoiced to find his flute still there. He felt also the precious diplomas certifying his passage of the teacher entrance exams. Then he heard an unfamiliar rustle of paper notes. Some money. He smiled ruefully. His mother. Where had she found it? He must write to her as soon as he had got safely away. Once he was enrolled at the school.

A riot of birds called to each other around the hills of Tralibane. This lonesome place felt like a heavy blanket weighing him down. He set his jaw and climbed out of the old ruin.

"Goodbye," he called back to the gloomy interior.

There was no reply.

The Priest And His Boots

Bantry, County Cork, Ireland, 1865

"Come in. Come in, Daniel," the Canon said as he opened his door. "Goodness, it's early."

Mute, Daniel followed the priest into his large home.

"Can I get you anything?" the older man enquired over his shoulder. "My housekeeper doesn't come until much later in the day."

"No. No, thank you."

"To be honest, I don't have much need of her," he said. "I like to manage these things myself."

The priest was still unshaven, his collar awry. His unkempt clothes made him look like an overgrown schoolboy.

"Well, sit yourself down there," he said as he ushered Daniel in.

The front room was covered in papers and books. Daniel had to clear a worn armchair before sitting down heavily. Despite everything he cannot help but notice the disheveled state of the room. Their own house always had the good room kept pristine. His mother would not have approved.

"Daniel," exclaimed the priest. "You look in an awful state. Are you sure I can't get you anything?"

Daniel hung his head.

"A cup of tea," announced the Canon. "It'll set you right."

Father Sheehan retreated to the kitchen. Daniel sank back into the armchair, feeling sore all over. His clothes and hair showed signs of sleeping rough. He eyed a large lithograph of the Acropolis on the wall.

"There you are."

The Canon returned with a teacup and brown bread and jam on a tray.

21

He perched the tray on a stack of books overflowing the table before Daniel. Daniel gave the tray a blank look, hunger warring against his regrets and misgivings.

"Go on," urged the Canon. "I can't understand how you Corkmen are always so reluctant to take a favor from another fellow," he chuckled. "You won't be forever in my debt or anything."

"Thanks, Father," said Daniel.

He slugged back tea.

"Although I am a transplant to this county, I am growing very fond of it. I'm thinking of starting up a literary and historical society here someday…"

The priest's tone was shy, far off. Only half-listening, Daniel wolfed down the bread. He barely stopped to wash it down with more tea. The Canon dropped the subject and sipped his own tea in silence. Daniel noticed the pause and looked up.

"I had a fight with my father. He won't let me go. I've left home."

"Oh." Canon Sheehan's features fell. "That's unfortunate. I did not think it would come to that. Poor John O'Neill. Do you think it would help if I spoke to him?"

"No, Father. My mother tried and he wouldn't hear of it. He has no care for what I want. Only thinks I should be a farmer like the rest of them."

The Canon sighed.

"And what do you want?"

"Anything but that. I want to be a teacher. I've passed the exams."

"College is an expensive route to take. Without parental backing, I can't really help you I'm afraid."

The Canon stuck out his big lower lip and set down his teacup.

"Have you thought of letting things cool down a bit? Think of your poor mother."

"No, Father. I'm a man now. I want to make my own way."

"Of course," Sheehan nodded. "Well, there's always the seminary. Our Bishop Delaney is a friend of mine. I could help you there."

"The Brothers?"

"Yes, Daniel. It's not such a bad life."

The priest looked around his untidy front room with a chuckle.

"You can do alright. Look at me! An intelligent fellow can do well in the church in this country. I was always mad for books and study, like yourself. That's why they made me a Canon. The church encourages it. Keeps a fellow distracted."

Suddenly, the boy burst out crying and stood up.

"I didn't want to leave like that. And my own brother…"

Father Sheehan's face went pale. He got up and awkwardly tried to comfort Daniel.

"Now, now. It all looks terrible right now but it will be fine. Wait until the day you come back as a man of the cloth and impress them all."

Daniel pulled himself away and wiped his eyes. He took a deep breath.

"You're right, Father. Thank you." He heaved a sigh. "I really am sorry for all the bother."

The Canon shook his head with vigor.

"Don't you mention anything of bother. Sit down there and finish that. In the meantime, I will write up an introduction to Delaney for you. He's in Blackrock, so you'll have to get to Cork. The mail should be going out from town soon."

Daniel collapsed down onto the chair, relief and gratitude getting the better of him.

"Thank you so much, Father. I don't know what I would do today only for you."

The priest made a dismissive sound as he bustled out, searching for his good stationery.

The New Mail Coach

Daniel tramped down School Road and out onto the broad stretch of Market Street. The remains of the recent mart were still evident. Only a stall or two was left as stray dogs picked at discarded rotten produce. A drunk sprawled asleep on the grass. For a moment, Daniel wondered if the man was dead. Daniel hurried past the dark and opaque windows of the workhouse. He checked the address again on the letter he had added to the precious store in his bag. Canon Sheehan had stuffed money into it and shyly refused to take it back. Chapel Street still slumbered as he strode down to the post office where the postmaster was just opening up.

"I'd like to book passage to Cork," said Daniel.

The wizened old dwarf favored him with a skeptical eye.

"Would you now?"

He disappeared back inside.

Daniel stared at the empty door for a minute then marched in after him and found the cantankerous little man behind a desk piled with papers and parcels.

"I have enough to pay for a trip to Cork. When does the coach leave?"

His voice rang out stern in the dusty shop.

The old postmaster looked affronted for a moment, mouth open. He considered the angry young man for a long while before replying.

"Eight o'clock."

"Is there a place to wait?"

"A place to wait?" He wondered aloud. "Her Majesty's Postal Service does not generally provide *waiting rooms*."

"Never mind."

Daniel handed over his money and walked outside. He had an hour. Time for one last look at the town—a quick tour of the harbor and a last longing gaze into the window of the music shop. When Daniel returned the red and black coach was nearly loaded. An overweight guard in a tattered scarlet and gold uniform idled by the carriage, elbow resting against the butt of a matchlock musket. A few other passengers were already squeezed inside.

"You'll have to sit up on top with the driver, sir."

The postmaster added the last with a sneer. Daniel had little choice but to climb up.

The driver was silent as Daniel climbed up beside him. One of the horses whickered with impatience. Daniel tucked his bag under the running board and settled in. The guard took a long time hauling himself onto his seat at the rear of the coach after the mail was secured.

"Aye up," said the driver to the horses.

PART ONE: SEA

Without ceremony, Daniel left forever the town of his birth.

★★★

Their pace was slow but steady, the road rough in patches. Once, they had to stop to clear a branch off the road. Daniel helped while the guard watched them. No words were exchanged between the driver and Daniel, who was too enthralled by the countryside rolling by. On road signs were places only heard of in the names of tunes: Dunmanway, Ballineen, Ahiohill. He wondered what tunes they might have there.

"We've a bit of a stop in Bandon," announced the driver.

Daniel started.

"Bandon?" he asked without any idea what to say. The driver had only responded to earlier questions with grunts.

"Yeah. Big town. Heard of it?"

Daniel just stared back at him.

The driver erupted with laughter.

"I'm only rising you. Do you know the saying: 'Bandon, where even the pigs are Protestant'?"

Daniel nodded to the familiar joke.

"You're awful serious for a youngfella. Where are you off to this fine day anyway?"

"I'm ah. I'm going to Blackrock to enroll at the Seminary. I want to be a teacher."

"A Brother?"

"Yes. I suppose so."

"Hah! Had them for a while. Cruel feckers they were. Half the reason I ran off from home. The other reason was my old fellow was a nasty drunk."

He glanced side-long at Daniel.

"Looks like you might be striking out for yourself in the same way."

Daniel made no reply, only frowned into the distance.

"You get to see a lot of different types up here," continued the driver. "I don't know about joining the Brothers but a clever fella like you could do well in the Navy. I was a sailor myself for many a year. Navy has teachers as well you know."

"Really?"

"Oh yes. Look, we're stopping at Queenstown today. Go down to the Navy ship and ask them."

"I might."

"Navy has no problem if you like women. Not like the church."

Daniel got lost in thought again. The driver cocked his head, awaiting a response.

"Sorry," replied Daniel. "How long were you in the Navy?"

"Eight years. It was tough mind you. But saved me from the gutter. Saw a lot of the world too. More than this arse-end of it anyway."

"I could give them a try."

"Like I say. Anyway, we're not going to Blackrock this run. The Seminary can wait another bit."

Daniel paused in thought for a long while. He turned to the now friendly driver.

"Do you like music?"

By the time they reached Bandon he was sore from playing while the carriage jostled along.

A Soldier And A Sailor

Queenstown (Present-day Cobh), County Cork, Ireland, 1865

There was a large gash at the top of the steep hill where land had been cleared for the new Catholic cathedral. Below it, Queenstown's ranks of solemn terraced houses looked out to sea and the military fortress on Spike Island. Between these, the *Hawk and Hastings* creaked with the gentle motion of the sea. Daniel walked up the gangplank and onto the gleaming deck. Uniformed sailors busying about deck paid no attention to him.

"Where is the commanding officer?" he inquired.

"Wot's that, son? We don't speak Oirish," replied a seaman.

"I. I was speaking English."

"Eh? No Oirish!" he shouted. His words were pantomime slow.

A few of the sailors were listening now. One laughed.

"You men, what is this delay?"

The loud voice carried down from the poop deck. The merriment ceased.

"This here gentleman would speak with you, sir," announced Daniel's antagonist. With a cruel glint in his eye, he inclined his head toward the officer descending to them.

"Well. What is it?"

The officer took in Daniel and the state of his clothes. He did not appear impressed. Daniel smiled, swallowing his nervousness.

"I have come to inquire whether you have any teaching positions open. I have my teacher's qualifications with me."

"Teaching positions?" the man repeated. He looked as if Daniel had asked for directions to the moon. His uniform was all gold braid and brass buttons, the cloth deep cerulean blue.

"Ah yes. Well, that is to say. I have passed the entrance exams, sir. I am not yet fully accredited."

"Her Majesty's Navy is not currently seeking any teaching staff."

A snicker erupted from Daniel's previous tormentor. The officer disregarded the sound.

"Hmph," he grunted. His voice went quiet. "You may enlist, if you wish."

He bent a little closer to Daniel, waiting. "Do you wish to enlist?"

For a moment, Daniel was flustered. All his earlier resolve and plans evaporated.

"Enlist?"

Most of the sailors stopped pretending to work and watched the exchange. Daniel stood up straight and faced the officer.

"Yes! I do want to enlist."

"Very well. What age are you?"

"Sixteen years old, sir."

The officer humphed again, turning away.

"Private, escort this man from the ship."

Daniel watched the retreating form in confusion. The sailor gripped his arm and started shoving him down the gangplank.

"Yer too old for us. Can't join the Navy if you're over sixteen, stupid Mick."

With that, he pushed Daniel hard onto the dock. Daniel stumbled onto the dirty wood, banging his knee. He picked up his dusty satchel and retreated along the busy wharf.

Shandon Bells

Cork, Ireland, 1865

Daniel wandered bewildered around Cork city, through the noisy bustle of Patrick's Street to the bridge over the broad river Lee. He paused on the new bridge to admire the ships lining the quays like carriages, a winter forest of masts and spars. Unused to sleeping rough and hungry, he was drawn to the spire of St. Anne's. It was the one landmark he knew—the steeple an upended telescope above his destination. He walked up the hill on the north side of the city, crazily humming a jig to himself. The streets here were steep and narrow with watchful curtains. Urchins at one corner crouched over a selection of little steel balls.

"Watch where oo're going, boy," they yelled at him. "We're trying to play ballahs."

Daniel mumbled apologies as he left the narrow street onto the square. Before him loomed the ornate entrance to the Butter Market. The place was busy with farmers, merchants and inspectors, conversing in the falsetto accents of the city. He was last here when his father took him when he was eight or nine. They traveled all night, cart loaded with stubby wooden firkins. He had watched with awe the weighing of the barrels in the round building called the firkin crane. It was shaped like an upturned tub and still struck Daniel as unreal. The inspector had looked down his nose at them before putting a # symbol on the tubs: Fourth grade. One stroke for each grade. Business done, no delays in the big city were allowed before they were back on the road home again. Looking back, he had imagined hiding in one of the wooden firkins to be shipped off to some distant exotic place.

There he was. Sean Hennessy. In intense conversation with a cluster of men. He didn't expect to see him but if he were anywhere in Cork it would be here. These days, Hennessy brought their butter to Cork on consignment. Daniel could just walk up to him and be back home by tomorrow.

"Come back, langer!"

A child tore through the crowd chased by a shopkeeper. Daniel slunk back to the shade of the colonnaded wall. A young woman bumped against him.

"Aren't 'oo a flah?" she said. "Fancy a go?"

She could be older than Daniel, perhaps younger. Her face was clumsily painted, her dress tattered. The buttons of her bodice were open. Daniel averted his eyes from her half-covered breasts.

"What do you mean?" he asked.

"A shilling and you can have me in the graveyard."

Her eyes darted up to the church.

"No," he said. "That wouldn't be right."

She shrugged.

"Feck off for yourself then."

Daniel recoiled and hurried away. Once he was out of her sight, he lingered where the firkins were lined up by grade to be collected for shipping out from Queenstown. He couldn't see Hennessy anymore and was too ashamed to try and find him. He felt menaced and confused by all the different people here. Disheartened, he looked back up at the black clocks of St. Anne's spire, shook his head and left.

★★★

The bishop's palace sat sedately on the banks of the river Lee. Daniel was ushered into the drawing room, considerably larger and better appointed than Canon Sheehan's, by a secretary in clerical garb. An old man rose slowly from an ornate chair and approached the youth. He proffered a hand adorned with a large gemstone. Daniel stared at it. Surely he shouldn't shake hands with a bishop.

"You are supposed to kiss the ring."

The voice was reedy but not particularly affronted.

"Oh. I'm sorry, your Eminence."

Daniel did the necessary veneration.

"At least they taught you the proper terms of address. Well, sit yourself down Mr. O'Neill."

Bishop Delaney shuffled back behind his desk. Daniel slipped into the

29

chair across from him. He noticed the opened letter before them.

"Father Sheehan speaks very highly."

It was almost a question, the man's voice sounded so querulous.

"Thank you, your Eminence."

"And you have your entrance exams passed?"

"Yes, your Eminence. Here are the papers."

The ringed hand received them weakly.

"Very well. How do you feel about joining the Christian Brothers as a teacher? It is a life of chastity and poverty."

"I would like to. I wish to be a teacher. I've always had good teachers. Your Eminence."

Delaney waved away the salutation and sighed.

"Please. Father is sufficient. Many turn away from the seminary after the first six months. Are you sure of this?"

"I am Father."

"Hmm. I am not so sure. You are still very young. Younger I think than what this certificate attests."

An inquisitive eye to Daniel who looked down at the desk.

"Why not come back in a year or two? After you have grown a little?"

Daniel looked back at the prelate in surprise. He hadn't expected this.

"Canon Sheehan has been a great example to me. I would like. I would like to be as well educated as him."

Thin white eyebrows arched.

"Would you indeed?"

"I would, Father. And a vocation. I have a vocation for the priesthood."

Looking down, there was a slight pitch to Daniel's words as he lied but his voice held firm. The bishop did not speak for a long while. A clock ticked loudly. Finally, another sigh.

"Perhaps you are not as immature as you appear. I think you will be more than capable for the Brothers. Sheehan would not put any urchin forward."

Daniel looked up in hope. Delaney looked away.

"Come to North Monastery tomorrow early. Before ten, I should say. I have to be away to Cloyne afterwards. Indeed, you are lucky to have caught me. In any case, I will make sure you are set up with Father Burke."

"Thank you. Thank you, your Eminence."

"You may go. I will see you tomorrow."

Daniel stood and turned to go.

"And O'Neill?"

There was a sudden hard edge to the bishop's voice.

"This is a commitment for life. There's no going back on it."

Daniel nodded, retreating from the drawing room.

The Jolly Corkonian

The boarding house room was riddled with damp. The bed, an evil stain fouling the humped mattress, smelled like something had died in it; but it was much better than a ditch.

"Are the sheets clean?"

"Clean enough."

Daniel clenched his teeth as tiredness threatened to overtake him.

"I'll take it, Missus. Just the one night."

The woman sniffed as she took his money.

"No other visitors and no food or drink in the room."

She closed the door, leaving him in the dank gloom. He searched for a place to hide his bag. The only precious things remaining were his flute and books. The bishop had held on to his papers. He assembled the wooden flute and began to play. Tunes flooded out of him. A dam burst and he played ferociously: reels, jigs, even an air he hadn't played in years.

"Oi! No noise in that room!"

The landlady's voice came muffled from below-stairs. Daniel stopped, flute poised over his lips. He took a deep breath and found the other half of the air gone. Sighing, he disassembled the flute and tucked the parts into his coat. He stowed his bag under the bed and went out.

Along the Mardyke, a warm light came from the window of an inn: *The Fox Hunters*. The painting of the fox and hounds was amateur. Inside were mostly university students out carousing, a thin fellow on the tin whistle in their midst. The innkeeper raised a skeptical eye as Daniel approached the bar.

"What are you having?" he asked.

"Oh, just food for me."

"We have stew for a ha'penny."

Daniel nodded and sat in a quieter part of the room. The food arrived and he consumed it, savoring every morsel. The drunken students sang bawdy songs and the odd chuckle escaped from Francis, despite himself. Eventually he left his solitary spot and went over to the others, asking if he could play along on his flute. There were looks of amazement followed by acceptance and laughter. Daniel had never heard anything like them in Tralibane but he quickly picked up the simple melodies of their ribald tunes.

After an hour or so the crowd thinned out. His companion player put down the tin whistle and laughed as Daniel trilled off a quick reel.

"Hah! Way better than my poxy whistle."

The remaining drunkards laughed.

"We know how you got the pox on it too," retorted one wag. "Go on and buy him a drink then!"

"Well," agreed the skinny whistle player. "What'll you have?"

Daniel put down his flute.

"Oh," he said. "I don't drink."

His statement was followed by expressions of shocked amazement.

"Don't drink? And you're a student?" the thin fellow inquired. "You must be a student?"

"I am. I will be. Tomorrow I start across the river at the Seminary."

"No! Your last night of freedom and you can't even drown your sorrows. Lads, he's a teetotaler like Father Matthew."

Another round of laughter. One of the group intoned:

The smell on Patrick's bridge is wicked,

How does Father Matthew stick it?

Followed by the raucous chorus:

Here's up them all says the boys of Fair Hill.

Daniel smiled to himself as he joined in, his troubles forgotten for the first time in days. They didn't bother him with drink again.

★★★

"Come on out! You've missed your breakfast."

A great dust-swarming shaft of sunlight streamed into his dreary room and stood at the foot of Daniel's bed. For a long moment he stared about, unsure of where he was.

"I said come on out now. I'll call the peelers if you don't."

Banging at his door. The landlady. A late night. *The Fox Hunters*. Leaving home. All the details flooded back. Daniel groaned.

"Alright. I'll be out in a minute."

He pulled on clothes that were the worse for wear. Opening the bedroom door, he can't believe he slept so long in that sepulchral bed.

"I said you had to be out by nine."

"I'm sorry. Haven't slept properly in days."

"That's no concern of mine. Out you get now. Unless you want another night?"

"No. No, thank you."

She came into the room, nosily checking everything.

Finally, Daniel remembered.

"The bishop!"

He grabbed his bag and raced out of the boarding house, the landlady's cries faint behind him.

"Bishop, me arse!"

Across the bridge again. Belly empty, he hurried up the steep hill to the North Monastery. The red brick of it loomed ahead of him as he ran. He couldn't help, despite his rush, admiring the contrasting bands of sandstone brick around the windows. Inside, wide stairs swept up from the main hall, dark oak paneling everywhere. He spotted a tall older boy and rushed up to him.

"Is the bishop still here?"

"The bishop?" asked the youth, cheeks raw with acne. "I think he's gone."

Daniel's heart sank.

"Can I speak to the Head? Father Burke, I think."

The boy shrugged and motioned for Daniel to follow. They walked to an office at the end of the hall.

"This fellow wants to speak to you, Father. Says it's about the bishop."

Inside, a man in a long black soutane stood at the window. He was staring with indifference out at the city and the river.

"Yes? What about the bishop?"

The priest arched an inquisitive eyebrow.

In a moment, realization dawned on Daniel. Something was wrong in the way the light cast itself on the priest's dusty clothes—the oppressive heavy silence of the school.

"Well?"

"I think I've made a mistake."

Father Burke shook his bland head, not understanding.

"I'll be going now," said Daniel. "Sorry to bother you."

Out On The Ocean

Salt spray stung Daniel's face as he stared out at the receding shoreline and the hills and spires of Cork faded away. Canvas flapped, ropes strained, timbers groaned and men cursed. Around him bustled the crew of the barque *Anne*. He leaned back into his task of polishing the brightwork. His hands were already red from rubbing brick dust into the cleats, bollards and other metal trimmings on deck. It was tedious work but he was happy to be at it. He could get nothing in Cork over the last week and had run out of money. Squally clouds scudded past.

★★★

"Why should I take you on?"

Watson, the English Captain, had quizzed him on the dock.

"I'll work hard."

"Any experience on a ship?"

"No, but I want to go to sea. I want to leave this city and see the world."

"I see," the man smiled. "We would be happy to have you as a passenger. Fare is not so expensive as all that."

"I can't pay."

"By Admiralty Law, no one's allowed travel free on the seas. You must pay a fare or we must pay you for a service."

"I can work."

The Captain paused for a moment in calculation, appraising the youth.

"I will give you three shillings when we arrive in Sunderland. You will have to do whatever my second mate needs of you—swabbing, whatever it may be. Think you can handle that?"

"Yes, sir."

"Good. What is your name?"

For a moment he hesitated. Then he looked straight at the Captain.

"Francis," he replied. "Francis O'Neill."

"Welcome on board the *Anne*, Francis O'Neill. Maybe we'll make a sailor of you before this voyage is done."

"Thank you, sir."

"Mind if I ask why you are in such a hurry to leave Cork?"

"I've nothing to keep me here and, like I said, I want to see the world."

"Parents? Family? Trouble with the law?"

His tone was one of idle curiosity.

"As I said, there's nothing to keep me here."

"Very well then." He clapped Francis on the shoulder. "Up you go. Mr. Dukes. See if you can put Mr. O'Neill here to some use."

★★★

Francis soon learned to make himself look busy or face the ire of Mr. Dukes. Despite this, he was enthralled by the mechanics of the ship, the indecipherable arrangement of the sails and spars above him. He daren't venture up the rigging like others on the crew but he watched with awe as they scuttled up the three masts to reef the sails. Their language was unfamiliar as well—so many things to learn. When the men were unfurling the sails before departure, they sang shanties. It made the work easier. He wondered if any of them had a fiddle or fife and tunes to be traded. He would wait for the night for that. *Why had he not given his old name?* He shook his head, took a deep lungful of sea air and looked back for the coast. He was surprised to find it gone.

CHAPTER 2

I'm a Poor Rambling Boy

Sunderland, England, 1865

"Unroll that hawser from the bitt," Mr. Dukes yelled at Francis.

Francis looked about in complete incomprehension.

"Ah! You crimson cur," cursed the second mate as he scrambled over to unfurl the thick rope.

"Now, now, Mr. Dukes. You were as green once surely," called Captain Watson from the quarterdeck. "Jones! Assist Mr. Dukes please."

A nearby deckhand jumped to assist in mooring to the wharf.

"Don't look so crest-fallen, Francis," the Captain said. "A few weeks voyage does not make you a sailor."

He walked stiffly down to the young man.

"Forty odd years I have been before the mast and I myself am still learning. These new steamships for example."

He shook his head.

"I saw one in Queenstown, sir. It was hauling coal. Had sails and a funnel."

"Blamed contraptions. I am to take command of one soon. Company orders."

"Is that so, sir?"

Watson made no response but to stroke his silvered whiskers, one eye on the men setting up the gangplank.

"Sir, we had an agreement before," supplied Francis. "When I first came on board."

The Captain nodded. He handed Francis the promised money from a billfold in his coat.

"So, you are arrived at Sunderland. And you are sundered from our service. What do you mean to do now?"

"I will find another berth. A good berth."

"Ah, very good. I recommend you be at the docks early. There will be captains looking for apprentice hands. You may use my name. Size up the ship before you take up with her is my advice to you. Same as with a woman.

And… Avoid steamships."

"Thank you, sir. I am very obliged for your help."

"Not at all. You're a good lad. You'll do well, I can see."

They shook hands. Then, without another word, Francis grabbed his bag and started to walk off the ship. Looking back, he saw Mr. Dukes spit overboard.

"Wager he'll be drowned within the month," Mr. Dukes said.

"Now now, Mr. Dukes. Now now."

The Captain called out to Francis's retreating form.

"Avoid steamships!"

★★★

One of the sailors on the *Anne* had told Francis cheap lodgings could be got on Flag Lane, but the entrance to the lane was so narrow it had no sign. He had to ask several times before finally finding the alley between a pair of grim warehouses. The street was a scattering of cobblestones amongst muck and puddles where peddlers laid out their pitiful wares. A grimy assortment that looked to have been picked from the low tide surrounded one toothless wretch. Further along were a couple of dingy taverns, the exterior of one with a drunken balladeer bawling a song at the entrance. Another establishment was fronted by a table with three cards on it. The tout asked all and sundry to try their luck. Francis skirted these diversions, finally settling on a lodging house towards the end of the lane. The peevish landlord looked on Francis with scorn but took his money readily enough. He ushered Francis up to his room—a long garret with four beds in it. A lump of a man snored in one.

"This one's yours. Any mess yeh pay for. Door closes at nine."

Dejected and weary, Francis flopped down on the bed staring up at the mural of cracks on the ceiling. It was not at all like his simple but clean room in Tralibane with its shelf of books where, in the quiet of the daytime, he could slip up and read. He thought of his mother and siblings, even Johnny and his father. He hadn't thought much about home on the busy blur of his first voyage. What were they doing now? Were they thinking about him? He turned his head toward the window and the noise of the street below.

The glass was lumpy and smeared, making everything distorted. The outside noise sounded like discordant music, a mockery of true melody. He failed to hear a tune in his head to counter it. Instead, he opened his dusty copy of Chapman's *Odyssey* and tried to read.

A loud fart erupted from the far bed.

★★★

The tiny kitchen of the place was crowded, the table occupied by a rowdy bunch who guffawed loudly at anything resembling a joke. Francis waited patiently for his turn at the stove, a big woman in a dark shawl ahead of him.

"Ahem," he murmured as she stirred her slumgullion.

She ignored him.

"Excuse me," he tried again.

"She's deaf," shrieked one of the gang at the table. Their aggressive laughter was almost pitiable.

The woman turned to Francis slowly after he tentatively tapped her shoulder.

"I. Just. Want. To. Fry. This. Herring."

He motioned at the fish on his plate.

"You'll have to wait your turn then, won't you?"

She turned back to slowly stirring the pot. The table erupted with hoots of derision.

★★★

"I've no money left to pay you," Francis informed his landlord a few fruitless days later.

"No money, no bed," the landlord replied.

"I'll have work soon. I know it. There are no ships in town right now. August is a quiet spell."

"What kind of fool do yeh take me for? As soon as the first ship comes, I'll not see yeh again."

"No. I'll find a way."

The landlord looked at him expectantly.

"Yeah?"

"How much'll you give me for this?"

39

Francis reluctantly produced his black wooden flute.

"That? I wouldn't give a ha'penny for it. Try the pawn on Castle Street. Take your bag along. Don't come back if yeh can't get anything."

Francis took to the street, his shoulders slumped. After a distance, he settled at one corner of the alley and decided to play. In vain hope he opened the cover of his bag before him to take contributions. He started with a favorite hornpipe. For the first time in days, a slight smile came to his lips as he pursed them over the tune. He warmed to his task and started into another hornpipe: "The Rights of Man".

For an hour or two, he played all sorts of tunes. A flood of them as if he were unburdening his soul. After a mournful slow air he stopped. He had got nothing but hostile glances from passers-by the whole time. Hungry, he put down his flute and looked it over.

"We'll have to say goodbye now," he said softly. He dismantled the instrument and stowed it into a leather pouch.

★★★

Francis glanced at the three golden balls on the sign above the door before studying the window display. Inside were all manner of knick-knacks: snuff boxes, silver teapots, ill-matched ceramics, a flat iron, a scuffed telescope, children's shoes, even a couple of fiddles and a tarnished flute. Despite his misgivings, he couldn't help but marvel at the treasures and trash stacked and tagged without any regard to order.

"Buying or Selling?" a large oily-haired man demanded from a high perch behind a counter. Francis blinked and recalled where he was. And why he was there.

"Hurry up now. Haven't all day."

"My flute. An Irish flute. Given to me by my father."

He handed it over.

"Yes, yes." The pawnbroker massaged the inside of his fat cheek with his tongue as he regarded it.

"Thruppence."

"No! This is a family heirloom. It has played some wonderful music. It's worth at least a shilling."

The man's laughter was heavy with condescension.

"I'm sure. Sixpence then. Last offer."

Francis took the money.

Over the next few days, he came back to the shop several times, each time describing the value of every book as he sold it, bidding it a mournful farewell. A ritual with the smug broker. None came to as much as the flute, which sat beyond reach in the window.

★★★

"Cast off the spring lines!"

With that shout, the *Jane Duncan* slowly untethered from the wharf. A single figure ran through the crowd and made a leap onto the departing deck to a general cry from the sailors on board.

The first mate grabbed Francis by the scruff of his neck.

"Explain yourself, you bla'guard, or over the side you go."

"Was told you're looking for apprentice seaman. I came as quick as I could."

"Maybe we were. Maybe the spot's been filled."

"Forgive me, sir. I'm trying to improve at being on time."

The mate motioned him towards the railings, making to push him over the side.

"Wait! I've already sailed. Under Captain Watson on the *Anne*."

"Never heard of 'im."

"I can't swim," exclaimed Francis. "If you throw me over, I'll drown."

The mate considered this for a minute. They were far enough out from the wharf now. He relented.

"Never learned meself neither," he admitted. "We do need more apprentices, as it 'appens. Captain Andersen'll have to approve you, mind. An' if you don't pull yer weight, we'll leave you at the first port of call. I'm first mate. Name's West."

"Thank you, Mr. West, sir. I'll work, you'll see," Francis said. "Where are we headed?"

"Egypt."

A broad smile broke onto Francis's face.

Miss McCleod's

Alexandria, Egypt, 1865

Francis wiped his mouth with the back of his hand, watching the trail of his vomit merge with the sea beneath him. He swallowed slowly a couple of times, blearily noting how fast the sick disappeared in the wake of the ship. Leeward, the rock of Gibraltar looked like a crouching animal. Staring at it made his sea-sickness worse. A flurry of color out of the corner of his eye. In the nearby rigging, a bright eye regarded him: turquoise feathers with a jacket of rusty red. Francis approached the bird carefully. Its breast beat heavily but it did not fly off. If he reached out, he could catch it…

"O'Neill, what are you doing?" asked Captain Andersen.

The bird disappeared out to sea.

"A bird, sir. It was tame."

"Oh, it will die. Likely got blown out to sea by that last storm. They try and rest on the ships."

Francis looked out to the sky where the little creature disappeared.

"Sorry, sir. I was feeling queasy."

His superior snorted.

"No time for sightseeing now. When we arrive in Egypt, I have a special task for you."

"What is that, sir?"

He indicated a small dinghy lashed onto the deck.

"You are to be the bosun of this fine craft. I require you to take me back and forth to shore."

★★★

Staring at the multitude of bleached white and yellow sandstone buildings lining the sweep of the bay, Francis spotted the odd minaret spire poking out between them. To the east, a tall finger of stone pointed to the azure sky.

"That must be the needle," he said softly.

"Well spotted, O'Neill," remarked Andersen, leaning next to him at the rail.

"Captain," exclaimed Francis. "I'll get right back to work."

"At ease, young man. At ease," said the Captain with a chuckle.

Andersen had taken to the serious young Irishman after he proved to be a quick study. The Captain gestured to the distant obelisk.

"It is indeed Cleopatra's needle. She put it up for her Antony. He must've had a fine one himself, eh?"

Francis gave an obliging laugh to the Captain's remark.

"My encyclopedia had an engraving of Cleopatra's needle as one of the seven wonders of the world. I've always wanted to see it."

Andersen grunted.

"You ain't in Cork now. This is much bigger scale. You got Christians, Jews and Mohammedans. Even a few religions I'm not too sure of. All sorts in Alexandria. Be careful though, especially in the market. They'll rob you blind given half a chance."

Francis gaped at the white city, the buildings laid out like sand castles on the Bantry strand.

"The famous library is gone too, isn't it?" he murmured, suddenly regretting his lost encyclopedia in the Sunderland pawn shop.

The Captain nodded.

"It don't have no docks either. That's why we've taken anchor out here."

He straightened up from the railings.

"Now then, Bosun," said the Captain. "You'll scull me ashore, where I'll arrange a scow to start our unloading."

★★★

The scow was as ugly as its name—broad-beamed and flat-bottomed with coal-stained canvas sheets. A battered tin chute teetered over its hold from the *Jane Duncan*. The Arab laborers Francis rowed in from shore filled tubs with coal and sent the black greasy stones clattering down the chute. Never had he seen skin as dark. After several hours in the blazing sun, their gaffer allowed the crew some respite. They drank deeply from a water barrel in the relative shade of the wheelhouse. Francis approached them with some hardtack left over from the crew's lunch. They accepted his offer but did not eat. Francis looked at the nearest of them puzzled. The man pointed at his belly and shook his head, smiling.

"Ramadan. Ramadan," he repeated, bowing nervously.

43

Francis nodded, baffled by the response.

Later, they rowed back to shore, the pink sun setting over the citadel on the western promontory of the bay. Once close, they pulled the tender up onto the darkening beach. One of them produced Francis's gift. With a solemn bow to Francis he shared it amongst the others. They ate without speaking in the warm gloom, an occasional smile and nod to Francis. He could think of no reply. Instead, he bowed awkwardly before returning to his little craft.

★★★

The souk, ringed by awnings from dusty buildings, had stalls laden with lemons, figs, dates, spices and other produce—all watched by turbaned men chatting to each other. A camel brayed above it all. Francis burped in unison, the hot *hawawshi* he bought from the vendor not settling in his stomach. He wiped his brow, heat getting the better of him. The Captain was on an errand and had let him roam the city. He retreated quickly from the fishmonger section, the smell overpowering. Towards the back of the market he found stalls of brass goods and rug sellers. A hurdy-gurdy buzzed and droned in one shady corner. Francis listened to it for a while before his heart leapt with excitement. He had spotted a bookseller.

The stand was covered in books, new and old. Some were without covers and mildewed. Francis started thumbing through them.

"You are English?"

He looked up in surprise at the young woman sitting behind the stand. In his excitement, he had not noticed her.

"No! No. I'm Irish."

She laughed, her long thick hair part-covered by a thin cotton veil.

"It is the same. Is it not?"

"Um," he stumbled for a moment, looking away from her. "How do you? How do you speak English so well?"

"My father sent me to the British school. He wanted me to know what we were selling."

"Oh. I see. That's. That's nice. I think…"

She cocked an amused smile at his fluster.

"I need to practice. The British girls at the school would not speak to Egyptians and especially not a Jewish one."

His eyes widened. He dared a look at her olive skin, arched eyebrows, long slender nose.

"But tell me about you? Why are you in Alexandria?"

"The *Jane Duncan* is my ship. Oh, I mean, I'm a sailor on her. We're only here for a few more days."

"Such a short time," she exclaimed. "What do you think of our city?"

"Beautiful. It is beautiful. I've never seen anywhere like it. The buildings…"

Her generous laugh thrilled him.

"You do not sound like a sailor."

He reddened and ducked his head.

"I'd like to be more than a sailor. I want to study. Maybe teach. I could. I mean. I could help you with English."

She looked away from him and down at her books.

"That would be nice. I must work the stall today but perhaps tomorrow. I could show you, oh how do you say it, the city of the dead."

Francis started.

"The city of the dead?"

"Yes. Yes. It is quite beautiful and you English love it. *Necropolis*."

"Right. Of course. My Captain mentioned it. He said the gardens were nice."

"You will speak English and I will show you."

"Thank you. That would be lovely."

"Take this," she said, plucking out a book. "It is worn but it speaks of Egypt and her old writings."

She handed him an *Account of the Recent Discoveries in Hieroglyphic Literature and Egyptian Antiquities* by Thomas Young.

Francis held the tattered book with reverence. He was at a loss for words. Again.

She laughed some more.

"It never sells. There is no romance or murder in it."

"I couldn't take it. And I probably can't afford it."

"It is not a sale," she said. "It is a loan. If you like it, perhaps you will buy."

He looked at her, holding the book to his chest.

"Thank you. I'll read it closely tonight."

She shrugged.

"Come meet me here tomorrow early. I will close up and take you. You had better have that all read."

"I'll try. I don't know how far I'll get." He paused. "Oh, what's your name? Mine's Francis."

She gave him her sweetest smile, a strand of unruly black curls across her face.

"It is Zakiyah."

Castle Donovan

On a nearby sea wall, a turbaned soldier put his gun down and prostrated himself, facing the spreading yolk of the rising sun. Francis, absentmindedly coiling heavy rope, watched from the ship. The distant cry of a muezzin broke across the morning hush.

"Francis," called Andersen. "Get the tender ready to take us ashore. I've more business with that damn chandler."

Captain Andersen was an early riser. Francis stifled a yawn as he went to the side where the tender was secured. He had been up most of the night with Zakiyah's impenetrable book.

"Yes, Captain. Sir, I'd like to send a letter. Where should I go?"

"A letter is it? The British Consul is your best bet."

"Thank you, Captain."

Francis hauled the little boat alongside and started to hop on board.

"Consul's not far from the officer's club. You'll find it. Got a sweetheart to write to?"

Francis wobbled precariously, distracted by the Captain's question.

"Ah, sir! You nearly had me in the swim."

He had to brace the little vessel with his feet, holding the ladder for Andersen.

"I just want to tell my family where I am. They haven't heard from me in a while now."

The Captain chuckled as he descended.

"Very good. Anyway, I'll let you have some time to yourself. Don't want to spend all your time in Alexandria stuck in a book."

Francis smiled as he pulled the oars towards the shore.

★★★

"Thanks again for the book."

Zakiyah placed it in a box beside her closed up stall.

"How did you like it?"

"It was very… complicated. I think he figured out some of the hieroglyphics though. And that Cleopatra. She was something."

"Oh yes. She made emperors do her will."

She cast her dark eyes downwards.

"We read Shakespeare's play at school about her. It was difficult and wonderful to read. But what are high-row-gliffs?"

She faltered on the word.

"Hieroglyphics," Francis paused between each syllable. "From Greek. Meaning picture writing. The ancient Egyptian script. No one understands all of it."

She said some quick words. He looked back at her in confusion.

"I thought you knew Greek? We have many here in the city."

"It sounds so different when you speak. I've only learned to read it really."

"Perhaps I will teach you some, too. First, we will go to the tombs. There are many high-row… picture-writings there."

"Will your books be alright?"

"Hah! Do not worry. This is Alexandria, a haven for books." She nodded to a nearby girl walking up to them. The teenager studied Francis, then burst out laughing. She said something quickly and returned to her stall.

"Salah will, how do you say, keep an eye for me."

Francis pretended not to notice that something had passed between the women. He followed Zakiyah out of the busy souk.

★★★

Francis paid the entrance fee for two. They walked the gardens together in silence, the plants unfamiliar and strange. A hand-painted sign saying "Catcombs" caused a nervous chuckle from Francis. Zakiyah gave him a quizzical look.

"It's just," he said. "It should be 'cat-a-combs'. That means a comb for a cat. To brush hair."

Zakiyah laughed as he made a combing motion.

"That is too good. Cats are like gods here. Cleopatra shaved off her eyebrows when her favorite one died."

She paused at the dark entrance.

"This place is called *Kom el-Shuqafa* in Arabic," she said. "Here *Comb* means mound as in Mound of Shards. I do not know why it is called that."

"You are very smart, Zakiyah. You're the one doing all the teaching."

She smirked.

"Perhaps." She cocked her head to one side. "The sound of your voice is so different from the other English I have heard."

"The sound?" Francis asked.

Their eyes met and his heart skipped.

"Oh, you mean the accent. Yes. Well, Ireland is very different from England. We have our own language and music too."

"I see. I enjoy it. There is a music in the way you speak."

They were quiet for a minute.

"Then let us comb the cat," Zakiyah announced as they reached a spiral stairway into the ground. She took his hand. Francis gulped and followed her down. The touch of her hand was wonderful and strange.

★★★

The cool vestibule was a welcome relief from the midday heat above. A statue that could be Greek, Roman or Egyptian observed them without comment.

"Over there," said Zakiyah, indicating a dank hall with stone couches. Past a dim lantern, Francis could make out a mildewed frieze of a dark woman with wings. "That is where they would have feasts for the dead."

"Feasts for the dead?"

"There is a better word, I would say. But it is where they would celebrate their lost ones."

"A wake. That's what it is called."

"Ah, awake. A funny name for those who will sleep forever. We say the *kaddish* at our burials. It is a mournful prayer."

Her skin was warm honey in the lamplight.

"Through there is the Hall of Caracalla. It's said to hold the bones of many young Christians killed by that emperor."

"That's terrible," murmured Francis.

"Perhaps. There was blame on both sides."

Francis thought it best to change the subject.

"What's down there?"

A set of broad steps led away from them.

"Tombs."

The walls were lined with deep slots.

"Just think of how old all this must be."

Zakiyah made no reply. Francis noticed light streaming in from the far end where men were working. They hauled away sandy soil up to ground level.

"*What are they doing?*" he asked.

"They dig up older parts of this city. And everywhere in this city is old. I think they use it for, what is that word, weight on the ships."

"Ballast? But these are graves. From ancient times."

Zakiyah shrugged.

"Come. We can walk past back to the gardens."

As they ascended, Francis noticed a small paper-thin skull—a discarded eggshell amongst the sand and gravel the men were loading into wooden baskets. It was probably a child's. He followed Zakiyah to a bench in a quiet corner.

"Just think," he said, sitting down beside her. "Someone from long ago to be dug up and carted off like that."

"It is sad," she replied in an uninterested tone.

"In Ireland, even the poorest farmer will not desecrate an ancient grave. We call them fairy forts."

"You sound upset, Francis."

"I'm sorry," he leaned back into the shade of the giant palm. "Maybe I'm homesick."

She took his hand again.

"What a surprise you are," she exclaimed. "I knew you were no simple sailor when I saw you looking at books instead of drinking on the waterfront. Such strong feelings you have!"

She leaned forward and kissed him. His eyes opened wide in amazement then closed at the experience. After a long while she withdrew, studying him. The kiss was so electric that he still felt her lips. Astounded by the feeling, he leaned forward and kissed her back. She pulled away, remembering something. She wrung her hands and wouldn't look at him.

"What is it?" he asked, reaching for her.

"I am so sorry, Francis. My fiancée…"

"Your fiancée?"

"I couldn't tell you. I should have but…"

She gulped back her words.

"I must go."

She stood up and started to leave. He reached for her, his hand on her wrist.

"Wait, Zakiyah. It's alright. Just sit. We've been talking of me the whole time. Tell me about him."

Reluctantly, she sat back beside him. The entire story spilled out. Her father had approved the marriage. He was a good man. She would marry him but she was afraid. She had not expected to meet another and besides, why did marriage have to be for life? Were they not just having fun together? She loved talking about serious things with him. At this Francis's heart jumped and they kissed once more.

"I really must go."

She stood up, looking away.

"Wait. Please. At least can you meet me again?"

"Tomorrow. After dark. By the citadel gates."

In amazement, he watched her slender form leave the gardens. He could

50

not quite believe everything that had happened. He kept looking around in disbelief all the way back to the ship.

★★★

"Engaged!" the Captain erupted. "Well, I warned you to watch out for thieves. Sounds like this one robbed you of more than your purse."

"Ah, Captain. She says she didn't mean for this to happen."

Francis stared out over the city, not seeing the choppy waves battering the shore. All night he felt the faint echo of their kissing.

"Ha! She says that, does she? Easily said. Never trust a woman, O'Neill. Besides, what future can you have? An Egyptian? And a Jew at that?"

"I know, sir. You are right."

His voice was surly.

"There are sailors with wives in every port. Tends to be more trouble than it's worth." He put a hand on Francis's shoulder. "Leave her to her own people is my advice."

Francis nodded his head.

"You're right, sir. I would like leave to see her one last time. To tell her."

Andersen considered for a while, a skeptical look on his face.

"Come with me to this chandler first." He indicated the ledger in his lap. "He says I've not paid for all the supplies we purchased."

★★★

The chandler's shop was on a short dusty street not far from the harbor. The large glass window contained a jumble of ship supplies: spools of rope, brass compasses, binnacles, barbed hooks, awls, bells, mallets, fittings and signal flags. Inside, behind a long counter of worn dark wood were shelves cluttered with axes, lanterns, oilskin hats and rows and rows of leather-bound ledgers. A big man with curly greased hair looked up as they entered.

"Mr. Popolani," said Andersen. "This is my accountant, Mr. O'Neill."

Francis straightened himself, taken aback.

"Nice to meet you," said the chandler, taking his hand. "I am Apollo Popolani."

"Francis O'Neill," he replied. "Apollo. I didn't expect a name like that in Egypt."

51

"My people are Greek. There are many of us in Alexandria. Even the city's name is Greek. Neither have I heard of Captain Andersen having an accountant," he added.

The Captain made a thin smile.

"What is the problem, Mr. Popolani?" asked Francis.

Apollo waved a sheaf of waybills he pulled from a ledger.

"These do not tally with what your Captain has paid me."

The various documents were laid out on the counter. Francis examined them, lost in the details. The two men observed him in silence.

"Oh," said Francis. "Here's a problem."

The chandler bent forward.

"Yes?"

"This is a 7 but looks like a 1. If you tally those figures, you can see that it doesn't add up. Also here. That seems to be counted twice."

The large man scrutinized the page for a long while. Then he looked over at the Captain. "You have a good accountant."

"Yes. I was never one for sums in school. That's why I need him."

The men looked at each other for a long moment, then laughed.

★★★

The three sat in the cluttered little room behind the shop. Popolani produced a bottle of ouzo which he shared liberally with the Captain.

"Would you like a glass, Mr. O'Neill?"

"Ah, no. Thank you, though."

The chandler shook his head.

"Truly he is a good accountant." He looked over to Andersen who was sipping the milky liquid with a satisfied smile. "Will you part with him? I could do with someone with a good head for figures around here."

"Perhaps," said Andersen. "He definitely has taken a liking to Alexandria."

Francis reddened visibly.

"A certain book-seller's daughter has caught his eye."

Apollo raised an eyebrow.

"Then you must stay," he announced. "I will expect you to start work tomorrow."

"Imagine. Me living in the land of the Pharaohs."

"There are worse places than Alexandria, I suppose," said the Captain. "I could see you do well no matter where you settle."

"Here's to my new assistant," announced Apollo, raising his glass. Francis looked to Andersen, who smiled but declined the toast.

★★★

After a leisurely time with the chandler, they finally returned to the dinghy.

"Thank you, sir," said Francis. "Will I tell Mr. West of my promotion to accountant?"

Andersen ignored the mild jest.

"Came to me in a flash. If anyone would best that big Greek at figures it would be Francis."

Francis said nothing for a while. As they rowed alongside the ship he said, "I will go ashore tonight, sir."

"Very well. Don't tarry long though. And Francis…"

He had already started tying the little tender against the ship and had to turn back to the Captain.

"Make sure you return."

★★★

He struggled to get the little boat to shore. The wind had risen and choppy waves swelled about, threatening to capsize him. Still unused to small craft, he had a tense half hour before finally pulling the dinghy up to the rocks. He was drenched. Palm trees along the promontory road, lit by gaslight streetlamps, swayed in the warm wind. The nearby castle loomed in the half-dark. He gave a wistful look at the symmetric crenellated walls—so different from the half-collapsed mottled-gray Donovan castle he knew near Tralibane. Despite being soaked, he longed for the chance to explore. He spied her by the open gate. She rushed up and kissed him fiercely. It was almost aggressive—a challenge. Francis did not resist, his resolve melting with each moment. Eventually they broke off.

"You are so wet," she said.

"Rough sea," he replied. His voice sounded hoarse and distant. She studied his face. He was unable to break away from her gaze.

"I have a gift for you," she said.

She pushed a slim volume into his hand.

"It's a book?"

"Of course, books are all I have," she looked away. "This is *Antony and Cleopatra*. Long hours I took with it at school. But it is right for us."

He tucked the thin book into a dry part of his jacket.

"I wasn't going to come tonight," she admitted. "I was going to leave you alone."

He took a deep breath.

"We shouldn't be doing this, Zakiyah."

"I know," she agreed.

"You are to be wed."

"Yes."

She looked out at the sea.

"And I've nothing to give you. I was kicked out of home. Before this job I hadn't a penny to my name."

Suddenly she laughed. "You are not very good at this, Francis. Many men have spent their time telling me how good they are for me."

"What about him? Will he be good for you?"

"Shhh," she put a finger to his lips. "Follow me. I know a place."

★★★

Francis could not keep track of the route they took through the dark unlit streets. The empty café she led him to had shutters on the windows and cracked tiles on the walls. He could hear the distant hush of the sea. Scowling, a matron served them thick dark coffee. Zakiyah giggled like a schoolgirl. The matron disappeared to the kitchen in the back.

"The lady knows you?"

"Yes. She knows me."

She beamed widely, her voice full of mischief.

"Aren't you… worried?"

"I do not care."

She tossed her dark chestnut hair. The long wavy flow of it.

54

"I'll do as I please. My mother didn't want me to sell in the market but I do that too."

"The ship chandler Popolani offered me a job," said Francis.

"Here? In Alexandria? This is great news."

"Yes. He was very impressed with me."

"I do not doubt it."

She stirred her coffee, considering.

"Why are you called Francis?" she asked.

"It's a name in my family. A saint's name. Actually, my real name's Daniel."

"Daniel," she laughed quickly. "Why not use that name?"

"Daniel was the name of my brother that died."

"Oh."

"He was only a baby. I just want my own name. Francis is my second name. What about you? What does your name mean?"

"In English class, I was told it means the same as Catherine."

"Like the saint," he smiled, "Catherine of Alexandria. They taught us about her in school. It's one of the few things I knew about here before I came."

She threw back her head, laughing.

"I would say that I am no saint, Francis. And neither are you."

She kissed him then—a bittersweet coffee taste.

"We could be together," she said softly. "When you finish work."

She reached out her hand across the table. He did not take it. Instead he looked at her.

"And your fiancée? Would you still marry him?"

"Francis. I must do this. We could be together often. It is different here in Alexandria. You could meet him, even come to our wedding. It will be a big feast."

"I can't do that," he said.

"But why not?"

"Who owns this café?"

Silence.

"It's his, isn't it?"

55

"It is one of his."

"I should go," he said finally, standing up. His voice was hard, his mind made up.

"Stay. Please stay. In the morning we will talk properly. This is excellent news about your job."

Francis looked at her. In the morning? Her eyes were very still, looking back at him. He wished he could draw her picture, some way to remember her. He thought he heard music, urging him out. He felt the book in his pocket as he walked to the door.

At the door, he wondered at the punishment he would get for being so late. He turned to go back to her. She was crying alone at the meagre table. He had no ties. Why not set himself up here? Then he thought of her fiancée and his resolve returned. Quietly, he turned and closed the door behind him. He wandered disappointed through the maze of dark streets before finding the harbor again.

The Banks of the Black Water

Constantinople, Ottoman Empire, 1865

"Your turn aloft, O'Neill," barked a sailor into the hatch.

Francis stumbled out of his bunk, fumbling for his clothes in the gloom. His nightclothes were still damp after his recent dream about Zakiyah. Ashamed, he had feigned sleep to avoid the others' mockery, missing the thin breakfast gruel they called skillygalley. He did not mind too much as the crow's nest still made him queasy.

"Time to take your post above us all," muttered rat-faced Grimes from a far bunk.

"You're welcome to the spot," replied Francis.

"Oh no. Captain wouldn't have anyone other than his star boy," said Grimes. "Besides," he added with a snigger. "We know you like to play with yourself up there."

Francis ignored him and dragged himself up from the hold. Taking a deep breath, he looked up at the mast stretching to the sky. A stiff breeze struck Francis as he climbed the rigging. Even with ballast, the *Jane Duncan* was much lighter and making good time. He settled himself into the nest. He had learned not to look down at the distant deck beneath him, rolling in the sea. His back to the mast, he reached for *Antony and Cleopatra* in his pocket. No one would know if he read or did anything else up here. He flicked through the book's pages looking for a picture that might conjure Zakiyah to mind.

He stopped cold when he noticed she had written something inside the front cover. He could not make himself read it. Some day he would but not now. Suddenly, he felt the sensation of kissing her again and shivered. *Why had he frozen and not stayed?* If he read what she wrote then it would be final. Over.

Frustrated, he put the book away.

They had left the open Aegean and were threading through the Dardanelles to the sea of Marmara. It was Francis's duty to watch for obstructions in the narrow straits. To distract himself, he tried to appreciate the vertiginous view—distant hills and tiny fishing villages. On one rocky cliff he spied a flash of white columns. He reached for the brass spyglass and studied the half-collapsed temple. Grecian? Some columns still stood unconcerned beside their toppled neighbors. Which gods owned it? He imagined a limpid Oracle making pronouncements from the steps. He stared at it for as long as he can until it melted into the haze behind him.

★★★

Billows of black smoke roiled from the out-sized stack of the hearse-black tug as it approached their ship. From the crow's nest, Francis watched its progress out from the city. He put the telescope to his eye: the base of the green mountains on the far shore were speckled with buildings. He could see dots of other ships entering the straits of the Bosporus. Many were propelled by similar tugs to counter the forceful current swelling from the great black sea on the other side of the narrow strait.

"Come down from there, Mr. O'Neill," called the Captain.

"Yes, sir," answered Francis. He pocketed the spyglass and scrambled down as quick as he could.

"You've grown fond of that perch," remarked Andersen as Francis came

57

alongside, out of breath. "What were you doing up there?"

"Just surveying, sir. I saw temples along the coast. Wish I could have explored them."

"You are a funny one, O'Neill. Well, you'll have plenty of temples to see where we're going next. Constantinople requires us to stop and file clearance papers. The Sultan wants to know of our passage. You," he pointed at Francis, "are to row me ashore."

★★★

The broad waterway was alive with vessels from all corners of the world: tall ships, steamships, ferries, and a multitude of smaller craft. A caïque, the ornamented skiff of the Sultan's guard, slid by while opalescent jellyfish pulsed in the murky trash-streaked sea. On shore were buildings surrounded by plane trees, along with the odd needle of a minaret. Amidst the chorus of the city he heard yells and the rumble of vehicles and trains. Andersen shifted on the thwart across from him.

"Quite a sight isn't it, Francis? Best not to gape for too long."

"Oh sorry, Captain. I've not seen the like of this place before."

"The hinge of the continents," the Captain announced, a gleam in his eye. He stabbed at the horizon, rocking the boat

"North, south, east and west!"

By now, Francis was used to the Captain's outbursts.

"Look at that," Francis said, enthralled by a sprawling complex of buildings.

"The Sultan's palace," supplied the Captain. "The Seraglio. Topkapi is their name for it."

Shining marble walls. Clusters of spires and domes. The hint of opulent gardens.

"Beautiful," he breathed.

"It is. They would cut out your eyes if you ever got in to see it. The jewel at the tip of the Golden Horn. The main part of the old city of Stamboul."

The Captain paused, lost in his own memories. "Best heave-to now," he said finally. "The Sultan's port guards are a sulky bunch."

★★★

PART ONE: SEA

The tender was tied to the wharf along with a plethora of other craft. Francis's job was to "keep an eye on it," but he set out to explore the city as there was little risk of anyone swiping the dull thing compared to the other vessels. The mid-day smells assailed him—a faint citrus tang to the heavy air. Other savory odors came from the stand of a flatbread vendor. Crippled men, some missing limbs, lined the street begging for alms. Many of the windows were grilles cut in repeating patterns, allowing the heat out but no view in. Outside a barber shop, dark-eyed men in fezzes smoked from a narghile, sharing the long pipe. They watched his passage with intensity. Officers of the Sultan's army passed in their peacock uniforms.

In the courtyard of a mosque, he saw men in flowing white robes, dancing a strange twirling dance. Their arms were outstretched as they spun, eyes closed in mild bliss. He paused under the shade of a plane tree to watch. The music was provided by a magnificently mustachioed old man playing on a large bowl-backed lute. The tempo of the piece varied from languid to frenzied. The rhythm was as important as the melody, if not more so. Long passages were repetitive and hypnotic. Francis noted the slow modulation of the music's mood from solemn and mournful to excitement then back again. A bell sounded from within the mosque and, without a word, the dancers slowed their dizzying progression before stopping. They bowed and beamed at one another before filing into the building, the music continuing for a while as they departed. Eventually the old man put the instrument down, stood up and stretched. There was no hat to reward him. Besides, Francis had neither money to give nor flute to play. Francis was tempted to try talking to him. Instead, he retreated to the wharf and his duty.

★★★

An oppressive mood settled on Francis as they left Constantinople and headed north on the Black Sea: 175,000 square miles of bleak water with no island or shore to break the monotony. The heavy weather added to his woe as a low bank of storm cloud followed them. Difficult as it was to put her out of his mind, the excitement of his encounter with Zakiyah had curdled to regret and misgivings. Perhaps on the way back he could seek her out? But the *Jane Duncan* would have a full hold of linseed from Odessa

59

then and no need of heading that far south. Perhaps he should sneak a look at the inscription to *Antony and Cleopatra*? He reached for the thin leather copy under his bunk.

"O'Neill," came a call from above deck. "West wants you on foredeck."

He left the book behind him on his narrow bunk.

Put On Your Clothes

Odessa, Russia, 1865

"Jesus Mary and Joseph," shouted Francis. "Look at that."

The Potemkin steps swept down to the docks. A statue of a man in a toga dominated the apex. He loomed larger than the varied collection of people walking up and down the immense steps.

"Francis! Such strong language from you."

The other men laughed courteously at the Captain's jibe. The *Jane Duncan* was anchored out beyond Odessa's long pier. Fine wedding cake buildings lined the hills of the city. The men stood at the railings, gawking at the sights.

"So different from Constantinople, eh West?" Andersen remarked to his first mate.

The mate only grunted in assent.

"Although there's a chap in a fez," said Andersen. "A *tarboosh*. Across from him one of them Russian hats. Every kind here. It's like somewhere in America. This town was hardly built fifty years ago."

One of the sailors threw his eyes up to heaven. A mild chuckle from another in response.

"Shut up, you lot," growled West. "O'Neill. You'll be taking the Captain in."

★★★

"Sailors are narrow-minded fools," grumbled Andersen as Francis sculled him across the blue-black choppy water.

"You watch what happens to that gang, Francis," he indicated back to the ship with a jerk of his head. "Once we get back to England, every penny they earn will be screwed, pissed and vomited into the gutter."

"I won't be doing that, sir."

"Oh really? Alexandria so quickly forgotten?"

Francis said nothing but the Captain spotted the young man's cheeks redden. "What are you going to do once we're back home?"

"I don't know, sir. Back to sea, I suppose. I want to see more."

"That's good. First, why don't you stay on with me when we're finished in Hull? Mrs. Andersen'll be joining me in Sunderland and you can stay with us for a while."

"Thank you, sir."

Andersen stared out at the horizon.

"And you don't have to *sir* me when we're on our own. I value your company, Francis. You're an educated lad who could do a lot better than this."

"Thank you very much, Mr. Andersen. I never expected to see so much of the world. Egypt and now Russia."

"Yes. And you've learned more than just geography, eh?" he cackled. "But don't sail for too long. You'll end up living from port to port like that crew of mine. We're better than that lot. Find a good woman and stick with her."

"Like Mrs. Andersen?"

The Captain's bushy eyebrows raised and he sighed.

"No. Not like her at all."

★★★

The rough and brutish Cossack stevedores reminded Francis of the most downtrodden itinerant laborers from home. There were women amongst them, wiry and quick. Faces lined and closed, they took the grain from the men and used hand scoops to fill every spare cranny of the hold.

"Fill it to the deck," West yelled down at them. "If that linseed shifts at sea, we're scuppered."

The Russians continued without a word. Francis wondered if they even heard, they were so unresponsive.

With the shadows lengthening, the workers stopped for supper. Their meal was coarse, consumed quickly and without any pleasure. Near Francis, a bear of a man stretched himself, muttered, then proceeded to cast off his dusty clothes.

Francis gaped at the naked Cossack.

61

Ignoring everyone, the man scratched at his groin, climbed a convenient barrel, then jumped into the sea with a roar.

"What are they doing?" asked Francis. More men disrobed and cast themselves into the sea. They sported like schoolboys in the black murk.

"Bath time," remarked an old sailor.

The women talked quietly amongst themselves. Not one even glanced in the direction of their naked male companions.

★★★

The noon sun bore down heavily on the decks of the laden *Jane Duncan*. The monotony of the return journey on the Black Sea made Francis restless and disappointed, tormenting himself with alternative scenarios with Zakiyah. Even the sight of steep green hills above the glittering Bosporus did not lift his spirits.

"Why are we stopped here?" he asked West.

"Bighouse bay? Good anchorage. Haven't been cleared yet, have we? Sultan's Lah-de-dahs have to sniff around for a bit. Take a nice back-hander too, they do."

Francis nodded and sighed.

"Somethin' eating you, O'Neill?"

"No, sir. Just the heat. I'm not used to it."

West pointed across the bay to the nearby shore.

"That's the continent of Asia over there," said West, friendly for once. "All the times I've been through the strait an' I've never set foot on it."

Francis stood on the railings, shading his eyes to look across.

"You're right," he said, flashing a grin.

"What you taking your shirt off for?"

Francis stripped down to his small clothes. Shoes were tossed to one side.

"I'm off to Asia for a bit."

"Wha? Oi! Thought you couldn't swim."

West was alongside him at the railing.

"I pick things up quick," he said before barreling into the sea.

The shock of chill water sloughed the leaden feeling from him. He surfaced to look up at the ship. Then he started off with even strokes. It was no different from the strand at Bantry. Fifteen minutes later he was lying on the white sand watching the ship shift slightly on the swell. The heat was pleasant now after the cold water. He walked about for a bit, dripping wet. Shading his eyes, he noticed an ornate mansion overlooking the bay. It ignored him with an aristocratic air. He laughed up at it.

"Asia," he announced to the wind.

The Sailor's Return

Hull, England, 1866

Francis stood up straight in the stuffy office, his sailor's duds as tidy as he could make them. He was a head taller than West, who stared angrily off to the distance. Captain Andersen sat between them, a ledger book, quill and ink before him on the table. He set out a stack of coins and notes from a drawer.

"That should be sufficient, Mr. Grimes," he said.

"That ain't right," replied the sailor, scowling at the pile. His forearms were smeared blue with tattoos.

"Oh? You took your articles in May last, did you not? That would be according to the rate agreed upon."

Grimes considered for a moment, eyeing West who glared back. Francis stiffened. He had been told to expect trouble. Grimes bit his lower lip before taking the money.

"What about O'Neill there?" he asked after taking his time counting it. "What rate's he getting?"

"Mr. West and Mr. O'Neill are staying in the company's employ," the Captain said. "They will attend the ship here in Hull until we can charter a tug to take her back to Sunderland. Thank you for your time, Mr. Grimes. Send the next fellow in."

★★★

Francis was glad to stretch his legs on the main street of Hull after standing in the shipping office for most of the morning. Twice now he had done the Black Sea route. Hull felt small and mean after the grand eastern cities he had seen. How different from when he first arrived in England with

63

hardly a penny. A small uniformed band played at a bandstand in a nearby park. Men in brown suits, women in long dresses and large hats attended the performance as children chased about laughing. Francis stood watching it for a while. The music was loud and martial, but it was still music. Of all the things he ached for, he missed playing music most. He asked directions from a nearby audience member who regarded him coolly but replied. Francis strode out of the park and up the high street.

★★★

"That fiddle is worth more than four shillings," said the shopkeeper.

"That's all I have," replied Francis. The shopkeeper laughed, giving Francis hope.

"You say that like I have to sell it to you."

"Maybe not," Francis agreed as he studied the instrument—a gouge on the left cheek was poorly varnished over. He noticed the strings were new. Francis put it back down.

"Alright then," the other man relented. "But there's no case for it."

"That's alright. I can figure that out."

★★★

Mr. and Mrs. Andersen entered the tearoom, busy with the clatter of delft. Francis stood up from the corner table. A fussy waiter had put the dirty sailor as out of the way as he could.

"Ah. There you are, Francis," the Captain said. "My wife. Mrs. Andersen."

Tiny and sharp-eyed, Mrs. Andersen ignored Francis's outstretched hand.

"I thought you said he was younger," she snapped.

The Captain laughed apologetically.

"I am today just sixteen, Missus," said Francis as they all sat down.

"Why, you should have said," exclaimed the Captain.

"It's fine, Captain. I got myself a fiddle."

He lifted it up from where he had it propped in the corner.

"Well, give us a tune then."

Mrs. Andersen narrowed her eyes on her husband.

"No. No," said Francis. "It's years since I played. I'll have to practice more."

64

"I should say so," she agreed. "No-one wants to hear that horrible racket sailors call music anyway. And in a hotel too."

"Francis is very taken with music. Aren't you, my boy?"

"I am. My family's very strong in it."

"Oh, that Irish music," she said with disdain. "I've heard that in Sunderland. I thought my ears would split. What terrible noise!"

Francis stifled a smile.

"Terrible stuff surely," he agreed. "In Constantinople, I heard even stranger. The music was so powerful, men in long white dresses whirled around all day listening to it."

Mrs. Andersen's eyes went wide. The Captain looked at her with apprehension. She barked a sudden laugh.

"Mr. O'Neill," she said. "Tell me more of your adventures."

★★★

The *Jane Duncan*, void of cargo or ballast, sat high on the water as a steam tug hauled her into the harbor. West and Francis watched from the empty wharf, squinting at the early sun's rays. Francis hugged himself, surprised at how cold it was for late summer. Only the Captain and his wife were on deck. At the wheel, the Captain inclined his head as she berated him.

"The Captain's captain," murmured West in a deadpan voice.

Francis grinned back. They could not hear the argument over the hissing of the steam tug. He found himself daydreaming of the first time on the Bosporus—that black tug churning the water before it, smoke obscuring the city on the shore. He tried to recall the unusual rhythm of Turkish music but snapped alert as someone gestured from the back of the tug. They had stopped, but the ship was still coming in too fast.

"Captain! Pull away! Look out, West!" he yelled.

The distracted Captain could not hear them over the noise of the tug. Francis reached for one of the cork buffers lying in a pile behind him and threw it to West who, slack-jawed, watched the ship's inexorable drift towards them.

"Take the fender. West!"

West snapped to and took the other end from Francis. The peeling paint of the brig's side was only a couple of feet from them. They scrambled to cover the pier edge with the fender as best they could.

"Captain!" they yelled. "Hard away!"

The Captain finally looked away from his wife, her face all annoyed puzzlement. West jumped clear in time but Francis, so intent on finding another fender, was bowled backwards by the inexorable hull. With a crunch of rending timbers, Francis was thrown hard onto the dock.

All he could see was black with yellow concentric circles, some with vicious looking spikes.

When Sick Is It Tea You Want?

Sunderland, England, 1866

Clop clop clop.

The banging came from inside his skull, a never-ending hammering.

Clop clop clop.

Eventually, the sound—hooves on cobblestones from an open window—receded but the throbbing remained. Francis slowly came to in a cavernous hospital ward. The ward was mostly empty apart from a few wheezing old veterans in metal frame beds and thin sheets. The walls were dull white. The stringent smell of carbolic overlaid a hint of decay. He noticed a pale man with an enormous goiter staring at him. The man never blinked. A white enamel dish of urine lay on a table between them. Francis made to sit up but could only shiver with pain. He felt at the lumps on his head through the bandages and groaned.

"Where am I?" he called out.

No answer.

"What is this place?" he rasped louder.

A plump nurse tutted her way over to him from a distant desk.

"Mr. O'Neill? You really have to stop this noise."

"Where? Where am I?"

"Why, the marine hospital here in Sunderland."

"Sunderland?"

"Yes, they brought you back in the ship. You were in nasty shape. The doctor will be by on his rounds presently. You had a visitor but we thought it best not to rouse you."

Francis's mouth gaped as he tried to process all of this.

"You should rest now. Here. Take this water."

★★★

In his dream, his father sat next to his bed. Old John rifled his gray hair with one hand. In his other hand was Francis's fiddle, the smashed body hanging loosely from the neck. Only catgut held it on. Francis turned away.

On the other side of the bed, Zakiyah regarded him with a slight smile. Dark wavy hair a contrast to her white cotton dress. She bent forward to say something. Francis strained to hear.

★★★

"And who have we here?"

The voice was reedy and thin. Francis opened bleary eyes to observe a small man, scant wispy hair held in place by a mirror disc on his head.

"Francis O'Neill, sir. Knocked off the *Jane Duncan*," murmured an aide.

"Ah yes. How are you feeling, O'Neill?"

Francis stared at the little man suddenly leaning over him. Before he could respond, the doctor's dry fingers were opening Francis's left eye.

"Look into the center of the mirror. There's a good chap. And the other eye. Very good."

He lifted the bandage across Francis's forehead and peered under it. He muttered at it for a moment before snapping back erect.

"Minor fracture of the cranium. Rectifying normally. Hmmm?"

Francis looked at the silent nurses and attendants before realizing they were expecting something from him. The doctor fixed him with a skeptical eye.

"Oh. I'm fine now," he lied. "Thank you, sir."

"Any double vision? Headaches?"

"Not any more. I've had some odd dreams…"

"Good. That's a fine scar on your head. You'll wear that badge of naval service for a long time to come. But."

He paused. The attendants leaned in.

"You very nearly died. So. I wouldn't complain too much."

He pivoted quickly, aiming for the next bed. The group hurried to follow in his wake.

"Two more weeks of bed rest I should say," he called back. The attendant scribbled a note before giving Francis a stern look.

★★★

"You have a visitor," announced the nurse. "A Mrs. Andersen."

Francis straightened himself, sitting up in the bed. His head still felt heavy and his vision swam.

"Mr. O'Neill."

He wondered if he should stand, frustrated to find he still could not.

"I'm sorry. I can't... get up."

"Yes. Understandable."

A pause. She looked around the ward and shook her head slightly.

"The Captain?"

She frowned at him and her nostrils flared as she considered the question.

"My husband is no longer officially of that title. Mr. Andersen will suffice."

Francis was lost for words.

"The company has seen fit to relieve him from duty owing to the recent," she sniffed, "incident."

"I'm sorry to hear it, Ma'am."

Her facade cracked.

"He's utterly miserable. Impossible to live with! He wanted to come but has been indisposed. He said to give you these."

She laid a bundle at his bedside: the book, his fiddle.

"The owners were most irate. They even mentioned pressing charges. Imagine!"

Francis doubted any charges were to be laid on his behalf.

"My husband was most insistent you be well-treated. He has interceded for you. These hospital expenses are of no concern and you are to be taken on the next voyage."

"I am," he struggled, "very obliged."

Sparks swarmed in his eyes.

"When does she sail? Next month?"

68

"Friday, I believe. Only minor repairs were needed. We no longer have any direct contact, of course."

"Today is Wednesday? Two days! But I'm not able to sail."

"Oh yes. We have assurances that you are to be kept in convalescence whilst on board. No strenuous tasks."

Francis made a noise of disbelief. She stood to go, waiting on him with an expectant air.

"Thank you, Mrs. Andersen."

"Pray don't mention it. My husband said he is sorry that it turned out this way but to remember him well."

"I'll try."

Mrs. Andersen scrutinized him.

"Are you sorry you left her?"

"Who?" he asked, amazed at the question.

"Zaky... whatever. The girl. Your Cleopatra."

A thin lizard smirk as she eyed the book, all he has left of her.

"Yes."

"Good. Remember that and it will stop you from being a sailor. It never ends well. Think of my husband."

She wrapped a light shawl around herself.

"Have a good voyage," she said and strode out of the ward.

The Sea Captain

"Jennings. Get him up here."

Jennings stepped down the gangway to aid Francis's ascent. Still bandaged and fighting off nausea, Francis clutched at his belongings as he limped forward.

"Come on then," encouraged Jennings. He was about Francis's age, perhaps younger, with sandy hair and a slight squint. Francis leaned on him as he once more boarded the *Jane Duncan*. The deck was busy with a new crew. The new first mate eyed Francis's bandaged head with overt skepticism. West had decided against re-enlisting.

"Who's this then?"

"Francis O'Neill, sir."

His voice was faint.

"Injured recently. Owner says I'm to convalesce on board until able to work fully."

"Conva-wha?"

"Get better, sir."

The mate wheezed in exasperation.

"I don't know how I'm supposed to get anything done with you lot. Better show the patient his cozy bed then, Jennings."

Francis shuffled below decks. Jennings came behind him, all questions.

"How'd ya do your head in?"

"Is it true the old Captain let his missus helm and smash the ship?"

"What's Egypt like?"

★★★

Jennings left Francis rolling about in pain to assist with leaving port. When he returned later, the daylight from the hatch showed a green tinge to Francis's face.

"You alright?" asked Jennings.

Francis could only dumbly point at an enamel chamber pot floating in the bilge. Jennings looked over and back, then rushed forward with it. Just in time, Francis heaved into the cold guzunder. When the convulsions stopped he sat up, gulping back air. The rancid smell of lamp oil and vomit nearly made him sick again.

"Francis?" Jennings queried, his voice uncertain.

"Yes."

"That your name? Ain't that a girl's name."

"Yes. As well. Frank if you like."

Francis rubbed his eyes. Although his queasiness had subsided, he felt every roll of the ship. The creaks and groans of the timbers sounded louder too.

"Jennings?" he asked. "What's your first name?"

"Bartholomew."

Francis muttered a minor swear.

"Too long. How about Barry?"

"Alright."

"In Cork, you'd be called Finbarr. What age are you?"

"What?"

"How old are you?"

"Sixteen."

"Sixteen?"

"Dunno. Thirteen maybe."

A distant rumble above decks.

"Did you hear that?"

"Captain says a storm's coming. Got to prepare."

"Oh. Thought it might be my head."

He could almost make out the youth's face in the gloom.

"Got a right bang, didn't ya? Ever been with a girl?"

Francis laughed.

"Maybe," he replied. "You?"

"I got a girl. We ain't done anything though. Kind of she kissed me. What's it like? You know?"

Francis exhaled slowly.

"I don't know."

"Don't know! Them older sailors go hooring all the time."

"I know. Saw it in Odessa."

"Should I do that? To practice?"

"Barry?"

"Yes?"

"What's your girl's name?"

"Charlotte."

"Would you like to bring her the pox?"

"No. Suppose not."

Francis settled into silence. His head had improved enough to dwell on Zakiyah again. The more he thought about her, the more he tortured himself. He could have stayed that night. *What was wrong with him?*

A crash came from above followed by shouts for all hands. The hatch lifted, wind and rain howling at the opening.

"You two," called down a terse voice. "On deck. Orders. We need those sails storm-reefed."

"Coming," said Jennings.

"Him too."

Francis tried to rise.

"He can't. He's too sick."

"Don't care. Why should he be in a dry bunk while the rest of us are hauling in the gale?"

"He's in a bad way. Chucked his guts just now."

Jennings pointed to the chamber pot.

"Christ! Alright. Get out here you."

Jennings sealed the hatch, leaving Francis to collapse in the darkness. The fitful rolling of the ship echoed his suffering.

★★★

Light bloomed briefly as the hatch creaked open. A rat scuttled in the dark. Francis was aware of having slept—dark painful dreams.

"How you doing, Frank?"

"Uhh. How long've I been out?"

"About a day now. Watch wanted to get you out there again. Had to fight them over it."

"A day… Thank you."

"Eaten at all?"

Francis thought about it.

"No."

"Got some fruitcake here from Charlotte. Reckon she'd want you to have some."

Francis's stomach growled at the mention of it.

"Here."

It was thick and rich like earth, with a heavy dark odor.

"Oh, that's good. She's a good cook."

"Thanks," a shy note in his voice.

"You might have saved my life, Barry."

"Ah well. Got to look out for each other, right?"

72

★★★

"I just can't have you below decks all the time."

The impatience in the mate's voice threatened to erupt into anger. He tapped at the bulkhead with an awl.

"Sir, it's just I'm unsteady on my legs. Maybe I can helm? Lean on the wheel."

The mate snorted.

"You done it? Before?"

"Aye, sir. In the Black Sea."

"Andersen trusted you?"

"He did. I'd do a two-hour trick at the wheel sometimes."

"Huh. Pity he didn't keep you at it or he mightn't have crashed her. Well, you'll do your whole shift there then."

"But, sir. That's eight hours."

"None of the rest of this miserable crew have much experience. You can see straight, can't you?"

Francis considered telling the truth.

"I can."

The Liverpool Hornpipe

Bowling Green, Scotland, 1866

Francis leaned on the helm as Barry Jennings approached.

"Barry? Come to replace me?" he asked, without taking his eyes from the sea.

"Hullo, Frank," the young man replied. "Yes. My turn."

Francis shrugged before handing over the wheel. He glanced skeptically at Jennings.

"We're coming up to Bowling Green. Mate says the anchorage is good but watch the current from the Clyde river."

"I'll be fine, Frank."

"Careful is probably what you want to be."

"I will be."

He sat down on a high coil of rope next to Jennings, wiping his weary eyes.

"Sick of it?" asked Barry. "You've been helm most of the trip."

"Ah, I don't mind. Like it actually."

"Even that fucker of a mate says you're good at it."

"Now, Barry. Couldn't you come up with a better word?"

Barry smiled. "He'd still be a fucker."

"Maybe. I'll get them to trim the sails. Don't want to come in too hard."

"Before you go," Barry lowered his voice. "Have you thought about what comes next?"

"A bit," came Francis's guarded reply.

"Rest of the crew are to be let go but we apprentices kept on," whispered Barry. "D'ya want another trip with him?"

He nodded down-deck to the mate.

"I know what you mean," said Francis, rubbing his forehead. The still-pink scar only itched now.

"And the Captain's changing again," Francis sighed. "I don't feel much obligation to them."

"Then let's escape. Bunk off!"

"Shh! I wouldn't mind getting on a ship for the east," mused Francis. "China or Japan. Don't fancy another year on old *Jane*."

"Let's escape this shitty boat."

Francis grinned at his younger companion.

"Alright," he agreed. "I'll ask Jack or one of the other sailors for some money. They'll be paid soon and flush. Be ready for first thing in the morning."

"What about these?" Barry indicated their sailor garb.

"I don't know. Cover them up or put other clothes over them. If we're spotted, we'll be marched right back here. Now watch how you steer! That shore is coming hard."

★★★

In the dawn gloom, Francis observed long skeins of mist draped along the mirror-still river. The countryside was quiet but for early birdcall. His stomach did a nervous turn as he waited for his companion. A figure shambled forward.

"Name of God," exclaimed Francis. "What're you wearing?"

"An old blanket," said Barry, stifling a laugh. "And you? What's that in your pockets?"

"Extra pair of shoes. Whisht! Mate will be up soon."

As silently as they could, they descended to the tiny riverbank landing. Every creak of the gangplank reverberated in the still morning. The top of the sun peered down the river at them.

"Walk casual," hissed Francis, shouldering his bag.

"Nice Spring morning," replied Jennings, affecting a saunter.

"Not that casual. Keep it quiet."

Jennings looked around seriously.

"Sorry. How far do we have to go?"

"I don't know."

He looked back at the ship, a dark outline in the gloom. The fiddle he had sold to Jack, an older sailor who took it with a shrug. Francis sighed and looked upriver.

"There."

A ferryman punted a broad skiff towards their bank. They quickened their steps towards him.

"Good morning."

"Ain't right morning yet, is it?"

"Maybe not. Where're you headed?"

"Skelmorlie, about a day upriver. Cost yeh tuppence."

He looked them over suspiciously.

"Each," he added.

"If we row, how much?"

"Sailors are ye?" he asked, glancing at the ship downriver.

"No. No," Barry said. "We're apprentices!"

"Ah, he means we're off to be sailors. How about tuppence for the two of us? And we'll row."

The ferryman grunted his sour assent. Francis quickly handed over the money.

"We're heading for Liverpool."

"Aye. There's a morning train from Skelmorlie headed to Greenock.

Get a steamer from there to Liverpool. If ye can afford it."

The ferryman spat in the river, squinting at the rising sun.

"Are ye coming on or not?"

★★★

Every lit window in the little hamlet of Skelmorlie stared hard back at them. It had been a long three-mile walk in the dark from the little jetty.

"D'ya think he knew?" Barry asked.

A dog barked in the distance causing them to stop. They continued, speaking in whispers.

"I'd say so. Whether he'll let anyone else know is another question."

"Think we'll be flogged if we're found?"

"Depends on the new Captain. That mate might."

"Didn't he already try and kill you in that storm?"

"We better find a spot for the night. Come on."

"I'm starved."

"Better hungry than flogged."

★★★

The old widow who owned the inn fed them cold potatoes and turnips. Afterwards, they locked themselves into the musty room. They had to share the bed.

"In the morning, we'll get that train," Francis said into the dark. "Then off on that steamer."

"I wonder if they're looking for us."

"Could be."

Barry propped his head on an elbow.

"You never really told me about the woman in Egypt."

"No. Never did."

"Ah, go on. I'm going to sail off there and find me a dusky beauty of my own."

"What about Charlotte?"

"Ya're awful straight, Frank. D'ya know that?"

"I don't know."

Francis paused for a long while, looking into the dark. The dreams he still had of Zakiyah... He could still conjure up the physical sensation of their kiss, of her touch on his hand.

"Years ago, I fancied a girl," Francis broke the silence. "Katie was her name. Oh, she was something. She would come to our place for the dancing and I'd sit near her."

"Ya kiss her?"

"Hah. No. Whisht and let me finish the story."

"Alright."

Barry settled back down in the dark.

"So I sat next to her one night. I put down my flute."

Barry snickered. Francis ignored him.

"Tried to ask her to dance."

"And?"

"Nothing. Couldn't ask her."

"Ah, that's just the nerves."

"Don't know. I couldn't do anything. I'd never... frozen like that before. She stopped waiting for me to speak and eventually danced with someone else."

"Ya missed your chance."

"Then I left. I took off out into the hills. Didn't come back until the next morning. No one said anything at home."

His voice trailed off.

"But the woman in Egypt?" urged Barry.

His companion leaned close, eager.

"That was different. We went to see these tombs and maybe I froze then too. But she. *She* kissed me."

"Lucky."

"Yes. No. I suppose. Later, she wanted me to stay and I ran off too."

"What? You're a funny fellow, Frank."

Francis went silent, lost in thought.

"I'd have been right in there," said Barry. "If I'd of fancied her."

Francis couldn't reply.

"Listen," continued Barry. "Lot's of lads are all talk about girls but can't do anything. Don't you be worrying about it."

The uncomfortable silence slowly lapsed into sleep.

★★★

The whistle of the locomotive pierced the morning. The widow un-locked their bedroom door at dawn, saying something unintelligible in her thick northern accent. They were already awake and skulking in the room, afraid to step outside.

"Come on! We have to get on that train," Francis said.

They ran through the street, feet stomping dirt. Skelmorlie was dom-inated by barren hills, looming over them. They hurried to the little rail station where a great black steam engine hissed impatiently—a sleek bull in a tiny enclosure.

"Two for Greenock."

The drowsy ticketmaster did not even look at them. They scuttled on board, settling onto the hard wooden benches of the rear carriage.

"I think we're alright," said Barry.

A tremendous huffing as the engine got underway. As the little village slipped away, Francis could finally relish his first train ride.

"They might have our description out in Greenock," he cautioned. "There'll be plenty of shipping men around the docks. We'll find out where the steamer is but wait until the last minute before we get on."

"Christ, you make a good criminal."

Francis laughed.

"We're not clear yet."

★★★

The drover cursed at his sheep—addled animals baulking at the gangway to the steam packet.

"Hup! Hon now. Hup!"

He trashed at them in frustration. There were too many for one man to herd. Francis came forward from the barrels they were hiding behind, his companion close behind.

"D'you want a hand?"

The drover looked at them with relief before caution clouded his features.

"Ye're not out to rab me are ye, Paddy?"

"He's no Paddy and neither am I," called Barry as he tried to cut off one angle of ovine escape. Green sheepshit slicked the wharf.

"All we want is passage to Liverpool," said Francis.

"Alright then. My crew left me when they got wind of the inn back in town. Help me unload 'em in Liverpool as well and I'll vouch for yer passage."

Relieved, Francis and Barry clumsily corralled the skittish animals on board.

★★★

Before Francis realized how much bigger it was, he almost mistook Liverpool for Cork. The teeming Merseyside was all stone wharves and warehouses—crowded with cattle, drays, sailors, runners and street urchins. Three-masted ships swayed above the chaos. Their steam packet had stopped trashing the waters and was drifting into its berth. The night on board with the sheep had not been restful and both young men queasily assisted the drover. After an hour, he released them, pointing up a broad street with tenements and taverns cheek by jowl.

"Vauxhall'll have a sailor's boarding house, I shouldn't doubt."

Without another word he turned away. Before long they found a rundown boarding house, a cloying smell of boiled meat coming from its kitchen. Francis eyed the place, brooding on how similar these places all were. The landlord bid them wait in the front room. They dropped onto a crude bench with hay-stuffed pillows.

"We did it, Frank," said Barry with enthusiasm. Before Francis could reply the door opened and a spry man stepped in. He had voluminous side whiskers and wore a bright red waistcoat with gold nautical buttons.

"Chaps," he fixed his eye on them as if guessing their weight. "I've been looking for you."

They jumped up. Francis was too worn out to make a run for it.

"Sir, we didn't mean to…" he replied in a meek voice.

"Don't mind that," said the man, cutting him off. "I don't care what you've been up to. My name's White. Shipping master on *The Antiope*. She's a full-rigged clipper bound for the East Indies."

Barry's eyes went wide.

"We've just finished our tour," he enthused. "Will ya take us?"

"Only need one though."

He pointed at Barry.

"It's you."

Barry's face lit up. Then he looked to Francis.

"I don't want to leave my chum."

"Not to worry. Plenty other ships looking for hands. He'll be fine."

Francis looked away, out the window.

"Go on then," he said to the bleak tenements outside.

Barry paused, realization dawning on him.

"Good luck, Frank," he said slowly. "You'll be fine. I'm sure you'll get a ship soon. Maybe we'll see each other again?"

Francis didn't answer, just kept looking out the window.

"Come on then," snapped White. "I sail at noon."

Francis finally looked at his young friend.

"Lucky so-and-so," he said, hiding his emotions. "Wish I was going East. Thanks again. For everything."

The shipping master made an impatient cough. Without looking back, Barry followed him out.

Francis sat back down on the bench with a sigh.

CHAPTER 3

The *Emerald Isle*

Liverpool, England, 1866

A half clipper in model and a packet clipper in rig, the Emerald Isle *hails out of New York and is the largest vessel built at Bath, Maine. She is somewhat full bodied, sharp, and heavily sparred. She is a three-decker but also has a forecastle deck with two large houses for a galley, storerooms, and crew's quarters and a small cabin abaft the main hatch. The first lower deck contains a steerage cabin with a double tier of staterooms on each side running forward to the main hatch. Each of these staterooms has eight berths. This graceful ship has a figurehead of a dog in the act of leaping. Her stern is half round with a carved moulding which has the Harp of Erin in the center, an American Eagle on the right, and a dog on the left. Underneath are written the mottoes on the Irish and American coat of arms:* Erin-go-Bragh *and* E Pluribus Unum.

—From Tapscott's Line

"O'Neill, isn't it?"

"It is, sir."

A trim man peered at Francis in the doorway of the galley.

"Name's Farrell. Chief steward of this fine ship. Captain says you're to be my assistant. Uniform fit alright?"

The stiff navy wool caught Francis across his chest and was too short for his long arms.

"Fine, sir."

"Good. Your job is distributing provisions. Staterooms have their own dining area and steerage eat where they are. Do what you're told and before we know it the five weeks are up and we're landing in New York. Questions?"

"Sorry, sir. Are you an American? I've never met one. I mean. You're the first…"

"Pennsylvania born and bred," interrupted Farrell. "Ever been?"

"This is my first time going to America."

"I envy you. Soon you will step foot on the finest country in the world."

"That's good, sir. I take it by your name that your people were Irish.

Were they from Cork at all?"

"Don't know or care. You'll find out quick that no one in America cares about that."

He fixed the surprised Francis with a stern look.

"To business. Been told we have 876 Mormons on board. Most of 'em Danes. Know what a Mormon is?"

"No, sir."

"Me neither. Some new religion." Farrell stared accusingly at Francis as if it were his invention. "They'll have to eat what's put in front of them, same as everyone else. Don't take any arguments. I certainly don't want to hear any. Also, no fraternizing with the passengers, O'Neill. That means you don't eat, drink, smoke or *anything* else with them."

"I understand, sir."

"Good. Oh! Almost forgot. We are to put in at Queenstown. Cursed water distiller's broken down. We'll have no fresh water for this lot if they can't fix it. You'll get a few days leave."

Francis stared at him, surprised by the unexpected news.

"Well?" asked Farrell. "Anything else?"

"Cork? I, ah, I didn't expect to get so close to home. May I have an advance on pay to visit my family?"

Farrell shrugged.

"I see no issue. Talk to the bursar. Make sure you're back in time though. Don't get drunk and forget to come back."

"I won't, sir. Thank you."

"Very well. Now into that galley and get stuck in."

★★★

The early morning train left Queenstown to journey all the way to the new station in Dunmanway. Train travel was still novel to Francis—especially seeing Cork countryside fly by. His exhilaration wore off when he got on the mail coach for Bantry, crowded with sullen unspeaking passengers who glanced at him with suspicion. A stranger. Although everything was the same it felt disappointing: drab and small compared to everywhere he had seen.

The Convent of Mercy scrutinized him without mercy as he walked by on the road up to Tralibane. He felt too ashamed to call on Father Sheehan and continued on the quiet road. Finally, the old house was before him. This at least felt unchanged, thought Francis as he inhaled the familiar smells of the farmyard. He knocked on the door and his mother answered. She was dressed in black, hair suddenly streaked white.

"Oh Daniel," she cried out. "You came back. You came back."

She leaned on him in the door, crying like he had never heard her cry.

"Mam," he consoled her. "'Course I came back."

She wiped her eyes and stepped back to look at him properly.

"Look at you! You're a giant of a man now. We got your letters. What places you've been. What's that?"

She reached up to touch the scar on his forehead. He blinked.

"It's nothing, Mam. I'll tell you all about it. I can only stay the night though. My ship is out for America in a couple of days."

He led her into the parlor. Johnny was smoking a pipe in their father's chair.

"Welcome home," he said.

"Sit down, Mam," Francis told his upset mother. He ignored his brother.

"Where's Daddy?" he asked.

And then he knew.

The story came out in a jumble: Her widow's weeds. The funeral where the priest neglected any mention of his father or his life. They had tried to send news but had no address. How she woke up with him cold beside her. She wept again as she told him this last detail. He had said he felt a bit sore before bed.

Johnny was head of the household now. He didn't say much. He didn't have to.

"I'll gather the neighbors and have them over," Johnny said, leaving them.

His mother's face brightened.

"Yes," she called to him. "They'll want to see Daniel before he goes to America."

★★★

The neighbors came. Francis stood by the fireplace like a statue of a saint, the whiskey bottle labeled *Allman & Co.* beside him on the mantelpiece.

"Where were you now at all?" asked old Timmy.

"Alexandria, Odessa, even Asia."

"Asia! Now what part of America is that?"

They were all wary of him. The scandal of his departure. His father's sudden death. His poor mother.

"My Seamus looked up to you something fierce," an older woman said to him.

He could not place her. A student's mother? But she looked so old.

"Is he here?"

"Gone. England, we think. Sure, why would he stay? There isn't land good enough around here to feed a snipe in the summer. And now you off to America not long after your own father's wake."

Solemn assent came from everyone in earshot. Francis nodded his head, not knowing what to say. He felt their emotions as they snuck looks at him: fear, resentment, curiosity, anger.

He realized he was the one being waked.

By this time, old Timmy had had too much drink and badgered Francis for a few words. Reluctantly Francis stood up and a hush descended.

"I don't like making speeches but I won't be here long," his voice faltered. "I- I've missed you all. I'm off to America in the morning and don't know when I'll be back."

He stopped, afraid he might start crying. Timmy broke the awkward silence.

"Let us not talk about that, Danny," said Timmy, his speech was slurred. "I want you all to remember my old friend John tonight. He was fond of a drop and very fond of music too. He had a song you all know he liked to sing. It's a happy song, not a sad one."

Francis, somewhat recovered, was pleased to see his mother's brief smile.

"I'd like you to sing with me now."

It had been a while, and the Irish was rusty in parts but they all joined in.

Agus bímis ag ól, is ag ól, 's ól.
Bímis ag ól is ag pógadh na mban.

★★★

Before dawn, his mother thrust a Tilly lamp into the room to rouse the unspeaking brothers. They barely fit into the small room.

"Johnny," she insisted. "You'll take him to Dunmanway in time for that train."

Johnny, still in his nightshirt, roused himself—a malignant look in his eye.

"And you'll give him the money you owe."

He muttered something and left the room.

Francis stood up. He had gone to bed dressed, just in case. He followed his mother outside.

"I've missed you, son. It means so much you came back."

"Of course, Mam."

"Will you come back again?"

"I'll try."

She stared at him for a long last moment. She knew. She blinked at a few tears before handing him a small bundle.

"It's not much. Food for the journey. Those ships are death, I hear."

"Don't worry, Mam. The crew's mess isn't so bad."

"Danny, I want you to know. Your father always regretted it. Letting you go like that. He just couldn't see beyond farming, you know."

"I know, Mam."

"If he could see you now. You'd have made him very proud. Keep writing to us. Don't forget now."

There was nothing more to be said. He hugged her one last time and then mounted the wagon where his brother sat in aggressive silence. Francis kept looking back as his mother diminished and disappeared from view. Past the Tralibane bridge and out the road to Dunmanway they went—birds raucous in the early morning.

★★★

With still an hour before the train departed, the station was quiet. Francis peered into his mother's parcel: a large round of cheese, a bag of flour, a jar

85

of jam, an unmarked bottle of poitín. He noted with delight the dull black gleam of a wooden flute.

"Better be going," grunted Johnny. He would only look at the cart-horse's rump.

Francis stepped down. They had hardly spoken the whole way, the silence a reenactment of their previous violence.

"It's all yours now, Johnny. Look after our Mam."

His eyes narrowed as he turned to look at Francis.

"It was always mine. You couldn't put up with what I have to. Swanning off around the world. I'll never have that chance."

Francis stared back.

"You could if you wanted to. Farm's yours now. You could sell it."

Johnny gave him a baffled look. For once, they realized how little they understood each other. With a sigh, Johnny fished some money out of his pocket.

"Here, there's your money. Don't be coming back any time soon."

The Merry Sisters

"Mr. O'Neill!" Farrell called out as Francis ascended the gangplank. "I feared we might have to leave without you."

The chief steward broke away from the group of men clustered around a machine on the aft deck.

"Good morning, sir," replied Francis. "I came back as soon as I could. I had to comfort my widowed mother."

Farrell cocked his head but said nothing. The only sounds were seagulls screaming and the clattering of shrouds in the wind.

"Sorry to hear it," he replied finally. "Best get your gear stowed below. Passengers are due back before sundown and will want feeding."

Francis made a slow nod of obedience. He looked past his superior to the machine beyond.

"Is the water distiller fixed, sir?"

Farrell let out a sigh. He pointed at the contraption next to a guilty-looking mechanic.

"They can't fix the temperamental thing. We're taking on extra water but there won't be enough."

"We are still to sail?"

"Captain says yes." Farrell gave him a worried look. "Nothing for it. Now below you go. I need that galley cleaned."

★★★

Once they cleared Queenstown harbor, a shiver ran through the ship as the unfurled sails caught the wind. From below deck, Francis pictured the men scrambling over the ratlines high above. In the dimness of steerage, he dispensed hard tack and yellow India meal to taciturn Scandinavians—families of simply dressed people with beautiful blond children. A bluff man with a barrel chest rose from his bench.

"This food is not good," he complained.

He indicated a bowl, a mixture of tack and meat the steward called "Dog's Vomit".

"It is crawling with bad things."

"I'm sorry," answered Francis. "That's what the people in steerage are allotted."

"We have many children. This cannot feed them. And the water. It is stale."

"I will tell the steward of your concerns. What's your name, sir?"

"I am elder Hans Jensen Hals. You will tell him?"

"I promise. Perhaps we can get you better rations."

The man huffed in disbelief. Francis made to reply but then he saw her, a mass of auburn curls piled on her head. The Mormon elder continued to speak but Francis did not hear. She wore a red shawl. Perhaps he heard her speak first, the lilting accent of Clare.

"Thank you again," mumbled Francis, distracted. "I'll be sure to tell the steward."

Elder Hals glared as Francis walked away and over to her group.

"Where are you from?" he asked the oldest man.

"Feakle. East Clare. Do you know it? Not too far from Ennis."

"I've heard of it," he lied. "I'm Francis O'Neill from Tralibane. It's in

West Cork, not far from Bantry. We're famous for music in our part of the world."

"Not near as good as ours," the red-haired woman said, joining the conversation. "Our fiddlers are the best for dancing to."

Francis smiled hugely but his tongue found no words. Her eyes were hazel.

"This one," said the older man. "Who should have introduced herself, is my daughter Anna. I'm Fergus Rogers. And this is my wife Nora along with our other daughter Julia."

A girl younger than Anna tilted a coquettish smile.

"Very nice to meet you."

"Ah, it's so good to hear an Irish voice," said Mrs. Rogers. "We don't know what these people are saying at all. And the English sailors are even worse. Some of the things they say!"

"They're a rough bunch, alright. Here's the food I have for you. It's awful stuff though."

Fergus looked at the rations in horror.

"We didn't know. The waybill said it would be better."

"Do you not have any extra yourselves?"

Frightened silence was the only reply.

"It's a terrible long journey. I can bring you a bit on the quiet."

"Oh no," said Fergus. "Don't be doing that."

"Shush, Daddy," said Anna. "He wants to help."

"Thank you, then. If you're sure."

Francis looked around, his tone serious.

"It will be quieter after port watch. Bring some others up on deck and meet me. I'll see what I can arrange."

★★★

The hand-written card on the door bore the inscription: *Hubert Murdoch Sr. & Hubert Murdoch Jr.*

Francis put down his tray and knocked, the murmur of conversation silenced.

"Yes," an irritated voice responded.

"Your supper, sir."

The door whipped open. The man was about Francis's age, pale with vivid red hair. A bald older man, his father presumably, smoked a pipe in an armchair.

"Bring it in then," the young man snapped.

The stateroom was well appointed with elaborate carved wooden finials. A porthole to the sea and a deck prism bore shafts of light through the limpid smoke. Francis noted the younger Hubert was quite short.

"As I was saying," his father said, light gleaming on his bald pate. "The challenge is to find opportunity within a crisis. When the fire burns off, where is the best ground to sow?"

Francis paused, unsure if this was addressed to him.

"Yes, yes. Obviously." The young man's voice broke a little with emotion. "But how to do it? Look at the country we have just left. Famine brought great opportunity. Removed millions of peasants. Yet the place languishes priest-ridden. So much opportunity squandered."

Murdoch Sr. inhaled his pipe with relish. It was dark wood with a large copper ring above the bowl.

"In any case, the principles of Reverend Malthus are proven correct again."

"Excuse me," Francis interrupted. "Your dinner."

Hubert Jr. regarded him with cold blue eyes.

"Over there."

He indicated the table.

"Many died terribly in the great hunger," Francis could not help muttering, putting the tray down.

The two men looked as shocked as if the table had spoken.

"Certainly, they did," replied young Hubert finally. "And why was that?"

"The blight and the landlords."

"Incorrect. It was because there were too many to feed. But you have a brain. So, think it through. What should they have done?"

The intensity of the young man was unnerving.

"I don't know," Francis said. "They couldn't do anything. They were starving."

"Pah! Typical wishy-washy response. *They* should have finished them all off. Cleared all the land of a troublesome peasantry."

He studied Francis and the tray of food with disgust. His father was standing now, regarding Francis with the same cold eyes.

"Enough now, Hubert. Nothing to be gained from antagonizing them."

Francis was breathing slowly. He straightened himself and addressed the senior Murdoch.

"I will be informing the Captain that you are smoking in your cabin. It is not allowed."

Silence. Young Hubert erupted into high-pitched laughter.

"The Irish revolution at last! By all means, inform our good friend the Captain."

Francis walked out of the stateroom, the back of his neck hot with shame and anger.

★★★

Francis scrounged what he could from the galley, along with some from his mother's supply. John Brennan, an older sailor and sometimes fiddler, was also coerced into bringing extra food.

"That bad water'll be their downfall," Brennan had concluded when Francis told him of the passengers' plight.

Later, they met behind the wheelhouse. There were a couple of other Irish families along with the Rogers. The ship made fair headway in the intermittent breeze.

"Ah Francis, good man yourself," exclaimed Fergus when he spotted the covert supplies.

"It's not much. We'll try to get you more later. Take care you only drink boiled water."

"Oh, this ship is a curse," wailed Mrs. Rogers, pale and distraught. "One of them foreign children is taken sick."

"Now, now, Mam," soothed Anna.

She turned to face Francis.

"Thank you."

He found himself unable to reply but managed to smile at her directness. Her father made to thrust money into his hand.

"No. No. I won't take it."

Brennan chuckled at Francis's embarrassment and opened the *poitín* from Tralibane.

"Might as well make a bit of a hooley of it. The Captain's abed."

Young Julia Rogers grabbed the bottle from him.

"That sounds grand to me."

Anna and her mother looked at her in shock.

"Why not a bit of music?" cajoled Julia. "We can dance. I've heard you sailors all play a bit."

Brennan laughed aloud.

"Francis," he said. "Did you not hear the girl? Go below and get your flute. My fiddle's in the big locker."

"Well, I don't know," said Francis. He noticed a small smile from Anna. The tilt of her head. The deck lurched beneath him without having moved.

"It'll be fine," said Brennan. "We'll keep it low."

They played into the night. John Brennan was not as fluid a player as Francis but played quietly if he fell behind. For the first time, Francis understood how playing music had the added benefit of sparing you from the horror of dancing. As the others danced, Julia called at them for "Reels now" or "Jigs" depending on the set. The drum of their feet on the deck kept the rhythm. In the middle of "The Silver Spear" he happened to look up and spotted Anna studying him.

★★★

Elder Hals looked hollowed out, his face so pale it was almost green.

"They have sent you?" he asked.

"Yes, sir. The Captain felt it should be my punishment for... associating with the passengers."

"The Captain. He will not come?"

"He is afraid of fever."

"What has he said of the behavior of the sailors towards our daughters?"

"Nothing, sir."

The man wiped his eyes. Francis noticed a thin sheen of sweat on his forehead.

"They are over here."

He led Francis to the far end of the cavernous hold where the Mormons were gathered around two small bodies dressed in white clothes. He remembered the first time he witnessed death as a young boy—a cow collapsed from redwater. The animal had shuddered for a while before going stiff.

"A bit of a fit," his father had muttered in disgust.

Hals murmured in Swedish to a few of the men who bent down to move the corpses. Francis fumbled with the roll of canvas, sick to his stomach.

"They must be wrapped in canvas before going aloft. Captain's orders."

He kept his voice as emotionless as he could. Hals stared in anger before nodding with weary resignation, giving quick words to the other men. They grimly took the stiff cloth. Hals was seized by a sudden vehemence and grasped at Francis.

"Who will know how they have died? Will you remember? Will your ship record how these poor souls were lost?"

Francis shook his head dumbly. The elder calmed. He straightened himself and gave Francis an absent-minded pat on the lapel.

"I do not blame you, son. This will be recorded. In the final reckoning all will be held to account. Even your Captain."

He turned to his people and spoke in Swedish. Francis assumed he was repeating this message. Many of them were too hungry or too sick to respond. Francis helped the others lift the little bundles aloft. To his surprise, some pilgrims managed a quiet hymn as they left.

If the Sea Were Ink

Francis stood on deck with the dazed passengers. A misty drizzle engulfed the becalmed ship like a wet wool blanket. It wasn't just the weather; it was the deaths. One after another until the Captain had ordered everyone above deck. A select, or not so select, few scrubbed out below with sea water.

"How're you holding up?" he asked Anna. Something about the gloom helped him overcome his shyness.

Her smile was quick despite her looking so pale.

"Only fair. Our Julia." She rolled her eyes. "She's being difficult. She disappears some nights. Mam frets and Dad just says nothing."

"I can tell the men to keep away from her."

He tried to sound dark and threatening.

"Oh, don't do that. You've gone to enough trouble for us. Julia can look after herself. Although, she stayed in her pallet all last night and had to be dragged out this morning."

She made a small sigh.

"The poor craiturs of foreign children are in an awful way though."

Francis nodded while surveying the damp, covering everything. He turned to her.

"They made me go down to get the bodies," he said, voice quiet. "Because we had music the other night."

"Oh, Francis. That must have been terrible."

"Worse for them." He looked away. "Their elder is going through an awful time of it. I couldn't..."

"What is it, Francis?"

"I wasn't able to properly stitch up the shroud on them. I was told to but... I couldn't."

She reached out and touched his hand, her touch was soft and fleeting.

"Don't blame yourself," she said. "A dead child is a terrible thing. Your Captain was cruel to send you down."

They did not say anything for a long while. Francis had to think hard to break the heavy silence.

"Did you see how they sing at the funerals?" he ventured. "Unlike any Protestants I've known, they celebrate at death. A bit like an Irish wake, I suppose."

"You'll be converting next," she said.

He brightened when he saw her smile. There was something in the way one side of her mouth turned up and her eyes widened.

"They don't drink at all though. I was at a wake in Bantry once that was drinking for a whole day."

"And what about you?"

"Oh no," he looked down. "I don't drink. My father was an awful man for it so I've no interest. I would like to know more of that song they were singing though."

Now she laughed.

"You really are mad for music."

"Yes," he agreed. "Especially when it's music from home."

Their eyes held for a second. Then his expression darkened as he recalled their circumstances.

"Home isn't home anymore though, is it?"

He looked away at the bedraggled crowd of exiles on the deck.

"No," she sighed. "Where will you go when we reach New York?"

"Stay sailoring, I think. I'd like to say some day that I sailed around the world. What about you?"

"We're to stop in Brooklyn, for now. Then we might venture west. My father wants to farm again."

"That sounds like a good life, Anna."

"Will you keep in touch? Write to us of your adventuring?"

"I will. Course I will. Though I don't think it'll be very adventurous."

He stood up without meaning to.

"We'll be delayed by this calm a few more days though." His words were quick and nervous. "Keep your food hid. Tell me if there's any thieving down there."

"You're awful good to us, Francis."

"I want to ask you something."

"What is it?"

"Hmm. I. Well."

"All below," bellowed the mate. "All passengers to return below."

A meek murmur of complaint came from the crowd, hopeless faces regarded the bleak hole of the hatch.

"What did you want to ask, Francis?" pressed Anna.

"It's fine. You should go down with them."

She tilted her head then nodded. Francis cursed himself as he watched her small form descend below. *Had she really touched his hand?*

★★★

A shout woke him. Lying in his bunk in a half-dreaming state, it sounded like a whoop of exultation from a dancer. In the darkness, other sailors groaned and grumbled at the disturbance.

"Man overboard," came a distant cry.

Francis yanked on his uniform. Above deck was confusion—no one at the wheelhouse. The wind had picked up again, waves slapping the sides of the ship. A gang of men pointed lanterns over the side, straining to see in the dim gloom while others restrained an older woman screaming at the sea.

"My babóg is gone," she wailed. "She's gone."

Francis pushed through the crowd to the men holding Anna's mother. "What's happened?"

"My babóg," she cried. "She's gone, gone."

Anna pushed past the bystanders with her father.

"What's happened, Mam?"

"Julia's gone. She's gone in the sea."

Shock overtook relief then settled to guilt. His first thought had been that it was Anna.

"Wait!"

Francis spied John Brennan and another sailor hauling on a rope by the railing.

"Lend a hand!" he called, dashing alongside to help them. A gasping Julia emerged clutching a cork vest. They pulled her over the rail where she collapsed onto the deck, sodden clothes in disarray about her. Her copper hair was stuck to her head like seaweed. For a terrible moment nobody approached, then Anna and her mother rushed to her.

"Doctor," shouted her father. "Someone get a doctor."

★★★

The medical officer covered her in a blanket. She coughed violently after sipping from a proffered brandy flask. The men congratulated Brennan on his quick wit. The cork vest was usually forgotten—an untrusted device like the water distiller.

"How did it happen?" asked the doctor. "What was she doing above deck?"

"He pushed me." Julia's voice was faint. "That young Murdoch fellow. The one in the quality room. I didn't want any more to do with him."

"Nonsense," thundered a strong English voice. The elder Murdoch, pipe in hand, stepped forward.

"I can vouch for my son. He was in our berth the entire time. He wouldn't go near any Irish trash."

Fergus Rogers lunged at Murdoch but was held back by Francis.

"Pay no attention!" shouted Francis. "The Captain. We need to get the Captain."

Murdoch regarded them, an implacable set to his jaw. Anna kept a hand on Francis's shoulder while he helped lead her parents away.

The First Night In America

New York, USA, 1866

"I'd let the whole thing lie, if I were you." John Brennan furrowed his heavy brow as he pulled on the oars. Francis watched the receding *Emerald Isle* from their little craft. Although crew were released, the vessel still lay in quarantine off the squat hump of Ellis Island. Across the water sat the dour Castle Garden building in the Battery. Brennan told him it was where the passengers had to enter the country. He pictured a weary Anna being processed there, surrounded by her upset family.

"The Rogers have suffered a terrible wrong, John. That Murdoch fellow should be prosecuted."

Brennan ignored this.

"Been to New York before?" he asked.

Shaking his head, Francis peered properly through the gray morning drizzle at the looming city—swaying masts of ships before distant tall buildings. This new city gave off a vague feeling of unwelcome.

"Can be a risky place," continued Brennan. "You're not in Cork now. Look. Captain told me to take you direct to the sailor's boarding house. The boss'll be by to get you another ship out soon enough. It's a good house on Oliver Street, owned by a Dane. He's married to an Irish woman called Bridey Reid." Brennan chuckled. "Bridey's a tough lady. Wouldn't take his

Danish name. I know her people distantly."

"Thanks, John. I'll have to go to the police to follow up on Julia's attack. I promised Anna I would. That crook of a Captain won't do anything."

"Fond of Anna, aren't you? I spotted her looking at you when we had the hooley."

Francis looked into the water shyly. Brennan made another small chuckle. "She your sweetheart?"

"No," he shook his head again and looked away. "Not with all that happened on board. She said I could write to her though."

"That's something. Do you know where they'll be?"

Francis's gaze darted all over the dim bulk of Manhattan looming in the dusk, as if he might find her address there.

"She only said Brooklyn. Do you know where that is?"

Brennan laughed aloud now.

"I do. It's across the harbor from where we're going. I know another boarding house over there. I'll stay there and get word to you when I locate them."

"We'll need to know their address to testify to the police."

"Oh, yes. The police."

Brennan fell silent, considering his words as he pulled the oars through the bleak cold water.

"They've been wronged, sure enough," he said eventually. "But there's nothing you can do now. That girl is fierce lucky to be alive. Look out for yourself is my advice."

★★★

A lamplighter busied at his task as Francis wandered up the quiet street. He was lost. In the murk of the unfamiliar city, he had mixed up Brennan's instructions.

"Excuse me," he enquired of the scruffy man. "I'm looking for 66 Oliver Street."

"You a sailor?" the young man asked, leaning on his pole.

"Yes. It's a boarding house for sailors."

"It's too early to be heading for your hunky, friend. What about a tavern?

97

I know one where the ladies sort out sailors quick."

His leer was grotesque in the green gaslight.

Francis just looked at him. The young man shrugged.

"Oliver Street's back that way."

He pointed with his pole.

"Funny. A few more of yous sailors just came by looking for the same place. Tried to tout them to *The Seahorse* too, but no good."

"Yes?"

"You run, you'll catch them."

Francis took off as quick as he could, canvas bag heavy on his back. Around the corner was a street of rundown brown-brick buildings with black windows. A few men waited on a stoop. He recognized one from the *Emerald Isle*—a taciturn American who rarely spoke.

"Hullo," he called. "Weston, isn't it?"

The group pulled apart at his call. Weston slipped past him.

"No," he replied. "And you ain't O'Neill, neither."

"What?"

Francis looked around in confusion. A big man with cauliflower ears spat on the ground in front of him.

"We don't know you. You don't know us. But we'll take what you got."

Suddenly, Weston was behind him, pinning his arms back. His breath, reeking of alcohol, felt hot on Francis's neck.

"Here's a message," he hissed. "Forget everything that happened on that ship. No making trouble. Forget everyone you knew on there."

The big man stepped forward to rifle through his pockets, taking what money Francis had. A third picked up his canvas bag.

"We're just robbing you. Next time, if we recognize you… Well. Could be a lot worse."

Furious, Francis jerked his head back, connecting with Weston's nose. His captor grunted with the sudden pain but didn't let go.

"You being smart?" asked the big one with the mangled ears. He punched Francis hard in the gut, making him gasp with the sudden pain.

An upstairs window rattled open and a lantern came out.

"Who's making all the racket? I'll get Olaf down to sort ye out, so I will."

An Irish voice. His assailants muttered to each other. Weston pushed Francis and he sprawled hard onto the pavement. A feeling of ridiculous relief overcame him when he looked up to see number 66 beside the door. The men laughed and cursed as they made off into the night.

★★★

Francis had pulled himself upright by the time the landlady made it down to the front door. She was rake-thin with a pinched sour face, mouth pursed with distrust.

"Be off now," she said sternly. "My husband will be down in a minute."

Francis steadied himself on the iron railings. He couldn't straighten up.

"Are you Bridey Reid?" he wheezed.

She looked at him closely.

"You know me? Be gone now if you're going to be causing trouble."

"John Brennan. He's a friend of mine. Said to stay here."

"Brennan, is it?" She sniffed. "He owes me money."

She considered for a long moment before relenting.

"You might as well come in so."

★★★

His stomach roiled every time he moved in the bed, twisting himself around the pain and the broken bed springs. Cold sweat drenched his shirt, the only one he had now. There was a moldy smell to the ancient pillow. He gave up trying to sleep. Dim pre-dawn gloom edged the thin curtains. Outside was the din of New York, sounds had not stopped all night—drays on the street, train whistles, shouts. He despaired he would never see her again. What if those brutes found her or her family? Images raced through his mind: her sister dancing and laughing, calling on them to play faster; small bodies wrapped in canvas they threw into the sea; Murdoch's cold blue eyes, a sneer on his lips.

Francis turned to the wall and sobbed quietly. Everything was gone: money, books and fiddle. The frustration and shame hurt as much as the pain in his side.

The Stormy Voyage

Miss Anna Rogers
Care of Mrs. Brigid Reid
66 Oliver Street
New York, New York
November 1866

Dear Anna,

I am writing this in hopes that the good landlady of 66 Oliver Street can pass it on to you. She has many contacts amongst the Irish people in New York so hopefully when you are settled in Brooklyn you can get acquainted. John Brennan, who helped save Julia on the Emerald Isle, *has promised to try and get in touch also. I am sorry we had to part under such terrible circumstances and I hope that you and your family are bearing up well. Someday I will see that justice is done for poor Julia. I tried to contact the authorities in New York about the matter but have had my own struggles. Suffice it to say that after my first night in America I had nothing to my name but the shirt on my back! Fortunately, I wasn't in New York long before an opportunity presented itself on the* Louisa Anne. *She is an aging schooner, not much better than the dreary packet ship we were fated to meet on. Before I knew it, I was bound for Brunswick in the state of Georgia. We were loaded with yellow pine lumber destined for St. Croix in the West Indies. What a world traveler I have become!*

By comparison to the portion of the world I have encountered heretofore I did not think much of Brunswick. It is about a half-dozen houses clustered around a sawmill. Perhaps someday it will erupt into another Odessa or New York. Who can say? The little hamlet is at the edge of a bayou. A word I had not heard before. It is a flat marsh or swamp with an ill-defined stream running through it. And yet our boats had little difficulty navigating there. It was August and the sun blazed over our heads all day long as we loaded dimension lumber on board from the mill's raft. Most of the crew, including myself, were laid flat by the heat and exertion. A negro hired to work with me showed great consideration by taking up my tasks while I recovered. I had encountered some of his kind in Egypt but was unable to converse in their language. This man Bob has been through some awful times. His stories of cruel treatment by his masters remind me of the troubles of our own country.

PART ONE: SEA

Our hold full, we soon sailed out into the open sea. Within a day we encountered a hurricane. You cannot imagine how frightening it was to see a great mass of black clouds off to the east descend with speed upon our schooner. The strength of the winds was enough to make me think we were not going to survive. Because of my experience, I was sent to the helm. To be honest, it was as much a matter of holding on with another fellow in a futile effort to keep her steady as the sea flung us about. The rest of the crew manned the pumps all the furious night. There was no rest as the water crashed over the pines braced and chained to the deck. The Captain assured us there was little risk of sinking as our cargo was lumber. However, my fear was that it might come loose and slide off in the tempestuous violence, taking us down with it. Although some was lost, it was not until we finally found our way to St. Croix and unloaded the remainder that we found three large rat-holes below the line. Water had been pouring into the hold the entire duration of the storm!

The storm having passed, we made haste south. Several days later, off the coast of Florida, a pair of eagles circled our ship. Given these great birds' love for high places, it was no surprise that one of the pair perched on the lee gallant yardarm. Although I had been at the wheel, I watched the bird as closely as I could the entire time. At eight bells, being relieved from duty, I made up my mind to capture our noble visitor and climbed aloft as delicately as I could. I hope you will not think me fool-hardy but these last couple of years at sea have made me very nimble on the rigging. I was as close as the jaws of the yard (where it is attached to the mast) before he showed any interest in my approach. I slid along as quietly as I could, stopping every time he moved. One arm on the beam, my bare feet on the rope, I had only the other arm free. He peered at me as the ship rolled over a high wave and raised his wings to depart. That was when I lunged for him. I managed to grab him under the wing and clasp him to me. It was tricky enough to get him down from there with just the thin footrope and the yard to hold onto. To tell the truth, apart from the great height, it wasn't much different from getting my mother's rooster down from the rafters of a shed when a boy. We made a pet of the great bird and fed him rats and canned meat. The Captain is an American and took great delight in him.

I hope you do not find my tale too gruesome, Anna. I liked how we were able to speak freely to each other on our voyage together. You said you liked my "adventure stories". Anyway, the West Indies are beautiful and lush. The fish so abundant they

101

jostle one another out of the water when we throw scraps overboard from the galley. Their brilliant colors make our northern fish lackluster by comparison. On leave in St. Croix, I was able to hire a local to take me for a tour along the coast. He pointed out every species of tree, tamarind and coconut palms grow wild everywhere. He also showed me the fine houses of the sugar plantation owners high up in the mountains. I was told that these owners were mostly of Irish ancestry, being descendants of the Irish shipped out as slaves by Cromwell. Although they came here as slaves, they have no problem keeping slaves themselves. I saw many of Bob's dark brethren engaged in back-breaking work in the fields.

Once we entered the town again, I was short on time so bid farewell to my guide. Dusk descends quickly and early in that latitude. However, hurrying back to the tender that was to carry me back aboard, I spotted a large cat sitting in the second window of a small house. I remembered the rats crawling all over the Louisa Anne *and the damage they had wrought. Thinking this a rare opportunity and perhaps overly proud of my success with the eagle, I climbed a rough wall and reached out for the creature's tail hanging over the ledge. I swung him off the sill and endeavored to grab him to me. What a strange music of hissing and squealing followed next! Not least of which were my own expressions of pain as the forepaw of the terrified tom found my right knee. Before long, all four paws and his teeth were buried in my flesh. I had the wharf in my sights, so I gritted my teeth and half-limped half-ran to the waiting craft. With great effort, I managed to throw myself onboard and yell to my fellows to push off. The cat let go after we were in. I think his desire for freedom was not as strong as his fear of water. Later, he proved an able rat-catcher and regularly provided for the eagle. He never took to me, however.*

I have no more "great adventures" to report from my West Indies trip. We took on a load of coarse salt from a group of coral islands. It was dreary work loading the stuff in the sweltering tropical heat. The trip back was uneventful enough, although I had hoped to see you when I returned here to Mrs. Reid's. I'm shipping out soon on the full-rigged ship Minnehaha. *It will be a long stint. The ultimate destination is Yokohama, Japan. I am excited by this opportunity of a long voyage to foreign countries. I'm sure I will have many good tales to relate when I return, should you wish to hear them. I do hope you get this, Anna. Please write back to me if you do. I will return to 66 Oliver Street in hopes that you will. Although we knew each other for only a short time, I think we shared more than just a common understanding. Please let me know if you feel the same way. I do enjoy this traveling the world but it gets awful lonesome sometimes. And of course, I would like nothing more than to hear of your own adventures in America.*

Yours sincerely,
Francis

The Pleasures Of Hope

Boston, Massachusetts, 1867

"Call me Hickman." The first mate extended a sunburned hand to Francis.

"Thank you, sir. Francis O'Neill. Many call me Frank."

Hickman chuckled to himself.

"What do you think of her, Frank?"

He indicated the elaborate sails and masts of the full-rigged ship above them.

"A real beauty," said Francis. "I look forward to steering her."

"You have experience at the helm?"

"I do, sir. On several ships. But it'll be my first time on a four-master."

"That's fine. We want to make good time with the trade winds across the Atlantic then southeast to cross the cape. The *Minnehaha* is a heavy ship, though. Sure you can handle it?"

"I'll do my best, sir. I helmed my last ship through a hurricane off the Carolinas."

Hickman made to reply but his expression darkened as he looked beyond Francis.

"Captain on deck," he announced.

Francis stood up straight, surprised at the abrupt change of tone. A dour man, walking with a slight limp, appeared out of the Captain's quarters. His beard, in the Shenandoah style, was black streaked with gray, a stark contrast to the pallor of his cheeks.

"Hickman," he barked. "Stop loitering and prepare for sail."

"Aye, sir."

The captain fixed a young cabin boy with a glare. Francis noticed the Captain's eyes were red-rimmed and slightly bulging.

"What is your task?" he asked the boy.

"I don't know, sir," came the timid reply.

With surprising speed and vehemence, the Captain cuffed him. The young fellow tumbled back, blood trickling from his ear. A strange gleam lit the Captain's glassy eyes.

"Anyone else not know what to do?" he intoned, turning about.

A general scramble followed as everyone made to look busy. The Captain looked around again before trudging back to his door. Francis helped Hickman tend to the pale-faced boy.

"You heard Captain Burleigh," said Hickman, his face a mask. "Everyone back to work now. For you Frank, that means taking this boy below." He lowered his voice. "Clean him up and see if you can get him something out of the galley."

Francis nodded, leading the frightened youth away.

★★★

Francis, busy at stitching canvas, looked up briefly at the coast gliding past—a horn of rock looming over a desolate shore. His mind was elsewhere, trying to recall the second half of a jig in a minor key.

"First time crossing the cape?"

Hickman's voice surprised him; he had been too engrossed to notice the man's approach. Francis simply nodded and returned to his work.

"Bit of a letdown, isn't it?" said Hickman.

Francis shrugged.

"Heard of the *Flying Dutchman,* Frank? They couldn't get a pilot to land here."

Hickman indicated the headland.

"So they sank. The ghost ship is supposed to haunt hereabouts. Never able to land."

"That's a good one. Why had they no pilot?"

"The Captain murdered him. He doomed the ship and crew."

"Sounds like a story we might be repeating."

Hickman pursed his lips instead of replying.

"I've had a number of captains now, sir." Francis whispered. "None as bad as him."

Hickman shrugged.

"Careful, now," he said with a note of reprimand. "There are different ways to have discipline. Bully is one. Burleigh hails from Cape Cod. They're a stern lot out there. This is my third voyage with him. First time, he was quiet as a mouse. Halfway through the second, he changed overnight. Swain slopped his boot and he damn near killed him. Not sure why. He raves, you know. At night. I sometimes hear him accusing himself in his cabin."

Francis said nothing to this revelation.

"Let's hope," sighed Hickman. "We don't end up like them Dutchmen, eh?"

★★★

Once the *Minnehaha* passed the volcanic peaks of the St. Paul and Amsterdam islands, strong gales blew them far off course south towards Australia. Cruelly pushed to their limits, the crew made it to the Java sea through the Sunda Strait. Here, they were becalmed daily. Without good anchorage in the shallow waters and unable to steer, they drifted. The cruel tropical sun baked the timbers. So oppressive was it that Captain Burleigh assented to draping the deck with canvas to stop the men wilting in the torpid heat. Francis had never experienced such torture. The Captain seldom appeared on deck. When he did, he stood outside the canvas shade. He snickered and muttered at no one in particular, unnaturally pale in his funereal black clothes.

Francis stirred himself from under the makeshift awning. It was not much cooler there but at least he did not have the risk of Burleigh. The tar of the deck squelched beneath his coarse rope sandals. All hands were employed twice daily wetting down the deck and hull for fear of warp. Sometimes Francis was overcome by a fear that the entire ship would dissolve in the ferocious heat. Once, his vision swam and he nearly collapsed, having to steady himself against a spar.

"Sail to starboard!" came a shout from aft.

Staring to the horizon, Francis made out a squat ship with articulated sails. A Russian sailor strode up to the railing and squinted through an eyeglass.

"What kind of ship is that?" asked Francis.

"Junk," replied the Russian in his terse manner.

The Russian said his name was Thomson but Francis did not believe this was his real name. A wiry beard bristled from his face and his eyes were a severe blue. He had served in the Confederate navy, perhaps they had made him change his name. His speech was full of extra vowels he tried to suppress without success. Francis once asked him if he had been to Odessa and how he had liked it. Thomson had laughed violently, choking on his tack.

"Junk?" echoed Francis, puzzled.

"Pirate," he barked. He rushed to a cabinet by the wheelhouse, beckoning Francis to follow. The magazine was full of carbines. He thrust one onto Francis. The stock was hot, as if it had just been fired.

"Tell them," Thomson shouted at Francis, now shook awake from his torpor.

"Pirates!" cried Francis, running up and down the deck.

The ship woke from its heat-induced slumber, men gathering at the railings to gawk at the distant ship. More experienced hands took the warm rifles, their faces grim. A mute Francis followed Thomson to the little cannon on the poop deck. Thomson expertly angled the black iron barrel toward the junk.

"How do they move with no wind?"

"Watch," commanded Thomson. "They have oars. Many crew below."

The ship was more distinct now, the sails like the leathery wings of a malevolent bat. There were few men visible on the narrow deck but Francis could make out the oars.

Hickman ran up to them.

"A big one," he remarked, his calm voice incongruous.

"How will they attack?" Francis asked. Sudden bile rose in his throat, his heart pounding.

"They will draw alongside us. You won't hardly see them until then. They carry long knives and throw stinkpots. In this heat I shouldn't wonder if we won't go up like a bonfire. Ready, Thomson?"

The Russian nodded. He had the little cannon primed.

"Wait until they are well in range. That pea-shooter won't make much impact but at least it'll show we mean business."

"Mr. Thomson," came a querulous voice rose from the lower deck. "Do not dare fire on them."

Captain Burleigh limped towards them.

"Captain," said Hickman. "Our meaning is to deter them."

For a moment Francis feared Burleigh would strike his first mate. Hickman stood ready.

"Do you want them to kill us all?"

The Captain sounded near tears. Francis forgot the nearness of danger to wonder how all the bullying bluster had deserted the man.

"Sir, we have our orders," said Hickman. "Before they board we are to put up as much resistance as we can. Once they board, we are to surrender."

"I'll no longer be dictated to by those mandarins on Merchant's Row, half a world away. Or by you," Burleigh spat back.

"Those." The Captain gestured to the looming junk. "Those yellow savages'll cut our throats once they get the chance."

Hickman said nothing. Burleigh turned to Francis.

"You," he shouted. "Get down to the wheelhouse and initiate evasive maneuvers."

Francis looked to Hickman for confirmation.

"We have no wind, Sir."

"You'd better make some then," shouted Burleigh.

Hickman remained silent.

"I can fire now," said Thomson, through gritted teeth.

Hickman paused for a long moment. Burleigh stared both of them down. His eyes might have erupted from their sockets.

"Go forward, Frank," directed Hickman. "Tell them to raise every inch of sail. See if we can stir ourselves."

Francis dropped the carbine and left without waiting for further orders. On his way he noticed a pennant twitch. A light breeze. He decided to turn back to tell his superiors.

"They can't take me. I can't be taken." Burleigh was blubbering. He leaned on Hickman's sleeve. Thomson was looking away.

"They might not even be pirates…" Hickman was saying to placate him. The Captain kept sobbing despite the wind rising around them. Wide-eyed, Francis rushed forward, rousing the crew to action. Nobody questioned his sudden authority. Slow as a mule pulling a laden cart, the mild breeze pulled the big ship forward. It was a long time before the junk receded to the horizon.

★★★

At the helm, Francis struggled to steer to course, his chart indicated reefs all around.

"Anything?"

Hickman's shout was faint above the wind. A chorus of "No" and "Nothing" was his reply. The noon sun blazed hot despite the breeze. Men were aloft on every available cross-spar, others hung off the bowsprit and crowded the railing of the forecastle.

"Look for a break in the waves. The slightest sign. Howl it out," boomed Hickman up to the men. He ran back to Francis.

"Steer clear at the first noise," he advised.

Francis frowned at the redundant direction but only nodded. Hickman looked askance at Burleigh standing in the shade, silent. Hickman shook his head and ran forward.

The sea was covered in foamy white caps from the fresh wind, sunlight glinting on the water.

All at once the world stopped—an ear-splitting grating as the bow ground onto a reef. Francis felt the shock of reverberation through the helm. He spun the now useless wheel. The feeling of no control frightened him most of all.

"We're reefed! Reefed," he cried.

Burleigh let out a scream. He pushed Francis violently away, clutching at his lapels.

"You fool," he screamed. "Why did I ever let you at the helm?"

"S-sir," stuttered Francis. "We knew the reefs were here but you told us to sail on."

Burleigh stared at Francis. There was murder in his eyes, but then his face crumpled in fear. He covered his ears at further sounds of the reef tearing the hull.

"It's my fault," he wailed. "We're sinking."

Hickman returned. He had directed the men to examine the wreckage.

"There's parts of the keel floating in the sea. Doesn't look like…"

He stopped at the Captain's howling.

"Hickman," entreated Burleigh. "What will become of me? If we don't sink they'll murder me for this. I just wanted us there on time. They've been hounding me for years and now they have me."

"Captain Burleigh," Hickman said in a soothing voice. "We won't sink and no one is after you. Here. Frank will take you to your cabin. He'll have the cook bring you something."

"What will become of me?" his broken voice pleaded.

"Frank," whispered Hickman. "Take him down. Get cook to make a strong brandy to calm him. The man's nerves are gone."

Francis approached Burleigh apprehensively.

"Come along, sir. Mr. Hickman will see us off the reef."

"You're in their employ," he snapped at Francis. "I know it."

"Go along to the cook," said Hickman to Francis, catching Burleigh by the arm. "I'll lead the Captain to his quarters."

★★★

They were anchored off Batavia, the city a vague smudge on the horizon. They had limped along as far as they dared before sending out a party. Francis and Fred, a sailor from Bruges, kept Burleigh drunk in his cabin. When not in a stupor he railed against both of them. They had kept his door locked with a plank.

On deck, Francis helped bring onboard Hickman's party. They brought a small Asian man clad only in a simple cloth. He gave a cheerful nod to Francis before plunging off the deck. Francis watched with growing horror as he didn't resurface.

"I don't think he'll make it, sir," Francis said, rushing to the railing.

"Oh, I know these Malaysian fellows. They live underwater."

"Why thank you, sir," came a musically accented voice. The diver had re-appeared behind them, water streaming off his brown chest. "You are most understanding of my special skills."

Francis nearly fell overboard.

"How did you…"

Everyone laughed at his obvious shock.

"Hah! You came up the other side," Hickman said.

"That is so, sir. As you were saying, I truly can live underwater."

His impish face was pock-marked, thick black hair slicked back on his head.

"Well, Mr. Peh," asked Hickman. "How does it look under there?"

"She has taken quite a pummeling, sir. There is no doubt of it. However, I think the structure is sound. I am the best assessor and diver in the world. That is why your company hired me, of course."

"Yes, our company only hires the best," Hickman said dryly. "The pumps have not been under pressure since the crash. It seems we can continue. Thank you."

"You are most welcome. Will you be sailing to port?"

"No, no. We have delayed long enough. Mr. Jack Burleigh will be joining you, however. I have secured a place for him in the naval hospital. Frank, see Mr. Peh to the tender and await them."

"Yes, Captain Hickman."

★★★

Burleigh, hands bound, stared ahead glassy-eyed as they seated him onto the little boat to be winched down the side of the ship. Francis and Fred prepared the oars. Hickman sat on the thwart furthest from Burleigh.

"Madman," came a shout from amidships. "You damn near killed us all!"

Burleigh winced at the accusation. When their craft reached the water, he gave one last look at the high wall of the *Minnehaha's* hull looming above them. He turned to Hickman.

"You'll never be a captain," he threatened. "I'll see to it."

"I'll see you rot in that Batavian dump."

Burleigh's eyes widened in surprise. He started to reply, but crumpled, burying his face in his hands.

★★★

Francis and Fred were surrounded by the market's rainbow of color— flat baskets of indescribable spices, fruits and vegetables. Hawkers loudly touted their wares. The two men, ignoring the sights and odors assailing them, chatted idly as they walked.

"He was a cruel one, alright," agreed Francis.

Fred shrugged. He was small and stocky with a head of black curls.

"I have had tougher captains. He was, how you say, *lâche*. Coward. This is worse."

"And he cared nothing for his crew. I'm not sure about his replacement, though. Hickman."

"Someone had to take over," said Fred. "Did you want to do it?"

Francis's only reply was to look at a nearby stand.

"You like? Monkey. They good pet."

The stand owner pounced on his brief interest. The aroma from his large clove cigarette was overpowering. A small monkey with leathery features swaggered in a cage.

"He looks just like Burleigh!" exclaimed Fred.

"He good one," said the wizened stall-keeper. "Very nice."

"I don't know," said Francis. "I don't think Hickman would approve."

Despite Francis's protestations, Fred insisted on buying the creature. The seller opened the cage and it leapt onto Fred's neck.

"Hey," laughed the Belgian.

"What should we call him?" asked Francis, stroking the animal's thick fur. The monkey preened in appreciation.

"*Bien sûr,* Burleigh is his name."

"No. Hickman would never allow *that*. Let's call him Jack."

"Make it Jocko—a good French monkey's name."

The Boys From The East

Yokohama, Japan, 1867

The broad port of Yokohama bristled with activity. A cluster of Western ships, the *Minnehaha* biggest amongst them, lay in the harbor surrounded by Chinese junks and smaller Japanese sampans. The latter were flat-bottomed and sculled by breechcloth-clad men perched along the ship's side. Conical straw hats were their only other clothing. A couple of these vessels approached Francis's ship before they had even dropped anchor. Beaming sailors called up to them. The crew responded enthusiastically but without understanding.

The wooden buildings of the town were all steep-sloped roofs. A few aloof European-style buildings near the wharf looked out of place, distancing themselves from the cheek-by-jowl native buildings. Francis could make out steep fields give way to pine-covered mountains beyond a severe wall cutting the peninsula off from the mainland.

★★★

"*Dokkoi! Dokkoi! Dokkoi!*"

"*Soooo-RYA!*"

Francis gaped at the men straining to move a stone-laden cart up from the wharf. They wore as little as the men on the sampans—rags around their foreheads to gather sweat and thin loincloths around their waists. The leaders responded energetically to the chant from behind.

"*Dokkoi! Dokkoi! Dokkoi!*"

"*Soooo-RYA!*"

"Why do they not use horses?" asked Francis.

Thomson shrugged.

"Too much cost. Only samurai have horse."

They walked up a steep narrow street. Everywhere were awnings covered with Chinese writing, the lettering bold and baffling. People passed quickly in cumbersome wooden sandals, sneaking glances at the tall pale foreigners as they passed.

"These people," the Russian gestured vaguely. "Peasants. Samurai rule."

"Samurai?" Francis asked.

"Warriors. Come! I take you to a friend."

Thomson's friend was a Portuguese sailor who had married a Japanese woman and opened an *izakaya*, an inn, over a year ago.

"Is good food," insisted the Russian as they approached. "And more..."

★★★

"*Irashaimase!*" called out a voice as they ducked into the little restaurant at the front of the building. Inside was dim and busy. Behind the high counter stood a portly Western man wearing a *yukata*. He squinted at the new arrivals, wiping his sweaty brow.

"Thomson," he exclaimed.

The Russian nodded and sat at the counter. Francis followed, taking in the spartan surroundings.

"Good to see you, José," growled Thomson.

"You too, my friend. Who have you brought along?"

"This is Francis."

"Francis O'Neill," he supplied, extending his hand. "From Ireland."

"An Irishman! What a pleasure. I am José Eduardo Santos Melo Tavares Silva," he pronounced grandly. "Although here they call me Ho-shi. Originally from Bilbao. I fished off Irish waters many years ago."

He bowed to Francis. The latter withdrew his hand in confusion, sketching an awkward bow.

"He is a good one, Thomson," said José with a laugh.

"Yes," agreed Thomson. "He was useful when our Captain went mad."

"Mad!" José produced three tiny cups and an earthen jug. "On the *Minnehaha*?"

"Yes," he frowned. "We have new Captain now."

Thomson slugged back the little cup and clapped it down onto the counter. He looked over at Francis who was timidly peering into his.

"Saké," he said. "Is good."

"I don't normally drink," Francis demurred.

The Russian looked at him in disbelief. "Is rude," he grumbled.

"It is fine," said José with a magnanimous air. "Portugal is a holy country too. At least on the surface."

"Pah," Thomson spat. "Catholics."

He pronounced the word with distaste. Francis and José exchanged a look.

"No, no," relented Francis. "I'll try it. It smells very... different."

"It is wine made from rice. This one is called *gen-mai-shu*. Very. Best. Saké."

Francis gingerly sipped and grimaced. It was fiery on his throat.

"Ha," said Thomson, clapping him on the back. "Is good."

Francis frowned at the laughing men and drank some more. He thought it best to drink quick to be rid of the foul taste. Thomson kept filling their cups.

"Tomoko," called Silva. "*Tabemono*."

A slight young Japanese woman arrived with a tray. Her long black hair was fastened in a bun on her head. Her skin glowed with exertion from serving the customers. She carried small black and cinnabar bowls of rice, pickles and fish.

"Please try," said the proprietor. "You will like Japanese food. You are my friend as you are Thomson's friend. It is years since we sailed so we must celebrate."

Thomson grinned, his gruffness gone.

"We had some good times, José."

The men reminisced while saké flooded Francis's senses. Looking up from the confusing chopsticks, he found the room spinning about him. He staggered, half-rising and sent a bowl clattering to the floor.

Thomson grabbed him and settled him back in the chair.

"I'm sorry," Francis said. "Not used to this… this strong wine. I think I need to lie down."

The room would not steady itself. He felt like getting sick.

"That is fine," José said. "Tomoko, *o-kyakusama wa futon ga hitsuyo*."

Tomoko nodded brusquely and took Francis's hand. He stumbled after her.

★★★

The tiny room had a *tatami* straw mat floor. Faint mildew obscured the simple patterns on the sliding *fusumu* screens. Tomoko opened one and retrieved some straw filled bedding and laid it out on the floor. Francis looked at it in confusion.

"*Futon,*" she said, as if to a child. "*Futon.*"

He bent down and crawled to the futon. The sudden change in altitude had a negative effect. Tomoko must have noticed the change in his features. She quickly provided a wooden bucket for him to vomit into. She giggled as he fell back onto the bed.

★★★

He dreamed of someone chasing him. He could not see who, but their laughter was cruel. Everywhere was black as pitch. He felt his way from room to room trying to escape. He heard children crying in agony but could not find them. His body trembled all over, every shiver burning cold.

★★★

The room was dim when Francis woke with a start but he could make out Tomoko sitting on her legs across from him. His body trembled but it felt external to him, as if the room itself were shaking.

"*Jishin,*" she said, without emotion.

A plaintive cat mewled in the distance as the tremors subsided. Francis laid back on his side before propping himself up on one elbow.

"Was that an earthquake?" he asked, voice shaky.

She said nothing. A faint scent drifted from her thick ebony hair, gleaming in the scant light from the shuttered window. Francis sighed.

"I'm sorry, Tomoko. I don't speak your language. I am sorry for making such a mess here."

He indicated the bucket and made an awkward motion.

She shook her head, looking at him.

"*Dai-joubu?*" she enquired.

Francis was totally at a loss what to reply. He could only repeat.

"Die Joe Boo?"

She said no more, only sat, indifferent as a cat.

"What do I say?" Francis asked, as much to himself as to her. "How can I tell you everything? I have been in ships all over. Lost my family and home. Storms and madmen. I fell in love but I've lost her…"

He sighed again before continuing in a tone of self-pity, "I feel more and more lost with every day."

She stared ahead as he delivered all this, a waiting servant. He marveled at the elegant almond shape of her eyes. He noticed the slight parting of her kimono. As if sensing his gaze, she looked up at him, a cold challenge in her eyes. Francis looked away.

"José?" he asked. "Can I see Ho-shi?"

She nodded and got up, sliding the door closed behind her.

★★★

After an interminable time she returned, small *sori* slippers making a whispered shuffle. She studied him, ignoring the sounds of José stumbling along the tiny hallway behind her. José spoke quickly to her in Japanese. Her response was formal, the words icy. She looked directly at Francis as she spoke and it struck fear in his heart. Francis gathered himself and stood up.

"I'm terribly sorry about the mess I've made," he said.

"No. No. It was the drink. It's not for everyone," said the older man. His own words were slurred from alcohol. He pulled Francis down to the futon with him.

"Sit. Sit." He indicated Tomoko. "What do you think of Japanese girls? Are they not the most beautiful? This one. She's an outcast. If you can believe that? Father's a tanner. Even the peasants shun her. Tomoko! *Onegai. Suwate!*"

She sat beside them; her face betrayed nothing.

"Feel her hand."

José fumbled for it. He grabbed Francis's own and forced them to clasp. Francis resisted.

"Feel it," came the other man's sudden aggressive bark.

Francis did. For a second her eyes met his. A castle wall. Then she simpered coquettishly at her employer. Francis withdrew his hand quickly.

"Thank you for all your hospitality. I really must be going now."

José's laughed.

"Japanese girls and Japanese drink. Looks like you can't take 'em."

To Francis's horror she laughed too—a glistening crescendo. Francis went to the sliding door.

"Thank you again. I'll be off now."

"Go. Go. Thomson had to go too. You missed the boat."

He broke down laughing at this. Francis bolted from the inn. Her cruel gaze remained with him as he hurried down the Yokohama street.

★★★

Looking helplessly across the dark water in the late dusk, Francis could just make out the *Minnehaha* anchored in the harbor. He considered stealing a boat but recalled Hickman's warning about the harsh justice of the Japanese. He took off his shoes, tied the laces together and put them around his neck. He would never find Anna if sharks devoured him here.

The warmth of the water was a surprise. For a while, he swam at an even pace. Some distance from shore, he paused to tread water and rest. A nearby hump appeared in the water against the lights from the shore. He dived back down and opened his eyes. It was too dark to see properly but he imagined thousands of moving shapes. Something butted against him and a sudden terror overtook him.

Francis swam for his life. He could not see or hear anything but the beast had to be right behind him. He trashed toward the ship, mind full of panicked thoughts of getting bitten. He remembered the chandler's shop in Alexandria—the shark jawbone of razor-sharp teeth.

He pulled his body forward, unsure of when it would strike. Unbidden, a rhythm came into his swimming. A fragment of a tune he repeated to himself.

Bímid ag ól is ag pógadh na mban.

His father's song. Over and over.

Let us be drinking and kissing women.

Despite his peril, he pondered the correctness of the English version.

Bímid ag ól is ag pógadh na mban.

The water was complete blackness. He could see lanterns up on the deck. He made out a sailor. He wondered if it devoured him here would he have a chance to cry out? Would anyone hear?

A hard slap on his right hand.

It was the hull of the *Minnehaha*. The shock was too much. He sank helpless into the deep dark murk.

Bímid ag ól is ag pógadh na mban.

He propelled himself upward, his chest near bursting from the effort.

117

Surfacing with a gasp, he weakly found his way to the Jacob's ladder amidships. For a long time, he held onto it. Sharks may take him but he could go no further. Finally, with great effort, he hauled himself up.

"I'll never drink again," he swore.

★★★

"Ha," barked Thomson when he saw Francis. "You had good swim?"

Thomson's blue eyes had a vibrant gleam as he regarded Francis's damp clothes.

"Why'd you leave me?" mumbled Francis. "I was in a bad way. Those people…"

"Is not my fault," chuckled the Russian. "Had to go. I don't like being on land with earthquakes. Oh, what you missed. José showed me geisha house. Very fine women."

Francis said nothing.

"Very fine," repeated Thomson, with heavy emphasis.

"Very good," Francis said dryly. "Did Hickman notice I was gone?"

"No. Third mate is mad, though. Said to give warning."

Francis shook his head.

"At least I made it back alive. I'm not going in that water again. A shark near got me."

"Sharks? No sharks this far into bay."

★★★

After several tedious days watching the Fairbanks scale as coal was unloaded, Francis was back on shore leave. Pausing in a busy arcade, Francis studied with wonder intricate lacquerware arranged on a little stall: bowls that stacked perfectly within bowls, cabinets and boxes with multiple drawers. All were covered in delicate scenes of trees, mountains, dragons and flowers inlaid in gold over black, cinnabar and red.

"Beautiful stuff, isn't it?"

Francis looked up in surprise to see an Englishman about five years older than him, prematurely balding with a round smiling face.

"Yes," agreed Francis. "Not sure I can afford it though."

"Oh? Perhaps we can see about that. I know old Jun, the owner of the shop. He owes me a favor or two. My name's Malcolm. With the British legation."

"Nice to meet you," said Francis. "What do you do here?"

"Mostly translation. Had to learn Japanese through Dutch. Only dictionary I could find. Longer I'm here the more I realize we need a proper one of our own. Sorry. I'm rambling on. What's your name?"

"Francis O'Neill."

Malcom scrutinized the sailor.

"The honorable O'Neill," he announced with a laugh. "In Japanese an 'O' before anything is a term of respect. *O-kané* is money. *O-saké* is alcohol. But I digress. What brings an Irishman all the way to Japan?"

"I'm aboard the *Minnehaha*," Francis gestured back toward the bay. "She's out of New York. I would like to take something of this place back there."

"Sweetheart, eh? *Jun-san, iimasu-ka?*" Malcolm called into the little shop behind the stall. A canny little man peered out. Wizened and hunched, he greeted Malcolm with great excitement. Upon seeing another foreigner, he bowed deeply, smiling at Francis's shoes. After a long exchange between them that Francis couldn't follow, he pressed a small cabinet into Francis's reluctant hands.

"Jun says it's a lady's desk. Has a secret compartment."

Francis marveled at it. The old man gently showed him the trick of it. He closed the compartment—a serene landscape scene on the glossy black lid.

"Oh, it is fine. How much does he want for it?"

"He won't take anything," Malcolm said. "They are terribly generous over here."

Francis made an awkward bow. He thanked the old man profusely as they bid farewell.

"You must let me thank you, though," Francis said to Malcolm as they walked down to the harbor.

"I say, got any books to share?" asked Malcolm. "We don't get too many novels out here."

"Back on board I have *The Woman In White* by Wilkie Collins. I liked the way the crime was solved in it. I have a couple of others…"

"Sounds intriguing. I have worked my way through all the Thomas Hardy I can stomach. Perhaps we could trade?" asked the civil servant with excitement. Francis gave him a serious nod.

"I have an appointment on the British clipper *The Lookout* this afternoon," continued Malcolm. "Any chance you could bring them over? Should be near you."

"This is our last leave." Francis frowned. "I'll figure something out."

★★★

"No ech… extra leave!" hiccupped Sampson, the red-faced third mate. There was a warm smell of whiskey off his breath.

"But it's Sunday afternoon, sir."

"No! Ay've a good mind to put you aloft to scrape the… masts and pulley blocks," he threatened.

His rheumy eyes wandered in his head as he was distracted by an imagined noise.

"Wait there while I check the bow," he slurred.

Francis watched perplexed as Sampson staggered to the stern. The mate took a nip from a flask before leaning over the side. He teetered there, in danger of falling in. Francis hurried beside him and took hold of his shirt. Sampson struggled and slipped over the railing. Francis braced himself to the rail while trying to hold onto his bulk.

"Help! Man overboard!"

For an awful minute he held on, feeling Sampson slip away. Sampson's eyes bulged in his ruddy face as he trashed about, terror bringing him to sudden sobriety.

"Hold steady," called Hickman as he rushed near and reached down to help haul him in.

"What the hell is going on?" asked the new Captain.

"Said he had to check the bow," replied Francis.

"This is the stern, Sampson."

"Oh. Got turned around."

Sampson gave Francis a black look. Francis only shrugged.

"Ah," said the mate. "Let me show you what I meant, sir."

Sampson lead a skeptical Hickman away. Francis used the distraction to return to his quarters and wrapped a couple of books as best he could in canvas. With spare rope, he fashioned a rough harness for the bundle and gingerly balanced it on his head. Quietly, he slipped down the ladder. The water held no fear for him now when there might be new books to be had. Within fifteen minutes he was on the forecastle of *The Lookout,* carefully unwrapping his parcel before Malcolm.

"Remarkable," enthused the latter. "Had no idea you would swim across. Thought you were an officer, you see."

"What's this one?" asked Francis, holding up one of Malcolm's books.

"That? *Under the Greenwood Tree* by Hardy. Not as dreary as others of his. Don't know if you'd like it though, an awful lot about fiddle music..."

"Oh!" Francis said, excitement in his voice. "That sounds excellent."

A boat rowed out from the *Minnehaha* as they debated the literary merits of their pooled library. Thomson hauled aboard, staring in wonder at them.

"Books," exclaimed Thomson. "You brave sharks for books but have no time for drink or woman."

"I thought you said there were no sharks."

There was real alarm in Francis's voice. The Russian shrugged.

"Shark is nothing to anger of Hickman. I cannot help you this time. I am not allowed to row you back. You must swim."

"Can you at least take this book back for me?"

He handed Thomson *Under the Greenwood Tree.*

★★★

Francis was chained to the mast as punishment. Sampson leaned over him threateningly. His eyes had the focus of revenge.

"Make a monkey of me in front of the Captain, will ya?"

Jocko, already chained after being caught thieving from the galley, shrieked.

"I saved your life, sir." Francis murmured to the officer.

"I'll have yours! Bread and water rations. Three days."

Satisfied, Sampson left Francis chained. Francis noticed Hickman on the foredeck, eyeing him darkly. A forlorn Jocko sidled against Francis, whimpering. Francis sighed and stroked the monkey's soft fur.

The Green Island

Baker's Island, Pacific Ocean, 1867

The *Minnehaha* rolled softly in the mild warm breeze, Francis enjoying his turn at the wheel. Ballast was the main cargo, making the craft light to pilot.

Hickman stepped up beside him.

"How is she faring, Francis?"

"Well, sir. Nice and steady going."

"I considered leaving you in Yokohama," Hickman said. "After that display."

"Yes, Captain." said Francis, looking to the horizon.

"You understand the need for discipline, don't you?"

"I do, sir," answered Francis, voice slow with controlled anger. He was still sore from the chains.

"Good. Don't give me call to regret keeping you on."

"I won't, sir."

Francis considered reminding his new Captain of Burleigh's discipline. He had a sudden giddy urge to punch the man.

"MAH-yo! MAH-yo!"

Their conversation was interrupted by loud bird cries echoing from the hold. Hickman shook his head and cursed.

"What manner of birds are they at all, sir?" asked Francis, changing the subject.

"Not sure. Never was one for ornithology myself. 'Asiatic Pheasants' is what the waybill says. Smelly things."

"Beautiful and exotic they are. I've never seen birds like them."

"You're a curious bird yourself, O'Neill. Quite the literary sailor. Anyway, I hope they please Queen Emma in Honolulu. She is apparently quite partial to them. Saw her once at an officer's ball. Beautiful woman. Half native, half English."

"The queen of the Kamehamehas," said Francis. He relished the sound of the word he had learned from Fred. Hickman raised a skeptical eyebrow.

"Yes. Well, we won't have time to call on her in Hawaii. Once we unload these damn birds, it'll be straight off to scrape birdshit off Baker Island."

★★★

Despite watching out for it, the tiny island crept up on him—only three miles around and a mere ten feet above the sea. Francis checked the chart. A quarter of a degree north latitude, nearly on the equator. He had a fanciful image of a great iron span across the ocean, over the dull treeless island. They were close enough now to make out the main inhabitants: frigates, noddies, terns and boobies circling and squabbling over the barren roosting ground. Their gray, white and black feathers were a grim contrast to the cages of brightly plumed exotics unloaded at Hawaii. The excrement deposited everywhere was the sole reason for their journey.

At Hickman's shout, the sails were adjusted to slow the big ship. Francis turned the wheel hard toward a cluster of large iron buoys on the west of the island.

"What's the plummet?" he called.

"Over ninety fathoms," replied Fred from the railing at the end of the poop. Bemused, he held up the end of the measuring line.

"No fear of a reef then," murmured Francis.

"Tie us down," shouted the Captain after the sails were fully trimmed. A couple of men jumped off the bow and swam to the nearest buoy. Francis, steering finished now, noticed three iron cables secured the buoy to permanent anchors deep below. The nearest man grabbed a hawser thrown out to them before all three started straining on the line, hauling the ship in. Other men scrambled to secure the stern to another buoy.

"All valuable items in the lighters," ordered the Captain. "Best take precautions out here."

★★★

The sailors scrambled up the white and yellow smeared rocks, disturbing the raucous birds.

"*Merde*," Fred cursed under his breath, covering his nose at the nauseous stink. Once up from the beach, they surveyed the dreary landscape—flat and covered with withered scrub. Only a few ramshackle buildings broke

123

the bleak prospect. The wind cut without mercy across the desolation. A clapped-out white mare pulled a single flatcar along movable tracks. The fifty or so Kanakas hired in Honolulu surged past them to greet more of their brethren engaged in packing dry guano into sacks, their language sounding pleasant to Francis's ear. These native Hawaiians had entertained everyone on board with their contests of strength and agility: arm wrestling and racing up the rigging.

"Where's Burleigh?" asked a white man as he approached. He was tall and rangy with close squinting eyes.

"Are you Irish?" asked Francis in surprise.

The man studied Francis with deep suspicion.

"I'm Lieutenant McSweeney. From Londonderry. Who're you?"

"Francis O'Neill. Cork. I didn't expect to see another Irishman out in the middle of the Pacific."

McSweeney snorted.

"Where's yar Captain? These damn Kanakas will spend the time lolling about if you let 'em. An aye've a mountain of birdshit to load."

"Burleigh?" sniggered Fred. "He is locked up in Batavia."

McSweeney gave Fred a hard look.

"This island is a tough place," he said in a low voice. "'Specially for jokers. You'll not last long out here, Mr. Frog."

"Mr. Burleigh was… taken ill at Batavia," supplied Francis. "Mr. Hickman is our Captain now."

"Hickman! How did you lot ever make it out here alive?"

They led him to their new Captain. After a brief discussion, the sour McSweeney took him to Lake, an English sailor in charge of loading the freight. Governor Johnson, a native of Wisconsin, was also found. Steiner, the taciturn German cook, prepared a meal for the Caucasian bosses of this outpost of humanity. The rest of the crew and the Hawaiians were not invited.

★★★

All next day was the tedious work of unloading of ballast—rusty scuttles and small scoops their only equipment.

"Get yer backs into it," yelled Sampson. "We have seven hundred tons of gravel to move."

Francis and Fred hauled the heavy scuttle along the deck. They were startled by the ship heaving suddenly beneath them.

"What's that, Captain?" Francis asked as Hickman ran to the side. His covered eyes scanned the sea.

"Ocean swell. Most likely the storm that missed us the other night."

He grimaced, working his jaw.

"Fred. Wilkes. Go down to that buoy with another hawser. Let's fasten her down best we can."

With a grateful sigh, Francis's companion abandoned the gravel to join Wilkes on a tender out to the buoy. Another deep wave caused the bow to violently rise upward. The lines creaked with the strain.

"Swell from north," shouted Thomson.

He threw another line to Wilkes and Fred on the buoy.

"Make her fast," he shouted.

Francis looked around in confusion. The air was calm and fresh, yet the sea roiled as it had in the hurricane off America. It was like a silent monstrous hand pounded the ocean out of view.

Another giant wave and the boat pitched steeply, stern in the trough with the bow high in the crest, accompanied by a tumultuous rending sound and a snap. Shouts came from the men aft. Francis watched helpless as Fred and Wilkes were tossed into the air. The undercarriage of the buoy snapped off like a fastener from a saddle.

"Man overboard," he shouted. "Fred can't swim."

Young Wilkes, unlike half the ship, was a strong swimmer. After surfacing, he swam swiftly to where the Belgian's hat floated in the water. He dove down and retrieved the spluttering Fred, pulling him up by his hair.

"Cut loose all boats," yelled Sampson.

The atmosphere was excited but calm as the sailors freed the boats and started crowding into them. The ship plied back and forth, now that the unmoored bow was at the mercy of the deep swell. A ripping crunch came from aft as one violent wave pummeled her against the rocky coast, adding to the damage from the reefs off Java.

"Abandon ship," called Hickman from the big lighter, already in the water. The ship bucked violently like a crazed bull. All hands scurried to get onto the nearest small vessel.

Apart from Francis.

"O'Neill," screamed Sampson. "What the bloody hell are you at?"

They watched Francis tread the dangerously pitching deck.

"Books," said Thomson, his voice half dismissive, half in awe.

"No," a bedraggled Fred said with a cough. "He already stowed those."

"He can stay on there if he wants," growled the mate. "Push off!"

The almost swamped boat pushed off to more sounds of splintering timber. On board, Francis found the little monkey still chained to the mast, hiding under loose canvas.

"Poor little fellow. They were going to leave you here."

The monkey's eyes were big with fear, reminding Francis of a terrified child.

Francis looked about for the key. It had to be kept out of reach as Jocko was clever enough to unlock himself. All the deck was a jumble from the tossing about. Giving up on finding it, Francis took a hatchet and started to chop at the mast. He looked up at the great high timbers swaying above him. He redoubled his efforts until he had hacked off the bolt securing the chain.

"Now that's done," he said. "But how are we to get off?"

He had never been entirely alone on a ship before. In a sudden calm, he took a moment to admire the graceful curve of the deck and the white wings of the disheveled sails. The calm did not last. Another calamitous crash came as a new swell pushed the ship against a rocky ledge. Francis guided the frightened monkey onto his shoulders, looping the remaining chain into a pocket of his shirt. With much chattering they made it down the ladder along the side.

With one last look up the black wall of the hull, he pushed off into the swirling green water and swam for shore.

Here's Good Health to the Piper!

The men stood in small clusters at the shore, barely visible beneath the canopy of unfamiliar stars. The birds, apart from an occasional shrill call, were silenced by the crashing waves. The sickening odor of excrement was everywhere. Francis, eyes accustomed to the darkness, spotted the bulk of the ship listing to one side. "She's breaking up."

There wasn't much sound at the end, compared to when the hull and masts were hammered onto a ledge of stone in the swell. No one spoke as the two main pieces of their ship disappeared into the black.

★★★

After a spectacular rosette sunrise of pink and orange streaks of clouds, the men stirred themselves. They had huddled together all night on the rocky beach. Hickman walked past, crestfallen, with Sampson following like a lost pup. Sampson was shaking all over, either from fear or delirium tremens.

"What's the Captain going to do?" asked Francis.

"Not captain anymore," replied Fred. "He has no ship."

The bleakness in Fred's voice surprised Francis.

"Yes. I see that. Of course. But he will have a plan to organize things. Won't he? Look at how he fixed Burleigh."

Fred shrugged.

"There are things washed ashore," said Francis. "Let's see what we can scavenge. Come on, Fred."

The bulk of the wreckage was concentrated on one section of the shore. Birds screamed while cursing men retrieved what they could from washed up casks. Some just sat watching the sea.

"There's driftwood over here," shouted Francis, urging the lethargic Fred to action. Together they hauled a gnarled and twisted piece over to other scraps of wood.

A Kanaka appeared next to them and grabbed the heavy log. He wore light clothing over his copper skin.

Francis nodded, accepting his help. The Hawaiian had heavy brows and wild wavy nutbrown hair. They deposited the log near a pile the other sailors were building.

"Thank you," said Francis.

The Kanaka said nothing. He regarded them for a moment before leaving to scour for more.

"They're feeling bad for us," Fred said. He sat down again on the pile. "They have no room in their cabin. No extra food. And we will die out here."

Francis had no reply to the raw despair in the Belgian's voice.

★★★

Francis crawled upon the sharp black rocks toward a single nest separated from the rest. He ground his teeth to set to his purpose, ignoring the squealing squabs within. A couple of blue-footed boobies wheeled above, but neither bothered him. Earlier, he had tried another nest and several furious birds attacked screaming. He had hunted for an hour before finding this isolated nest. With a rush, he grabbed a couple of the white furry creatures. He squeezed them tight in his fist before dashing their heads on the rock. Grim, he repeated this a couple of times, ignoring their siblings' helpless cries.

He walked back to their ramshackle shelter. Thomson looked up from a meagre fire. He was trying to boil sea-spoiled oats in a can.

"What is that?" asked Thomson, peering into the mess in Francis's hands.

Francis dropped them to the ground.

"Squabs. I don't know. Maybe we can fry them."

The Russian regarded the clump of blood-stained white downy feathers. "Maybe."

He tasted the oats and spat them out. "Pah! Over there is other can."

Francis labored over the young fowl for a long while, cleaning their scrawny bodies. He lay them into the blackened can. After roasting the oily bodies over the fire, he covered them in pepper and vinegar the cook had spared from his meagre store. With the eagerness of hunger, he bit into one.

"Oh God," he exclaimed, spitting the rank mass onto the ground. Thomson abandoned his oats and reached for one. He took a nibble and chewed for a while, considering. Then his eyes widened and he spat the foul stuff out.

"Yes. Bad."

Francis lay back on the ground. Their rough lean-to was just an accumulation of debris from the shore. It was precarious and cramped.

"Some of the Kanakas catch fish in shallow pools."

The Russian gave an unimpressed grunt.

"Maybe I should try and get…"

"Where is he? Where is he?"

Fred had returned panic-stricken. He looked all around the shelter.

"Who?" asked Thomson.

"Le singe. Jocko!"

"This stupid monkey. It is gone."

Fred ignored Thomson. Francis had to grab him by the shirt to keep him from wandering on. "He'll show up, Fred. He can't go anywhere."

"Have one of you eaten him?"

Francis was shocked by this change in the sailor. His eyes were red-rimmed and there was a nervous quake to his voice. Fred hadn't been right since his near drowning.

"Maybe lie down for a bit there, Fred. This coat is dried out now. You could lie under it."

Francis guided the Belgian, who was trembling with a fever, back into the shelter. Fred laid under the torn woolen jacket, staring at the sky.

"Hunger and shock. Can kill you. I saw this in Russia," Thomson said.

The Belgian made no response. Francis swallowed, bile rising as he recalled the vile flavor of the squabs.

"I'll go out to try and find something else."

★★★

"I'm afraid you will have to make the best of it. Our food supplies were stretched before the wreckage."

The corpulent governor straightened his old-fashioned frockcoat as he addressed the assembled men. A pale Hickman stood at his side.

"My lieutenant, Mr. McSweeney, will ration out what we can spare. You must endeavor to make it last as long as possible."

Irritated by his new task, the hard-bitten Northerner gave the crew a baleful look.

"Captain?" called Francis. "How long will we be left out here?"

Hickman narrowed his eyes at Francis but did not respond. He looked out to sea, as other voices called out questions. Governor Johnson thumbed his lapels, waiting for silence.

"All former officers of the *Minnehaha* are to reside with me," he said, in his heavy pompous voice. "The brig *Zoe* is due to arrive in a week or so but may be delayed due to storms. As I say, make the best of it. Come, Mr. Hickman."

With that, the governor turned away. Hickman made to follow, then turned back to his former crew. The governor ignored them, leading away a small procession of McSweeney and others. A few of the former crew clustered near.

"I know things are bad, men. They will be worse for me back home, you know. Burleigh went mad and then we lost the ship. Merchant's row will not be happy, I can tell you."

"What of us?" asked Francis. "What if that ship doesn't come? We might starve on this rock."

Hickman gave Francis another hard look. "Like the governor said, we will give you all the food we can spare. The ship will come."

"How will we fit on it? There are thirty of us. They won't be prepared for the extra."

"It's all I can do for you."

"It's not much," Francis said, frustration in his voice. "We'd better find something for ourselves. Come on."

Hickman chewed his lip as his former men walked away. He was left alone, watching the seagulls tirelessly scan the water.

★★★

"A week? We could make," said Thomson. "Two weeks? I think a couple might die. Any longer? Well…"

He looked over at Fred huddled under the shelter.

"There's got to be something else we can get," mused Francis. "So the gannet are foul. What about the bigger ones? The frigate birds?"

Thomson shrugged, gnawing on hardtack. A weevil squirmed in it.

Thomson swallowed regardless.

"They nest on the bare rocks on the far side of the island," said Francis. "Away from us."

No response from his comrades. Francis sighed and walked away. The wild grass felt coarse under his bare feet as he walked along. Further in from the shore there were few sounds other than the distant hush of the sea. He recalled the secluded dunes near Bantry strand. Apart from all the birds, he wondered if there were any other creatures. Rats, probably. A single bird swooped by, a kind of curlew. He stopped to look after it.

"First land bird I've seen. Back home it would be a sign of rain. Who knows on this strange island?"

He fell silent. So now I'm talking to myself, he thought. *First sign of madness*.

"Fred might plan on dying out here," he muttered. "Not me."

His words to himself were hurried. Despite his depressing prospects, he disliked talking to himself. It made him feel ashamed. He hurried on in silence. Unbidden, words came again.

"Mrs. Andersen might have been right. Life at sea." He stopped, exhaling sharply. "I've enough of it. If I do make it off this rock I'm going to try and settle down. Find Anna and settle down."

His belly made an angry sound, the only response to his plans. Over a slight rise were more rocks. They were not as plastered in guano as at the other end of the island.

"Grawghh! Gowan! Gowan! Gaagrghgh!"

The frigate birds, although bigger than gannets, were shyer. They scattered at his yelling. After much scrambling about, he found a semi-digested fish deposited alongside a nest of fledglings. Swallowing several times in desperation, he gulped it down raw. He managed to consume another before collapsing on the rocks, stomach curdling. He had to dry heave several times before the sweet release of vomiting into a rock pool. He wiped his mouth and lay down on his back.

"Jesus, Mary and Joseph," he cried. "Help me through this. I promise I'll pray more if I make it out alive. Go to mass. I know I haven't been. Just save me."

He started crying to himself, sobbing like a child—his face a rictus of anguish. He made more silent promises to God. He had only so much energy for self-pity, so he got up and staggered down to the beach. His legs wobbled as he wandered along the broad white strand. Tide was out. Pelicans, gray and white, fought for the best roosts on twisted and worn timbers half-submerged in the wet sand, skeletal ribs of ship corpses. He stumbled about the beach but found no food.

★★★

Over a week later and still no sign of the *Zoe*. A gang of sailors made a desperate foray on the Kanakas' quarters in the night. They covered their bodies in bird excrement to ward off insects and frighten the better-fed natives. The Kanakas jeered and taunted them in the darkness. Finally, Hickman came with a pistol and fired it into the air. They left, calling back curses on him.

"Savages," yelled the ex-Captain to the dim forms retreating into the night.

★★★

Francis woke with a start. Morning sunlight again. He was surprised he had slept, he was so plagued by constant hunger. His vanishing dream had been vivid, no images only a lively reel with a melody he ached to recall. He sat up and looked around.

"Where's Fred?" he asked the Russian lying next to him. Thomson stared back. His sunken eyes piercing blue in the pallor of his face, cheeks prominent as starvation set in. His face was still streaked white and green with guano.

Thomson shook his head. He had not seen Fred leave. After a while, they stumbled down to the shore. McSweeney was distributing a little water and rations with a dour mien. There wasn't enough for half of them.

"Fred. Anyone seen Fred?" asked Francis of the others in line.

Nobody replied.

By mid-day Fred's corpse washed up on the beach. For some reason it was naked. The Hawaiians wouldn't go near the dead body. McSweeney picked Francis out from the crowd.

"You. O'Neill. You knew him. Need help burying him, so I do. Extra tack in it for you."

Francis considered for a moment. He saw the cruel glint in the Derryman's eye. The pain of hunger in his gut was even crueler. Francis nodded.

"Good. Thought you'd come 'round. Suppose Mr. Frog wasn't that smart in the end."

There was delight in McSweeney's voice.

★★★

Midday on the eleventh day, a sail was spotted from the north. In his hungry delirium, it looked to Francis like an immense ship as it hove into view on the dark green sea. He imagined nine-foot-tall giants reaching for rigging thick as his arm. In truth, the *Zoe* was a medium-sized brig almost entirely crewed by Hawaiians, including mate and boatswain. Broad-bellied, even for a brig, with gunnels that drooped low in the water. The main deck was crowded with listless men. Once moored to one of the remaining iron buoys, their Captain rowed alone to shore in a tiny cutter.

"Let me help you there," called Hickman, running into the surf to help him out of his little boat. His counterpart said nothing. Big-jawed and taciturn, he let Hickman pull him in while he took in the dregs of Hickman's former crew.

"What happened?"

"Wrecked by a swell," replied Hickman. "My ship went down on the rocks over there. I would like you to consider…"

"Can't take 'em," interrupted the other.

"What? But they're starving. We've already had one fatality."

"Already full. Had to take on extra crew at Howland island to the north. Wrecked by the same storm."

"Won't you have more space when you unload supplies?"

The Captain only grunted a reply before walking off towards the governor's cabin, leaving Hickman standing alone.

★★★

After a promise of pay from an extra supply run, the Captain of the *Zoe* agreed to take them. The former officers were accommodated in a cabin but

133

the remaining crew were relegated to the hold. Large water tanks filled half the gloomy interior, mostly empty and covered in old canvas like drums. A portly Hawaiian mate indicated they were to sleep on top of these. He stood on the ladder, steadying himself from the rolling sea. He stayed near the square of daylight and fresh air, avoiding the stench of unwashed starving men.

"Inna day you goin get one biscuit of da tack and one cup of da tea," the mate instructed them, as he indicated the meagre provisions laid out below his feet.

"We're starvin'," called a sailor. "How long we going to be in here?"

"It plenny good stuff," retorted the mate. "Twice a week you goin' get a good meal too. 'Bout thirty days we goin be fo' Hah-va-hee."

Groans came from the darkness as the mate shrugged and retreated. Thomson picked up a square of pale ship's biscuit and handed it up to Francis.

"What's the tea like?" asked Francis after giving up trying to chew through the hard gray tack.

Thomson ladled him some of the black liquid. There was only one shared cup. Oily and viscous, the smell was diabolical. After a tentative sip, Francis handed it back.

"I'll not be drinking that muck."

Thomson stared at him and then swigged it back.

★★★

The former crew were so weak they rarely went on deck. Francis found it hard to stir himself out of the malaise and slow descent into shared illness. One night, he heard the distinct shrill of a flute. Realizing how long it had been since he last heard real music, he found the strength to venture above deck. A younger Kanaka played a simple hymn, without variation. He played the short melody over and over while others on the busy main deck ignored him. Francis sat down by his side. The young man put down the instrument and looked at the pale hollow-eyed sailor across from him.

"I never learn but one tune at the church," he explained.

His smile was disarming. Francis said nothing but reached out for the flute. The Kanaka shrugged and handed it over. Francis turned it around with reverence before putting it to his lips.

"Soldier's Joy" followed by "Yankee Doodle" followed by "The Girl I Left Behind Me".

A ring of Hawaiians gathered around in appreciation. He stopped, suddenly weak from the exertion.

"You feed dat boy up," instructed an older sailor to Francis's companion. "He play right well."

The other grinned and produced a wooden bowl of half-eaten salmon and poi. Francis blinked at it, trembling at the sight of proper food. The Hawaiian nodded encouragement.

"What you name?"

It took Francis a while to mumble it as he devoured the food.

"Too bad how they treatin' you, Frankie." He pointed to himself, "I'm Mikala. You goin' stay up here come mealtime fo' now on. I'll share with you if you teach me how to play dat flute."

For a moment, Francis was overcome. The flute and its music were a line lifting him out of deep black silence. Francis reached out to touch Mikala briefly on the shoulder.

"Hum one of those Hawaiian songs I've heard you sing." His voice was hoarse. "I like the melody."

One or two others joined in as the Hawaiian sang. His belly full, Francis picked up the flute and quietly joined them.

Closing his eyes, he thanked the music.

CHAPTER 4

The Kid on the Mountain

Honolulu, Hawaii, 1867

Once the *Zoe* dropped anchor in Honolulu, the native crew scurried about clewing sails and preparing for shore. Benign giants of pine-covered mountains looked down at their work from beneath huge castles of cloud. A cutter made a lazy progress towards them on the warm breeze.

"Blasted doctor took his time getting here," the Captain muttered to Francis. "I need these sick men off my ship."

"Yes, sir," said Francis. "Hopefully we'll all be released from quarantine."

The Captain studied him, one eye arched in surprise. As Francis was one of the few healthy white men, he gruffly treated him as an equal.

"Don't worry, O'Neill. You and a couple of others will walk off. I'll make sure the doctor sees to that."

"What happens to the others?"

The Captain shrugged.

"Likely hospital for a spell." He shrugged. "For all I care, they can die as long as they're off my ship."

Francis said nothing. He contemplated the other ships and the harbor.

The captain nodded grimly to the largest one, a barque lying not far off.

"That beauty's the *Comet*. I know her Captain. Abbott. I'll put a word in for you."

Before Francis could be grateful, the Captain was gone, striding towards the company boarding the brig. The crew on the distant *Comet* practiced furling and unfurling sails. It reminded him of an elegant bird preening its feathers.

★★★

They opened all hatches to let as much light as possible stream into the dank hold. Wraiths groaned as they were hauled before the doctor. Someone coughed weakly in the dark. Francis helped move the men along.

"Open."

Thomson stared at the old physician, his sailor garb just rags hanging off his hunched frame.

"Please, Thomson," said Francis. "He can treat you at the hospital."

The proud Russian looked at Francis with a flash of anger.

"He? He is a fool."

The doctor nodded and they forced the Russian forward.

"Thomson," pleaded Francis.

The fight went out of him and he opened his mouth with meek obedience. Francis leaned close.

"We have been through so much," he whispered. "When you get better look me up. I will try and get you a berth on the *Comet*."

He said nothing but took Francis by the hand briefly before being led away.

★★★

Honolulu town was an odd mix of warehouses, poor native dwellings and fine residences skirted by broad verandahs. Francis gaped up at a banana tree, giant leaves obscuring a chandelier of green fruit. Cats were everywhere, lolling in the shade and scrounging for food. Mikala broke from a gang of his fellows to approach Francis.

"Are you hungry, Frankie?" he asked. "There's a good China place nearby."

"Chinese food?" Francis asked with suspicion.

"Yah. Plenny good. Come on."

He led Francis through the hot streets to a low building surrounded by long three-cornered flags of yellow silk. Inside the busy spot was clean and neat. A small man, hair in a queue and wearing long Chinese robes took Mikala's order. He soon returned with dumplings, fish stew, noodles and bowls of rice. Francis offered to pay but was waved off.

"Play for my family at the village later," insisted Mikala, gulping down his food.

The hunger that plagued him on Baker Island vied with mistrust of the exotic fare. He took a tentative bite of stew. To Mikala's great amusement, it wasn't long before he had eaten all before him.

★★★

Francis and Mikala padded quietly along the black volcanic sand, the air so hot that all sounds, even the sea, sounded muted and dull. Past the sandy

138

shore was a dense multitude of different shades of tree and plant: banana, coconut, guava, papaya, mango and tamarind.

"This is paradise, Mikala."

His friend made a grateful little bow.

"Yah. Iesu has blessed us. Easy living here. Come on now, here's my village. Soon time fo' church."

They turned off from the beach to a hamlet with a scattering of low huts thatched with taro leaves. Broad-leaved banana trees provided shade around the simple white wooden church. A cluster of hefty barefoot women called out to them. They wore colorful robes and fanned themselves constantly. Mikala responded with "Aloha" followed by a string of incomprehensible speech. Francis recognized it as Hawaiian from hearing it spoken onboard. He did not understand many words but the cadence made sense. Many of the men wore broad straw hats, trimmed with ribbons and flowers. Children ran around everyone, playing excited games—Francis was amazed to see one or two of the youngest naked. Other men, lightly clad as Mikala, waited outside the church. Francis, beginning to wilt in the heat, wiped the back of his neck. One of the older men, his beat-up hat elaborate with ribbons and flowers, said something in a low voice. All the others laughed.

"He say you wanna get inside 'fore you melt," said Mikala.

They greeted Francis's vigorous nodding with more laughter.

As everyone wandered into the church, a simple hymn from a small choir wafted on the air. Francis was struck by a memory of buttered brown bread in the kitchen after mass. The crowd chatted agreeably, discussing the weather. Even though the present environment couldn't be more different, he felt suddenly at home. He spied a large dark woman in a florid dress fanning herself in front of him. He was pulled back to the strangeness of the place and briefly overcome with homesickness. He set his lower lip in a frown and took his place inside.

★★★

After the service they sat on the ground in a shack belonging to Mikala's extended family. Sunday fare was simple, a large calabash of fish, fruit and the ever-present poi. A cock crowed brazenly in the yard. One woman nursed a baby at her breast, while her sister picked nits from her hair. Nobody was too excited by Francis's presence. He was soon forgotten after the initial introductions.

The ground trembled beneath them. The child started mewling like a frightened cat as her mother stood up. Voices quiet, they motioned for Francis to follow everyone outside. They stood in the village clearing as the palms swayed without wind.

"An earthquake?" Francis asked Mikala.

"Yah. Plenny bad one too. They say Mauna Loa's not done yet, erupting on the big island all the time. The lava's so choke she making a new island."

The shaking soon subsided and people started to disperse.

"We had one in Yokohama," said Francis, trying to sound knowledgeable. "Can you see the volcano from up there?"

He pointed up to the distant peak of Diamond Head.

"I don't think so. Might see some smoke."

"Will you take me?"

"You crazy haole! Too far. Anyway, you're not supposed to do nothing on Sunday."

Francis grinned.

"I'm shipping out tomorrow. How else will I get to see a volcano?"

★★★

Following Mikala's directions, Francis found himself staring at the base of the mountain. The climb up from the sea face was steep, even treacherous in parts, but he was determined not to be deterred, hauling himself up the brittle gray porous rock covered in dry green and yellow vines. He tried to make the final ascent on a wall-like cliff face but fell down several feet, scraping his hands and knees. Tropical birds, their song unfamiliar, called out at his lack of caution. He laughed aloud as a brightly colored lizard scurried past. Not that long ago, he was scrambling for food on a desolate rock. Now here he was climbing in paradise. Nevertheless, he took a more circuitous route to the top.

The sun was past its zenith when, wiping his brow, he gazed down on the sweep of Honolulu bay, sky beyond merging into the sea. He could just make out the steeple of Mikala's little hamlet far below. Behind him was the basin of the extinct volcano, the deep valley inside the mountain dense with scrub. From his pocket he pulled out some crumpled paper along with a ship's pencil to draw the scene.

How long since he had last drawn something? As he sketched the interior of the dead volcano, he was reminded of a ringfort not far from home. His headmaster said these ancient forts were built by the fairies and were always on a height to see everything for miles around. What were the fairies around here like? He imagined them much more ferocious. He frowned at his final sketch, he was out of practice. A sudden fear gripped him: could his ability to play music also fade?

Past the mountains of Oahu a thin trail of smoke rose to the clouds. He pictured the lake of fire and smoke of Muana Loa, terrible sulfurous vapors choking every breath.

The Lady Behind the Boat

"Ah, Mr. O'Neill. Won't you sit here next to me?"

Francis ducked under the awning strung by the steps to the poop. It was to allow for passengers on the *Comet*'s deck to lounge without getting sun-burned or too much in the way. They had been stuck in the doldrums for several days now. Like the passengers, Francis found himself hunting for shade as he went about his business on deck.

"Mrs. Hoitt," he replied. "Captain Abbott mentioned you wanted to speak to me."

"Yes, yes. Do sit down. You're too tall to be stooping under this moldy canvas."

He sat down next to the lady, trying to make himself comfortable in the narrow deck chair. She was portly, dressed in an extravagant gown of deep crimson with excessive lace. A strong scent of lavender masked a faint sickly tang.

"Won't you try some iced tea?" she nodded toward a jug. "Ice? Tea?"

She chuckled, her eyes were alert and intelligent. He was surprised at how earthy she sounded.

"Yes," she said. "Our Dr. Beck is quite the epicure it seems. He cannot abide the standard ship fare. Somehow, he has gained access to the ship's ice store. He promises ice cream before we reach our destination."

Francis poured a small measure into a cup. She laughed again at his nervous grimace.

"What do you think?"

"It is fine and cool. Give me hot tea with milk and sugar any day, though. Thank you, Ma'am."

"Oh please. Julia. And I will not continue with this 'Mr. O'Neill'."

"Francis. Frank, if you like."

"Francis it is then. Has the Captain explained my purpose in interviewing you?"

"No, Ma'am. I mean Julia."

"I am engaged by the San Francisco paper the *Alta* to report on this monstrous volcano." She sighed. "But I am primarily to provide a travelogue of this excursion. The flavor of the local and so on. I am looking for someone with some experience of the natives and their customs."

"A travelogue?"

"Yes, a sort of novel based on actual events."

Francis nodded. He noticed she had a copy of George Eliot folded in her lap.

"Haven't read him," he said. "I really like Thomas Hardy."

"Really? I find him... dreary. But a sailor who reads? Can't believe it."

"Many do. You'd be surprised. Not much else to do at sea. Especially on my last ship—everyone but the Captain spoke Hawaiian."

"Our Captain Abbott says you can speak their tongue."

"A little bit. I've always been good with languages. As supercargo, I have to check waybills in the transfer of freight. It helps to be able to speak a bit to make sure everything's right."

She frowned.

"My readers won't care about supercargoes and waybills. Tell me how you picked up such a language in the first place?"

"Oh, I was marooned on Baker Island. A cruel barren place. The

Kanakas—that's what the Hawaiians call themselves—one of them be-friended me as I could play the flute."

She sat up, wide-eyed.

"Now that's a story! You're a musician?"

"Ah. Not really. My family have always had music."

"How interesting! But tell me, how did you come to be marooned?"

Francis gave a terse outline of his adventures while Julia listened in amazement. He paused to take another sip of the cool tea. It wasn't so bad really.

"Where else have you been?"

"Oh, Japan, Russia, Turkey, Egypt, America, England and Ireland of course."

Julia shook her head.

"My goodness! Why Francis, you should be the one writing. I can hardly stand the sea-sickness on this voyage and you calmly sail around the world having thrilling adventures."

He reddened and looked at his tea.

"Don't know about that. But I've always loved books," he said. "There's nothing in life like what you read there. What about you, Julia? Do you just write for the newspaper? I mean. Not *just* the newspaper. Books."

"No," she replied, smiling at his fluster. "Not *just* the newspaper. In my capacity as deputy super on the California state school board I have compiled numerous stuffy documents and reports. However, I am working on a book of quotations, practical and inspirational. It is not Eliot," she waved the heavy book in the air. "But I believe nobody has put together a collection like it."

"That is an excellent idea," Francis agreed. "Very useful."

"Thank you." She fanned herself with the book. "Now, tell me more about your Kanakas."

"I've a friend. Mikala. I think his name is a form of Michael. He took me to his village. I'm sure I can get him to take you when we get to port. I've been to their church."

"They are Christian?"

"Oh, most of them are. They told me of an American missionary that visits regularly."

Francis paused. Mrs. Hoitt motioned for him to continue.

"Anyway, you'll see for yourself. They are a most friendly people. Very hospitable despite their rough circumstances."

Francis had a sudden vision of this fine lady amongst the Hawaiian villagers, very different from the barefoot women with long untended hair. A quiet chuckle escaped despite himself. She frowned.

"I'll have you know I'm no stranger to rough circumstances."

There was sudden steel in her voice.

"As well as my duties on the school board, I often assist our church—a Methodist church—in picnics and benefits for the indigent of San Francisco."

"Oh, but the Kanakas are fine people." Francis said to placate her. "They're living in paradise. Very different from San Francisco, I am sure."

"Paradise," she repeated and paused, considering. "What of this volcano? Have you seen Mauna Loa?"

He shook his head.

"I've not been to the big island. I believe you'll have to charter another boat there. But you can see the smoke and I've felt the ground shaking from it."

He noticed her features blanch in horror.

"Ah, you'll be fine. I've heard the worst of it's over. I would like to go up close to see it."

"I'm beginning to regret this entire endeavor," she said with a theatrical sigh. She could not hide her curiosity about him though. "Perhaps you shall see the volcano on another stint with the *Comet*?"

"Oh no, I've been on this side of the world too long. I would like to sail around South America someday. I might want to settle down in New York, eventually. Somebody I know there…"

His voice trailed off gruffly.

"How wonderful," she said, her smile encouraging. "This has all been most informative. You must tell me how you progress. We may correspond through the offices of the *Alta*."

Francis took her proffered hand.

"Thank you, Julia. I will look for your report on the volcano in the paper."

She smiled again.

"It should appear in my column in a month or so. Should I return alive!"

He noticed a disgruntled look from one of the officers passing by.

"Well, I should probably be getting back to work. Thanks again for the tea."

As he departed under the awning, he could not resist a final request.

"I wonder if you've any books to spare at all? Is this George Eliot any good?"

The Shepherd

California, 1868

Francis had little luck in San Francisco, despite the city's name. He had tried for weeks to get work on a ship to take him back to New York but could get none. Money running short, he chanced on an advertisement in the back of Julia Hoitt's newspaper: *Shepherds wanted: Norman Salter's Ranch, Salter's Ferry, Tuolumne County. 50 miles out from Stockton.*

He boarded a steamer for Stockton that night. Late the next day, he was in a stagecoach trundling into a small cluster of buildings on the Tuolumne river.

"Salter's Ferry," shouted the driver.

Francis startled awake. For a minute he believed he was on the mail coach from Bantry. Should he go back home and patch things up with his father? His mind cleared and he realized where he was. He looked out at their destination, a narrow two-storey red brick building with a long wooden hitching post in front. The sign read Stage Station and Post Office. Beyond, a ferry skiff was moored at a broad arm of the river. The surrounding land was flat and empty, the immense Sierra Nevada mountains on the horizon, stretching into the azure of the afternoon sky.

His companion in the coach was a Scotsman named Bill Anderson who insisted Francis call him "Scotty". Also heading for work on the ranch, he had befriended Francis on the way. Scotty stirred himself and yawned, handing the ravenous Francis an apple from his bag.

"Think I can send a letter from here?" asked Francis after munching his thanks.

"Canny see why not," replied Scotty, squinting at the building. "Who's it for?"

"Someone in New York," said Frank.

"Oh ho? 'Someone' is it?"

Francis said nothing.

"I'll see abou' wetting my whistle while you do that. Don't tarry long, Frank. Salter's farm's a bit of a walk upriver."

★★★

Norman Salter leaned on the gate of the corral surveying hundreds of sheep wailing and bleating in the dusty enclosure. He occasionally berated a man at the far corner.

"Goddamn it, John," he yelled. "Stir about or they'll be all out that gate."

John shrugged before making for a far wooden gate.

Salter did not turn to Francis and Scotty as they approached.

"Damn river Indians," he groused. "Live on catfish and jackrabbits. They ain't worth the bullet to shoot 'em."

He spoke to them from the corner of his mouth. Francis looked at Scotty who raised his eyebrows in response.

"Good morning, Mr. Salter," said Scotty. "I've brung you a fresh hand. He might be able to help out round here."

Salter turned to study Francis, his lower lip bulging as if swollen. One side of his face was scarred, the left eye glass. It stared away from them.

"Name?"

"Ah, Francis. Frank O'Neill."

"Know sheep?"

"Somewhat. I grew up on a farm."

"Where? You ain't American."

"Ireland, sir. County Cork."

"Huh. Long way to come. I'm from Missoura myself. Any Irish I've ever met are as lazy and shiftless as John Owl over there."

"I'm a hard worker, sir."

"We'll see. You vouch for him, Scotty. Your problem if he leaves us high and dry."

"Och, he's a fine man." Scotty said, trying to laugh it off. "You'll see, Mr. Salter."

Salter turned away and spat a brown stream into the enclosure. Francis realized he must be chewing tobacco. He addressed them again without turning back.

"Got eight hundred wethers that need herding to pasture up in the Sierra. You start tomorrow. Get over to the bunk house to drop off your things."

No more information was forthcoming. Scotty nudged Frank and they retreated from the ranch owner.

"John," yelled Salter, behind them. "Show the tenderfoot how to herd, will you?"

★★★

"What do you know about herding sheep?" asked John.

His brown face was lined and leathery and he had long greasy black hair tied in a tail. His vowels sounded soft and strange to Francis.

"I haven't done it much," admitted Francis.

"Ain't much to it," John replied with a shrug. "I can show you in the morning."

He looked away.

"Anyway, that bastard Salter will have me running around 'til after dark. Still got a few hundred to squeeze."

Francis nodded.

"What kind of Indian are you?"

"Paiute," the older man cocked his head. "You know my tribe?"

"No. Never heard of them."

"Mostly live on the plains. We gather for fishing around this time of year. Whole tribe. Long overdue."

He scowled in Salter's direction.

"No more talk. Tomorrow, I'll show you."

★★★

The next day came with such intense heat, Francis imagined he could see the stubby plain grass wilt and blanch in the sun. The sheep were skittish and intractable, making Francis wonder if it was the weather or they could

147

sense the intentions of the men to castrate them. Salter barked orders at all, man and dog alike.

He approached an unsure Francis.

"Where's that Indian? He showed you the ropes yet?"

"No, Mr. Salter. I've not seen him."

Salter cursed. The light glinted off his glass eye. "I knew he was fixing to light off. Shouldn't have paid him. Right. You'll just have to figure it out yourself. Head out about half a mile toward that small wood. Bring back what you can."

Francis nodded, an unsure look on his face. He looked for Scotty's help but he was busy applying tongs to the nether regions of bleating sheep.

"Go on," rasped Salter. "I don't pay you to stand around idle."

★★★

"Hup! Go on now. Hup!" Francis waved his hands. The sheep looked away, watching him from the corner of their strange eyes. He tried to encourage them back towards the corral. Every movement only caused them to run in an opposite direction. How many years had he done this with cattle? Yet here he was after a futile half hour of chasing about with nothing to show for it. The terrain was nothing like home, broad flat plain instead of parcels of small fields marked by ditches and stone walls. No fence or boundary line hemmed in these half-domesticated creatures.

He shouted in frustration, making a go for one of the herd. It skittered off, raising dust with its nimble hooves. Defeated, Francis sat down in the dirt, the hat Scotty loaned him between his legs. He wondered when the next stage back to Stockton was. Salter would abuse him but anything would be better than sitting here in the heat and sheep shit.

A whistle pierced his reverie. Scotty rattled a feed bucket at the entrance to the enclosure. He whistled again. Woolly heads turned, ears pointing at the sound. One scrawny specimen started off toward the feed.

"Stay put," shouted Scotty. "When the rest follow, stay back. Just urge the stragglers on. Don' rush 'em."

Francis watched in bemusement as the tide turned. The bulk of them headed for the promised reward. He picked himself up and dusted down

148

his trousers. With a sigh, he urged the stragglers forward.

My Lodging Is On The Cold Ground

Sierra Nevada Mountains, California, 1868

"Gid morning." Scotty quietly set the dimmed lantern down beside Francis. In his other hand, a tin plate laden with lard beans and sowbelly—a tarnished copper spoon sitting in the middle of it. Stars were still visible in the sky.

"What time's it?" mumbled Francis, trying to wake up.

He dragged himself out from his rough blanket, clothes bag doubling as a pillow. His back was sore from sleeping on the ground. He had woken many times during the night from unfamiliar sounds and discomfort. He groaned at a sudden back pain.

"Shoosh," whispered Scotty ferociously.

He removed a cigarette from his mouth.

"Must be about five. Go on, get that in yer belly. I have coffee back at my fire. Keep it quiet though. Two flocks of three thousand sheep'll be scurrying about for feed come dawn. You can snooze at midday when they cluster in the shade."

Scotty left Francis to gobble down the food in the dark, surprised at how delicious it was.

★★★

Francis darned the tear in his trousers with Scotty's needle and thread, glad of the cool of the black oak. A battered pot simmered over their little fire. Scotty stood up and walked over to study Francis's clumsy stitches.

"Your mam must have been very good to you. I dinny think you've done a lot of that work."

Francis put it down in frustration.

"What can I do? The pair I've on is nearly as bad!"

"Hah. Good thing not too many women out here. They'd no' be too impressed wi' the cut of you."

"No. I suppose not."

"Have you any girl at all? Mebbe whoever yer sending letters to in New York?"

149

Francis frowned in annoyance.

"Aha," said Scotty. "Tha's a long way away. Knew a sailor never spoke of a sweetheart for fear of bad luck comin' to her. But we're no' at sea now."

"Have you any music with you?" Francis asked, changing the topic. "I thought I heard harmonica playing back at Salter's bunkhouse."

"Mebbe I do."

Scotty grunted as he reached in his bag for a small harmonica. He gave it a few tentative puffs before sitting down on a fallen log away from the fire.

"Know this one?"

A lively hornpipe erupted from the little instrument. Francis sat up straight listening, cramming it into his memory.

"That's a fine one. What's it called?"

"'Off to California' I think it is. D'ye like it?"

Francis pulled out the leather case of the flute he had bought in San Francisco, assembling it with speed before Scotty's amazed gaze.

"Play it again until I get the air of it."

★★★

Aggressive squirrel chatter came from above. Scotty's dog barked at it. The men had to put down their instruments with the racket.

"Shoosh now, Vicky," said Scotty, patting the dog. "You'll fright the sheep."

Francis stood up, shading his eyes to squint into the leaves.

"He's a grand gray one," said Francis. "Looks like he'd devour a sheep given a chance."

The squirrel's complaining increased. Vicky snarled and snapped back.

"Bet I can get him."

Francis was onto the low branches in a moment.

"Mind yerself there, Frank."

The squirrel's noise stopped in shock as Francis clambered level to him.

"Give yourself up, Mister Squirrel," he intoned. "You're surrounded."

One indignant bulging eye stared back as Francis crawled closer. The squirrel reconsidered his affront and sprang from the tree. Vicky was after him as soon as he reached the ground. The squirrel made for the hollow log where Scotty perched, the dog barking in anger.

"Vicky," shouted Scotty. "Stop it now."

Francis hung down from the branch and dropped to the ground. He reached into the dark hole of the log as Scotty tried to calm the dog.

"Ye mad eejit," exclaimed Scotty. "He might have rabies."

A broad gray brush appeared in Francis's fist.

"I've got a piece of his tail."

The creature's chittering echoed loud from his new holdout. Scotty had to crouch beside the dog as she nosed at the hole. He spotted sheep scattering away from the trees.

"Shit! I knew that would happen. Dog frightened 'em."

"I know what to do," Francis said quietly.

He pulled a stick from the fire, poking the brand into the squirrel's retreat. There was a blur as it leaped back out onto him. Dog barking and Scotty cursing, Francis dropped the burning stick as he jumped back. The squirrel disappeared up another tree.

Sudden silence.

"Where's it gone?" Francis asked, looking around.

Scotty stared back at him, eyes-wide, before doubling up with laughter.

"What? What's so funny?"

Perplexed, Francis stroked the dog's soft black head. She looked away, nonplussed.

"Yer trousers! Yev really fixed 'em now."

The stick smoldered over a black hole on the seat of his trousers.

The Sheep On The Mountain

It took weeks of herding before the mountains began to get close. They were sometimes joined by White, who steered the supply wagon and the senile mule pulling it. White took this as a sign of his authority over the others, who mostly ignored them. This night, he insisted they take a pass to a spring near an old mining town he remembered prospecting from years ago. Scotty had disagreed but was overruled. Instead of having the sheep at the creek before dark, they spent the whole moonlit night chasing about, cursing White and his shortcut. At dawn, one of the mustang sheep found a break down the edge of a steep canyon. Before Scotty or Francis could do anything, the rest of the bleating mass followed. The men rushed to the edge, instead of seeing the sheep plunging to their death, they were relieved to see the herd lapping at a thin stream that cut through the gulch.

★★★

"Hallooo!"

The call echoed up along the narrow canyon. Francis stirred himself awake; Scotty lay corpse-like beside him. Although hungry, weariness had gotten the better of them. Without even changing clothes, they had laid their bedding on the spot while the flock drank. The sun was not yet high.

"Scotty?" called White. "Where are you?"

Francis caught the faint echo of White's voice on the wind, he gave Scotty's shoulder a light shake. His companion opened his eyes, passing a hand over his face. He stood slowly.

"Where are ye?" he shouted back.

Eventually, White appeared across the gulch. Francis could just make out his stooped form.

"What took you so long?" he called across.

Even at a distance, White's voice was distinctly petulant.

"All night we've been on the wild goose chase you sent us," shouted back Francis.

No reply.

"Ach, don't bother," muttered Scotty. He laid back down, turning about in his bedroll.

"Aren't we going to go over to him and get food?"

"Aye. You go. I'm right knackered."

"Pancakes and bacon over at the camp," White yelled through cupped hands. "Already cooked 'em for the others."

Francis needed no further encouragement.

"Where is it?" he shouted back.

White's only response was to gesture along the gulch. He turned away, disappearing from view.

"If I don't go, I'll eat one of the sheep," said Francis.

Scotty turned in his bedroll.

"I'll watch the herd," he grunted. "Bring back some grub, will you?"

Francis got up and straightaway started to run in the indicated direction. The taste of raw squib on Baker Island rose in his gullet, reminding him he never wanted to be that hungry again. He slowed to a jog as he came to a single street of desolate buildings, some with caved-in roofs, others missing doors and windows. One or two were once fine facades. There was a bank or a saloon, alongside a barber shop with a still brightly colored barber's pole. The entire street was uninhabited, wooden sidewalks petering out to nothing. A pair of crows took to the air, cursing his arrival to all who would listen. Hunger briefly forgotten, Francis walked slowly along the street. He stopped for a while staring at a midden heap in front of an abandoned school.

A thin line of smoke came from behind one of the buildings. Francis hurried towards it, sudden fear coming over him of the ghosts in this place. It was only dispelled by the familiar sight of White's wagon. The cookfire smoldered near a scavenged pine table set out in the open, the remains of breakfast laid out on it. There was no sign of anyone else. In the eerie silence, Francis hunted through the wagon. Upon finding an open can, he could contain himself no longer, drinking the thick batter directly from the can.

★★★

"Oh, Frank. Tha' was a near enough thing."

Francis had returned to Scotty an hour later with a stack of pancakes, cold bacon and a large tin of coffee. Not even the smell of the food had roused Scotty at first, stretched like a corpse where Francis left him.

"A near enough thing," he repeated, munching with satisfaction.

"That other crowd didn't even leave us much," complained Francis of their fellows. "I had to scrounge this up from what was left."

"Aye. White's an odd one. Probably'll complain to Salter that we sent 'em astray. On his orders."

Scotty shook his head.

"That mining camp," said Francis. "Was it a town once?"

"It was, aye. I forget what it was called."

153

"Anyone live there now?"

"One or two, mebbe. All mining up here's dead. Only sheep now."

He washed down the food with a gulp of coffee.

"And look at ye. A right herdsman now! Graduated up from hunting squirrels."

Francis smiled broadly.

"I don't know, Scotty. I prefer the sea to this. Can't get lost on a ship."

"I suppose. Though you can get lost at sea easy enough."

Scotty's voice trailed off as squinted at the dirt. He bent down to examine a disturbed patch of ground.

"There's something…"

Francis joined him to look at the ground.

"What is it?"

"Bear tracks. They don' like sheep much but they're known to maul lambs. Time we got moving."

The Humours of Whiskey

They trudged up the rising mountains, urging the sheep before them. Francis had a system for easing weariness and boredom: he leaned on a tall stick to the opposite side of the foot going forward. Sometimes, when he stumbled, he would lift the stick for a moment until his feet caught up. It was like playing a long E or G at the end of a tune so everyone could catch up before playing again.

The dry plain of Salter's farm was a month away, minuscule somewhere beneath them. The trail was edged by sugar pine, height magnified in the rarefied air. Francis felt suddenly light-headed. The herd felt it too and stumbled forward with a false energy, rushing ahead to the level of the pass. Tossing aside his stick, Francis whooped and ran after them. Scotty gave a knowing look to White in his wagon, the latter as impassive as his mule. The sheep, followed by Francis, spilled into the high valley, a meandering stream bisecting the green sward. Massive mountains, thick with trees, surrounded them. At the valley's near end, a simple log cabin lay at the forest edge. Francis couldn't understand this sudden thrill. The blue sky and pristine paradise around were part of his elation. Yet under it all he felt false, a sense of impending crisis. He stopped running and noticed the sheep too breaking out of their gallop, a sudden constriction came to his chest. As if struck, his knees gave out from under him and he crumpled to the grass. He lay there, breath shallow as spots appeared before his eyes. All he could do was listen to the interminable bleating of sheep and watch the occasional puff of cloud drift by.

"Are you right, Francis?"

Eventually, Scotty drew near.

"What happened to me?" he asked in a faint voice.

"Some call it mountain madness. No' everyone gets it the same. Just rest there and you'll be fine. I'll bring the canteen over."

An ashen falcon drifted aloft. Francis could only lie still, listening to Scotty fussing with supplies. After a while, White's wagon creaked by. He paused, looking down his nose at Francis.

"Looks like them others beat you to the cabin. You'll be sleeping outside while we're up here."

Francis's heart sank as he watched the odious White urging the mule away.

"How long is that, Scotty?"

"Till autumn I s'pose. Rest there. We'll have grub goin' in no time."

★★★

Francis woke in the dark of their first night, unaccustomed to the rushing sound of the stream. Overhead, a blanket of stars stretched across the sky. A distant light from the little cabin meant the others must be still awake. Playing cards, he guessed. Francis stood and stretched. The sickness of earlier worn off, he felt a real weariness after the weeks of climbing up to the mountain. A sheep bleated in the distance followed by murmuring discontent from its peers. No sign of Scotty. Must be over at the cabin too. The silence and stillness blossomed as he tucked himself back in. The sun was well over the trees when he woke from profound sleep.

★★★

After a breakfast of cold beans from a can, Francis walked around to learn the lay of the land. There was no sign of the other men. Already he'd had to break up the flock stupidly clustered around one spot, destroying the pasture. He made plenty of noise yelling at the sheep. Still no response from the other herders. Sweating, he realized from the itch in his armpits and crotch that he hadn't bathed since San Francisco. Near to the cabin, a large log crossed the stream. Functioning as a bridge, it had a smooth worn look to it. Francis sat on it, regarding the fast-flowing cool water. He dipped his hands in to wash his face. *Freezing.* He was surprised to feel the beginnings of a scraggly beard. He regarded the backs of his hands, brown from days in the sun. He could not see his reflection in the stream but his face must be just as leathered.

He took off his boots and stockings, so far past salvation they smelled like rotten cheese. He dipped a toe in. At first the cold was shocking but the feeling soon faded. He looked around. Nothing but mountains, sheep, trees. He took off his belt and trousers, placing them on a rock. Back at the log, he unbuttoned his shirt and lifted it over his head. Naked, he was just putting his shirt down on a far part of the log when he wondered how his belt came to be there. Hadn't he left it over by the rock?

The rattlesnake basking in the sun raised its diamond-shaped head. The dull black body was patterned with pale chevrons. Francis froze. A sudden flash came to his mind of a detailed engraving of a snake from his encyclopedia. It was near enough he could make out its individual scales. Lidless eyes stared back at him. A tongue flicked in and out as if in anticipation. Terrified, Francis stared at the rattle the snake was raising like a weapon. Should he move? It was close enough to strike. Scotty had warned him about the dangers of getting bitten. Amputation or death. He stood as still as he could.

The door to the cabin opened and the tall figure of Watkins, a herder from Kentucky, emerged in undershirt and britches. He made for the stream to urinate.

"What the devil you at there?" he shouted at the naked figure of Francis.

The snake raised its head.

Francis dove into the water. Can snake swim? He felt along the bottom for a stick, finding one caught in the shallows. He jumped out of the frigid water, looking about. The snake had uncoiled on the log. Francis pinned the head with the end of the branch. It arched its body, trying to escape, curling along the stick and rattling furiously. The reptilian movement repulsed Francis.

"Help me," he called out. "There's a snake here."

Watkins strode up to him, fly unbuttoned. His face was grizzled with white stubble and his skin had a yellow pallor, eyes rheumy and yolk colored.

"Ain't this a fine scene!"

Francis was conscious of his nakedness. The snake trashed beneath his stick, attempting escape.

"Help me," he repeated. "It's a rattlesnake."

"You don't say," drawled Watkins. He drew a knife from his belt and slashed it down on the snake's head, half-removing it. The maw remained open, forever attempting in desperation to bite its attacker. Venom dripped out. After another cut to sever the head, Watkins proceeded to skin the creature while the body still spasmed and whorled about. Francis pulled on his trousers in haste.

"This here rattle's bigger than your John Thomas!" announced Watkins with a cackle. He held up the unusual appendage, hands covered in ichor.

"Thirteen rings," Watkins said with a whistle. "Haven't seen one that big in a long time."

"What's going on here?" asked Scotty, joining them. He stared from the decapitated snake to a half-dressed shivering Francis.

"Well, Mister Scotch, I've been saving Adam here from the serpent."

Watkins laughed aloud, wagging the rattle at Francis. Francis looked abashed, shirking away from the thing.

"Ah, now," reassured Scotty, "Watkins is only having a bit of sport with you. Go downstream from the cabin to wash. There's trees and the water's deep. Rattlers don't like too much shade."

Francis nodded and gathered his clothes, ears burning at the laughter of the other men.

★★★

The night brought cool air through the valley. It caused the embers of the campfire to glow.

"D'ye no' want to join us tonight?"

Scotty was returned from washing enamel plates in the stream. There was a slur to his words.

"What are you doing?" asked Francis.

"Watkins been working through those bottles of rye White brought up. Keeps losing at cards."

Scotty winked.

"You could make some money there."

"I'll stay down this end with the sheep."

"Suit yerself," said Scotty. "Boring company they tend to be."

Another night alone under the stars, the sound of his flute practice mingling with the stream.

★★★

Francis woke late again. No sign of anyone. After another scant breakfast he rushed out to the flock. Several had wandered from the valley to a neighboring grove. Whistling to Vicky, he ran after the miscreants. A group of sheep stood sniffing at bushes with bright waxy leaves. They skittered off at his approach. Francis inspected the tiny black berries under the leaves, making a soft oath to himself. He ran for the other men, the dog barking in confusion behind him.

Francis banged on the door of the cabin. No response came from inside but muffled curses. Francis pushed the door open.

"Poison laurel," he shouted. "The flock's got into a bunch of it."

He had spoken before he could take in the debauched scene before him. The single room was in disarray: a chair on its back, bottles and cards all over the floor and table where Scotty's harmonica glinted at him. Men lay half-clothed on the floor grousing and stirring themselves. A rifle with a tarnished brass receiver was propped by the door. Watkins rose from the one bed in the corner.

"Hellfire," he thundered. "What you doin' waking us, Nancy boy."

Francis was taken aback. He stepped back over the lintel, unsure of himself. Watkins reached for his knife and stood up in a drunken fury.

"I'll have your blood, Irishman! I'll teach you to disturb real men."

A part of Francis wanted to turn and run, down the mountain and far away. Curse the sheep and these drunks. Instead he reached into the corner for the rifle, cocked it and pointed it at the advancing Watkins.

"It's a fight you want?" he asked. "Come on."

Watkins sobered at the sight of the rifle. He stood there, considering. Scotty rose from the ground. He pulled back the murderous Watkins.

"Easy now. The lad's only trying to save the sheep."

The others were standing now. Watkins's eyes were wide and rolling as he railed against the cussed Scots and Irish. Francis did not falter, staring down the barrel at him. All at once, the fight went out of the Kentuckian. His jaundiced face slackened and he dropped the knife.

"Put that sixteen shooter away, kid. You might hurt yourself."

Watkins collapsed onto the bed. Francis pointed it at the ground.

"Leave him," Francis said. "We've got to get those sheep out of the laurel or they're all dead."

The other men stumbled out after him. Francis did not return the rifle. After some frenzied herding, they gathered into a pile the corpses of four poisoned sheep, their tongues distended and black.

"I will tell Salter the cost is to come out of Watkins's packet," said White.

Roll Her on the Mountain

After a dull summer in the mountains, Francis stumbled back down half-remembered trails, weary from the drudgery of herding. The sheep often tried to bolt but he was wise to them now and quick to wallop them with his stick when they strayed. The September sun was still strong but setting earlier. Through the trees a great lake spread across the plain before them. He stopped short, alarmed that they were turned around. Were they on the wrong side of the mountain?

The water of the lake shimmered with an unreal glint. A mirage, he realized. He remembered seeing something like it on the African coast, from the rigging of the *Jane Duncan*. He jumped up and down a little but it did not change. After some time, he did not know how long, the unreal lake dissolved into wavy quivering air above the parched plain. He walked on quietly, plagued by a longing he couldn't quite place.

★★★

Watkins, on the back of White's wagon, was much diminished by delirium tremens. White shook his head often in admonishment, deriving great pleasure in describing Salter's retributions. Francis could not help smiling to himself.

"Buggers have got a whiff of water," Scotty yelled from across the slope as hundreds of sheep careened down the rise between them. They were strong from pasturing in the high valley.

"C'mon," shouted Scotty.

Francis ran along with the sheep. At times he wondered how far he would fall were he to trip. The sense of danger did not concern him as he ran around rocks and branches laughing aloud, urging the sheep on. They cried and mewled in their desperation for water.

For an hour or two they ran with the flock, the wagon left far behind. They were brought to a sudden jolting halt at a half-dried creek. The sheep skipped from pool to pool, drinking only a little from each at the excitement of abundance.

Scotty wheezed next to him when he finally caught up. Vicky gulped down water alongside the sheep, too thirsty to heed her presence.

"That's me done for," panted Scotty.

Francis noticed sheep nosing at white chalky spots separate from the thin river.

"What're they at over there?" he asked. "Will they be alright?"

"Aye. That's them stopped for the day too. Alkali. Salt Licks," he explained. "No budging 'em now."

Francis scratched his head, tiredness overtaking him.

"Will we stop here for the night?"

"There's a good enough camp down the river a ways. White'll be by wi' our stuff later."

"But who'll mind the sheep?"

"I dinny know, lad. I'm done for."

The older man walked away along the riverbank, not looking back. The dog cocked her head in consideration before following. Francis sat down on a stone, wondering what to do. Out of nowhere, a small boy with raven black hair walked up.

"Hello," said Francis.

The boy made no reply. He must have been rolling in dirt, he was so covered in it. Francis noticed his skin was a light coffee tone.

"What's your name?"

The boy shrugged.

"Come away from there," called a voice from behind them.

The native appeared from the trees. He wore torn breeches and a tattered gingham shirt.

"Oh," said Francis. He stood up. "Are you Paiute?"

The man nodded, making no move.

"Um. I'm Francis O'Neill. These sheep belong to Norman Salter. I met one of… one of your tribe early in the season. John Owl I think his name was."

A flicker crossed the brow of the taciturn man.

"Well. I wonder could you help us at all? Bill Anderson—Scotty. My partner and I, are exhausted from chasing these sheep. He's gone to camp over there. Could you mind them while we rest for the night? We can feed and pay you in the morning."

The boy picked his nose as the older man considered Francis's proposition. Without thinking, Francis reached for the snake rattle he had kept in his pocket.

"Will this do as payment?" he asked. "It has thirteen rings."

The man cocked his head, taking the severed appendage with solemn reverence. He held it high, rattling it rhythmically while dancing and yelling.

"Hulla hulla hu! Hulla hulla hu!"

This went on for a whole minute with Francis watching in amazement. Then the solemn child burst out laughing. The taciturn man's face creased as he joined in. He had to put his hands on his thighs to control himself before giving the rattle back to Francis.

"Now we've done our rain dance," he said. "We can look after your sheep."

"Oh good," said Francis.

He wasn't sure if the mockery was over but weariness had the better of him.

"Just make sure they don't go too far, won't you?"

★★★

That night the camp was quiet. Their supplies were meagre on the return, White being extra mean with their portions. Too tired to object, the men collapsed to sleep once the sun set. There was an unexpected chill in the early autumn air despite the honey glow of the dusk. As soon as he laid down and closed his eyes, Francis felt himself falling down the mountain to the thunder of thousands of cloven hooves. The sensation was almost real and slow to leave. All night, he slept fitfully, despite his exhaustion.

He woke, feeling raw and anxious. After a quick breakfast of watery oatmeal in near dark, he hurried back to the flock. The sheep whickered and grunted in the cool dim morning, many still sleeping. Up on the riverbank glowed the embers of an abandoned campfire. Stretched on a rudimentary spit were the remains of a wether, fat still dripping onto the fire. He looked about for the man and his child but they were long gone. Francis sighed and crouched down next to the carcass. Shaking his head, he pulled off a hank of mutton, devouring it to ease his hunger.

Far From Home

Miss Anna Rogers,
6 Saint Felicitas Avenue,
Normal,
Illinois
March 27, 1869

Dear Anna,
I am writing to you from New York, not far from where we last said farewell, about
3 years ago. At the time, I promised faithfully to write regularly. Although I kept my

side of the bargain, I find that my former host, the landlady at 66 Oliver Street, did not. In fact, Mrs. Reid has proved to be a true criminal. Not only did she present me with these same letters when I saw her but now she refuses to return the $200 I left in her safe-keeping after I returned from South America. This was all my savings since I first landed on American soil, including the balance of my wages from the Minnehaha. This money grudgingly paid by the company agent as we had been shipwrecked off Baker's Island (more on that anon!).

I am at a loss as to how to retrieve my savings from her. Initially, she said she had used the money to pay off a pressing bill. Now she is pretending I never gave her the money. Twice now I have learned the hard way not to trust people with money and have resigned myself to being "stung". She must have had some twinge of conscience for at least she had the grace to return (already opened!) my earlier letters to you, recounting my adventures up to my stint herding sheep in California late last year. I apologize for this weighty correspondence and the lateness of it. It would almost make a book, all together like this. You may wish to stop and read the other letters now so this latest one will make sense in sequence…

I hope you enjoyed them. Reading back through them myself, I can scarcely believe some of the adventures I have had. Baker Island was the tightest squeeze of all, to tell the truth. Rest assured it has left no lasting mark though. How strange it is to be writing to you directly at last. Maybe I always knew in my heart that Bridey Reid couldn't be trusted and that those letters were being written to myself as much as they were to you. I should add that John Brennan sends his regards to you and your family. He was the one who passed on your new address and the welcome news that you were hoping to hear from me. John also gave me some of the story of how you headed west. It sounds like you have many adventures of your own to tell. I would dearly like to hear them.

It would be remiss of me not to continue my adventures up to this point. I found myself back in San Francisco last October, with a telegram from Brennan that he had made contact with your family. I suppose I should let you know that this was a matter of some interest to me. Although I had resolved to sail no more when I went herding sheep, I still needed a way to get back to New York. Besides, I had precious little luck before as the sailing trade is dominated by Scandinavian captains who look after their own kind. Lucky for me, Scotty had a contact from his sailing days with the first mate of the Hannah and accompanied me from Stockton to San Francisco. Truthfully, I believe Scotty was more interested in spending his wages in an inauspicious part of town called 'The Barbary Coast' than making introductions for me. We bid farewell on the dock after he had spoken highly to the mate on my behalf. I do not believe we will meet again.

The first mate was himself a very unusual character, not least of which being his pronounced hunchback. He stood on the deck of the three-masted barque ordering everyone about. Upon being accepted for employment, I asked the whereabouts of the Captain. This angered him no end and he ordered me to work straightaway saying he was to be appointed Captain soon. A nearby sailor sniggered at this but, being new, I did not pursue the matter. I was only interested in finding my digs on this new vessel. Our voyage was to involve picking up logwood in New Mexico and circling Cape Horn to deliver it to New York.

Below deck, I was directed to my bunk by a barrel-chested Welshman named Jones. He laughed when I asked about the Captain, telling me the real Captain had been dismissed for drunkenness and it was the hunchbacked mate who had ratted him out. I groaned inwardly, thinking here I was cursed, yet again, with a bad Captain. If I were ever to lead a crew, I surely know how not to do it. Jones must have sensed my dismay, as he smiled and told me that our new Captain had announced to the crew that all hands were to dine on shore this evening. Perhaps this was a bid by the hunchback to curry favor with the crew. Both Jones and I knew this ploy was bound to backfire.

Sure enough, the night was long and noisy with crew returning at all hours in worsening states of inebriation. The turnout in the morning was of a sorry lot, some wincing visibly as Jones clanged the bell calling them to assembly. In a loud cheerful voice, Jones announced to all that he was the new Captain and had a signed letter affirming his captaincy. The hunchback exploded at the affrontery of this. When Jones calmly asserted his authority, the man rushed belowdecks. It was the third day out to sea before we saw him again, under horrific circumstances.

I hope you won't be offended by the next section, Anna. I would spare you the gory details but for I remember how understanding you were about the dead children I had to handle on the Emerald Isle. Imagine my horror at being faced with another cadaver to be stitched into canvas. This time it was the hunchback mate. He had crawled into a dark corner and taken his own life by consuming a quantity of the logwood dye remaining on board from the last voyage. His was a terrible end, judging by the agony written on

164

his face. The other men, including our new Captain, were visibly shaken by the sight of his bloated body. His tongue was distended and horribly stained. God forgive me, it reminded me of the poisoned sheep I saw up the mountain. No one wished to handle him so the task of preparing the corpse fell to me. I did as best I could, considering my lack of experience, and wrapped him from view. Only then would the others aid me. We loaded him onto a plank and carried him topside. As we had no chaplain, the task of saying final words fell to his former enemy, Captain Jones. Without further ceremony, we consigned him to the deep.

The most terrible part of the story was yet to occur though, for the corpse would not sink. It bobbed back out of the water, the hunchback's ruined features peering out from the canvas. The sea was calm and the breeze light, so the body was visible for a long while. The Captain had to threaten flogging to stop the men gawking at the spectacle. I felt ashamed as I must not have weighed him down enough.

In any case, we made our way further south. We were soon overtaken by a hurricane. This one even more ferocious than the one I told you about off the coast of Georgia. There was much scurrying about in the dusk, reefing sails and battening hatches. Jones wanted someone to go to the lowest deck to secure everything but no one would go. When he demanded to know why, it came out that they were afraid to enter the spot where the hunchback committed suicide. They feared he would not rest as a ghost because his body did not sink. Sailors are a superstitious lot. It is ironic that the hunchback finally got to be captain of a sort, the men fearing him in death more than the living Jones.

There was nothing for it but face into the storm. It was night when it hit us full force, wind howling as the deck pitched and rolled. The waves were like walls, everywhere you looked. I was helping at the bilge pump when we heard an unnatural boom, a noise so loud it was obvious over the storm. The men around me stopped pumping in fear. "It's the hunchback!" exclaimed one. The only answer was a cacophony of crashing and banging. My first thought in the general panic that ensued was to get the Captain. I had to feel along the railing in the stinging rain and high wind, waves washing over me as I crawled along to the poop. All the while, a thunderous booming continued beneath me. Under a lantern by the wheelhouse, I found Jones. He was screaming at a man to stay at his post or there would be no one at the helm. By the lantern's light, I made out the young sailor's features. He was pale with fear.

"What the J**** is going on below?" yelled the Captain. I answered that I *didn't know. As I shouted my reply, the wind died suddenly. A hurricane is a giant vortex, the center of which is an eye of calm. We took the opportunity to make for a small trapdoor by the foredeck. The helmsman stayed at his post, terrified. Again, the Captain excoriated what men were nearby, trying in vain to get them to descend. Finally, I agreed to go, reasoning the former mate's spirit had the least reason to take against myself. Jones thanked me and held the lantern over the gaping square of black.*

Down I went.

Those tombs I told you about in Alexandria were bright compared to the blackness down there. I had no proper ladder to hold onto, only stanchions that were hard to find in the pitch black. I clung to the Captain's lantern with one free hand as I descended. Halfway, I almost lost my grip as the calm passed and the storm recommenced. Hurrying down, I was nearly crushed at the bottom by a large unsecured barrel. So, this was the spirit come to haunt us? I am sure my companions above thought me possessed by the devil when the sound of my laughter reached them.

Days later, anchored in shallow waters six miles out from Culiacán, there was much joking about the whole event. The Captain was grateful for my efforts and made sure my duties were sparse. An older sailor and I fished off the side as the others brought aboard logwood. The large gray fish we caught made a grotesque gulping sound as we pulled them out of the water, so we called them grunters.

Later, we were lodged on the edge of the town in a small house of wattles daubed with clay. The roof was of large palm leaves. The man hosting us was a Spanish sailor married to an Indian. They were extremely hospitable, serving us the most delicious coffee. Life was simple and unhurried there as in Hawaii and I was sorry to leave.

Back at sea and further down the coast of South America we spotted a shoal of flying fish. I must confess I did not believe they were real when I read about them as a child in that favorite book I told you about: Goldsmith's History of the Earth. *Yet here they were. They glided above the sea with a wobbling grace, tails barely touching the water.*

Cape Horn was a bitter spot but this was its mildest season, summer there being our winter. Heading back North, I was taking my turn at the helm when we struck something. I frantically checked the charts. We were just off the Falkland Islands in clear water. I veered to port, not knowing what to do. Another bang against the hull, less severe this time. I spotted a large black mass moving away from the ship. A flume of spray erupted from the whale's giant nostrils. The giant tail appeared as it dove away.

"Flukes ahoy!" shouted a sailor from the bow.

Taking the helm, the Captain appeared beside me. He ordered everyone to trim the sails saying there must be a school about. I abandoned the wheel to assist with the tying down of canvas. In truth, I wanted the best vantage to view the immense creatures. I had spent four years circumnavigating the world, skimming along the top of their watery domain. The sight of them frolicking and crashing in the sea was my abiding memory as we pulled into view of Sandy Hook some weeks later.

This seems like a good spot to conclude my adventures. I hope you don't mind the length and quality of my writing Anna. I have been at sea a long time and am glad to put it all behind me. Currently, I am applying to work with my oldest brother Phillip as a stevedore in Erie, Pennsylvania. I read in the Boston Pilot *alluring letters about farming in your part of the country. I too should like to take my chances out there. Would you like to meet again? John Brennan, the old rascal, said you might have a beau out there. If that is so, I apologize for the forward nature of this correspondence. I refuse to believe it to be true! Please do reply, even if you are so engaged. I dearly wish to hear from you again.*

Sincerely,
Francis

PART II
FIRE

CHAPTER 5

The Tongs By The Fire

Chicago, Illinois, 10 October 1871

"How're you doing, Ann?" Francis called her Ann now but thought of her as Anna. She did the same with Frank and Francis.

Anna groaned as she navigated from the tiny bedroom of their tenement flat.

"Take your time," he said. "Sit down there by the table."

Francis fussed over her as she sat down, brushing him off.

"He's been rolling inside of me all day," she chuckled.

"Now, now. We don't know it's a boy," Francis insisted.

"He kicks around enough that I think it's a He."

"Could be *she* takes after her mother. Another dancer from Feakle," he said with a grin. "Only another month 'til November. Then we'll know."

"Oh…" she squirmed with discomfort instead of saying more.

He frowned and went to their ancient black stove, worrying about how pale she was.

"A cup of tea might help?"

She shook her head.

"No. Too soon before Mass. I'm already changed and ready to go."

"I'm sure nobody'd mind if you skipped it. So close to…"

She gave him a look. He slugged back his tea.

"Well then. Let's be off."

★★★

The autumn afternoon was dry and windy. They took their time getting to Saint Pats. Francis was glad of the late Sunday service, priests in Ireland were never so accommodating. Anna had been up half the night and would never have been able for it first thing. He took a side glance at her from their hard pew. *His wife.* The idea still surprised him almost a year later. He recalled the rickety wooden frame Methodist church in Bloomington. How his father would have hated that, even though it had been the only option for their ceremony.

To think he had despaired she would never look at him again. Right after Bridey Reid had conned him out of his money. After several rough months working as a navvy with his brother on the canals in Pennsylvania, he headed west. He didn't care if she had someone or not. But why had he been so stiff and awkward when they finally met? By then he had a job as a district schoolteacher in a town near where she worked. He hated it. Give him South Sea pirates and hurricanes any day over a classroom full of boys. And he had thought he always wanted to be a teacher.

Finally, at the Knox county barn dance, screeching fiddles and people stomping around them, he muttered to her over the noise and crowd:

"Ahm, Anna. Would you? Maybe you'd like to?"

"Yes, Francis?"

"Go along with me?"

She laughed her lively laugh.

"Come over here!"

He was so surprised, she had to drag him out onto the dance floor.

"*Dominus Vobiscum*" intoned the priest, his back to them. The murmured words died in the dim of the church. Francis started from his reverie, getting a dark look from Anna as the crowd muttered the response. He joined in hastily.

★★★

"Jesus, Mary and Joseph! What's that?" she asked, pointing to the evening sky.

Drapes of red hung between nearby buildings. There was a strange bitter smell on the wind.

"Can't be the sunset," Francis said. "It's to the north of us."

The other parishioners stared about, some curious, some alarmed.

"Maybe we should head home," said Francis.

She ignored him, furrowing her brow at the spectacle.

"Let's go see what it is. Go up to the river."

A crowd of people headed along the street northwards. Francis looked ahead to see Anna purposefully following them.

"Ann! Go easy now," he called, racing to catch up to her.

PART II: FIRE

★★★

Across the river, the fire blazed. The neighborhood known as Conley's Patch was mostly single-storey wood frame buildings, stables, sties and sheds alongside shebeens and bawdy houses. A single fire boat pumped futile water into the conflagration. People swarmed towards them over a nearby bridge, shouting and cursing, holding onto hastily grabbed precious possessions. The crowd in front of Anna and Francis jeered and catcalled at the boat, their voices sounding mostly Irish.

"They're drunk," Francis muttered in disgust.

"Their homes are gone," replied Anna, edging forward.

A sudden flume of water splashed against them, the force knocking them back. Francis's senses left him for a moment. He could not understand this deluge of water. It swept his young wife from her feet.

"Ann!"

He went to her, lifting her up as the powerful hose played on others in the crowd. She coughed and gagged, trying to wipe the tarry water from her mouth. The river was unspeakably foul.

"Why?" he called. "Why are they turning the water on us?"

A nearby man shook his head.

"They'd rather put us out than the fire."

Most of the crowd were backing away from the hoses. All at once, the wind rose. It carried embers into the air, some landing on the surface of the black river. The water was so sodden with oil that patches of it stayed lit. One large ember wafted onto the fire boat, setting the canvas alight. Hoses stopped as the men struggled to extinguish the new danger.

"Come on," shouted Francis. "We should get back home."

Anna winced in pain as he helped her up. Over their heads, embers lofted hundreds of feet into the air, carried along by gusts of hot wind.

★★★

"It'll never come across the river," insisted Mrs. Maloney, their neighbor.

"There's a good chance it already has," said Anna. "We saw firemen stopping just down the street. Best prepare for the worst."

Mrs. Maloney put her hand to her mouth and retreated into the hallway.

Anna stiffly went to sit at their table.

"We should gather what we can. Just in case."

Francis nodded several times, distracted by the weakness in her voice. He tore around their little pair of rooms gathering what he could: the few extra dollars under a floorboard; their good clothes; the japanned box with the gold and cinnabar scene of birds, his engagement gift to her. He hid their money behind the false panel in the latter. He rushed out to the kitchen with everything stuffed into a cardboard suitcase.

"Our worldly possessions," she said with a trembling smile.

"Now, Ann."

She burst out crying. He rushed to her with his handkerchief. She took a deep breath and pushed it away, wiping her eyes with the back of her hand.

"I'm grand. I'll be fine now. It's just all emotions from the baby."

Francis stood up, unsure of what to do. He put his hand through his hair.

"What do you think, Frank? Will it come here?"

He chewed on his lower lip as he looked out the window.

"I can see the shop on the corner on fire. These buildings are like tinder. They could go up any minute."

"Right. Where can we go that's safe? Maybe check into that new Palmer House on State Street?"

She asked the last question with an ironic chuckle. He frowned. He was afraid to look back at her, worry for her and the baby clawing at him.

"If it's as bad as this, even there won't be safe. I think I know where to go."

★★★

Red rain fell all through the night. Prairie winds whipped the flames across the city, settling equally on humble shack and stately building. In no time at all, offices, banks, theaters, even the great courthouse, were devoured by an insatiable beast determined to return the city to the plains. Gusts of hot wind blew blazing houses onto other houses. People yelled and ran through the infernal heat and light, stomping on large rats appearing from under the wooden sidewalks. Firemen, trying to face the blaze, found the water blown back in their faces.

People went to the one refuge they could rely on. With escape to the north and the west cut off, they turned to the lakeshore and the Sands—the former slum recently cleared by the mayor. Looking westward, the night sky was lit spectral yellow, bright as mid-day. Francis watched a woman cry out in despair. She wore two fur coats and dripped with jewelry. Waist-high in water, she screamed at her husband. He ignored her, wading further out to escape the heat buffeting them. The howl of the fire-driven wind drowned her screams.

"Should we go into the water?" Francis yelled to Anna.

"No. There's shelter behind these rocks."

Her face was closed, lips pursed tight. What was she thinking? Afraid of the answer, he asked anyway.

"Is the baby alright? How do you feel?"

She made no reply.

He crouched next to Anna, sitting on their battered suitcase. He held her as the city burned down before them.

The Young Woman's Lament

Calvary Cemetery, Evanston, Illinois, 1871
A white sandstone marker bearing the following inscription:

John Francis 1871

O'NEILL

Mrs. Anna O'Neill,
461 South Jefferson,
Chicago,
Illinois
December 4th, 1871

Dear Madam,

Thank you for your recent correspondence. The Chicago Relief and Aid society have considered your petition for support in the wake of the events of the tragic fire on October 11th. It is indeed tragic that your son, born a month later, only lived 10 days. However, it is not our belief that your child's unfortunate demise is in any way related to the fire. Your petition states the child "burned with a fever he caught on that terrible day." While regrettable, the two events cannot possibly be connected. As the mandate of our society is to assist those displaced and injured by the conflagration, we are unable to provide the full assistance you request.

We also interviewed your husband, Mr. Francis O'Neill, who explained that although currently unemployed, he is healthy and more than likely to find work once conditions in the city improve. Chicago has many worse cases than yours, Mrs. O'Neill, and we have only limited funds to disperse, despite the charitable donations we have received from across the country.

We do understand how difficult conditions are for you currently and will recommend you for receipt of a Wheeler & Wilson sewing machine. Through dedication and hard work, you may use it to provide for your family, including any new additions which, no doubt, will come in time. Just provide this letter as proof at our head office and your name will be put on a waiting list.

Regards
David Havelin
Secretary,
Relief & Aid Society

The Butcher's Apron

Packing Town, Chicago, January 1872

Francis shivered in his thin coat. He had woken in the dark and slipped out of their rented room to look for a job. Not easy in a city with so many still destitute from the Fire.

The leaden sky was split by a smear of rising sun. Another freezing day. The snow that fell weeks ago was still everywhere. Despite the weather, it felt warm near the cattle and pig pens, steam rising from the dumb beasts. There was at least a square mile of livestock pens. Beyond them were the factories, squat long buildings surrounded by high chimneys belching smoke. Every day, hundreds of thousands of animals were crammed together, brought in by rail to be slaughtered, rendered, stripped, boiled, packed and canned in the distant low buildings. He hugged himself. The coat was better suited as protection from wind and rain on deck, not the damp cold that whipped in off the inland sea they called The Lake. How he would love to be at sea again. Moving. Going somewhere rather than lining up for work in this foul place.

Had he really given up his job as a teacher for this? It had been easy to find work in Missouri. In Chicago, unless you were connected, you could end up like the animals in these enclosures. It had been exciting at first, newly married and Anna's family near enough to them. Archey Road in Bridgeport even reminded him a bit of Bantry: unpaved roads, small shops close together, lots of Irish. But months without finding a job had taken their toll. He soon learned the social strata that made up Chicago. There were people destined for the high buildings and glamorous department stores of State Street and Michigan Avenue. The Irish, Germans and all the other new arrivals were not welcome there.

He swallowed his bitterness, mouth dry from want of breakfast. He had to find work soon or else both of them should leave. Back to Missouri? The school director was a Galway man and would surely take him back. How terrible would it be to teach those monsters again?

He looked about at the crowd of eager, nervous, tired men. Hundreds of them waiting and how many would find work today? One, two, five? One day a cart had rolled up and the nearest ten or so had piled on, not looking back at those left behind. A temporary job fixing broken pens, he had heard later when trudging home. At the yards, men rarely spoke. He heard that bosses spied on them from the windows, watching if anyone was too friendly. They wanted the men as dumb and frightened as the steers and hogs in the pens.

The Kent and Hutchinson packinghouse door opened. The crowd straightened themselves, slowly surging forward. Two men emerged to face them. One was a tall aproned man with a thick mustache, followed by a shorter man, hat in hand. They spoke as if nobody was there.

"I vant five more men for ze cellar, Granger," said the mustached man.

"Yessir, Mr. Schmidt," Granger said, glancing around. "Shouldn't be a problem. What will they be doing?"

Schmidt's eyes were crystal blue. He scowled at Granger.

"The usual, of course," he said. "Dressing hogs and pounding ice. Try to get Germans. Better vorkers."

"Yes, of course, sir," Granger said in a mollifying tone.

Without another word, the boss turned back inside. Granger looked after him, a sneer curling his features. He turned and stepped into the yard. The men all started speaking at once, different accents and tones announcing their fitness for work. Francis said nothing but hung back a little at first. He slipped into a cluster of Prussians near the front.

Granger held up his hands. The crowd quieted.

"Alright. I can only take five. I've got a lot of work on this morning so here's what I'll do."

Instead of further explanation, he darted forward with his arms wide. He hugged two of the Prussians near Francis. Sensing what was happening, Francis surged forward with another pair. The men smelled stale up close. The four managed to fit themselves into Granger's grasp, pushing Francis back. He managed to squeeze back between them. One of them shouted in German, denouncing him. Others tried to fit into the narrow circle, pleading and yelling.

"Enough," shouted Granger. "I have my men. The rest of you go home. Come back tomorrow."

He lined the five up by the wall, inspecting them.

"You," he barked, scrutinizing Francis. "German?"

178

Francis straightened himself.

"Sure, what does it matter?" said Francis. "I will be when the boss is around."

The one who denounced him earlier wore a shocked expression, complaining bitterly in German.

"Alright. Alright," laughed Granger. "Maybe you can explain to these sausage eaters what is going on."

"How much is the pay, sir?"

"$1.75 a day. Any problem with that?"

"No. Thank you, sir. That's... That's great wages. I'll explain it to them."

Granger turned away without a reply, his mind on the morning's work.

★★★

Francis staggered in the door to her. It was late. He was covered in blood.

"Frank," exclaimed Anna. She drew back, afraid for him. Afraid of him.

He collapsed onto a chair.

"What happened to you? I've been worried about you all day."

His face was pale under the smears of blood. His hands were covered with it.

"Did you? Did you get in a fight?" Her tone changed. "Were you drinking?"

He looked at her. Finally, he spoke.

"I got a job," he said.

She sat down next to him.

"You have? That's great news altogether."

"It's only a dollar and three quarters a day. Slaughtering pigs."

He fished the coins from his pocket and let them clink onto the table.

"Is it hard work?"

He nodded.

"Never known work like it. Breaking stones on the Erie canal was easier. At least that was clean. Those hogs..."

His throat constricted and he had to swallow.

"The hogs come in hooked to a chain and we have to kill them quick. The chain doesn't stop. A few of mine were still squealing when they were

179

taken on to the next set of men. The blood gets everywhere."

"Francis, come on now. You've work again. We can start saving. You won't be doing this forever."

"Ah, we'll never get anywhere on that."

He gave a dismissive nod to the money.

"And you're not even making a dollar a day on the piece-work you get."

She looked down at the table, he didn't notice his words had hurt her. Silence stretched out between them until he finally spoke, voice distant.

"I talked to a foreign lad. A big fellow. I think he was from Lithuania or somewhere. He has his whole family, even his children, working in there. I'll not have any child we have condemned to that."

"You might become a musician?" she suggested, changing the topic. "You got paid at some of those dances in Missouri."

"Augh. There's no money in music. The music they want here is different from home anyway. I have to do better." He stared at his bloody hands. "Better than this."

"Do you want to leave Chicago?" she asked.

He took a deep breath. The thought of moving again calmed him down.

"Not yet. I like that we have family here. But I'll only do this awful work for a while. There's no future in it, Ann."

She took his bloody hand.

"You'll find other work, Francis. You're an intelligent man. Maybe as a clerk for one of the stores around. There are so many of them. Sheila Dunphy's husband is at one of them. Maybe he could put in a word for you?"

He tried a smile, coming out of himself.

"Yes. Can you talk to her for me?"

She nodded, then dropped his hand.

"Now, for the love of God get out of the kitchen and wash that off yourself."

★★★

Palmer and Fuller Planing Mill, April 1871
The blade swirled inches away from the operator's coffee-colored hand. The engine powering it lurked nearby, causing the stuffy mill to throb with its

presence. Shepard, the foreman, came by often to curse it and its stoker. The foreman saw himself as a priest whose main role was to remind everyone of their imminent demise from this machine. He delivered scriptures of doom to all in a cheerful tone. That morning, after first sermonizing Francis, he told him his new job was to keep the saw operator supplied. This involved maintaining a constant supply of untrimmed lumber for the vicious spinning steel. The wood came in on a narrow-gauge rail. It jammed often and Francis had to haul hard to pull it across the floor, all the time avoiding dangerous flying splinters.

"Know how much you earn yet?"

The machine operator's name was Sam, curly black hair prematurely balding. His dark brown eyes protruded a little. They were outside, eating from their lunch buckets in the thin spring sunshine.

"I'm not sure. Shepard was vague enough. I'm glad to be out of packing town though. Took me a while to find this job."

Sam snorted and wiped dust from his brow.

"I'm hoping I'll get a dollar fifty a day at least," said Francis.

A cloud came over Sam's features.

"The hell you will. That's more than I get." He spat and gulped down cold coffee. "Dressing hogs in packing town might be tough but pay's better there."

Francis was taken aback by the sudden change in his companion.

"You white boys are all the same. Always thinking you should get more pay than us."

"I didn't mean that," insisted Francis. "Foreman said it would be better than my last job. that's all."

Sam's face twitched and he scratched under his eye. Francis hadn't noticed the scars all over his arms before. Sam nodded in Shepard's direction.

"You go ask him. Tell me what he pays you out."

Francis frowned but said no more. He left the lunch pail and his truculent companion to walk over. The ganger was eating alone at the end of the long bench outside the main office.

"Mr. O'Neill, how can I help you?"

Shepard was in a good mood. Francis smiled briefly.

"I was wondering about my pay, Mr. Shepard. I'm hoping to get a dollar seventy-five a day based on what you said before."

"Oh no, no, no," said Shepard, tone as jovial as ever. "Every machine man in here would go wild if I gave you that. They may be black as the soot from that cursed boiler but they are smart enough when it comes to money. Come here."

Francis sat down next to him. Shepard leaned close, speaking in a low voice.

"I can do a dollar and a quarter a day for now. It's better than I give them starting. Keep that between yourself and myself, of course. You'll be a good man with lumber, I can see that."

"Thanks, Mr. Shepard," said Francis. He avoided Sam's stare as he returned to his work.

★★★

Francis weighed his options as he slowly pushed the heavy trolley towards the blade.

"Hey," shouted Sam. "You're taking your sweet time getting that lumber to me."

"Yes," said Francis. He stood up and faced him.

Sam cocked his head to one side.

"I guess you found out your wages."

"I did."

"And?"

"I think I'll be looking for new work tomorrow."

Sam shrugged, returning his attention to the spinning blade.

Were I A Clerk

Chicago And Alton Railway Service, August 1872

"How long have you been in our employment, Frank?"

"Over four months now, Superintendent McMullin."

McMullin, a lanky man in his fifties, leaned back in his leather chair. The superintendent's office was untidy, full of boxes of files and waybills.

A window streaked with dirt looked out onto the wide railway yard facing Halsted Street. Men hurried about the tracks as freight trains bearing the C&A stamp came and went.

"I started in May as trucker," Francis supplied as the super, lost in thought, looked out on the scene. "Then checker. Later I was made entry clerk at the door scales. I've lately been in charge of demurrage on coal and lumber cars terminating here."

"Quite the meteoric rise, I'd say," murmured McMullin.

"Thank you, sir." Francis hesitated before continuing. "But my pay is still the same at a dollar fifty. I think I've shown my worth to this company. I've even looked after John Beasley's route for two months while he was on vacation."

"Oh, John, yes." McMullin perked up. "My niece's new husband. Lots of promise in that young man. I believe they went to the Dunes for their honeymoon."

Francis took a deep breath.

"Yes. He's paid considerably more than me, Mr. McMullin. Yet I was able to do his work while he was away. Along with my own."

The superintendent sat up at that. His long neck ended in a small chin.

"What are you saying, O'Neill?"

"I'm not casting aspersions on John Beasley or anyone else."

Francis sat as straight as he could. He was nearly as tall as the man in the dusty suit scowling down at him.

"I just want to be paid properly for the work I do here. Mike Ryan, the head checker, lets me do night work so I can make a bit extra but it's wearing me out."

McMullin said nothing.

"The other day," continued Francis. "Reid, the agent, told me of a vacancy at this office due to a death. Today I got here to find it was filled. Why wasn't I even considered?"

A quick smile from the superintendent.

"Look. Frank. You're a good man. You must understand the way things work though. I can't just give people jobs based on how well they do. That

183

wouldn't be fair to the others, would it?"

Francis frowned.

"That's the very definition of not fair."

He struggled to keep his voice even. McMullin shook his head.

"No. No. No. Have you ever worked as a clerk before?"

"I haven't."

"There you go. You aren't used to the way these things play out, are you? It takes time to get ahead and you must prove that you really are a railway man. That you have what it takes. Don't worry though. The C&A is a wonderful place and will only keep enlarging. You've lots of time to prove yourself."

"No. Thank you," said Francis, standing up. "I think, you've proven yourself well enough to me. I'll not be working here anymore. I'm handing in my notice."

He walked out of the office, surprised to find the emotion he felt most was impatience, not anger or indignation.

★★★

Farwell and Company Dry Goods, October 1872

A man persuaded Weary Willie, with some difficulty, to try to work on a job for thirty days at eight dollars a day, on the condition that he would forfeit ten dollars a day for every day that he idled. At the end of the month neither owed the other anything, which entirely convinced Willie of the folly of labor. Can you tell just how many days work he put in and on how many days he idled?

"Mr. O'Neill?"

Superintendent Stearn called out to the busy room full of clerks. They were mostly young men, eager to get on in the burgeoning business. Francis stood up from his desk by the entrance.

"Yes, sir?"

"Can you come here for a minute?"

One or two of the others made malevolent smirks to each other at Francis's expense. Stearn ushered him into the room and closed the door.

He motioned to Francis to sit. A large portrait of John V. Farwell adorned the wall behind his desk. The company founder had a determined look as he scrutinized both of his underlings. It reminded Francis of the picture of Jesus, heart exposed in the bishop's office in Blackrock.

The puzzle had made the rounds of the office, eventually reaching Stearn's desk. Francis had supplied this teaser after easily solving the puzzle provided by Stearn himself. Stearn's overall role at Farwell's was nebulous, although he was the Superintendent of clerk exams.

"Ah. Yes," Stearn said as he sat down. He indicated the puzzle written in Francis's neat handwriting, a sheet of paper blotted with ink and scribbled solutions beside it. "Others have complained to me that you sent this around this puzzle as a mockery. How do you respond?"

"Mockery? Oh no, Mr. Stearn. I enjoyed the previous puzzle and just wanted to share another."

"Yes. Well. None of them are able to solve it," blustered Stearn. "Haven't had time to look at it myself but it seems a trifle ridiculous. And the tone of the thing. Well, it strikes me as inappropriate."

Francis cocked his head to one side, he spoke in a cautious tone.

"Yes. I didn't think of that side of it, sir. I took it from one of my arithmetic textbooks from Missouri. Perhaps if I demonstrated the proof using a quadratic equation." He paused before adding, "for the others, of course."

Stearn nodded, relief plain on his face.

"Yes, perhaps if you ran through your solution once so I may judge it appropriate or not."

Stearn jumped up to place a sheet of paper and a fountain pen before Francis. It only took a minute to run through the solution. Stearn was nodding all the time.

"Ah, of course. Very good. Very good."

He sat back down across from Francis, studying the junior clerk for a while.

"How long have you been here now, O'Neill?"

"Only a month or so, sir."

"Hmm. What are you on?"

"Two dollars."

"Not great is it?"

Stearn relaxed. He was in charge again.

"I was hoping I could have an advance soon," said Francis. "My wife is expecting and I am looking to save for a mortgage."

"Good. Good. Yes. Farwell's is a great place for promising young men like yourself. Our founder…"

Both briefly acknowledged the portrait staring down at them.

"He started with nothing as well, you know. Came up from Ogle county without a cent. Worked his way up as a clerk until this…"

Stearn gestured vaguely about the office.

"Now he gifts half of his money to charity and actively encourages promising young men. Such as yourself."

"He's a great example."

"Yes, indeed. However. I understand how difficult it must be to stand out. Even for someone of your intellectual prowess."

He indicated the mathematical puzzle.

"But that is only one aspect."

Francis leaned forward a little in the uncomfortable chair. Stearn made a sudden lunge, reaching his hand across the desk. Francis stared at it. Stearn pushed his hand closer. Francis took his hand, unsure what else to do. Stearn's grip was weak until he pressed one finger hard on Francis's knuckle. He raised his eyebrows in expectation. After a few seconds he released and asked,

"How would you respond if I said 'Boaz'?"

Francis's face betrayed complete bafflement.

"I'm sorry, sir?"

"Hmm. Never mind. Just a word."

He smiled to himself, satisfied.

"A powerful word though. Used by the most powerful people."

Francis had no idea what to say.

"Were you to be a member of such a powerful group, I could ensure advancement in this office. You would have to be accepted by this group before I could do anything."

"This group?" ventured Francis.

Stearn gave him a look as surprised as Francis's a moment ago.

"Why, you can't expect me to name them, can you?"

"Um. No... I suppose not, sir."

"Of course not. Well." He looked down at the papers on his desk. "I expect you have many things to be getting on with."

"Ah, yes," said Francis. He stood, realizing this was his signal to leave. Seizing the opportunity, he ventured a question.

"And the question of my advance?"

Stearn just waved him out, frowning down at the proof. Francis gave him a dark look and left the office.

The Devil's Dream

461 South Jefferson Street, Chicago, January 1873

"I'll be raising your rent by a dollar this week. If you can't do anything about it, you'll have to go elsewhere."

The landlady's voice was harsh as gravel. She stood out in the dark hall as she delivered her ultimatum. Francis could just make out her squat form. Women landlords were worst of all.

"Of course, Mrs. Wright. I'll do my best to get that to you. Of course."

"See that you do."

The last he saw was the grim set to her face as he closed the door, along with her final greedy glance in. He turned back to their single room flat: bare floorboards and bare furniture. "Extortion," he exploded. "That's what it is."

Anna looked up from the bed, baby nursing at her side. The infant made a surprised sound, threatening to cry.

"No. Sorry," he said in a mollifying tone. "Didn't mean to upset the child."

He was all fluster, unsure of what to do around the new baby. He was also called John Francis. It was a family tradition to reuse the name of a child who died, just as he had been named Daniel.

"Ah, Frank," she said, tucking the baby into the blankets and reaching for her dressing gown.

187

"The doctor said you were to stay in bed," he pleaded.

"I can't be staying in bed all the time. I feel too black lying here with the baby all day. Sit down over there and talk to me."

He looked at her. Here was something of the old Anna returning. He sat with care on the edge of the bed. Months after the first boy died, she would go days without speaking, as if he were not there. Not knowing what to do, he found himself avoiding her. He felt guilty, but he even stopped coming back to their miserable digs some nights, unable to face her silent despair and the memory of the little boy who had cried so much. Instead, Francis had walked around the dark streets: looking for other work, other places to rent, anything. From the shadows, he watched men brawling outside bars, heard domestic arguments. But he did nothing.

"I'm going back out to work," she announced.

"What? No. You're not right yet. And who'll mind the baby?"

She shushed him; the baby was starting to doze.

"Maybe my sister," she replied, whispering. "Besides, I have to. You heard that sow of a landlady. She'll have us out if we can't pay."

"It's because of the Fire. There still aren't enough places in the city." He shook his head and sighed. "I'll find another job at night."

"No, Frank. You work hard enough as it is. I can do it. I want to. It'll take me out of this."

She looked around their spartan room.

He had no answer for her.

"We have to have our own place," he said finally. "Now is the only chance we have. Otherwise, every bit of our money will always be leeched by landlords."

She raised her eyebrows, forehead wrinkled with weariness.

"Look at this."

He held out a much-folded handbill—lots on Halsted and Thirty-first were glowingly described in a large font.

"I could build it myself. By night. Gardner and Spry will give me the lumber on credit after my time on Lake Michigan with them."

She scrutinized the fine print on the paper.

"Frank, that's way beyond what we can afford."

"The main streets are, yes. But maybe if I ask the agent about a lot on one of the side streets. With fifty dollars down and eight percent interest it won't be much different from the terrible rent we're paying."

Her frown deepened. He found his heart jump with delight, any emotion at all was welcome.

"No bank will ever lend us that. And even if they do, how will we afford to build it?"

"We can do it," he enthused. "It'll be the same as when I helped my father build a shed. Some of the lads I used to work with at Farwell's said they'll give me a hand. Ann, imagine if we had our own place. Never to have to worry about some old biddy banging on the door whenever she feels like it. It'll give us a chance…"

He faltered.

"What chance?" her face betrayed nothing.

"For you not to have to work." He looked at the now sleeping baby. "To be able to mind little John properly."

Her eyes narrowed. For a second, he thought he saw anger. She erupted crying.

He rushed to her, held her to him. The baby joined in the crying.

"Ah, shush now," he soothed. "It'll be fine. I'm to meet the main real estate fellow tomorrow and arrange it all."

★★★

The snow was doing a good job of hiding the lingering devastation from the Fire. All over the city, there still jutted spandrels of half-demolished buildings, nagging reminders of the horror in the past. Francis picked his way through the slush on the margin of Halsted Avenue. Sections of the street were so ripped apart, there wasn't even a single plank to walk along. Many of the new empty lots were piled high with debris. In the middle of it all stood a single new wooden-frame home, paint still fresh. It stood apart like an apparition.

Francis knocked on the shining door, half-wondering if it was real.

"Yes," called a bright voice from inside. "Come in."

189

He walked in, marveling at the fresh decor. A fire roared on a generous hearth.

"Welcome to the home of the future," announced a red-haired man as he turned to face him.

Francis's jaw dropped. The recognition was instant.

"You!"

Murdoch stepped back for a moment, blinking.

"I'm sorry. I believe I was to meet…"

Francis rushed at him, grabbing the tweed lapels of his jacket.

"You were on the *Emerald Isle*! You near drowned my sister-in-law. And after. Your father had those men attack me."

Francis yelled into Murdoch's face. A dribble of Francis's spit covered the other's chin.

"Tell me why I shouldn't beat you senseless?"

Murdoch's pale face was impassive apart from a slight unruffled smirk, infuriating Francis even more.

"I believe you are mistaken," he said. "I am certain we have never met before. Perhaps if you calmed down a little, we could discuss this properly."

Francis took a deep breath. He looked around, shaking.

"Are you not Hubert Murdoch? Did you not travel to New York on the *Emerald Isle* about five years ago?"

"That was so long ago. Are you sure? I can't remember, to be honest. I've traveled so much. Besides what have you got to prove any of these accusations?"

"I can prove it," Francis said with truculence, cold anger coursed through him as he realized he could not.

"Let go of me," said Murdoch. "Now. Let us talk about this like gentlemen."

Francis held him tighter for a moment. He could see himself beating the man, taking out on him all the helplessness of the last couple of years, pounding his pallid face. He lifted his right hand, fist tightening.

"I can get you a good deal on a lot," Murdoch flashed a smile.

Francis's eyes narrowed. "What?"

"How are the banks treating you? Unskilled Irish? Can't imagine the mortgage offers are favorable." Murdoch stepped back from Francis's slackening grip. "Let me look after that. Perhaps we had some misunderstanding in the past. Forget it. I have sway with certain bank people. Now, you have a chance to improve your station. If you attack me, you throw all that away as I will have you thrown in jail. A criminal record will be the first step on your downward fall."

He pushed Francis's hands off his smart lapels, wiping the spit from his chin.

"Think instead of the opportunities that lie ahead. This fire has proved a boon to so many. It's cleared the way for a new city. One that doesn't care about where you came from. Here's your chance. Now, what is your name again?"

He looked down at a sheet on the lacquered table.

"Francis," he continued. "Don't throw your opportunities away on petty squabbling. You're better than that."

Francis backed away from this man. Up close there had been something repulsive about him, fascinating as the rattlesnake.

"Jail?" Francis asked. "You're the one that should be turned into the police."

Murdoch trilled his falsetto laugh.

"Oh, Francis! Please. Have you encountered the police in this town? Half of them are part-time crooks. The better ones are private, paid for by powerful men. You know better."

Francis stood back further, hands dropping wearily to his sides.

"Tell me about the lot," he growled. "It had better be a good deal."

Murdoch's smile was cold and thin as he clapped Francis on the back.

"Come. I will show you the site of your future home."

Farewell To Whiskey

James McParland's Saloon, Chicago, March 1873

A fury of music swelled from the back of the saloon. James McParland leaned on his counter, listening to them. He sometimes swished his glass of whiskey in time to the music. The tempo slowly increased until one of the fiddlers started on a different tack—general confusion ensued.

"Sorry. Sorry," apologized the fiddler. "Thought that one was followed by 'The Broken Pledge'"

Laughter and good-natured admonishment.

"Drink up there, boys," McParland called out with the lull in the music, his Ulster accent pronounced. "This is my last night of business and the drinks are on me."

A rousing cheer came from the musicians, followed by commiserations and toasts to his health. In the middle of the table, Francis was examining his borrowed flute.

"I'll sell it to you if you want, Frank."

The older man across the table studied him closely while Francis tested out the flute.

"That's too good of you, Tim. But I'm broke these days with putting the house together. I couldn't afford it."

Tim considered this before changing the subject.

"How're you doing as a builder?"

Francis put down the flute and sighed.

"It's hard work. Doesn't help that half my lumber was swiped by others on the street. There's nothing I can do about it though. They steal it when I'm gone during the day."

"You need a policeman," replied Tim with a chuckle. Tim Sullivan had been on the force himself for a few years now. As their friendship grew, he often regaled the younger man with tales of the job.

Francis shook his head.

"Thanks for the loan." He made to give the flute back to Tim. "Someday I'll have the price of one for you."

Tim looked at the flute for a moment, then shook his head.

"Go on. Hold on to it."

"What? No! I can't take it."

"Go on," Tim said again. "Before I change my mind. Call it a long-term loan. Give me a tune as interest."

Francis lifted the instrument up, wetting his lips in preparation.

"I hope you find this of interest," he said with a broad smile. He launched into "The Day We Paid the Rent". Soon, the others got the air of it and joined in.

★★★

Francis looked up to the gilt-inlaid mirrored clock on the saloon wall. One o'clock.

"God! Ann will kill me," he announced.

The group of musicians had shrunk to Francis and Tim, their numbers had dwindled as McParland's store of whiskey depleted. The owner sat down to the table with them.

"Just tell her you were building that house," he murmured.

Francis smiled back at him.

"You don't know what I'm dealing with. She'd never fall for that."

McParland took out a clean and starched handkerchief with an expansive gesture. He proceeded to use it to rub the outside of his right eye with his right finger. Francis watched this secret signal with bemusement. McParland gave him a keen look before pocketing the handkerchief with a sigh.

"You've lasted the longest of most of them," said McParland after a long pause. "You must have great strength for drink."

Tim stirred himself next to Francis.

"Hah! He hardly drinks at all is why," slurred Tim. With a grunt, he got up from the table and stumbled out without saying another word.

"Why is that, Frank?" asked McParland, once Tim was gone. "Not every day I'm giving out free booze."

Francis shrugged.

"Never took to it much. A drop's alright. My father was a bit too fond of it."

"Aye. But why stay here all night then?"

"Music," said Francis, grinning. "Anything to be playing music."

McParland shook his head.

"Why are you closing up anyway, James?" asked Francis. "The city's building back up. I'd say you might get this place back on its feet someday."

"Ah, I'm tired of being stuck in one place. I left a steady job in Belfast when I was younger than you. Went to England and America, wanting to get out of the steady thing. Where're you working now?"

"Clerk at Farwell's."

"How do you like it?"

"It's alright. Never thought I'd say it but I do miss the sea. I don't miss the traveling so much as being my own man. Plus, Farwell's is run by Masons. I'll never get anywhere there."

McParland took off his spectacles to rub tired eyes.

"Masons," he stated. "I'm guessing you've not encountered the Irish kind?"

"Irish kind?"

"Clan Na Gael mean anything to you? I'd say not given how you didn't respond earlier. They're a bunch of Fenians. They help some get jobs over here."

He took a deep swallow of whiskey.

"I've had no real luck with them myself. One reason I'm selling all this to become a detective."

"A what?" Francis was surprised at the Northerner's sudden secretive tone.

"Private detective. The firm's run by a man named Pinkerton. Not just in Chicago too. Says he'll send me all over. He has offices out East. Doesn't mind employing Irish, either. Pay's much better than a city cop."

"Huh? Sounds like a good idea."

"Fellow like you'd do fine there. Mind you, there might be some unofficial work you'd have to do."

McParland winked. Francis's lower lip massaged his upper as he considered.

"I've heard you can do well as a policeman in Chicago," Francis said, finally. "Look at Tim Sullivan that's just left. He's helping me put together the requirements to get in. Maybe if I don't get it, I might just take you up on that."

"Fair enough. Don't wait too long, though. City police department's always strapped for cash." McParland snorted. "Sure, not that long ago they were just a private force themselves. If there are enough Paddies and

194

Micks in this Pinkerton's, I'll let you know. Put a good word in for you."

"Thanks James," said Francis with a chuckle. "I should be putting in words for you. You're the one going out of business."

McParland leaned back in his chair with a smile, raising the last of his whiskey to toast Francis.

The Halfway House

461 South Jefferson St., Chicago, March 1873

"Come on, Ann. You can open your eyes now." Francis guided Anna, her hands over her eyes. It was just the two of them, her sister Julia was looking after John Francis. The other Bridgeport houses were rising quickly around their plot—all signs of the Fire erased in the raging boom of construction. A whistle shrilled out from the nearby railway embankment.

"Frank," she exclaimed. "The roof's finished!"

He kissed her quickly. She pushed him away with a smile.

"How did you finish it so quick?"

"Hans, the bricklayer from two doors down helped. Wouldn't take any money either. He helped me point the chimney."

"We can't not pay them," she said, her voice serious.

"Of course not, believe me I tried. He said to get a nice shawl for his wife."

"I'll make her one then."

Without another word, he held her hand and led her up to the door frame. The little patch of lawn was all muck and debris.

"It's not much," he admitted. "Just a big wooden box, really. I'll probably have the door made by next week. Some scoundrels around here keep stealing the lumber. I'm keeping it inside now which is a bit better—"

She squeezed his hand.

"It's marvelous, Frank. You've made this yourself."

She paused for several heartbeats, brow knitted in seriousness. When she spoke, her voice was serious and fierce.

"I've a surprise for you, as well."

His eyebrows raised.

"I'm expecting again."

For the briefest moment his heart fell.

"That's wonderful," he said, hugging her.

"Come on inside. Let's celebrate in our new kitchen."

She followed him into the small parlor, marked off from the rest of the house by chalk. Francis hadn't got to putting interior walls up yet.

"Sit down there on the 'kitchen table'."

He indicated a neatly stacked pile of lumber by the gap for a window. His mind racing over a million topics, he went about picking up tools, putting them down. Her smirk as she watched him was enigmatic.

"What name will we give him?" she asked, adding with a laugh, "Or her?"

"I don't know," he said, still bewildered. "I'm still getting used to the idea."

She nodded, looking around the dusty floor. She spied his flute and a crumpled copybook laid out on a crate.

"Do you practice much when you're here building?"

He looked away, shy about it.

"Yes. I didn't want to be bothering you with it. Before. I like practicing in the quiet."

Another wry smile from her.

"Go on. Play me a tune. Something to celebrate the baby coming."

His eyes widened as the implication returned. Then he went to the instrument, picking it up he sat beside her. He blew on it gently, adjusting the head joint until the A sounded right. He fidgeted with it as he thought about what to play.

"I'm not sure what…"

"Anything at all."

He pondered for a long time before starting. It was in jig time but slow and a little melancholy. He stopped after a couple of phrases, taking a deep breath.

"What is it?" she asked.

"It's called 'The Little Fair Child'. One of the lads at the saloon gave it to me. I swear he nearly cried after playing it. Do you mind it?"

"Go on," she said, although she shook her head.

He picked up the tune again, the flute sounding a little shrill in the empty house. Anna stood and started to dance, steps halting and uncertain.

"Wait," she said, voice stern. He paused, mouth half-open over the embouchure.

"You're not playing right, Frank. I can't dance to it."

"What do you mean?"

"It's like you're studying the tune while playing it. Stop that. Just play as if you were dancing it."

His mouth was still open over the flute.

"Go on. Try playing it as if you were in that dance hall at Knox county with a hundred hopping around you. And don't be so mournful either. Isn't it a song for a child?"

For a moment, his eyes filled with tears. He blinked and closed them, imagining the dancehall full of people. He started into playing again. His emotions calmed and he forgot everything: the stolen lumber; the dull monotony of his job; the landlady looking for more money; losing their first baby.

Anna danced on the fresh pine floorboards. Her laughter opened his eyes and he stopped to admire her.

Princess Royal

Criminal Court of Cook County, Chicago, May 1873

Judge Lambert Tree stroked his elegant long mustache. He surveyed his courtroom with disdain, regarding the gathering as a mob of drunken Lithuanians, stern Germans and shifty Irish. He wondered how long more before he could escape.

O'Hara, the clerk, rasped at the assembly for silence and order.

"Who is next?" he called to O'Hara, his voice lofty and distant.

"Frank O'Neill, your Honor," O'Hara responded.

Tree considered the tall stern-looking man before him, unruly hair half-tamed by a sheen of pomade, suit shabby and worn. His eyes were intense and discerning. He looked like a likely criminal to Lambert.

"Ever been in trouble with the law before, Frank?"

Tree pondered the question aloud, as if musing to himself.

"Ah, no, your Honor. If it pleases your Honor, although I'm down as Frank, I prefer Francis. That's my proper…"

"Who is to vouch for Frank?"

"I am, sir. Your Honor."

Tim Sullivan stood up in his full police uniform, only the top button of his tunic fastened. The large dull star of a police badge was pinned to his left breast.

"Officer Sullivan, isn't it? I think I had you before me the other day. Petty theft if I recall correctly. And now here you are bringing another criminal before me." Silence gripped the room.

"Pardon, your Honor? This isn't criminal court. Frank here is a fine upstanding young man. He…"

Sullivan spoke quickly, impatient to get this over with so they can get to the saloon and celebrate. He was anxious for a few drinks and tunes.

"Proceed," snapped the judge.

O'Hara stood up and began to read the document.

"Affidavit for Naturalization in the State of Illinois of the May term of the Criminal Court of County, in said County and State, in the year of our Lord One Thousand Eight Hundred and Seventy-Three. In the matter of Naturalization of Frank O'Neill…"

Francis tensed at his name. He didn't really mind Frank as a name. It was the fact that he was now officially Frank that galled him. Didn't he grow up as Daniel Francis?

"…that he resided in the United States five years and upwards, to wit: for the term of Seven years, including the three years of his minority, and in the State of Illinois for Three years…" continued O'Hara in a monotonous drone. Francis winced at this stretching of the truth. Tim had said it was common enough.

"…that it is bona fide his intention to become a citizen of the United States, and renounce forever all allegiance to every Foreign Prince, Potentate, State or Sovereignty, whatever, and particularly the allegiance and fidelity which he in anywise owes to The Queen of Great Britain and Ireland."

Frank smiled at the thought of the Queen as a Foreign Prince. He could sense Anna behind him, uncomfortable in the same gingham dress she was married in, now tight with her expanding belly. She shushed little John Francis fussing alongside her.

"Repeat after me!"

Francis snapped to attention.

"I, Frank O'Neill,"

"I, Frank O'Neill,"

"Do solemnly swear, in the presence of Almighty God…"

Francis repeated the words as the clerk doled them out. His voice did not waver. At the end, Judge Lambert signed the document and called next with only a withering glance in his direction.

★★★

Outside the court, they walked past a four-horse carriage with Lithuanians loudly scrambling back on board. Their language sounded harsh to Francis's ear. Each one held the same ornamented document as Francis. The seal of the President of the United States, now their equal under the law, was stamped upon it.

Tim Sullivan clapped him on the back.

"How does it feel? No longer a subject to the Queen?"

"I'm a subject to this queen," Frank said, taking Anna's hand. She smiled her one-sided smile and hefted the toddler in her arm. Tim looked away.

"Tree was in a queer mood today," he said after a pause. "Some days he refuses to accept the Lithuanians or Pollacks when they have no English. Ward bosses don't like that."

"If they can't speak English, how do they even know to get here?" asked Anna.

"Party stooges round them up. Got to have the votes."

Tim laughed at the frown on Francis's face.

"Don't worry about that lot. I'm sure you'll be a shoo-in to the force now you're a real American. Let's get out to Callaghan's saloon to celebrate. Hope you brought that flute. Don't worry, Ann. He's always the most sober one there."

★★★

The distant train whistle interrupted the quiet of their room. She turned over, discomforted by the baby stirring inside.

"Frank."

"I thought you were asleep. Sorry."

"No. I heard you come in."

"Sorry. Johnny's still asleep in his crib."

"Was it any good?"

"What? Ah, you know. A lot of the usual crowd. Tim was in great form."

"I feel so empty sometimes. Here in the house on my own."

He turned toward her unable to make out her features in the dark.

"But you have John Francis," he said in a loud whisper.

No reply.

"Ah now," Francis continued. "You know they don't like women in those places. I don't think you'd like it much anyway."

"It's not that. Ever since losing the first baby…"

"Whisht now, Ann. Listen. I won't go to any saloons anymore."

"No," she was angry at the idea. "That's not what I mean. You're not listening. Even when you and the baby are here. I just feel. Alone."

"I thought it was better with the new little fellow. I thought you were doing better."

"No, Frank. That's not what I'm telling you."

He went silent, unsure what to say next. She got like this before every baby. It was even worse after the birth.

"And the money problems we've been having," she continued. "Sometimes I just can't cope."

Her words and the flat tone cut through him.

"I'm trying my best to work things out," he blurted. "Tim says he'll help me get some names together for the next uptake of city police. You know that."

She turned away from him, saying nothing.

"Try not to worry about everything. I feel sure about this police job. Once I get that, we'll be able to fix all our problems. Move on from this."

200

She said nothing for the longest time. He listened in the darkness, holding his breath, wondering if she was asleep.

"I hope so, Frank." He heard her whisper. "I really do."

The Mason's Apron

Corner of Clark & LaSalle, Chicago, July 1873

The grimy cable car rumbled past the corner where Francis stood. He leaned against the black iron of a lamppost and studied the much-folded pages of the official document. His formal application to the Board of Police and Fire Commissioners was headed by Tim Sullivan's signature, along with four fellow parishioners. It included testimonials from a member of Congress, his Superintendent from The Chicago and Alton (hard-won from old McMullin) and even a recommendation, again thanks to Tim, from Chief of Police Elmer Washburn. On top of all the glowing reviews was a dark red stamp of one word in stark capitals:

REJECTED

As Francis stared at the word, it started to look like a cipher from an alien language, full of hidden meanings. It reminded him of the rusty cable car receding from view—a visible manifestation of some deep unfathomable network. What string was pulled, or not, to put that red stamp on his application? How could he go back to Anna with this news? How would he pay the mortgage after being out of work now for two weeks?

His mind wandered to his last unsettling meeting with Murdoch.

"I'm certain I'll be accepted onto the force soon," Francis had assured him. "The salary's a thousand dollars per year and I've a number of testimonials lined up."

"You know the only testimonials that matter are the ones with faces of presidents on them."

Murdoch smirked at his own witticism, making Francis clench his teeth.

"Have you considered our proposal?" asked Murdoch, voice like silk. "Mister Pinkerton could do with someone of your... ilk. It's a good company, as I'm sure your friend McParland can testify. It would certainly help with your current... insolvency. We have certain law enforcement needs

201

that you could help supply."

"What kind of needs?"

"Oh, security and such," replied Murdoch airily. "There is always the inconvenience of unions to deal with. We appreciate someone with intelligence who can still blend in with the common Irish. McParland is a fine example."

"Haven't heard from McParland since he disappeared back East."

"I'm sure he's on a very important task. What about Clan Na Gael? Know anything about them?"

"I don't have anything to do with that lot."

"You could have something to do with them. We could arrange that."

"How are you involved with all this anyway?"

Murdoch stared at Francis.

"Do not concern yourself with my involvement," he finally replied. "You may deeply regret it. I represent an organization whose power extends far and wide."

Francis gritted his teeth again, suspicions confirmed. Masons. For all Murdoch's posturing, he wondered how high up he really was. As he left, he had pictured himself as a cop hauling Murdoch before a judge: make him answer for what he did to Julia.

A horse whinnied in pain as a hackney driver took his crop to the animal, the noise breaking Francis from his reverie. He was about to correct the bullying driver when he was hailed from across the busy sidewalk.

"Why, Frank? What are you doing out here?"

Alderman Tracey, one of the sponsors on his crumpled form, walked over to Francis from the granite steps of the new City Hall.

Francis didn't know what to say. He ran his hand through his hair in a self-conscious gesture.

"Why aren't you out celebrating your appointment?" asked the alderman.

Francis raised the application and showed him the red stamp. The other furrowed his brow with lack of understanding. He listened with an out-thrust jaw as Francis relayed his tale of woe along with his fear at returning to Anna empty-handed.

"Come on in with me," announced Tracey, taking the papers from Francis.

The alderman's suit was impeccable, his black patent leather shoes recently polished. Francis followed him into the depths of City Hall, the ornate gothic style of the building designed to intimidate all who entered. Francis led Tracey to the office where he had received the bad news. A clerk at a desk by the door rose to dispel Francis but blanched at the sight of the angry alderman. They swept through to the secretary of the board who jumped up from his desk as if standing to attention. Tracey tossed the papers before him.

"Alderman Tracey," asked the secretary. "To what do we owe the pleasure?"

"Why was this man not been accepted? Is there not an appropriation of one hundred new men? He has my recommendation."

The secretary sat back down, considering options.

"Why, Alderman," he said. "You have got your man already."

"So I have," replied Tracey. "But I'm entitled to two. This," he indicated Francis, "is my second one."

A wave of relief washed over Francis at the consternation on the secretary's face. He stifled a smile as the bureaucrat harrumphed and gathered up the document for amendment.

The New Policeman

Monroe Street, Chicago, 17 August 1873

Francis pushed the heavy helmet back to scratch his jaw. All around him was chaos—buildings looming next to gaps of new construction. A maze of electric, telegraph and tram wires along with attendant poles obscured the heavy summer sunlight. There were awnings of all colors over shops, banks and saloons. Signs everywhere: "Goodfriend shirts", "Commercial National", "SMOKE".

Hansoms, horse-drawn omnibuses and carriages were backed up along both main streets by a cart overladen with hogsheads stalled at the intersection. Drivers and passengers spilled onto the pavement, yelling and cursing at the obstruction. Men in dark suits and caps, women in heavy frocks and hats watched the scene. Francis waded into the midst of it all, the heavy blue wool of his new uniform still chafing. After a month of traveling beat, he was still unused to it.

"What has you stopped in the middle of this street?" he called to a man pulling at a brace of carthorses.

Eyes wild and rolling, the animals tossed their heads about. One bled from the neck, stomping and resisting. The driver's hands were covered in dark horse blood. He turned to Francis, knife in hand. Francis's hand went straight to the club on his belt.

"This blamed horse won't get going. He's just stopped here. Stoppin' all of Chicago he is. I nicked his neck a little to let the pressure out. Get him goin' again."

The man's features were slack, as if drunk or simple.

"Alright. Slow it down now," Francis said. "I want you to put that knife down, right now. Slowly mind. I don't need you letting any more pressure off."

The driver regarded him with a confused look.

"What is it, officer? I ain't done nothing wrong."

"Right now, you're the cause of an obstruction at a major intersection. Now put that knife down or I'll haul you in."

The man slowly put the knife down, a scowl on his features at the injustice of it all. "Blamed horse is the cause of it all," he muttered.

Francis took the knife and tossed it in the wagon. He motioned other nearby drivers to the halted wagon of barrels, directing them to untether the frightened horses and use their own beasts to haul away the over-burdened wagon.

"How'm I going to explain this to my ganger?" the driver asked.

"Take it up with City Hall," growled Francis, stepping back from the center of the thoroughfare. He scratched again under his helmet strap. The obstruction finally cleared, he walked down Monroe Street, squinting in the early afternoon sun.

A loud bang. It came from everywhere and nowhere, at once. Francis looked back to the intersection. Traffic still moved, ignorant of the loud sound. The bare-breasted caryatids of Palmer House stared down unconcerned. Francis turned the corner at Clark and spotted a man dashing past pedestrians, pursued by another in a black suit. They were running straight at Francis.

"Halt there," shouted Francis, spotting the gun.

The man stopped, looking back at the other chasing him. The latter waved a revolver of his own, trying to clear people out of the way. The young man raised his pistol, blinked and shot straight at Francis—a quick blaze of fire spat from the gun barrel.

The blink saved Francis's life.

He had enough time to begin to dodge to the right. A sudden sharp slice of pain came under his left shoulder, followed by a coldness spreading all down his side. He put the fact of the bullet from his mind, as the young killer approached. Instinct made Francis reach for his club. Somehow, he raised the baton, bringing it in an arc down upon his assailant's pistol. He felt outside himself, watching everything from a distance. He noted how young his attacker was, hair untidy and eyes slightly crossed. The young man looked in confusion at his weapon on the ground, unsure of what to do. Then his pursuer was upon them, a burly type with jet-black hair to match. His brow was a single bar above his grim face.

"You've done it now, Bridges!"

He raised his gun at the young man.

"Nobody plugs a Chicago cop and walks away from it."

He said the last with relish as he studied the best spot on Bridges to place his lethal shot.

"Bloody Pinkertons," spat Bridges. "Always skulking around after honest men."

He cowered in anticipation. The detective laughed, savoring the moment. "No."

Francis still felt he was watching himself from outside. He spoke to confirm he was still alive. He put himself between them, left hand limp at his side, club half raised.

"Don't you shoot him."

He gasped as a sudden spasm of pain took him. The Pinkerton gave a disgusted sneer and tucked his gun into the depths of his black coat. Bridges saw his chance and made to run. With his good hand, Francis grabbed him by the collar and shoved him to the wall. Francis hoarsely cried to the gathered crowd for help securing the criminal, blood dribbling out of the left cuff of his police coat. In the confusion, the detective slipped away.

★★★

At the back of State Street station, Francis lay stretched on the Captain's desk, inconvenient blood pooling on reports and dockets. Outside the door, his sergeant fussed about.

"Where's this Bridges now?" asked the sergeant. "In a holding cell? What, and Frank bleeding out on my desk?"

Tim Sullivan peered in.

"How're things, Frank?"

Francis could only groan in response. His back arched with a sudden lance of pain.

"Doc's here now," Tim said, sounding contrite.

A young man bumbled in. He unclasped a set of wire spectacles and affixed them with care. He started with surprise at the sight of the wounded policeman before him.

"Oh," he proclaimed. "He's bleeding."

"Yes. They didn't tell you? Come on, Doc. What can you do for him? Try and get that bullet out."

"Help me get his shirt off."

Francis gasped with the pain. He passed out briefly as the young doctor's cold fingers probed the wound.

"Bullet lodged by the shoulder blade," muttered the doctor. "Going to have to leave it there."

Sullivan cursed under his breath.

"Sorry, Frank," he mumbled.

A moment of clarity.

"What? Will I make it? What about Ann? The babies? Are they…"

His voice faltered; vision shimmered into blackness.

PART II: FIRE

★★★

Next day, Francis was sitting behind the sergeant's desk, deadened arm in a sling. He traced the scar on his forehead, thinking of the Sunderland hospital nearly a decade ago. He glanced down at his bruised and bandaged left breast. Another trophy.

"Well done, Frank. Well done!"

The sergeant bustled in, a great mustache hid his mouthful of bad teeth.

"Thank you, sir."

"Yes. You'll get a good citation for this. And you're definitely off probation now. Full time. Doctor says you'll probably always have some stiffness in that arm. Couldn't get the bullet out."

"Will... Will I still be able to play flute?"

"What? Oh right. Sullivan mentioned that. No idea. Time will tell. Left arm anyway so you'll still be able to shoot straight. Go home now to your wife and child. Take a few days and rest. You'll be on desk duty until better."

"Thanks again, sir."

Francis stood. His entire body was stiff from the shock and the uncomfortable night spent at the station.

"Sorry about the mess in your office."

"Not at all," humphed the sergeant. His annoyance was plain.

Francis took his time getting to the door.

"And O'Neill?"

"Yes, sergeant?"

"You did well saving that Bridges's life. Damn Pinkertons think they can act as they please. Can't say he deserved it though. Especially after he put that hole in you. Do you want to go down to the cell with one of the men to give him a little of his own medicine?"

The thought lingered in Francis's mind, a flare of anger and revenge.

"I'll think about it," he said, before closing the door behind him.

207

CHAPTER 6

The Cliffs of Moher

Deering Street Station, Chicago, 1874

"Patrolman O'Neill. You and O'Mahony are in charge of the station this shift."

"Yes, Captain," answered Francis with a serious nod.

"Well then, I'll be off home to Mrs. Hubbard for supper."

"Very good. Very good, sir," agreed Pat O'Mahony, his big face a solemn mask. "Please give her our best regards."

The fastidious Captain gave the big patrolman a skeptical look. He paused, about to add something. He massaged the Herculean mustache on his upper lip with his lower, weighing the subtle insubordination of his inferior against the man's big shoulders and barrel chest. He reached into his uniform's top pocket for a scuffed silver timepiece. Francis had once noticed the inscription read *To My Husband George Washington Hubbard.*

"Good night then, gentlemen," he said, scurrying out the station door.

Francis and Pat erupted in laughter once he was gone.

"By God, Mrs. Wallace will be served early tonight," quipped O'Mahony.

"Ah, you're terrible, Big Pat."

O'Mahony grinned and clapped his hands on his thighs before raising his large frame from the small desk it was captured behind. He stretched for a moment before opening the desk drawer to produce a flute case.

"Are the Maloneys coming, Frank?" he asked.

"I talked to their father today. They'll be along later."

"Ah, good. We'll have a few flutes so. Keep the fiddles at bay."

"Would you play that one again?" asked Francis. "That jig in G."

He retrieved his own flute and screwed it together, sitting on the edge of O'Mahony's desk.

"I know a fair few jigs in G, Frank."

"Oh," said Francis, considering. "How did it go?"

He stretched the fingers of his left hand, wincing at the familiar stiffness in his shoulder. He played a tentative long D followed by two short B's.

"I have you," said O'Mahony. "'Out on the Ocean'."

He pushed back his chair and propped its back against the wall, taking a moment to arrange his bulk properly. After a few experimental puffs on his own instrument, he soon had his eyes closed, playing the catchy melody with a lively swing. Francis listened with his head at a tilt, half-smile on his face. Big Pat's tone was clear and full, his playing metered by his legs swinging like a double pendulum.

"A lovely tune," enthused Francis, once Pat paused. "The 'Cliffs of Moher' might go well before it. That other one you taught me."

"Off the cliffs and out on the ocean," agreed Pat with a broad grin.

"Where is it your people are from again, Pat? Not far from there, isn't it?"

"Liscannor, West Clare. Just down the road. A cold draughty spot in winter."

A sudden darkness came over his big features. He started to play the "Cliffs" at a mournful pace—the near shrill opening high notes descending to dark lows.

Francis studied his own flute, affected by the somber melody.

"Ann's from not far from over there. East Clare."

"Ah hah, they're all mad out there," Pat replied, humor returning in a flash. "Here's another reel from out that direction."

The station staffroom echoed with his lively playing. Francis joined in.

"What is all this now?"

A figure appeared at the door with a large broom in his hand. The music stopped and guilty silence bloomed. Michael Keating came forward into the gaslight with a cackle. Pat swore, wobbling on his perch.

"Keating! I thought for sure you were the Captain back. Get over here and join us. There's a long night there yet."

Soon the three policemen were busy at reels: "Happy Days of Youth", "Miss Wallace", "Little Katie Kearney" and "The Queen's Shilling". Big Pat led on flute with Francis's quieter playing accompanying him. Keating provided percussion with his broom, twanging it expertly on the chipped maple floor. The first time, they had mocked him for this, but once they realized how good he was they welcomed the unorthodox playing. Their evening filled with music as more joined them later.

Chicago slept a fitful sleep beyond the confines of the small police station.

The Stranger From Limerick

16 South Emerald Street, Chicago, Winter 1875

"Come on in, Jim."

"Are you sure, Frank? I don't want to disturb you."

"It's no bother at all. The children are after being fed."

Lanky Jim Moore made his apologetic way into the kitchen. Anna was busy with her sewing machine. Their two toddlers played on the floor with rough-hewn wooden toys made by Francis.

"Hello," she said. Auburn wisps escaped from the bun of her hair. "Sorry about the state of the place."

The young man gave her a shy nod.

"Ann, this is Jim Moore, not long arrived here from Limerick."

"Oh," she said, putting away some fabric. "My people are from outside Limerick. Feakle."

"That's County Limerick, isn't it?" ventured Jim.

"It most certainly is not," she admonished. "County Clare it is and always will be."

Francis laughed as Jim looked abashed.

"Now, Ann, don't be giving the big city man too hard a time of it. I've never even been up that way myself. Limerick sounds like a grand town."

"It is," agreed the young man. "Times are after getting tough again though."

He paused, leaving the rest unsaid.

"Frank," exclaimed Anna again. "Where are your manners? Let the man sit down."

"Of course. You can tell us all about it. Maybe even play some of those Limerick tunes you mentioned. Here, sit at the table."

"No, no. I couldn't," replied Jim. "I'll pitch here."

He sat on the wood-box Francis had made for beside the stove. John Francis toddled over with a little wooden train to demonstrate to the visitor.

"He loves trains," chuckled Anna. "I bring him over to the yards sometimes to watch them come and go."

Moore took the rough train in full seriousness from the child. He looked it over and nodded in approval. John Francis laughed at this and grabbed the train back.

"Get out of that now, Johnny," Francis said, picking up the child and returning him to where his younger sister played. "Jim didn't come over to be playing trains."

"Didn't he now?" Anna asked with an arched brow. "You are like boys with trains about those auld tunes."

"Never mind Ann," said Francis with a quick wink to Jim. "We'll have her dancing around the kitchen yet."

The young man smiled shyly as he regarded the young family.

"This is much nicer than the boarding house I'm at."

"That place?" asked Francis. "They've only the plaster on it with a few weeks. I can't believe they're renting it out without proper doors on. Rough part of the neighborhood too."

"The rent's cheap," admitted Jim. Again, he let the conversation falter.

"We're not long moved from our own first place," said Francis. "We're renting it out now. Built it myself so I make sure it's in good shape. Maybe you might lodge there?"

Jim swallowed and made a noncommittal nod.

"Well then, while we're waiting for a bite," continued Francis. "Did you want to play a tune or two?"

He drew his chair up close to Jim.

"Frank," admonished Anna. "He's hardly in the door. Give the young man a rest."

"Ah no, it's fine. I'd love to. The only thing is…" He frowned. "I've no flute. Had to sell it."

"That's no bother. Here. Take mine. I'll use a tin whistle."

Francis took his flute down from a high shelf along with the simple whistle. Moore couldn't help but laugh at the speed at which they were produced. He took the instrument and straightaway launched into a set of

212

reels. Anna and the children ignored the music as Francis listened transfixed. When playing, Jim was a different person than the diffident young man that first entered their kitchen. After he stopped for breath, Francis, full of praise, pressed him for the tune names.

"Names?" Jim asked, confused. "I can't think of the names at all."

Francis just shook his head.

"Go over those slowly while I try and get the air of them on the whistle. We'll figure out names later."

Jim Moore nodded with a wry smile. Others he could not name came to mind, his boss and cronies in Hell's Half-Acre. If they only knew he was in a cop's kitchen playing music. He sighed, regretting he would never return.

The Little Fair Child

Chicago, August 1876

John Francis was first to go, eyes sunken in his pale face. His body was cold now after the ravages of fever. How he had shook and screamed, gasping for breath, neck swollen enormously. The fool of a doctor could only recommend they buy ice to cool him.

His son. The sweet boy had already shown a love for music, tuneless tootling on the tin whistle to impress them. Already his memories of the child felt tarnished—precious sepia photographs rescued from fire. Shouldn't he be able to recollect every single minute of John Francis's life? He wanted to hide these memories away, protecting the precious moments from the light of recollection, lest he wear out what was left.

He should have been home more. He was always out, busy trying to make a go of it on the force by day and playing tunes by night. Ann often complained of his absences. It was worse when she said nothing, only hard silence. He made himself look at the other stiff cold little body laid out on the next bed. Poor little Mary. Just a year younger. She was so beautiful and perfect. Lively and roguish at times, like her mother. Like her mother was. What cursed illness was it that took them both? The doctor had muttered something about "possible diphtheria" and then his hand was out for money.

The *Emerald Isle*. The little Mormon child wrapped in a moldy canvas shroud. Were he and Anna cursed in some way?

Anna. He could hear her shushing baby Francis in the next room. Her voice dull and exhausted. At least their newborn had been spared. He can't stay in the room with the pair of little bodies any longer. Wiping his eyes, he took a deep breath and opened the door.

"How are you?" he asked.

No response.

"What do you want to do?"

"Do? What is there to do?"

The baby started to cry again, frightened at the tone of his mother's voice.

"I know."

He can't think what else to say. He sat down across from her, overcome by a sudden urge to run out the door.

"Help me," he said. "I don't know what to do."

Her red eyes regarded him, mouth a stubborn pout.

"I'll not lay them out here," she exclaimed. "I'll not do that again."

"I know," was all he could repeat. "There's that new undertaker. Mrs. McGreavy was laid out there..."

"I'll not lay them out here. I won't have that!"

The new baby screamed at her raised voice, his face going red with sobbing. They looked numbly at the child, the one that survived.

"Don't, Ann."

His voice was soft, an edge of tears to it. He stood and took the baby from her. Unable to console her, he put the child on his shoulder and stroked his small back. The baby's cries were convulsive sobs.

"Shush now," he pleaded with the infant. He started to hum a tune. What was the name of that one? "The Little Fair Child". He had played it for her years ago. When she was first pregnant with John. The name of his father. The name of their first. Thrice gone now.

The child calmed eventually. *He was so light.* Frail little body. The relief transformed into grief and Francis started to cry.

"Francis," said Anna. "Stop that. This is hard enough."

The look on her face was fierce. He nodded, swallowing hard.

★★★

Candles and flowers lined the little coffins. The funeral home was well-appointed and new, people kept arriving and wishing them well. Through the distance of shock, Francis observed everyone. Some were embarrassed by grief, some overwhelmed, others just nosey and inquisitive. The unctuous funeral director wore white gloves.

"Would you prefer an open or closed coffin?"

Anna had finally broken down at that question.

They'd said goodbye then and closed the coffins. He looked across at her, so pale and distant. He had a sudden recollection of a statue in the necropolis in Alexandria. Her sister Julia hovered nearby, helpless. Everyone wore black. How to get through this? When all these people are gone, they will have to return to the silent house.

"So sorry for your troubles."

"A terrible loss. So sorry to hear."

"You're holding up wonderfully. Awful tragedy."

"Sorry for your troubles."

"My deepest condolences."

"You'll make it through. I'm sure of it."

"Troubles."

"Loss."

"…"

Whistle and I'll Wait For You

South Halsted Street, Chicago, October 1876

Behind the broad windows of the barber shop, men stretched out in reclining wooden chairs. Before high mirrors and ornate lamps, quick brilliantined barbers stepped around their customers, making conversation and tending to hair and whiskers. Francis rubbed the back of his neck, feeling the length of his hair. It would only take ten minutes. A shave too, perhaps. The high door opened with a jingle as he entered.

"Officer O'Neill," called a barber from behind a counter. "What can we do for you today?"

"A trim, I think," said Francis, taking a seat beside a couple of other men wearing dark suits. They studied their newspapers, pretending not to notice him.

"I can take you right away," replied the barber, turning a chair around towards him.

Francis looked at the men sitting nearby. Nobody returned his glance.

"Ah no. I'll read for a minute. Let these men go ahead."

The barber smiled and ushered the next man forward with a flourish of a towel.

Francis frowned at the cover of the misnamed *Police Gazette*, a burlesque dancer arching a leg ensconced in fishnet stockings. He selected the *Daily News*, a seemlier paper, and scanned the headlines. A handwritten sign to his right read "Challenge Laundry Service". An older boy came through the shop pushing a handcart piled with soiled linen for the laundry in the basement. He loaded tagged bags into a dumbwaiter and cranked the black iron wheel, slowly lowering the clothes. Sounds escaped from the women working below: shouts, laughter, snatches of song. Francis jumped up.

"Hold it there, son," he shouted.

The barbers froze, cutthroats and sharp scissors poised in mid-air. The laundry boy blanched. His eyes darted to the smutty paper on the low table.

"I didn't do nothing with it," protested the boy, acne-scarred face pale with fear.

Francis ignored him. He tiptoed over, ear bent to the dumbwaiter. He strained to catch a faint sound of song wafting up from below—muffled shouts and laughter when the distant singer finished. After a minute of listening for more, he sat back down. From his pocket he retrieved a small Clarke tin whistle and repeated phrases from the melody, committing them to memory. The boy stared at him, mouth agape. The owner motioned for him to continue his job. He winked to the other barbers who smirked back as they returned to their clients. Business resumed as the policeman played quietly, smiling at the new tune.

The Scholar

Illinois Central Railroad, Chicago, November 1878

Francis's carriage was first behind the engine. Smoke occasionally obscuring his view, he looked out at the backs of houses, grain elevators and churches. He listened to the heaving train engine, picturing the men tending to it. Thankfully, the windows were shut tight against the late autumn chill. *Fall.* He must learn to call it "Fall". He had been sent to City Hall with a satchel of dispatches for the superintendent. Regular trips to City Hall were part of his new role as desk sergeant and he had all morning to make the journey.

He took off his helmet and rested it on the vacant wicker seat beside him. From the folds of his tunic he retrieved a crisp new Currier & Ives map of Chicago to marvel at. He had ordered it with the standard maps for his patrolmen. In truth, it was not really a map—the detailed engraving depicted Chicago stretching away from the sweep of the lake from the perspective of several thousand feet up. He was senior enough now not to have to justify such a purchase to Central. The illustration showed the Lake full of multiple types of schooners (he could name them all) and steamers. He traced the snaking line of the river from the red warehouses of the McCormick Reaper works all the way to the stockyards. The engraving included a forest of high smokestacks, their smoke and height obscuring nearby buildings. The many chimneys made the city appear to be built over an immense underground furnace.

He took his attention from the map and gazed out the window. The smoke parted again, showing more backs of buildings. Where was he now? Hard to believe the smoking ruin from seven years ago was gone, replaced by all this. He grimaced to himself. The Fire never left. Some days the smoky air made their little boy Francis cough up black stuff. With nothing to blame, Francis cursed whatever foulness had taken their three children. He needed to work his way out of Bridgeport to somewhere cleaner.

The track curved sharply and the vista of the Lake opened before him. Soon the Park was to his left, new piers and breakwaters stretched along the glistening water. A weak sun struggled to appear behind low clouds. He looked out to the horizon; map forgotten. It was mostly steamers now.

Why call it a lake when it was as big as a sea? Maybe they could leave the force and this city? To hell with his recent promotion. He sighed and leaned back. The rhythm of the train slowed as it neared the terminus—less of a reel and more of a march. Soon the iron and glass and ranks of trains at Great Central station were all he could see.

★★★

The morning was waning by the time he made it out of City Hall and over to Monroe and State Street. Ornate gold letters on the window indicated the establishment as Lyon & Healy: Booksellers and Music Supplies. He looked up the street to the corner where he was shot years ago, reflecting for a minute before he entered the shop.

The interior was cool and inviting with the quiet hush of books. He walked along the shelves, stopping occasionally to examine a volume. He stooped down onto his haunches to peer at a book at the bottom of a shelf. A very fine 1694 volume of

A

Collection

of

IRISH AIRS

FOR THE

FLUTE VIOLIN or FLAGEOLET

with new symphonies

Arranged as Duets or Solos

"Yes, Officer. Is something the matter?"

Francis looked up from the frontispiece engraving of twin seventeenth-century gentlemen playing flute, to the frowning man interrogating him. He straightened himself slowly. The man was dressed in a dull tweed suit. His lower jaw protruded, giving his otherwise bland face an aggressive appearance. His accent betrayed a Northern England edge.

"The matter?" enquired Francis. "What do you mean?"

"I mean to say," the man paused. "Is there something we can help you with? Some criminal matter perhaps?"

218

"Criminal matter?"

The man indicated Francis's uniform with his eyes.

"Oh," said Francis. "No, I'm just here to look at books."

The clerk's eyes bulged. "But you're a policeman," he blurted.

"Sergeant Francis O'Neill, to be precise," came the voice of an approaching man. "A regular customer and a fine flute player into the bargain."

The large and heavy-jowled proprietor reached out a hand which Francis shook.

"Lovely to see you again, Francis. This is Mr. Chambers. He started here recently."

"How are you Patrick?" asked Francis, ignoring the Englishman.

Chambers stared in disbelief.

"That's fine for now, Mr. Chambers," said Healy. "I'll speak with Sergeant O'Neill."

Francis cannot hide his smile at the clerk's flustered retreat. They were soon absorbed in discussion on a collection of books recently arrived from Healy's native Boston.

★★★

"Unfortunately, I must go," said Healy, heading for the door. "I'll leave you in the hands of Mr. Chambers."

"Now, don't let him bargain you down any further," Healy admonished his young clerk. "The prices we agreed are on that slip."

Francis affected a wounded look.

"Patrick, I could have you up for robbery on this deal," he said to the bookseller's disappearing back.

Francis turned to the confounded Chambers, who made a tepid smile. Francis enjoyed the bruised silence as they settled the account.

The Old Blind Bard

Deering Street Station, Chicago, August 1879

Francis absent-mindedly scratched at his nose while looking through the duty roster. He stood before the busy clutter of scuffed desks and cabinets of the staff room.

"Not much else today, lads," he announced to the men seated before him.

"Finally though," he said, looking up. "Allow me to introduce a new patrolman into our midst. Mr. Michael Houlihan. Stand up there, Michael."

A freshly scrubbed young man stood up from one of the far desks. He was lean with large expressive eyes, his new uniform hanging awkwardly on his lithe frame.

"Welcome to Deering Street Station," said Francis. "Michael will be starting on reserve duty from today."

A murmur of welcome, all heads inclined to his direction.

"Thank you, sir."

"Michael, I believe you are a native of Kilkenny originally."

"Yes I am, sir. Kilkenny town it is."

"We'll try not to hold that against you."

A loud groan came from Big Pat in his corner desk.

"Now then, Michael," continued Francis. "You'll find us a good bunch here. We've plenty of scoundrels and drunkards to deal with daily but these men around you are always here to help. Irish like you came here first to work on the canal that made this great city. Many others have come since but we're still the backbone of this area. Although," he added with a smile. "It might surprise you to learn that not every patrolman here is from Ireland."

A good-natured sigh from Lieutenant Schmidt.

"Furthermore, I've it on good authority that you possess special skills that aided your assignment to our station."

"I'm not sure what you mean, Sergeant," replied Michael, blushing under the scrutiny of his peers.

"Dancing. I've been told you're quite the man for it."

Michael's eyes widened with apprehension.

"That's true," he said in a careful voice. "I've even won competitions back home."

Big Pat's chair creaked as he leaned forward.

"Go on," he called out. "Let's see a few steps then."

The young policeman walked into the open area. He looked about at the expectant faces and shrugged before executing a quick set of jigs and reels, feet clattering on the smooth pine floor to provide rhythm. He stopped to look around with trepidation, wondering if he'd gone too far. The appreciative applause was led by Francis.

"By God," said Pat. "I'd say Mike here ought to go up and dance for old Murphy. What do you think, Sergeant?"

The slightest wink was transmitted to Francis, unseen by the young dancer.

"Who is Murphy?" asked Michael.

Francis raised his eyebrows, all seriousness.

"He's a bit of a legend here in Bridgetown. A blind piper of great renown. From County Clare originally. Lieutenant?"

Schmidt smiled complacently.

"Would you man the station while I introduce the new recruit to our local celebrity? I'm sure you've little interest in the matter."

A slow nod came from Lieutenant Schmidt.

"I'm off duty soon, too," announced Pat, pulling himself out from his desk with a grunt. "Haven't heard the legend play in a long time. He doesn't play for everyone, mind. But if Frank—Sergeant O'Neill—is going, I think he'll oblige."

★★★

A pack of mangy dogs retreated under the Archer Avenue bridge at the sight of the three policemen. Beneath the first arch was a precarious shanty, obscured by wild shrubs. The black foul water of the Chicago river churned nearby. Propped against the side of the rickety structure was a mildewed piece of wood with a rudimentary representation of a bottle and pipe daubed in tar. The door was open to the world. Francis ducked his head as he entered.

"Good day, Mr. Murphy," he called.

Inside were half-broken chairs and a low table. Arranged upon it were grimy jars of candies: sourdrops, hoarhound, and cat's eyes. Next to these delights were a few battered tins of tobacco.

"Who's that now?" called a wary voice from the back.

"Sergeant O'Neill. Here to ask a favor."

"Oh, Sergeant," came the reply. "Is it yourself?"

A small leathery man appeared from behind a curtain, hands and face yellow with filth. A shock of wispy white whiskers surrounded the black and broken teeth of his mouth. His eyes were directed aimlessly from blindness. He quickly pulled a curtain behind him but the policemen were still able to see rows of black bottles beyond.

"How's business, Tim?"

"Ah, terrible. Terrible. No wan comes out this way at all."

"Well, I've a new arrival on the force with me here. He's Michael Houlihan from Kilkenny. A great man for dancing altogether. Big Pat is here as well. We were wondering if you'd play us a few tunes on your pipes. Maybe Mike could step out to them."

The old piper's head shook while he considered the request.

"I'm not sure, now. Is he any good? A piper like me. Of my caliber, you know. I can't play for any wan. Nor any of that new stuff either."

"Ah, he's top notch, Tim," said Big Pat, gingerly placing himself onto the least broken chair. "He's won competitions! You play him some of that good old stuff. There's nothing like it."

"That's true enough, Pat. True enough. I do try and keep the auld tunes alive, so I do. Let me get my little instrument."

He felt along the wall until he reached a dark mass on a hook. The bag of his pipes was stained and the drones rusty, the chanter refashioned from bone. Soon Murphy was seated again. Michael watched in reverent awe as the blind man gathered the pipes around his crooked frame. He stopped for a full minute, pondering, before he started playing. It wasn't music that came out, but a horrific droning and rasping noise, no tune discernible from the random screeching. Occasionally, there came a gasp and pause as some part of the monstrosity failed and the piper had to mutter and fuss with the workings. Big Pat laughed soundlessly, shaking his head and covering his eyes. Houlihan's jaw opened in amazement at the surreal scene. Francis smiled broadly to the young man.

"Come on now," he said. "Show us some more of that fine dancing. There isn't piping like that left in all of Ireland."

Houlihan grinned back and launched into a slip-jig.

★★★

PART II: FIRE

The house was dark when Francis arrived home. Their street had been raised up several feet as part of the city improvements and he had to go down a set of wooden steps to get to their front door. He opened the door as quietly as he could.

Anna was sitting in the front room—the child in a daybed beside her.

"Ann. Why are you up? How's Francis?" he asked in a fierce whisper.

She did not respond.

Thinking she might be asleep, he went to the Tilly lamp on the mantle. It had a fine China pattern on the base that had appealed to him when he bought it at an auction. He lit the wick as quietly as he could. A honey-yellow light filled the room. Francis went to check on the child.

"Don't touch him!"

Her voice was dull and strange. He looked at her in confusion. Her face had filled out now she was six months pregnant.

"What is it, Ann?"

He could see the speckling of scarlet fever all over the child's face. *Why didn't he move?* He touched the forehead. It was cold.

"Leave him alone! Can't you leave him be?"

"What are you saying, Ann? He's not moving."

The truth began to dawn on him. He was all too familiar with the signs.

"Oh, God! No."

He went to Anna. Without meaning to, he shook her by the shoulders—wanting to shake this strange dullness from her.

"What's happened, Ann? The doctor said he was improving."

His voice was all panic and frenzy, fighting disbelief. A tear ran down her cheek.

"We've no children, Frank. I've failed again. The next one will die too. On and on."

She wiped her face.

"Little Francis is gone. He's gone."

He tried to console her, clumsily held her as shock set in. He kept repeating that it will be different the next time. Their next child will be strong. They were going to move out of this dark pit into a better house. His pay

223

was better now. They could afford it.

She said nothing.

He Left Us In Sorrow

Calvary Cemetery, Evanston, August 1879

The heavy air of the cemetery was noisy with cicadas. All the nearby trees were burdened with the big insects. It's only a reclaimed lagoon, Francis thought to himself as he looked about, no doubt the lake will be back in here in a hundred years. The cemetery was old by Chicago standards so there were no plots left near the entrance. It had been a long slow procession to their plot. The moist dark soil opened here again.

John Francis 1871
John Francis 1872-1876
Mary Catherine 1873-1876

O'NEILL

Another Francis to add to the list. Although unsaid, they had hoped better fortune for this child if named after himself. His mind turned over and over on pointless things: contacting the monument engraver to add the name, how much to give the priests, a recent string of burglaries. These details helped. Bury it away. The priest came to the end of the decade of the rosary, everyone murmuring along with him. Beyond the priest, the crowd was small. He looked over at Anna. She couldn't wear a mourning dress due to being so pregnant. A neighbor had lent her a heavy black cloak to cover her maternity clothes. He turned to Julia.

"Thank you," he said, "for coming out here."

Anna's sister's eyes were red from crying.

"Of course," she insisted. "Ann's very low, Francis. If we're not careful, she might lose this baby too."

They looked over at Anna, her head bowed like a sorrowful angel statue on one of the expensive plots.

"Why don't you stay with us?"

He had not planned to ask but the idea made sense.

"I'm not sure," she replied. "I've a position back home."

"Ah, don't worry about work. We'll find you something, there's no end of work here. Stay with us," he pleaded. "Help Anna."

She said nothing. Francis studied her. She had never been the same since their voyage over. Ever since, she was so quiet and reserved. His mother-in-law despaired of her ever finding a husband.

"Maybe I will, Frank," she finally said. "I'll need your help though."

He made himself smile. Move on from the grief. On to the next thing.

"That's good." He touched her shoulder lightly. "Now. Let's take your sister home."

She nodded and turned toward Anna.

The Fairy Rath

South Emerald St., Chicago, December 1879

Their new house was in the middle of a street. Close together, the houses were also recently sunk as the road was elevated, a trend all over the neighborhood. Francis struggled down the steps with a tea-chest full of their possessions. He navigated slowly, fearful of slipping in the wet slush. The early December snow was kept cool by the dark of the recessed lawn.

"Ann," he called out. "For God's sake be careful out here. These steps are treacherous. I'll get sand to grit them when I get a chance."

He had to haul the chest into the kitchen as the hall was full of boxes. Julia was liberally scattering a small ornate bottle of holy water around the room.

"What's this now?" asked Francis.

The sisters called it his policeman tone of voice.

"Don't worry, Frank," said a seated Anna. "Julia is just blessing the place."

"In case of pishogues," added Julia.

"Pishogues, is it?" he grunted as he put down the heavy box.

"That last house of yours was poisoned with them," she said.

Francis sighed. He hadn't bargained on this when asking Julia to join them.

"I'm not too sure about that," he began.

"How was it you lost so many children then?" she asked.

Francis's brow furrowed. This was dangerous ground. He tried to make light of it.

"I don't think pishogues are allowed over here in America."

"Why not?" asked Anna. "All your music made it over here. Why not those things too?"

Anna, face flushed, was sitting on the only chair to have made it to the kitchen table. He knew better to argue when both sisters had their minds set on something.

"Alright. Alright," he said. "There are a lot of boxes to unpack. Julia, maybe you can help me…"

Julia put the holy water down to peer into his tea-chest. A loud knock came from the front door.

"I'll get it," she said.

Francis arched an eyebrow at his wife as Julia departed. Anna only returned a blank look. He sighed.

"It's Mrs. Mooney," announced Julia from behind a tiny wisp of a woman as they entered the kitchen. She went straight to Anna, sitting down next to her and placing her hand on her forehead.

"How are you feeling, Missus O'Neill?"

"Ah, I'm fine. Julia is a great help to me."

The younger sister gave a bashful nod.

"Won't you have a cup of tea, Mrs. Mooney?" Julia offered.

"No, no. Thank you, Julia. I won't stay. I was passing so I thought I'd check in."

"The doctor was by to check on her earlier," supplied Francis.

"That fellow? He's an old leech, so he is. I'll be able to look after ye better than him."

Francis ground his teeth. Here was another topic where the women had ganged up on him.

"I'm sure the doctor will do fine when the baby comes."

Silence.

"Oh no, Francis," said Anna in a quiet voice. "I've decided to have Mrs. Mooney for that."

An angry rush of blood went to his head, he took a deep breath to steady his temper.

"I thought we agreed to have the doctor."

"I'm not sick, you know," she said. "We can discuss it later."

Her voice had a tone of finality. The uncomfortable silence settled.

"I suppose I'd better get on with the unpacking," said Julia.

Mrs. Mooney cleared her throat.

"I'd better be off as well. Don't you be helping them either, Missus. These two are more than able for it."

Anna nodded, her smile grateful.

"I hope you're not expecting her to be waiting on you hand and foot?" Mrs. Mooney asked Francis in a loud voice as she passed him.

He groaned inwardly, forcing a smile.

"Not at all. Thanks for coming."

The older woman nodded up at him. He felt like a schoolboy around her.

"Well, goodbye Mrs. Mooney," called Anna.

"Don't you be worrying, Missus," replied the old woman from the door. "You can send himself here to get me when the time comes."

Francis made an unconscious grimace.

"I'll show you out," announced Julia, ushering the older woman towards the door.

"Pishogues! She's an auld pishogue," he muttered after them. He could hear their chatter in the hall.

"Frank," scolded Anna. "Don't you dare. I'm fond of Mrs. Mooney. Besides, a neighbor of ours at home was never the same after finding eggs left in the straw. That's a sign of pishogues. Ruined the family, it did."

He scoffed, pulling delft wrapped in newspaper from a chest. He held up a plate, admiring the glossy surface striated with multicolored streaks.

"These will be worth something someday, you know. Got them for nothing after they were damaged in the Fire. The marks look quite remarkable now."

She snorted, pulling herself up with a grunt.

"You and your auctions," she said, going to move another box.

"Anna O'Neill! What are you doing? Don't you touch a thing. You shouldn't be lifting anything at all. The doctor and Mrs. Mooney at least agree on keeping you quiet."

"What harm when I feel fine." She took a deep breath. "It won't be so long now, you know."

He studied his wife as she sat back down, her full belly ill-concealed by a house dress.

"I'm glad we got out of the old place before... you know."

"I know. I feel sure a curse or something was on us there."

"I don't know about *that*," said Francis. "But the air does feel fresher here. Closer to the river. Not so near the stockyards."

"Frank," she said, her voice serious. "I want you to be sure to call Mrs. Mooney this time. Not that doctor. I want this one to be different. I feel stronger."

He pursed his lips together. Her face was fierce with determination. He sighed. Secretly, he was glad of this fight in her.

"Alright. I'll call her when the time comes."

★★★

Mrs. Mooney brought the tightly wrapped bundle to Francis in the front room. He had been pacing back and forth most of the night.

"Here she is now."

He parted the swaddling blanket—tiny face puckered like a fist.

"I'd say she's the spit of you," announced the old woman.

Francis couldn't help but chuckle.

"Julia Ann," he said. He stroked the little cheek. "Julia Ann is what we'll call you."

Julia came in from the kitchen, her cheeks flushed with excitement. She took the baby from the midwife.

"That's lovely, Frank," said Julia. "I don't know how to thank you."

The child started to wail, loud and strong. A flustered Julia tried to calm her. Anna appeared at the door, only wearing her shift.

"Missus!" erupted Mrs. Mooney. "You get right back to bed."

"She's hungry. I'll feed her."

"Give her to her mother," said Francis, smiling as his wife took the child and disappeared into the room. Julia sagged, wringing her hands.

Mrs. Mooney leaned in close to Francis. "This one's strong," she whispered. Francis's only reply was a rueful nod.

Caroline O'Neill's Hornpipe

North Clark Street, Lake View, Illinois, January 1881

"Come in. Come in, Sergeant."

Francis had his helmet under his arm, despite the chill winter evening.

"Ah, don't be 'sergeanting' me now," Francis replied.

Edward Cronin, in his quick bird-like way, ushered Francis into the small front parlor: music stands clustered before a few bare wooden chairs and a much-scratched piano. Sheaves of sheet music were scattered everywhere. Cronin was oblivious to the clutter.

"I apologize," he said. "I got used to titles like Sergeant and Captain when I worked at Camp Fry after the war. Very near here, you know."

Francis sat on one of the bare chairs. Cronin, without thinking, sat at the piano bench he taught his students from. Francis gave an inward sigh—a cup of tea would have been welcome. It was tiresome to come up to Lake View after a full day traveling beat.

"Were you at the camp long?"

"A good few years, yes. I never made a go of it as a weaver in New York before the war. That was my trade in Ireland, you see. Came out West looking for any kind of work and got a job in the kitchens of the prison camp."

He looked out the window for a long moment.

"Anyway, the Confederate prisoners were a bunch of ruffians. Despite how well we treated them. An awful lot were Irish, by the way. Fenians into the bargain. People often complained about the noise: the rowdy rebel songs. I suggested we make entertainment for them. The Cronin family has always had music."

"What kind of music did you play? It must have been Irish."

"Ah, like I say, they were a rowdy bunch. We mostly had Come-all-ye's and Kentucky stuff. What we put together was popular. But ever since then I've made a bit of name for myself as a musician."

"John McFadden says he heard you play around here, not too long ago. He was very impressed. Said I had to come out to hear you."

Cronin inclined his head in acceptance of the praise.

"It's not often I get to play the real stuff from back home. John's a fine fiddler too. I'm delighted to hear he enjoyed it. He mentioned you are becoming quite the collector of Irish music. To be truthful though, I don't remember that many of the old tunes."

Francis's heart sank. Perhaps McFadden was wrong or sent him all the way out here on a prank. He shifted in the uncomfortable chair.

"It's just a hobby," said Francis, shrugging. "Could you play one or two, anyway?"

Cronin shrugged his thin shoulders before reaching behind him for a fiddle, the bridge white with rosin. He plucked on the strings to check the tuning, ignoring the little cloud of dust. He tucked it under his chin before reaching around for his bow.

A sudden torrent of music rang out. Cronin's face was placid as a Sphinx as he used the full bow to sweep through hornpipes, slides and jigs. His style was airy and graceful, accompanied by slurs and ornaments every bit as exciting to Francis as the range of melodies played. Francis was afraid to move, lest the flow be disturbed. Cronin stopped after about twenty minutes playing.

"You probably know most of those, don't you?"

Francis swallowed before slowly shaking his head.

"Edward," he said, voice faint. "That was beautiful. I've never heard such fluid playing. And those tunes! I don't know any of them."

"Oh?"

Cronin gave a look of mild surprise.

"Do you have their names?"

"Names?" Cronin blew out his cheeks. "Now you're asking hard questions. I've a few names, I think."

"Never mind. Never mind. If you could play them slow, I might catch the air of them myself."

Cronin sucked air through clenched teeth in an expression of distaste.

"Play slow?" he asked, sounding offended. "Why, then we'd be here forever. Why don't I write them down for you?"

"You can do that?"

"Of course. Can't you?"

"Ah, no," said Francis. He hung his head a little. "I love collecting tunes but I can't transcribe to save my life."

"Well, how about you come back in a few days? I'll write down those ones and maybe a few others. You can give them any names you like."

Francis's eyes lit up with gratitude.

"Oh, that'd be wonderful. What can I bring to thank you?"

"Just bring your own flute. Share a few of your own tunes."

★★★

The next time there was tea. The cups were mismatched like the chairs but Francis did not even notice. There was also a new spark in Cronin's eye when Francis arrived.

"I must say I was surprised how many tunes came back to me," he confessed, after his wife was ushered out. "Not just Tipperary tunes but ones from all over. There were always different people passing through Limerick Junction. Because of the trains, you see. Here's a lovely one from back then."

He launched into a hornpipe in D. It fluctuated from high to low, back and forth in a rolling manner. Francis sat rapt.

"What do you think of that one?" asked Cronin.

"Didn't you play that last time as well? I think it might be my favorite."

He straightaway had his flute to his lips, playing out the opening phrase.

"Yes," said Cronin, "It starts with an opening question."

He played again the initial arpeggio.

"But the second part, the B part, has a low rumbling answer to it."

Francis essayed through the second half.

"You have it, Francis. Try a roll on that last bit. Gives it a nice finishing statement."

"That's a great one," Francis enthused. "What's it called?"

"No idea. How about we call it 'Francis O'Neill's Favorite'?"

"Ah, no. That would never do."

Cronin dipped his pen into the ink bottle on the little table and scrawled this title over the top. He handed the manuscript to Francis.

"If the right name ever comes to me, we can change it. It's a good tune for the style in my area. I knew a fellow from Donegal. Tremendous fiddling but it was so fast. If he played that hornpipe it would sound like this."

He ripped through the same tune—less ornamentation and more drive.

"Too little space for the nice stuff," said Edward with a chuckle. "Where did you say your wife was from?"

"County Clare."

"Oh well, they would be much slower then. A lot more bow if you're on the fiddle."

He started playing the hornpipe in a slower ornate style but broke off with a laugh.

"I can't even do it. I suppose the tune must fit the style. That's why you get different tunes in different places. Same as you get different styles."

He put down the violin, gesturing at the sheet music.

"Anyway, that's the way with tunes. They're all about the spot they're from and the dances and stories of that place. They generally have a first and second part. You know all this, of course. I think the best tunes are the ones where you can hear a question in the first part and an answer, or a response at least, in the second part."

"I know what you mean," said Francis, nodding.

Cronin pondered for a moment before putting the fiddle back under his chin.

"See if you can guess where this hornpipe's from?"

This tune came with a persistent question in the opening part, followed by an evasive explanation. Francis smiled throughout.

"Well, that might be from Cork," he ventured.

Cronin looked down, his hand trembling a little.

"Not Cork, no. But thank you for guessing there. The right answer would be Chicago, I suppose."

He fidgeted uncomfortably. Francis's eyebrows lifted in confusion, waiting for more.

"I wrote it," admitted Cronin, finally.

"Why, that's a lovely one."

"You're too kind, Francis. Since we've started playing these old tunes, I've had bits of reels and hornpipes in my head. That one came back out lately."

Francis clapped his hands on his thighs.

"That's wonderful. What do you call it?"

"Did you say your wife just had a child?"

"Yes, our second daughter. Caroline. We've two healthy girls now."

"Well, if a Corkman over here thinks it sounds like home, let's call it after her. How about 'Caroline O'Neill's'. A present for your little one."

"I'm honored," Francis said, solemnly. "I'll play it for her when I go home. There are four parts, aren't there? Can you do it again, so I get it?"

Cronin beamed, the nervousness of revealing his composition past. He scrawled the name onto the manuscript and took up his bow.

James My Thousand Treasures

Washtenaw Avenue, Chicago, February 1883

Edward Cronin shifted uneasily in his thin coat. The snow was coming down hard and he was frozen through.

"Really, Francis. I think we might as well give up. Are you sure the address is correct? Brighton Park is a disreputable neighborhood, in my opinion."

Francis smiled to himself, considering if he should lend the small older man his heavy blue police coat.

"Joe Cant says this man can play strathspeys like no other. That's a fair recommendation from a Scotsman, don't you think?"

"Yes," agreed Cronin in a sulky tone. "I suppose."

"Here it is."

The narrow little house was second from the corner. Francis stamped up to the door. His gloved hand muffled the knock on the plain pine.

"Yes?"

A barefoot child answered, wearing only a patched union suit.

"Good evening," said Francis. "Could we speak to Mr. O'Neill?"

The child looked them over with suspicion.

"Pop," he called out. "There're police here for you."

Francis laughed. Cronin just furrowed his brow and brushed snow from his fiddle case.

A large man of muscular build came to the door, face streaked with grime.

"Timmy, get back to bed," he said, shooing the child out of the way. His Belfast-accented voice was husky and blunt.

"How can I help you gentlemen?"

"My name's Francis. I'm an O'Neill, too. Never mind the uniform. My friend here is Edward. We're musicians. Joe Cant told us about you."

"Oh aye, I know Joe." He laughed. "Come on in so."

★★★

A ravenously thin middle-aged lady brought in a tray of teacups, her skin whiter than the china. She sideways studied the men.

"This is Kate. Kate Doyle. My mother-in-law," supplied James.

"Are you in trouble with the law?" she asked.

"Not at all, Mrs. Doyle," said Francis, rising to take the tray. "We're here for music. We've heard about your son-in-law's playing."

"Music?" she asked, voice excited. "Oh, he's a mighty man for that. We love to have music around here."

"Thanks Kate," said James. "I'll just have a few words with these gentlemen."

He steered the older lady out of the little parlor.

"Kate's an awful plucky woman," he offered in explanation as he sat back down. "She minds Mayor Harrison's children, you know. They're very taken with her."

An uncomfortable silence ensued. Cronin surveyed the simple front room with undisguised disdain.

"It's funny when you meet someone of the same last name," Francis said, breaking the ice.

"True enough," agreed James. "O'Neills are everywhere now."

"You never know. We might be related somehow," said Francis. "Anyway, Eddie and I've been gathering tunes for a while now and know a few good players around the city. We play a bit too. There's quite a few musicians on the force."

"Didn't know that."

James looked at his hands, raw and dirty under the fingernails.

"I'll be truthful with ye," James continued. "I haven't pulled out the fiddle much these last few years. The strings are gone from the old wreck of a one I have and I'm as rusty as can be. The work at the mill wears you down. Doesn't leave much time for anything else. I think Joe Cant led ye astray."

"Perhaps we should leave, Francis?" Cronin said, raising an eyebrow.

"Come on now, Eddie," Francis said. "Why don't you lend him yours?"

With reluctance, Cronin opened his case and handed over the instrument. James looked it over, scratching his head before taking up the bow.

"I'm not even sure what to play."

"Where is it you said you were from?"

"Belfast. But Banbridge, County Down originally."

"Maybe something from up there?"

He sat up straight and without further ado played a driving strathspey. Francis looked over at Cronin, a twinkle in his eye.

James paused after a minute or so.

"Augh, I'm terrible. My father would kill me for playing that poorly. I suppose you gentlemen will want to be leaving."

"Oh, no," said Francis. "I think we'll be staying."

The Proposal

City Hall, Chicago, May 1883

Francis jumped off the new cable car on Clark Street. Looking back at the departing trolley, he marveled at the pace of change downtown. His gaze settled on the massive bulk of the Montauk building a block away—the ten-storey monolith called a "skyscraper". He turned back to observe the ornate granite palace of City Hall before him, sprawling across a full city block: Randolph, Clark, Washington, and LaSalle streets. Grecian columns girded the entire complex along the second floor. He steadied his hat and checked the stars on his lapel. Time for his appointment.

★★★

Police headquarters were well buried in the depths of City Hall. Superintendent Austin Doyle's office lay beyond a pool of shared desks of uniformed men. Francis opened the smoked glass door to find the super standing by a plant. He put down a little watering can and offered Francis his hand.

"Good to see you again, Frank."

The Superintendent was a tidy man, neat mustache and hair graying at the fringes.

"Thank you, Superintendent."

Doyle waited for Francis to stow his coat and hat on the stand before directing him to a set of chairs before his large desk. Francis took the furthest chair. He was surprised when Doyle sat beside him.

"I've been very impressed with the quality of reports coming out of Deering Street. I think I told you that in the last general meeting."

"You did, sir. I am very grateful to hear it."

"I have to say that you have the best penmanship I've ever seen in a sergeant."

"I consider it an important skill, sir," agreed Francis.

"That's good. Same goes for the content. We don't have too many good writers on the force. Even with the fancy new machines, the hectograph or what have you, good writing always stands out."

He reached over the desk and pulled an official-looking document from the far side. He looked it over before handing it to Francis.

"That's why I'm transferring you to my office. I need a new assistant chief clerk."

It took Francis a moment for the implication to sink in.

"A promotion? To City Hall?"

"Of course, you'll miss your fellows at Deering Street but we need someone like you up here."

His first thoughts turned to the circle of musicians he had built up. He

236

took a deep breath.

"Thank you, sir," he said.

For a giddy moment he thought to say no, mind racing through the implications. The bookshops would be much nearer. They could still live on South Wallace so he would be near the music in Bridgeport. The two girls and the new baby boy were healthy. Those black days of the past would be over for Anna and himself.

"There's a raise," added Doyle. "I foresee great things for you in this department, Frank."

He reached out his hand again.

"Welcome aboard."

★★★

"Sorry I'm late, lads."

Francis rushed into Cronin's front parlor. James was seated uncomfortably in one of the narrow chairs. Cronin was in his usual position on the piano stool, wearing a peeved expression.

"Honestly, Francis," said Cronin. "I wonder if you value these meetings at all. You're always late."

Francis was taken aback. He took off his coat and put it on a nearby chair before answering.

"It's my new job downtown," said Francis. "I'm working late most nights."

"Congratulations again, Frank," said James in his gruff way.

Francis grinned at him, retrieving his flute from the depths of his heavy blue coat.

"How're things at the mill, Jim?" he asked.

The big man shrugged.

"I don't know. We had another strike lately. Foreman's threatening to lay us all off."

"It's early days, but I might be able to help you on that score. Ever want to be a policeman?"

James gave Francis a surprised look.

"I'd appreciate that," he replied.

"What are we playing, anyway?" interrupted Cronin.

237

Francis was surprised but lifted his flute to his lips.

"I've been thinking of this air all day," he said. "I'd forgotten it and I'm afraid I'll lose it again. Do either of you know it?"

He launched into a slow tune.

"'The Proposal'," said James, after Francis had finished. "A lovely air. My version's a bit different."

He drew his bow slowly on the first notes, dwelling on the beseeching nature of the opening phrase. Francis listened with a stricken look on his face. He lunged for James, grabbing his right arm.

"Good God," shouted Cronin. "What's got into you, Francis?"

Francis stepped back, raising his hands. James stared at him in confusion and surprise.

"I'm so sorry, Jim," he said. "I'm afraid that if I hear your version, I'll lose my own."

"Ah, that's fine," replied James with a shrug. "Why don't you just write both down?"

"He's terrible at transcription," Cronin said.

Francis sat down, burning with shame, he could not look at either of them.

"Here," said James. "I think your way goes like this."

He delivered the alternative air with ease.

"So, let me get that down."

He scribbled the notes down on a blank piece of paper, expertly scratching out quavers and crotchets. Francis watched with open admiration, abashed at his earlier outburst.

"Just to be sure, play the last part again," said James.

Francis lifted his flute and, heart racing, rendered the final phrase: the answer to the proposal. James jotted it down.

"Right. There you are."

He handed the paper to Francis.

"I don't know what to say," said Francis. "I think you just saved this air from oblivion. Or at least my version of it. My old teacher used to play it."

"I'll put my version down after it. I think yours might be the better of the two, though."

"Now I'll *have* to get you on the force with me."

"I'd not thought music transcription was a skill many policemen needed," joked James.

"Gentlemen," announced Cronin, standing up. "I think you should
go now."

"What? Why?" asked Francis in amazement. "We've only just started."

"I am tired of this. Besides, I have work myself early in the morning.
Good night."

He ushered them out of his home, the surprised men scrambling to
pick up their belongings. Outside, in the snow, they looked at each other
wide-eyed before bursting out laughing.

CHAPTER 7

The Wheels Of The World

5448 Drexel Avenue, Hyde Park, Chicago, April 1901

Francis opened his eyes to the dark of their room, the dawn light beginning to edge the drapes. He listened for a moment to Anna's soft breathing beside him. For years now he has woken early, before everyone else. She hardly stirred as he sighed and slipped out of bed. He padded across the wine-red Turkish rug to their separate bathroom, stretching and scratching himself. He liked this time, children all asleep, hours before work. He could go to his study to research music or take an early walk.

After quickly dressing, he tiptoed out to the hall. Rogers's door was slightly open. Francis peered in but couldn't make out his son in the dark. Rogers was sleeping late a lot, recently. Francis would give his daughters a hard time for that but baseball season had just started and the lad needed rest. Francis tiptoed down the broad staircase. Their front door was light oak carved with Celtic knotwork; the glass stained with similar patterns. He allowed himself a quick smile as he slipped on his shoes, admiring the patterns in the dim morning gloom. For Irish gentry long ago, a door such as this would welcome family, friends and musicians.

He let the door click quietly shut behind him. The sun was a bright beacon at the end of 55th Street. The shadow cast from the turret at the corner of their home bisected the dew on his lawn. His Irish architect had suggested sneaking an ancient Irish round tower into the design, knowing Francis's inclinations. Few spotted the reference. Birds called to each other in the early morning quiet. Francis set out for the University.

★★★

Still early, few scholars were about the campus—all gothic-arched buildings infested with ivy and gargoyles. Francis reflected, as he often did, on how wonderful it would be to quit the police and take up life here. He had enough money coming in from real estate that he might even do it in another couple of years. He stopped himself. Did he really think the university would accept him in any aspect other than senior police officer?

He had left school at sixteen. They wouldn't even take him as an undergraduate. Nevertheless, he attended every public lecture he could, particularly the scientific ones.

Eight years ago, when the hullabaloo of the nearby Columbia Exposition was at its height, he often escaped to one of University's lesser frequented quadrangles. Seated on a stone bench, he snatched what time he could to scratch down notes about Irish tunes and their history. It was rare that any of the millions of visitors would venture in here away from the classical splendor of the World's Fair or the more enticing delights of the nearby Midway Plaisance.

He had nearly been put in charge of policing the whole thing. *Thank God he had escaped that.* The press had gone to town on police involvement, with criminals and prostitutes plying their trade during the fair. Even Chief Brennan's otherwise impeccable reputation had been tarnished. No doubt there would have been efforts to taint Francis's name as well. In the end, Brennan had made Francis his chief clerk a year later to "clean things up." It had meant back to working in headquarters away from the clean air out here in Hyde Park.

Ring-ring-ring-rinnnggg!

Francis was pulled out of his reverie by a tinkling of bells and female laughter. He jumped back from the road as a flock of cyclists clattered past—young ladies in plaid bloomers, loose blouses and jaunty feathered hats. He shook his fist after them but they paid no attention. He muttered to himself about the misnomer of these new "safety" bicycles as he watched them turn the corner on 59th and onto Midway Park. Despite himself, he couldn't help chuckling. Even Anne, his youngest and nearly eleven, had one now. He had taken a spin on it to help her learn.

He reached the broad stretch of the Midway and scanned both directions. Should he go the short route through Washington Park or the long way through Jackson Park? It was still early enough. Lots of time before mass. Why not the long way? He set out along the empty park, humming to himself "The Wheels of the World".

A lovely fiddle tune. Now what put that in his head? Maybe the bicycles.

242

Eight years ago, the biggest wheel in the world had been right over there. Anna had loved going up in it. He had been nervous of the Ferris wheel at first, although the draw of seeing the machinery up close won him over. He had imagined the thing coming loose and rolling through all the stands and concessions and out into the lake—an enormous Catherine wheel of electric Edison lights ripping through Chicago. Once up on it, his fears eased. They had marveled at the whole world below: the buildings of the Loop and the boats on the lake sailing into the sky.

Thinking of the Ferris wheel reminded him of when he sailed the world. During the Fair, that world had come here. Many places he'd been to were uprooted and put on display in Chicago: Japan, Java, Egypt. There were even Indians, some mistaken for Pacific Islanders, in the Wild West show. A funny water carrier from Constantinople came vividly to mind. Francis had tried to ask about the music of Istanbul but the man couldn't understand.

The rest of the Midway was a cod—phony stuff like the belly dancing on Cairo Street. The fake Blarney Castle had made them all laugh. The uilleann piper, Turlough McSweeny, had been good, though. Francis had helped promote him. Where was that Ferris wheel now? He read in the paper a few years ago that it was rusting away out in Lincoln park. Now, there were only a few bare patches in the Midway left to show of it. He must see if Rogers could play "The Wheels of the World" on the fiddle.

Rogers. His only surviving boy. About the same age now as Francis had been when he left Tralibane. Living in the foul smoke of Bridgeport, it had been rough for Anna and himself, losing five of their ten children altogether. But look how it had turned out. Anna was much better now, mad for dancing still. She could never sit still. She had her dark moods but not often. And how the boy looked like her, especially when concentrating to play the fiddle. How right they had been to give him her maiden name. Francis had resisted at first. In the end she got her way, of course. Francis was Rogers's middle name.

His eldest daughter, Julia Ann, was a different story. She was so like him. Stubborn, they often clashed over minor things. She never took to music, though. She had married James Mooney last year. He was a fine policeman but no good at music.

He stopped and took a couple of deep breaths—to steady himself. It was a practice he taught himself years ago up on the masts of ships. Should he sit? He noticed a tramp asleep on a bench, a bottle peeking out from the pocket of his tattered jacket.

"Michael," said Francis, close to the man's sleeping face. "Haven't I told you not to stay out here? I'll let Sergeant Walcott know I saw you."

The vagrant blinked his eyes open, pulling back in fright. Francis loomed over him.

"Captain! S-s-sorry, sir," he stammered. "I was only resting a few minutes."

"Go on now. Here. Get some breakfast."

Michael took the dollar with gratitude.

"Thank you, sir. Thank you."

"I mean it," insisted Francis. "I'll let the boys know you're out sleeping rough again. Give me that bottle. Come on."

Despite everything, Michael thought twice before handing it over.

"Spend that money on food," ordered Francis. "Do you hear me?"

"I will. Thank you again, sir. I will. You have a good morning now."

Michael scuttled off in the direction of Dorchester Avenue. Francis uncorked and sniffed the near empty bottle. With disdain he poured it into the earth beneath the bench. He shook it out and pocketed it for later disposal.

"Evidence for the prosecution."

There was nobody around to hear him. He set off toward Jackson Park.

★★★

Jackson Park was where the real Fair had been, not the Midway. The park had been filled with ersatz classical buildings larded with pilasters, gleaming in the Chicago sun. Most of it was gone now, apart from a few depressing ruins lining the edges of the dull lagoon. He caught a whiff of something rotting as he strolled along the poorly kept paths. How different from the commemorative magazine he had, full of beautiful photographs of the White city: The Peristyle, The Electrical Building, The Manufactures and Liberal Arts Building. Every building had enthralled him. Now he looked about the abandoned park in disgust, the twisted and charred remains of the Horticultural Hall in the distance. He had heard rumors it was left to burn as an insurance scam.

He picked his way through a wooded island where everything was overrun. He noticed a single stone lantern, edges blurred by rain and moss. The remains of stone steps were nearby, all that remained of the Japanese garden. He wondered who had carried off the pavilion. He had tried communication with the confused natives back then, too. Nodding and smiling and bowing, the Japanese had politely indicated their lack of understanding.

He continued through the woods. Across the lagoon a truculent flock of ducks had fouled the steps up to the Palace of Fine Arts, the one mostly intact building left. Back then, crowds had alighted from a gondola and up gleaming steps to enter the grand hall. Now, parts of the roof were caved in and whole sections of the plaster facade were missing or damaged. They should bring those fancy architects on State Street down here to see these ruins.

He spotted a movement across the lagoon, a single figure scurrying up the steps to scuttle through the great doors. *Who could that be now?* More vagrants like Michael, no doubt. Francis walked quickly around the lake to the colonnaded ruin.

★★★

"Who's in here?" shouted Francis, his words swallowed by the gloom. He thought he heard a distant repetitive humming. The fluted metal columns supporting the high vault of the ceiling were all he remembered from before. His footsteps echoed as he walked the mildewed pine floor, broken glass strewn everywhere. His truncheon would be handy right now. The only reminder of the fine paintings and sculptures were faint marks on the barren walls and floors.

A movement to his right. "Come out," commanded Francis.

There was no response. Francis walked toward the sound. In a shadowy alcove, he made out a figure on a mattress. A stack of books served as a bedside table.

"You shouldn't be in here."

The figure sat up, suddenly illuminated by a shaft of sunlight through the broken glass roof. Francis saw a prematurely balding man in a shabby suit. Recognition struck them both.

"You?"

Murdoch's eyes were red-rimmed, his pale face shiny with sweat. Francis noticed several small green vials discarded amongst his rubbish.

"The cabin boy," muttered Murdoch. "Or am I dreaming again?"

Francis went over and shook him roughly.

"Get up now. What are you doing in here?"

Murdoch struggled to stand.

"How dare you," he said, affronted. "I'll have the law on you."

"What are you doing in here?" Francis repeated.

"This is my palace," he replied. "I have built a kingdom here."

Francis shoved him back down on the mattress.

"Murdoch? You're a tramp? Why, you're no better than the fellow I shooed out of the Midway earlier. Worse, even. At least he was only drinking…"

Francis's eyes went to the discarded little bottles.

"I can hardly understand you," said Murdoch. "The Irish are particularly indecipherable when emotional."

Francis inhaled deeply.

"What happened to you, Hubert? You used to brag about all your connections. Like with Pinkerton. Last I heard you'd left real estate. Do you know I've done well for myself there? I'm a landlord to several properties now, including that first house."

The man squirmed as if struck. His blithe manner dissolved and he started sobbing.

"I lost it," he whispered. "It's gone. Thought I knew the market. How it worked. Thought I had friends."

"Stop it," barked Francis. "How I remember you. All your talk. Scorning us on the boat over while you and your father had the best cabin. Where's your fine father now? Both so superior to the rest of us."

Hubert shielded his eyes from Francis's words with trembling hands.

"Let me tell you something," continued Francis. "I don't know what dirty business you were stuck in back in New York but you left me with nothing then. Just like you, now."

Francis stepped back, stopping himself before he went any further.

"Ah, you're not worth spoiling my Sunday morning. Clear out of here now or it's Dunning asylum for you. I'll be back with my men later and you'd better be gone. Do you hear me?"

Murdoch shrank into the corner.

"What did it cost you?" asked Murdoch, his voice bitter. "To do so well in this city."

Francis froze and turned back.

"Listen to me," shouted Francis. "Clear out of here right now or you'll be sorry. Hear me? I don't ever want to see you again."

Nodding miserably, Murdoch grabbed some of his meagre belongings, including some books. Francis's chest heaved with barely contained emotion as he watched him scramble away.

★★★

Francis was nearly out of the ruined building when he heard it, high-pitched screaming echoing from the rafters. He looked around for the inhuman sound, unable to tell if it was laughter or crying.

"You'll regret this," screamed the voice. "You will. And I'll get you too. I did it, you know. I set the fires that made this city. That was all me."

Francis stepped away from the Palace of Fine Arts. He thought about going back in and hauling him down to the station but something stopped him, an odd mix of disgust, pity and fear.

Julia Delaney's

The sky was the first thing Francis noticed as he answered the front door that evening, a sunset of salmon-pink and blood-orange flecks across a deepening azure. He had to squint to make out his sister-in-law, laughing at his uncharacteristic befuddlement.

"Why, Frank. Aren't you going to let us in?" asked Julia. "It's like you were struck by lightning. The way you're standing there."

"Sorry. Sorry, Julia. I'm starting to think I need glasses." He massaged the bridge of his nose. "And… I met someone today. Somebody from long ago."

His voice trailed off. *How to tell her?* Julia gave him a perplexed look. He covered it by stepping past her to greet her companion.

"I see you've brought this reprobate along with you."

"Ah, Jaysus," said Bernard Delaney. "Go easy on me now, Captain O'Neill. I'll surrender my weapon." The prematurely balding plump man walked up to the door, a large wooden box under his arm.

"Good," replied Francis. "There are people here who'll be very glad you brought that weapon. Come on in."

He ushered them into a front room with wide picture windows and pale green velvet drapes. Mahogany cabinets held expensive china and other decorative ceramics. An ornate carriage clock adorned the mantle. Most of the party were men in their Sunday suits, alongside a couple of clergy. The sideboard was replete with pastries topped with prawns, eclairs stuffed with cream and other canapés.

"Julia," called Anna to her sister. "You're here to rescue me from all these men."

Anna was dressed in a dark ruby gown which, after they had hugged, drew her sister's admiration. Francis itched at his celluloid collar. Julia glanced back to him.

"Did you want to tell me something about who you met, Frank?"

"Later. I'll have a word later," he said before turning to her husband. "Now, Bernard. I'd like to introduce you to the Reverend Doctor Henebry. Dr. Henebry is a renowned academic on Irish music and president of the Gaelic League."

Delaney smoothed his dark mustache before taking the bony hand of a gloomy cleric.

"Mr. Delaney," said Henebry. "I've heard much of your prowess from Francis. Perhaps you can be induced to play for us."

Delaney only rewarded the priest with a complacent smile.

"There'll be music for sure, Reverend," said Francis, with a warning look to his brother-in-law. "Dr. Henebry is from Waterford, Barney. He has done many great things for reviving the language and the music. That's why I'd like him to hear you play."

He turned back to Henebry.

"Sergeant Delaney is unequaled on the pipes. That's why I had to put him on the force. I even traveled to New York to entice him from a Broadway production of *The Ivy Leaf*."

"It took the hand of his sister-in-law to seal the deal," added Delaney, with a smirk.

The Reverend smiled thinly.

"I must say," added Henebry. "I would never have expected to find so many musical policemen here in Chicago. And with such profound skill in the tradition."

"Frank's the one to thank for that," Delaney said in a serious tone. "He's done a lot for the music over the years."

"Ah, now," Francis said. "I can't help it. Chicago has so many good players like Barney here or Sergeant Early over there, I have to support them."

"But what do criminals make of it?" asked Henebry.

"They're the ones he hires," quipped Delaney.

"Very good," chuckled the Reverend. "And I hear you have set up this Irish Music Club to further the cause. A most exciting development. You must ensure that only Irish is spoken as part of your practice. In the League, we believe it crucial the tradition be kept pure and isolated from any syrupy strains polluting it—anglicized tunes like 'Killarney' for example."

Delaney bristled at this.

"How 'pure and isolated' can we be all the way out here in Chicago?" he asked.

Henebry raised his eyebrows in mild surprise.

"Well, as you are all transplanted here from peasant origins, you're the best proponents of that purity."

"Reverend," interceded Francis before the reddening Delaney could reply. "We'll get Barney to start the music in a bit. Perhaps I can introduce you to Sergeant James O'Neill, my associate and chief scribe in our collecting work. When he's not doing police work, James occasionally sits in at the Chicago Symphony Orchestra."

The cleric was steered over to the big Northerner who accepted, with good humor, the priest's amazement at another musical policeman. Francis took Delaney aside.

"Barney," he admonished. "Will you go easy on the Reverend?"

"Agh, you and your academics. I've a good mind to play 'Killarney' for him. 'Peasant origins', how are you! I'm from Tullamore."

"Alright, alright," Francis said in a soothing tone. "Listen. I need help from the likes of Henebry to get my work accepted back in Ireland. Have you any idea how hard it is to collect material all the way over here?"

Delaney blew out his cheeks in an exasperated gesture but decided against pursuing the topic.

"Any idea who'll be chief now that Kipley's resigned?" he asked.

"No idea," said Francis. "Don't care either. I stay well out of all that politicking. I've no interest in it."

"I suppose. You're not that immune to it, though. You've always managed to stay captain even when the Republicans were in. Now Mayor Harrison's back in you might be the dark horse candidate."

"I would be the darkest of dark horses," replied Francis with a dismissive shrug. One corner of Barney's mouth raised in a small smile.

"Now what's all this about my agent out in Palos park?" asked Francis, his voice a little raised.

"He's looking for too much," replied Barney. "Besides, Palos is miles outside the city. Who's going to move out there?"

"Don't be thick, Bernard," said Francis. "With the new train station opening, the wealthy are going to be flocking up there. I've already done well with that agent. Listen to him."

Barney looked away, feigning lack of interest.

"Is it a loan of money you need?" asked Francis.

Barney made no reply.

"Don't worry about it," Francis said. "I'll have a word with Julia, later. Look, sit down there and get out the pipes. Eddie Cronin over there looks like he can't wait to play on his fiddle."

With a terse grunt, Delaney turned to his plain wooden box and proceeded to extract the complicated machinery of his uilleann pipes. Often mistaken for bagpipes, the uilleann pipes were a much more subtle but temperamental instrument. Francis was distracted by the arrival downstairs of his son Rogers, wearing a black velour pageboy suit with scarlet bowtie. He stood uncertainly at the door to the busy room.

"Look how handsome you are, Rogers," exclaimed Julia. "Oh Anna, he looks so grown up."

Rogers shifted from foot to foot in embarrassment.

"Thank you, Aunt Julia," he said. "Although I do feel a bit of a fool in this get up."

"Come on in, son," said Francis. "There'll be music soon."

Cronin brought Henebry over to them.

"This is my student, Rogers," Cronin said. "He is the second youngest member of The Irish Music Club. As I was telling you, Reverend, we have a great younger generation coming through now in Chicago. Rogers here can play fiddle with the best of them. He has a very good ear and can read and write music well. *Unlike* his father."

"Oh, he's the better of his father in many ways," agreed Francis. "Top of his class at St. Thomas's and captain of the baseball team."

"Aw, Pa," said Rogers. "Stop embarrassing me."

"Nice to meet you, young man," said Henebry. "We'll have to get you over to Ireland to learn how to speak properly, though. If you're to be a proper Irish musician, that is most important."

Rogers just gave an uncertain smile. Before the Reverend could add more, a deep bass drone filled the room. The source of the sound was the seated Delaney, gazing out the window at the darkness beyond. He looked completely unconcerned at the noise his pipes were making. Without looking down, he layered the melody of the "Bank of Ireland" over the complementing drone. He played the reel in a fast slashing style, commanding everyone's attention. Dr. Henebry listened, mouth agape, his sepulchral features transformed.

After a minute, he inclined his head to his host.

"Truly wonderful playing," he whispered, enraptured. "I've not heard

251

as good since my childhood."

He grabbed the fiddle and bow from Cronin's surprised hands and straightaway joined in. Rogers smirked at the offended look on his teacher's face and ducked out, returning with a pair of fiddle cases, handing one to his teacher. Francis gave his son a grateful wink and went to retrieve his own flute from a side cabinet. Father Fielding, the other cleric present, also produced a silver flute to join in. Soon the room was filled with vigorous playing—Delaney at the head of the pack, leading them along.

★★★

Julia had snuck out to the kitchen and was filling a copper kettle at the large tiled sink, half-humming to the muffled sounds of music. Caroline smiled at her aunt from where she was playing with her sister Mary. Julia made to speak to them but they skittered off upstairs, giggling to themselves. The door opened and music bloomed before quietening as Francis closed the door.

"Sorry, Frank," she said. "I just needed a minute. A cup of tea to settle myself."

"No, no. I'm glad I got you on your own. Fill that kettle for me too and then sit down here."

She gave him a sardonic smile as she complied.

"Barney says you'll be Chief Super yet. You've already got everyone else running around doing what you say."

He raised his eyebrows, a little offended but glad to see some of her old feisty self. "Your husband has far too many opinions," he replied.

"Oh, that he does," she agreed, staring at the kettle. "I scold him when he says that. We both owe you so much."

"Nonsense," he said. "The least I could do. Will you let me give you some money for Whittaker, the agent out in Palos? I'm sure you'll do well out of the deal."

She looked over at him, with real affection.

"Oh, Francis. Why're you so good to us?"

"Someday you'll have children and I want them to—"

She shot him an angry glance and he stopped.

252

"I don't mean to interfere," he said, in a conciliatory tone.

"I know Barney is a fine player," she said. "But he's only half a policeman and…"

She looked away in dismay.

"What is it? Has he been off again?"

"Just a while. A couple of weeks. I don't know where he goes."

"Oh, Julia."

He scrutinized her, chewing on his mustache.

"I'll get his superior to give him a telling to."

"He'll know it was you," she replied.

"Good. Look, you wanted to know why I help you? Remember the boat out here? The *Emerald Isle*. Seems like a million years ago, doesn't it?"

She nodded and frowned at him.

"I met him again," whispered Francis. "Him! Don't tell Ann. Promise. He's truly a sorry figure now—a vagrant with crazy delusions. I nearly had him arrested."

"Why didn't you?"

Her voice went as quiet as his, color drained from her cheeks.

"I don't know," he admitted. "I think we're all better off with him out of our lives. Who knows what he might say down at the station? Or what the press might make of a madman like that."

He took a deep breath and exhaled.

"I'd rather the children knew nothing of how we came here," he continued. "We've a good life over here, now. Don't we, Julia?"

Julia stared, noticing for the first time how gray he was getting. The kettle started a shrill complaint before she could respond.

The Chieftain

Washtenaw Avenue, Chicago, April 1901

Francis and James sat down in James's cluttered front parlor, table covered with notebooks and papers. Flute and fiddle were not yet out of their cases.

"What do you think of that?" asked Francis, thrusting a letter in front of James.

James scanned the paper, eyes widening.

"*Given the quality of the sample you have provided,*" James read aloud. "*Lyon & Healy would be delighted to undertake the publishing of this encyclopedic work.*"

Francis basked in the excitement of James's voice.

"They went for it!" erupted James. "I should never have doubted you."

"Not everything they publish has to be popular music," said Francis. "Besides, I've known Healy a long time. Bought enough music books there down through the years."

"Well done," said James, voice serious. He stood up and extended his right hand.

Francis took it, beaming at his friend.

"They've a real eye for proper editing, mind," said Francis. "That's all thanks to you. And I'm still no good at the transcription."

"Ah no," said James, shyly. "If you hadn't—"

"Never mind any of that. This calls for a bit of celebration."

"You're right," said James. "Kate," he called out. "Come on in for a minute. We've a bit of news."

James's tiny bird of a mother-in-law appeared in an instant. She had a bottle of Powers whiskey in one hand.

"I couldn't help hearing you lads shouting from the kitchen," she said. "Sounds like you heard the good news before I even had a chance to tell ye."

The two men looked at each other.

"How did you know about the publishers?" asked James, perplexed.

"Publishers? What? Don't you mean the Chief Superintendent job I talked to Carter about?"

"Carter?" Francis asked sharply. "You mean Mayor Harrison?"

"Oh!" she said, a hand covering her mouth. "Maybe I've said too much."

"Sit down there, Kate," said James, taking the bottle. "I'll make tea for all of us and we'll sort this out."

★★★

"I paid him a visit the other night," said Kate. Her blue-veined hand shook a little as she held her teacup, but her voice was firm." I don't get to see his children as much now. Since I've retired." She said the word with distaste.

Her interlocutors regarded her in stony silence.

"Anyway, I had to wait in the front hall to see him. Joe Malony's the officer assigned to guard them. He's there full-time since poor Carter senior was killed…" She took a sip and continued. "What an amount of dust there was in that front hall. I don't know what kind of yoke he has cleaning the place, but they're doing a terrible job."

"Kate," asked James. "What did you say to the mayor?"

"I only told him that Francis was the best man for the job. He had Francis on his list, you know. It was tucked away inside the pocket of his dinner jacket. He agreed you were a smart man. Ninety-nine percent on the civil service exam, highest score ever. But he said you had no political backing. And your report on the railway strike was considered *too* honest."

"I always wondered about that," murmured Francis.

"Go on," urged James.

"I said to Carter that I knew he wanted to be a reform mayor: clear out those boodlers from city hall. I said Francis was as straight a policeman as you could meet and a great friend to our family. He just kept nodding, like he does. Then I told him about the book ye're writing."

"You told him about the book?" exclaimed James.

"He loved the idea. Sure, I used to sing Irish songs to him when he was small. His father was mayor then and never home. Only way to get him to sleep. Anyway, like I said, he thought a police chief who wrote a book of Irish music was a great idea. It would go down well with the Irish voters he said. I told him straight, before I left to see the grand-children, you make sure and pick Francis O'Neill."

James covered his face with his hands, afraid to look up.

"So, I'm sure that's what he'll do," she concluded matter-of-factly.

Francis's eyes were closed as he shook with silent mirth. It took him half a minute to recover.

"I think you'd better get that bottle out, James" he finally said. "We've double cause for celebration."

★★★

Anna was at the front door when Francis arrived at the gate late next day.

"Frank," she called to him. "There was a messenger. With an official letter."

She stood there, breathless with curiosity and still in her Sunday frock. Wisps of hair escaped from under her disheveled bun.

"Oh?" he asked, walking up the path. "Where is it?"

She handed it to him.

"Did you read it?" he asked, frowning at the official stationery.

"Does it look like I read it? Isn't it still sealed? John Markham from Headquarters delivered it personally. Said no one was to read it but you."

The sides of Francis's mouth turned downwards as he studied the letter.

"Aren't you going to open it?" she asked, her irritation plain.

"Can't do that until I'm alone, can I?"

"Frank!"

"Look. I'm just back from the farm. Let me change out of these dirty duds and I'll open it in the library."

She gave him a thunderous look but said no more, departing for the kitchen.

★★★

The letter was watermarked paper, stamped in gilded ink with the seal of the office of the mayor. It instructed the recipient to be at the mayor's office at 5 p.m. tomorrow, 30 April 1901 and to come with bonds for the office of General Superintendent of Police.

It is recommended that you procure said bonds from a reputable bonding company instead of personal friends. Keep the news of your appointment to yourself, the ability to do so is a factor in the fitness of a man to fill a position of responsibility.

Signed Carter Harrison II

The document concluded with the Mayor's quick scrawl of a signature. Francis tut-tutted at the sloppiness of his hand, before chuckling to himself in wonder as he locked the letter into his desk's top drawer.

★★★

"What in the name of God was in that letter?"

256

Anna was brushing her hair by the vanity table, looking at him through one of the triple mirrors.

"Nothing," said Francis, closing the bedroom door behind him. "Nothing!"

She slammed down the silver-backed brush.

"How can you say nothing? Are you in trouble, Frank?"

Her frown was furious.

"Maybe," he said, laughing softly.

She pushed past him with an angry glare before dropping into the bed. She pulled the covers up, turning away from him.

"Fine," she said with an acid tone. "Put out the light then."

Hide and Go Seek

Harrison and Clark Street, Chicago, September 1901

Francis pulled his collar up to conceal his face. He already had the brim of his battered slouch hat—a relic of his shepherding days—as low as it would go. He was wearing heavy spectacles and the plainest clothes he could find. It wouldn't do for the new Chief Superintendent of Police to be seen frequenting Chicago's notorious Levee district. He snorted to himself. He knew the place well enough. He had traveled beat here several years back. But even he had steered clear of darker corners like Little Cheyenne.

With an expert eye, he studied the gambling halls, penny museums, gin saloons and brothels arrayed before him. Which were the expensive five-dollar houses versus the cheap joints? He knew which were supported and frequented by powerful aldermen and which were panel houses, out to con the Johns wandering around the street alongside him. A pair of pale skinny girls, their faces painted garishly, tapped on a large front window nearby, beckoning him with bright haranguing voices. He took them in with quick sympathy. He also knew well the signs of heroin. He walked on, past a small gang of leering young men eyeing the girls. Mashers, that was the name for men like them. He'd have cleared them quick were it not for this disguise. He gave a paperboy at the corner a nickel. taking a *Tribune* from him.

"Keep it," he said to the boy's fumbling for change. Francis ducked into a dark saloon and sat at the back, massaging under the brim of his unfamiliar glasses before scanning the front page.

Chicago Daily Tribune

Volume L.X.- NO. 254 WEDNESDAY, SEPTEMBER 11, 1901- 16 PAGES

EMMA GOLDMAN IN LAW'S GRASP
ANARCHY'S HIGH PRIESTESS, ARRESTED YESTERDAY IN CHICAGO
M'KINLEY SAFE: FAST RECOVERY NOW EXPECTED
High Priestess of Anarchy, Who, Czolgosz Says, Was His Inspiration, Found in Hiding in Chicago
FACES OFFICERS CALMLY

He studied her photograph in amazement. She looked like an older Zakiyah.

"She'd better be calm with Schuettler giving her the third degree," said the man who sat down across from him.

"What?" was all Francis could say, looking up in surprise at his mind-reader. He was annoyed he hadn't noticed the man reading over his shoulder.

"Didn't mean to startle you. Part of the job."

The man's shabby clothes belied his cultured accent.

"What do you have for me?" asked Francis, looking around with care. The decrepit tavern they had picked was mostly empty. He didn't like having to meet here but the man was undercover.

"Not much from our last meeting," said the spy in a business-like tone. "There was another incidence of drugging at Michael Finn's. I would suspect the proprietor for sure this time. The victim was from a well-off family and it will be kept from the press."

"I'll follow up on it. What about this?"

He indicated Goldman's photo on the front page.

"Colonel S. thinks there is more to the current Anarchist revival than meets the eye. That group hasn't been the same since the Haymarket bombing."

"He's right," agreed Francis. "So what's behind it all?"

"I think if you look closely you might have an idea."

Francis narrowed his eyes.

"What exactly does that mean?"

His companion sat back and shrugged. It was hard to pinpoint his age. Francis could have guessed anywhere from twenty-five to forty.

"Corruption reigns amongst the police despite your best efforts," said the man. "This anarchy scare is a fine distraction from all that."

"Yes," agreed Francis, with a sigh. "I thought we were keeping it all in here."

He gestured at the Levee with a nod out the window.

"But the more I'm in the job," Francis continued, "the more I find out. I had to move out a senior detective lately because he was in league with a gang of safe blowers."

"We heard."

"They've started investigating me, now they know I can't be turned by 'fixing' my taxes or any number of other schemes designed to pull me into their orbit."

Francis shook his head. The man opposite him made no response but turned the newspaper around and tapped the image of the High Priestess of Anarchy.

"She's a clever one, though," he said. "Led your finest on a merry dance. Walked past them off the train disguised as a little old lady. Then they thought she was a Swedish maid when they raided her safehouse. This was after we gave them the location. Idiots. That big beast Detective Schuettler has it in for her as a result. Best thing you can do is let the wind out of the whole thing. We're certain there's no connection with president's McKinley's assassin."

"Assassin? He's dead?" Francis asked, shocked. "I thought he was recovering."

The secret service man got up to go.

"Wait," said Francis. "What about that one I asked you about before?

Anything on him?"

The man cocked his head in query.

"The one you thought connected with your death threat. Murdoch, wasn't it? Nothing. Disappeared. We're not even sure he's in Chicago."

Francis took the newspaper and opened it, shaking his head as he read the misrepresentation of his latest press statement. The other slipped off without a word.

The Maid of the Golden Tresses

Harrison Street Police Station, Chicago, September 1901

"Chief O'Neill! We weren't aware you were coming." The desk sergeant's voice had a guilty ring to it.

"Where is she?"

"Who?"

Francis arched his left eyebrow.

"Goldman? The Anarchist?" The sergeant scrambled to answer. "Detectives Schuettler and Herts are conducting an interrogation right now. It might be best…"

"Take me down there," snapped Francis. "Who else is there?"

"No one, sir. Schuettler thought it best to remove the other prisoners given what a dangerous criminal she is."

Francis cursed under his breath, motioning for the man to lead him down the dank corridor. The cells at the back of the station were empty, heavy iron doors ajar. A metal frame cage was in the center with a small woman on a thin mattress. Schuettler, a large hulk of a man, stood smoking against the far wall.

"Hey," he called as the sergeant opened the iron-barred door. "We're not done here yet."

"Oh, I believe you are, Captain."

His cigarette dangled loose when he saw Francis.

"Chief," he said. "We'd no idea you were coming. This is the bitch of an anarchist."

"You're relieved of this case as of now, Schuettler," said Francis. "Along with Herts, wherever he is. I hold my detectives to a high standard and smoking in the cells is not allowed. Not to mention heavy-handed interrogations. There'll be disciplinary procedures to follow."

Smoldering cigarette on the ground, the detective swallowed and licked his lips. For a moment, Schuettler straightened his big shoulders, threatening. Francis gave him a dark look.

"Yes, Chief," he murmured. "I'm sorry. I'll have a report for you soon."

"See that you do. Now clear out, both of you."

Francis took the iron ring of keys from the retreating desk sergeant. Schuettler moved his heavy bulk out of the cell, sending a rat scurrying as the door clanged shut. Without a word, Francis opened the cage, bringing a chair. He left, returning with a pitcher of water and a cup which he filled and handed to her. She gulped it down before looking at him with wide eyes.

"I never would have expected such treatment from the chief of police," she said.

There was a slight Eastern European tinge to her words. He sat on the chair with a sigh.

"Emma, isn't it? I apologize for the behavior of my men. I'm not here to bully or coerce you. Perhaps I can even help."

"I doubt that," she said. "I'm pretty certain you police wish to have me hung for the attempt to kill the president. I've been held here illegally. I don't know how many days. Not allowed sleep and threatened brutally."

There was fire in her voice, despite the weariness. Francis was amazed by the resemblance to the girl he met in Alexandria thirty years ago. He couldn't speak for a few moments, lost in thought of how different life might have been. She observed his distant silence with keen interest.

"Chief O'Neill?" she asked with a little laugh, despite herself.

He coughed, pulling himself together.

"Why don't you tell me everything?" said Francis. "Your connection with this man Czolgosz. Your movements since the assassination. Just give me facts. Spare me any speechifying."

She hesitated, took another sip of water, then poured out her story. Francis would find out later it was mostly true, she only left out one or two friends who had hidden her.

"Unless you're a very clever actress, you're certainly innocent," he said with finality. "I think you are innocent, and I am going to do my part to help you out."

She stared at him with disbelief.

"Why?" she asked. "I thought all you police were rotten through and through—lapdogs to your capitalist masters."

He shrugged off the insult.

"We're not all lapdogs," he said, standing up. "I'll see you're moved out of this cage to somewhere more comfortable. And make sure you get better treatment."

He studied her tired face for a long moment.

"Remarkable. You remind me of someone I knew a very long time ago."

He stopped, as if to say more. She arched her eyebrows, waiting.

"Take care of yourself," was all he could mutter.

He retreated from the dingy room in a hurry, locking the main door behind him.

The Little Red Hen

City Hall, Chicago, April 1902

Francis's carriage pulled up to the back entrance of city hall, he stepped out and stretched, massaging his stiff left shoulder.

"Chief O'Neill," called out a voice, recklessly running across the busy street from a coffee shop where he had been waiting.

Francis's heart sank. He nodded to his driver to carry on.

"Finley Peter Dunne. *Chicago Tribune*," said the man, catching his breath. "We've met before."

Francis's brow furrowed; the reporter looked familiar.

"I certainly know who you are," said Francis. "but I don't recall meeting."

"Thanks, Chief. It was years ago. I was only a cub reporter and you were, I don't know, a regular cop back then. We were on this packed tram and the operator was humming away—some old song from Ireland. You grabbed him and stopped the tram! I thought you were going to arrest him.

Instead you made him sing the full thing slowly so you could get the song."

"I don't remember that," Francis said with an apologetic shrug. "I was only junior then. Speaking of which, why is the *Tribune*'s senior columnist out interviewing innocent policemen."

"Normally, I wouldn't," Dunne admitted with a grimace. "The papers are gone crazy over this Larken case…"

"Unlike some, I actually like your 'Mr. Dooley' column," interrupted Francis. "At first I thought you were mocking us but when you read between the lines."

"Yes?"

"Well, Dooley can say what he likes with that thick brogue."

Dunne smiled, taken aback. Francis turned towards the rear door.

"Sir, I didn't come to talk about my column."

Francis turned back with a wry smile.

"The Larkin case?" asked Dunne. "Any breakthrough on that?"

"No. Nothing."

"But you had a tip. You met Sergeant Dillon back of the yards."

Francis gave him a look of blank surprise.

"The stockyards, sir."

"I know where the yards are," growled Francis. "Used to work there. How did you know?"

"Can't reveal my sources, sir. Care to make a comment? Any arrests made?"

"No. No arrests."

"Can you tell me anything?"

Francis noticed another reporter hurrying over to them. Fuller from InterOcean. Francis eyed them both balefully.

"The call was unrelated to the case you mentioned. It was… a personal matter."

"Another investigation into police corruption?" piped Fuller, as if he had been there all along.

Francis took a deep breath to keep his temper in check.

"The call from Sergeant Dillon?" pressed Dunne. "My source said you were in an awful hurry to meet him."

Francis laughed a quick laugh. Fuller and Dunne looked at each other.

"You want a scoop, Dunne? The truth is Sergeant Dillon found a 93-year-old lady who had a tune. She got it from her grandmother. Neither of us knew it. A wonderful piece."

Fuller gaped at him.

"A *tune?*" was all he could say.

"Yes," replied the Chief, with a smirk. "'The Little Red Hen' is the name of it. I have the notes here."

Francis retrieved a small notebook, opened to a page with that title. Like a secret cipher, if was filled with a jumble of letters A through F. Dunne laughed at the other reporter's confusion.

"Well, I think I have my story," he said. "Thank you, Chief."

The Book Of Rights

City Hall, LaSalle Street, Chicago, 1902

As chief, Francis found it wise to arrive early to his office, before anyone else if possible. His first task generally was to sort through a mountain of crises from the night before. This morning he encountered only a solitary janitor as he hurried along the high-ceilinged corridors. Walking towards his section, he noticed a young man fidgeting by the door. His hair shone from being slicked down with pomade, eyes tired and puffy.

"Mac! Everything alright? What brings you in here? And so early?"

John McFadden held his bowler hat before himself, rotating it in consternation.

"I wanted to see you privately. In your office," McFadden said, voice quiet and guarded. "Please, Chief."

"What could you need that we can't talk about out here?" wondered Francis aloud. "Besides, I probably have a number inside who are waiting on one thing or another. I'm trying to have council up patrolmen's pay to $1,100 a year," he added in a lower voice. "They don't like it at all but Harrison's on my side."

McFadden only shook his head in response, giving the chief a forlorn look.

"Alright then. Follow me through."

Francis led him through three already busy rooms, answering several questions on different issues before reaching the security of his private office. As Francis closed the door behind them, the younger man let out a sigh of relief.

"Chief," he said. "I've lost the third part of 'Paddy in London'. Remember you gave it to me last night? I had it all when I went to bed. When I got up this morning, all I could remember were the first and second parts. Could you? Could you whistle the third part for me again?"

Francis's laughter was full of relief.

"All that cloak and dagger, just to get a tune?"

"It's killing me, Chief. I was sure I had it all."

"Sit down there and let me think."

Francis cleared the dossiers off his desk and sat down. It took a moment of humming to come to it, before whistling the whole tune out loud. Mac nodded along, eager recognition dawning on his face.

"Ah! That's it. A great jig it is. Is there any tune you don't know, Chief?"

"That's another one for the book for sure," Francis said with a satisfied smile.

"How many do you have now?"

"About eighteen hundred, we reckon. Still a good few to make a final decision on."

McFadden gave a low whistle of appreciation.

"How'd you manage to gather them all?"

"Years of careful work, Mac. I'll make sure 'Paddy in London' makes it in. I'll have to check with James O'Neill but I'm fairly sure it's there. Jim probably has the dots somewhere if you want them."

"The notes? Naw. They'd only confuse me."

He whistled back the last bit again.

"Aye," he confirmed. "I have it."

Francis leaned back in his chair, leather creaking.

"That was a great concert last night," said Francis. "Powerful playing from yourself and Sergeant Early."

"Thanks, Chief. We're doing well together as a duo. It was good of the

265

Irish Music Club to put us on stage."

"And my brother-in-law came on afterwards. What was that he was grousing about at the start?"

"Oh, we got Delaney nicely," McFadden said, flashing a wicked grin. "He has a 'pet' jig he likes to play first. He calls it 'My Former Wife'."

Francis arched a concerned eyebrow. The fiddler shook his head, chuckling.

"No, no. It's fine. Only Early and I played it right before he was to be on. Oh, he was rotten over that."

Francis said nothing, his mind elsewhere. He stood up and reached into a side cabinet to retrieve an expensive looking box and opened it on the desk. Inside were heavy brass plates wrapped in dark felt.

"The front stamp for the book," Francis said. "Came in from Lyon & Healy just yesterday."

"Ah, that's incredible," marveled McFadden. "That's going to be some book."

"Yes. I want it to be special. Do you see the Celtic scrollwork around the edge?"

"It looks beautiful, Frank. Never seen a cover like it."

"Beautiful, yes," Francis said with a pleased nod. "I want it to be the most beautiful book of Irish music ever. Even if it's going to cost me more than I'll make," he added with regret. "A terrible amount of work has gone into it. Back and forth with the publisher too. They had no idea what to make of the Gaelic font and reversed a few letters. Then there was the checking of keys and settings. Terrible amount of work…"

He traced the intricate engraving, lost in reminiscence.

"When they thought you were murdered, back in February," McFadden ventured. "It was working on the book ye were."

"Don't tell anyone this," said Francis in a low voice. "That news story was great promotion for the book. Whoever wanted me dead did us a favor. I used to try and keep our music work secret but didn't have to after that."

"Huh, that's true," McFadden said. "And remember we had that meeting about your book in the Music Club a while back? Did that help at all?"

"The 'inquest committee'!" Francis replied with a derisive snort. "That's what Jim O'Neill and I called it. No matter what we put forward to you lot, it never pleased everyone. Barney Delaney and Cronin were the worst, bickering over everything."

There was a hard edge to Francis's voice.

"Ah well," said McFadden, standing up. "That's musicians for you. They only agree when they're playing. I've no doubt but Messrs. Francis and James O'Neill will finish it with style and I look forward to buying a copy. Well, I'd best get on to work. Better warn my department about this pay windfall your cops are getting."

"You can keep that to yourself for now," warned Francis. "And Mac…"

He whistled the first half of the ending of "Paddy in London" and paused, waiting.

McFadden frowned for a second before completing the melody with a flourish.

The Midnight Dance

Washington Park, Chicago, July 1903

It was Anna's idea to celebrate with a picnic. Even their house wasn't big enough for the proposed crowd and the park, with its new bandstand, was not far. Julia, Rogers and the girls pitched in to help with the preparations. It was to be a celebration of their youngest daughter Anne's thirteenth birthday, his reappointment as chief and the book's publication.

O'Neill's
Music of Ireland
Eighteen Hundred and Fifty Melodies
Airs, Jigs, Reels, Hornpipes,
Long Dances, Marches, Etc.

Many of which are now Published for the first time
COLLECTED FROM ALL AVAILABLE SOURCES
AND EDITED BY
Capt. Francis O'Neill
Arranged by
James O'Neill

CHICAGO
LYON & HEALY
1903

Francis lifted the brand-new book, admiring again the gilt on the engraved cover. He remembered as a child being given a present of a leather-bound encyclopedia—the thrilling magic of it. He opened to the title page and inhaled. That new book smell was from his book. The sumptuous Celtic knot-work was reminiscent of the Book of Kells. He'd had to show the perplexed illustrators his copy of *Illuminated Celtic Art* as guidance. Best of all, he had never held a book quite like this. He opened to a random page, admiring the numbered titles.

1182	*Aisling Paidin Ui Riain*	PADDY RYAN'S DREAM	McFadden
1183	*Ceol Annsa Gleanna*	MUSIC IN THE GLEN	Cronin
1184	*Casog An Sitmaor*	THE PEELER'S JACKET	F. O'Neill

Then the notes. Lines and lines of notes like the tracks out of Union station. He smiled to himself at that idea. These tunes were Pullman cars of the finest quality. Jim and himself had made sure of that.

PART II: FIRE

Beyond the trees, the sound of music and laughter wafted over the chirping of crickets. Francis had slipped back to where the abandoned picnic was laid out, egg salad sandwiches spoiling in the late evening heat. From the deepening gloom emerged the green pulsing of fireflies. He had never seen so many out together, their fairy lights almost in tune to the human music. He listened to that far music. They were no longer playing tunes from the book. It was something modern he couldn't abide.

The sun was no longer visible above the trees of the park's broad lake. Holding the book, a sudden fear gripped him. This was all too good. The book will fail, the railway strikes will get out of hand, something worse will come. *It always did.* Generally, after the best of times. Remember that first night in New York? He had just met Anna and then lost her, along with all his money. Or when he was herding on the mountains. That mountain valley had looked like paradise but he fell down, the wind knocked out of him. He was distracted from his dark thoughts by a slight figure appearing from the trees.

"There's the birthday girl," he called, standing up.

Anne rushed to him and gave him a hug. Oh, these modern children of his. He hugged her back, glad of the distraction.

"Thirteen now," he added. "Not Daddy's girl anymore."

She made a face.

"I'd rather not be thirteen. It's boring."

"Really? Well, never mind. Between you and me, you'll always be my baby."

She smiled, plopping down onto the rug.

"Can you tell me one of those fairy stories, Pa? Like you used to."

"Which one?" he asked, grunting a bit as he sat down on the rug.

"I don't know. Those ones about them taking babies in revenge for people stealing fairy songs."

"What made you think of that?"

"Maybe all the music tonight."

Anne could be a bit odd sometimes. He despaired at how they had indulged her as the youngest. Her older sisters resented it.

269

"Not sure I can remember those ones anymore. Where's your present?" he asked to change the subject.

"The fiddle? Rogers has it."

"Does he? Thought he might. Don't you like it?"

"I do. I just need time to get used to it."

Her tone was unconvincing.

"Why don't you get your brother?" Francis said. "Have him bring it here and we'll try it out."

She got up with a dramatic sigh and ran off. The fireflies swarmed and pulsed over one bush by the water's edge. He watched their slow fireworks, mesmerized. What tune could you put to that? He rooted around in the picnic basket for a candle and a Lucifer. With a flare, he made his own little circle of light. He leafed through the book for a tune she might like on the new fiddle. Nothing too difficult. Rogers would run it off quick for them. He cursed and slapped at his forearm—bloody mosquitos. Never had the cursed things in Tralibane. No fireflies either though.

"Hi, Pa," said Rogers. "They're looking for you back at the bandstand."

Francis motioned to his son to sit beside him.

"They can wait. What happened to your sister?"

Rogers rubbed at a mosquito bite before sitting down.

"Ouch. They're bad tonight," he muttered. "Anne said you wanted me to play a tune with you."

Francis sighed and shook his head.

"What do you think of her fiddle?"

"It's a nice one. Bright tone."

He smiled at the young man's features glowing in the candle's dim glow. Of all his children, he could only speak with Rogers as an equal. It must be because of the music. He might look like his mother but he sounded more and more like his father.

"Are you pleased with the book?" asked Rogers.

"Pleased?" asked Francis. "My whole life…"

He stopped, taking a deep breath before continuing. He had to stare at the fireflies' silent dance to stop himself crying.

"My whole life, I've wanted this. Earlier, I was sitting in the dark just reading the title over and over. Years ago, I was about your age, I'd a chance to study in Cork. 'The College of Art and Design' I'd say to myself over and over. I was maybe too young to be admitted, just like you at St. Ignatius."

Rogers sat still as he could, surprised by all the revelations.

"I never knew that, Pa. Why didn't you go there?"

"My father couldn't afford it. I don't really blame him. He had it a lot harder than I did and never understood why anyone'd want more schooling. So I left my little five foot shelf of books…"

"And went to sea!"

Rogers finished the sentence in excitement. Francis looked from the fireflies to his son.

"You never tell us about that much."

"Oh, there's not much to tell. Main thing is I met your mother and ended up here in Chicago. And this."

He held up the book.

"I want to be a writer too, Pa," blurted out Rogers. "Just like you. When I graduate college, I mean. All those tunes. And all the stories you've told me about them but haven't put in there. We could put those stories into another book."

Francis blinked. He swallowed, unable to trust himself to speak. All he could do was point to a tune in the open book. Rogers took the fiddle under his chin.

"I'll think about it," Francis finally said. "For now, play that one."

His voice was gruff with emotion. In the candlelight, Rogers squinted down at the indicated page—a quick smile before playing with fluid grace.

The Fairy Queen

Iroquois Theatre, Randolph Street, 30 December 1903

The much beloved Eddie Foy applied the white pancake with professional ease. The tiny straw boater of his alter-ego, Sister Anne, was pitched at a saucy angle over his right ear. A pink ribbon accentuated, rather than hid, his balding pate. He sighed. One had to make a virtue of necessity. Reaching for rouge for his cheeks, he spotted a stagehand in the mirror.

"Sidney, darling," he called. "Could you get a seat for my Bryan down in front?"

His six-year-old son looked up from under the elaborate wig he had been given to play with. Sidney made a face in reply.

"I saw that," warned Eddie. "Go on now. The head manager promised him a spot up front."

"The house is packed," complained Sidney. "Won't be any spare. He'll have to go in standing. Way up at the back. There's about two thousand out there tonight."

"Don't you worry," tittered Eddie to young Bryan in his sweetest Sister Anne voice. "You won't be going up there, my dear. Go with Sidney now, sweet darling. Daddy's got to go on with big bad Bluebeard in a few minutes and doesn't want to get nice Sidney in deep trouble for not helping out."

The last was said with a menacing growl, making Bryan laugh.

"Not promising anything," said Sidney, flouncing off with the child.

"Bitch," remarked Eddie to his retreating form as he made a pout to apply crimson to his lips.

★★★

Although considered the finest theater in the country—old world palace foyer replete with marble and plate glass—backstage at the Iroquois was typical chaos. Eddie winked to Bryan who sat on a little stool by a switchboard in the wings. He was going to give Sidney hell for that. His little boy looked excited though. Gales of laughter came from out front as Bluebeard's ugly wives tiptoed around him. The house sounded packed even from here. It was always hard to tell with the lights shining in your eyes. Eddie gave a skeptical glance to the rows of painted scenery drops at the rear of the stage. He always expected them to come crashing down on someone. The audience would probably have eaten that up. Nothing could go wrong with a house packed with young children and their mostly female chaperones. Oops! There was his cue. Time to berate the old tyrant's simpering wives.

★★★

Eddie was half into the elephant costume when he heard yelling.

"Are the hands fighting again?" he asked Robert, barely recognizable in black-face for his role as Mustapha.

A loud crack reverberated through the changing room. Everyone stopped talking. Annabelle, queen of the fairies, let out a scream after a louder crash broke the silence. Suddenly, there was shouting everywhere. Eddie's first thought was for his son. He discarded the elephant legs and ran out to the stage. Sidney and another hand were beating at the scenery drops with brooms, coughing in the smoke. Flames arched up the painted canvas, devouring the gauzy scenes.

"It's no use," shouted Eddie. "Ring the fire alarm."

"There's none," yelled back the other stagehand.

"*What*? Where are the managers?"

"Bunch of them went to the saloon."

"Jesus," swore Eddie. "Go down to South Water street. There's a police-box down there, I think. Go on!"

Eddie looked around, squinting past the lights. He couldn't see much, only heard screaming and confusion. There was Bryan, sitting scared in his little stool.

"Oh, my boy."

He swept him up and rushed over to Sidney. The youth's pale face was streaked with soot.

"Take him," ordered Eddie. "I'm trusting my son with you. Use the Dearborn Street stage door. Every other door is locked to keep people from sneaking in."

Sidney gulped and took Bryan without a word. Eddie Foy ran to center stage. An octet of dancers was trying to finish their number despite the smoldering scenery behind them. Half the orchestra were standing, looking to leave. The nearest dancer jumped back in shock at the sight of Eddie in his underpants, pony-tailed wig awry. He pushed through their midst.

"Please everyone," shouted Eddie. "Try to stay calm."

The nearby floor-lights gave a grotesque cast to his painted features. His voice was barely audible above the gathering panic. From the stage edge he could see people shoving each other as they tried to escape the upper galleries.

273

"If everyone takes their time, we can all…"

His pleading words were drowned out by the shouting and screaming. Falsetto cries from children pierced the rumbling of adults running.

"There is no danger," he shouted again. "Just be calm everyone."

He gestured to Dillea, the bewildered orchestra leader.

"Play," he insisted. "Start an overture—anything. But play!"

Some of the remaining musicians began a tentative waltz. Dillea jerked his baton in time, following not leading. Eddie turned around to yell at the remaining hands.

"The asbestos curtain! Bring it down! Bring it down!"

They hauled at the ropes but the heavy curtain jammed halfway. The obstacle was the guide wire for the fairy queen's swoop over the proscenium. Eddie squinted up at it.

"Cut the wire! Goddammit. Cut it."

Dillea dropped his baton in fear, only a single violinist remained, his playing inaudible. The curtain swung back and forth as the air was sucked into the blaze at the rear. Eddie just had time to duck as it billowed out with the backdraft—a cyclone of flame erupting into the audience. The explosion singed his wig.

Eddie was the last one off the burning stage, looking back as the asbestos curtain collapsed with a thump. He took one last look into the auditorium, everywhere shadowed by fire. A young woman screamed as she jumped, or was pushed, from an upper balcony. Eddie closed his eyes in horror, the image seared into his mind. It reminded him too much of Annabelle, as fairy queen, and her big finale.

PART II: FIRE

POLICE TELEPHONE AND SIGNAL CO.

DIRECTIONS

—*—

PLACE THE POINTER
ON THE SERVICE REQUIRED
AND PULL DOWN THE LEVER

1. POLICE WAGON
2. THIEVES
3. FORGERS
4. RIOT
5. DRUNKARD
6. MURDER
7. ACCIDENT
8. VIOLATION OF CITY ORDINANCE
9. FIGHTING
10. TEST OF LINE
11. FIRE

★★★

Sitting in his office, Francis pulled a page out of the roller of his new Underwood and peered at it arms-length. The page was from his half-finished draft of the final yearly report to Council. He found himself needing glasses for reading now. It made him feel like he was falling apart. After the year gone by, why wouldn't he? He scanned his notes for the report: worst railway strike in years, the car barn bandits, designing new police badges. That last item had been an epic struggle over cost but Francis felt it had to be done. It was too easy for unscrupulous policemen to rub off the enamel and go unaccountable. He took a deep breath. At least things were quiet, now it was Christmas week. Plenty of time to get the report finished.

Markham burst in.

"Chief," he cried. "Bad fire at the Iroquois theater. Alarm just came in."

"The Iroquois?" asked Francis. "That children's show's on there, isn't it? Get Michael Dunn from the fire department on the line. Where's Schuettler?"

Markham rushed back out to the main office. Bluebeard at the Iroquois. Julia had taken the girls to see it a week ago. He pulled his heavy overcoat on and left the office. Assistant Superintendent Schuettler arrived at the far door. Francis had never fully trusted him since he'd had to reprimand him over Emma Goldman. Schuettler was capable enough though, and well connected.

"Get every man downtown over there," Francis ordered. "Markham, what other divisions can we get?"

Markham looked up from his call with the fire chief.

"First and Third would be the closest."

"Good. Do it. Get the Fifth down there too."

Francis called out to his men, halting their hurrying about.

"Anyone not on essential duty, finish up what you're doing and follow me."

★★★

Black smoke billowed out of the Greek facade of the Iroquois as Francis and his men arrived. Two fire engines grumbled loudly as they pumped water in from the nearby river. Incongruous spots of festive snow peered out beneath a layer of sooty ash. Francis found Michael Dunn, the fire chief, already directing operations by the entrance.

"Looks like a bad one, Michael," he said.

"Worst I've seen in thirty years," answered Michael. "We put it out quick enough though. Not even that bad on the ground floor. The balconies though…" He looked away and spat. Francis had never seen the usually jovial Michael look so grim.

"Going to need the help of every man you've got to clear out the bodies. Who knows how many hundreds are dead."

He bit off the last word and swallowed before continuing.

"In the balconies," Michael said. "There were stampedes with all the smoke."

"Leave it to me," said Francis. He turned to Schuettler. "You heard Chief Dunn. We'll need everyone to move the bodies. Lay them over there but don't let anyone near them. Pick the best men to guard them. Don't want any looting of effects. I'll lead a group into the first floor."

Something passed across the German's big features before he pulled his helmet down tight against the December cold. Francis turned away to gather men to himself. His actions were halted by the sight of a slight man wearing little but undergarments and a ridiculous wig. His face was streaked with stage paint and grime as he held a frightened young boy.

"Here," Francis said, taking off his coat.

"I couldn't take that," insisted Eddie Foy.

"You need it more than me," was Francis's gruff reply.

★★★

Gathering as many lanterns and stretchers as they could, Francis led his men up the broad ruined staircase to the first floor. Coughing and cursing, firemen passed them on the way down. Francis tried to push open the door but something resisted his efforts and he had to put his shoulder to it. He got it halfway open and made his way in. There was blackness along with an overpowering foul smell. He held up the lantern, covering his mouth, the light piercing the smoke. He realized it was children's bodies blocking the door: some of their faces crushed in by boots; others lay serene at twisted angles in corners; other faces were distorted from asphyxiation. Francis saw several with flesh torn from their limbs by the fury of the escaping crowd. He heard a patrolman vomiting behind him. He thought of his own children, buried under that rotten tree in Calvary Cemetery.

"Come on," he said, making his voice as steady as he could. "Be gentle. There may be some alive."

★★★

REPORT OF THE GENERAL SUPERINTENDENT OF POLICE OF THE CITY OF CHICAGO TO THE CITY COUNCIL FOR THE FISCAL YEAR ENDING DECEMBER 31, 1903

Office of the General Superintendent of Police,
Chicago, Illinois, February 1, 1903

...

Among the articles found in the theater were 195 pocket books containing $884.33. There were 33 sealskin coats and a miscellaneous lot of astrakhan, otter, mink, Persian lamb, bear skin and other fur garments

277

taken from the ill-fated play-house... Besides the articles enumerated there were 259 ladies' and misses' cloth coats, 93 men and boys' overcoats, 263 ladies' hats, 100 girls' hats, 66 mens' hats, 240 pairs of rubbers, 30 pairs of shoes and 50 opera glasses.

...

Respectfully submitted,
Francis O'Neill, General Superintendent of Police.

Rogers O'Neill

5448 Drexel Avenue, Hyde Park, Chicago, February 1904

"'The Shaskeen reel', played by Patsy Touhey." Francis marveled at the sound of his own voice coming back to him from the trumpet of the Edison cylinder phonograph. Anna, sitting on the other side of the machine, gasped with delighted surprise. This was the first one he had recorded. Patsy and himself had been half-afraid of the thing, spoiling two of the fragile wax cylinders as they tried to understand it. He resumed turning the handle and the stylus picked its way again along the wax cylinder. Touhey's intricate playing filled the library. The possibilities of the device had impressed him back in the World Fair over ten years ago but only now could he afford it. He had bought the full cabinet set. It took up a corner of his office, sleek and modern.

"I can't believe it, Frank," said Anna, after the tune finished. "It's like Patsy's here in the room playing for us."

"Quite the thing, isn't it? I'm making recordings of all the best players in town: Barney, Mac, Early. Eddie Cronin too, of course."

"Better not do it with all of them together," she said with a knowing smile. "Another fight might break out."

"So much for the Irish Music Club," he agreed. "I've had it up to here with that business. Have you heard the latest? They were fighting over whether to use green ink on the letterhead."

"Green ink? Sure, that would look awful. That club would fall apart if it wasn't for you and Jim."

Francis shook his head with annoyance.

"Keep this to yourself now but a certain brother-in-law of yours marched out of the last meeting in high dudgeon. This was after he threatened Cronin with his revolver, if you can believe that. It was all I could do to have the others swear to secrecy on it. Think what the press would have made of it!"

"Poor Julia," said Anna, almost to herself.

"I know," he agreed. "I'm beginning to regret ever introducing them to each other. Good musicians don't always make good husbands, I suppose."

"Oh, I suppose you are right there," she said with a sly smile.

He ignored her jibe and wrote Touhey's and the tune's name onto the blue case of the Edison cylinder.

"I don't know," he wondered aloud. "Why is it every time Irishmen get together, they end up fighting? If Ireland ever got Home Rule, I wonder what kind of mess they'd make of it."

"Good thing you're all Americans then," said Anna with a laugh. He grinned briefly in reply. Anna got up from the table.

"I think I'll go check on Rogers," she said. "He said his fever was getting worse."

Francis only nodded back, lost in concentration categorizing the next cylinder.

★★★

"Close the curtains, Ma," complained Rogers. "That light's too bright."

Anna stood by the dormer window.

"I just thought you'd feel better with a bit of light in here," she said.

Her son didn't reply, his athletic form writhed in pain on the bed. Concerned, she knelt beside where he lay.

"What's wrong with you?" Francis asked, appearing at the bedroom door.

"Don't know, Pa. All down my back hurts like hell."

Anna put a frightened hand on his forehead. "He's burning up!"

"I'll get Steigler."

★★★

"You must keep the room dark and provide plenty of water."

There was still a hint of his native German in the doctor's voice. Steigler was a heavy-set man who sometimes did official work for Francis. He sported prodigious mutton chop sideburns and wore a suit from the last century. They stood in the hall outside Rogers's room.

"He's not himself at all, doctor," whispered Francis. "He shouts and curses when we open the door and let the light in. What is it?"

"Mostly that is the fever. Very dangerous when it is in the spine."

"But can you tell what it is?"

"Meningitis. As I have said. Spinal."

★★★

All night long, they took turns sitting with him in the darkened room while he raved and arched his back with pain. His mother tried to soothe him with calming words while Francis fretted and paced. Their son's responses were addled and frantic. Towards morning he quietened somewhat. Francis relieved Anna and drowsed in the stiff chair alongside the bed. He had a vivid dream of taking him out to their farm in Palos Park when Rogers was small, his mother crying out to be careful. Laughing, they ran along a river—dappled sunlight through the trees like copper tossed on water.

Francis woke with a start. He hated that half-asleep feeling of falling. Early morning light seeped in around the curtains. He straightened himself, sore from the chair. What was that tune in his head? Must hum it for the boy to play on the fiddle. He looked over at Rogers, he was lying quiet. Fever must have broken. Francis stood. Best to leave him sleep. Get Ann to sleep as well. She'll be worn out with the worry. He reached out to pat his son's hand.

As soon as he felt the coldness he knew. Francis rushed to open the curtains. Cold white face. No breathing. He put his head to the boy's chest. Nothing. Boy? He wasn't a boy. He was a man. He's going to college. All the music they were going to work on. He stood up. He could not look down at his dead son. His thoughts kept stopping short. He couldn't think it through or reason it out. Wild, he looked around the room for a criminal. The one to take down who did this. *There was no one.* He gave out an animal cry, a howl of pain. He sunk back down in the chair where Anna found him, alone.

PART II: FIRE

The Redhaired Hag

Owennashingaun River, Meeting of Three Townlands, Tralibane, Cork, Ireland, 1855

Her hair was flame red, almost crimson. She stood, still as a heron, in the middle of the river. Daniel had been sent down the road to ensure the path was clear for moving cattle. He stopped short at the sight of the strange woman up to her knees in the fast water. He had never seen anything like her in all his young life. He hid at the corner by the ivy-clad bridge and rubbed his eyes, thinking he was seeing things. Last June he had hidden under the bridge's span to eavesdrop on the forbidden music of the pattern dance at the crossroads.

He blinked a couple of times to clear his vision, he had been up half the night listening to the music below stairs—fast reels and slides and polkas and the pounding of dancing feet—and fallen asleep with it all ringing in his ears. Was she out of his dream? He heard her start singing. It was a different kind of music: slow and bitter. As she sang, she cut at the water with a large pair of tarnished copper scissors, accentuating the song with each bite of the instrument. Her clothes were rags and pinned to her from the water. She must have been lying in it. He could clearly see her sharp ribs and slight breasts. She stopped her mystical actions with the end of the tune and flung the scissors to the far bank. A rivulet of urine down her scrawny thigh mingled with the river's waters.

"Hup! Gowan! Hup!" shouted his father as he urged the cattle towards the bridge. Daniel sank deeper into the thicket, too late to direct the cattle trudging past.

His father spotted her.

"Hey!" he yelled out. "I told you to clear out last night. Go on out of here now."

Her feral grin was malevolent. Daniel could not make out most of what she spat back to his father. It was Irish and he could only pick out a few of the words: *Curse* and *Fire* and *Children*. He recalled a sudden pause in last night's music—more shouting and cursing. Did he hear her voice then or had he dreamed it?

281

His father was threatening the law on her. Their dog Teague barked furiously, drowning his father's words. She brushed back her bright matted red hair and turned her back on them, stepping out of the river. She picked up her scissors, along with a small bundle, and loped off into the bushes edging the field. His father cursed and tried to quiet the dog. The cows were out on the main road now, gate unopened by Daniel. There'll be hell to pay. He decided against appearing and asking his father about the foxlike witch. Instead, he stayed hidden in the brush. Over and over, he hummed her strange tune to himself.

As We Go About Our Work

Dum-de-dum

Anna's grief was different from his, deeper but quicker. A part of her couldn't fully feel the loss of a sixth child, having already lost five small ones. For him it was the opposite. Rogers had made it. He wasn't a child anymore. He told her he would never again play music in their house, not even on the phonograph. He would give the recordings to Michael Dunn for safe keeping. No more visitors over to play either. Rogers had been the second official member of the Irish Music Club. Now he was gone, Francis wanted nothing more to do with it.

She only nodded when he told her all that. Julia took the girls away to her house, all eyes red from crying. Jim O'Neill, face as white as Rogers, arranged the removal of the body with Steigler. Mayor Carter Harrison even called to pay his respects, Kate Doyle beside him. They wore black, weary faces offering commiserations. He was told he needn't come into the office. Stay home. Recover. He could only nod in reply. There was nothing to say because nothing was going to be the same.

Dah-dee-dum

The funeral mass was celebrated by Archbishop Quigley. More than a thousand attended at St. Thomas the Apostle Church. Even the sight of Rogers's young friends as pallbearers for the black coffin could not break through the hard numbness enveloping him. Francis went to work the next day. Anything would be better than at home with all the weeping women.

282

PART II: FIRE

Dum-de-dum

He let everything return to normal, on the surface. The house was silent but always there was this tune. He found himself humming it all the time. It haunted him: in the quiet of the house, on the crowded tram, in the busy hush of headquarters. Weeks and months blurred together. He functioned in a dull efficient way: gave an address to the International Chiefs of Police; attended the anniversary of the Iroquois tragedy; saw Harrison's retirement and Edward Dunne made the new Mayor. He was there, but distant from it all. Always that air stuck in his head, allowing no other tune to enter. He had on time for any music but this one. If he could only put a name to it.

De-dah-dum

Dunne's inauguration came amid the worst days of the Teamsters' strike. Francis was called into the new mayor's office. Was he going to stay on as chief for a third term? He almost didn't hear himself reply no. The new mayor cursed him, said he needed Francis. The strike was tearing the city apart. Francis said he would think about it. Next day, he appointed Chicago's first black desk sergeant, a man named William Childs who had done very well in the civil service exam. At his interview, Childs answered an irritated "no" when Francis asked if he had any musical talent.

De-dum Dah

Francis met the mayor again and told him he would see out the strike but not a day longer. The Secret Service met Francis, warning of a new anarchist group preparing explosives should the army be called in. Dunne and his circle wanted to bring in the troops. Francis had to fight them every step of the way. He felt like a boxer in the final round, just trying to stay standing. He argued that a city as great as Chicago should never resort to the army to protect its business.

Dum-de-dum

At the mayor's office, some fancy lawyer friend of Dunne's, Clarence Darrow, openly sneered at him, accusing Francis of wanting to protect the corrupt police force. Francis just stared back. In the end it was a close thing. The army were on their way when an agreement was finally brokered. He could have done with a thousand extra men to replace the striking teamsters.

283

Like his men, Francis had worked around the clock, snatching sleep a few hours a night in his office. Even with the hollowness inside, he recognized that Dunne was setting him up to take the blame for the whole fiasco. To hell with him. When the strike broke, Francis would hand in his resignation.

The Templehouse

Mount Olivet Cemetery, Chicago, June 1905

Dum-de-dum Dah-dee-dum Dum-de-dum

De-dah-dum De-dum Dah Dum-de-dum

"Frank!"

"Hmm. Yes?"

"Stop humming that thing."

"What? Oh. Of course."

Anna gave him a stern look. It was her way of showing she was worried about him. They were in the main carriage of the funeral cortège. Behind the coffin. He couldn't help admiring the sleek black polished wood of the carriage housing Rogers's casket, silver trimmings glinting in the warm June sunlight. Once he stopped humming, he could hear the crunch of the iron wheels on the cemetery gravel. A crowd of mourners clustered around the new mausoleum before them, far fewer than attended Rogers's real funeral a year ago. It had taken a full year to design and build the crypt. The Grecian columns mimicked a temple he had seen in Alexandria. The slope of the roof came from his father's cow shed. He smiled grimly. It was the finest and biggest tomb in all the vast stretch of Mount Olivet cemetery.

The frieze beneath the cornice was deliberately left blank. His own name would be engraved there some day. When he joined Rogers.

The carriages crunched their way past the crowd and came to a halt. He helped Anna out. Barney was there with Julia. James Early and James O'Neill nodded to him, wearing their best sergeant uniforms. Francis spotted big wreaths from the college, the city, even the Irish Music Club. He wondered briefly how much they had bickered over the cost and realized he didn't care. He took in all the faces awaiting them and all the Irish names on the headstones beyond. How many of the mourners here now would be around him forever? His daughters alighted from the next carriage. Julia Ann's husband James Mooney was also there in uniform. Little Frank, their son, broke free of his father and ran up to him.

"Grandpa," he asked with excitement. "Are we going to ride the horsey?"

The crowd held its breath.

Francis swept up the five-year-old.

"Later, big man," he whispered to the boy. "Just have to finish this first."

★★★

"Well, I'm glad that's over with," said Anna. They were back in the carriage, rolling out of the cemetery.

Francis didn't reply, only kept looking out the window. All the rosaries, blessings, incense, sermons and speeches had taken nearly two hours. Their carriage turned onto Fairfield Avenue. Francis stared out at the people going about their business on the busy street. A motor car gurgled past them. More and more of the things were on the roads. He hadn't realized this part of the city had grown so much beneath the gray outlines of the distant skyscrapers.

"You know," he said to her in an off-hand voice. "I can't feel a thing. I can't…"

She reached out and touched his hand. The black crêpe of her mourning dress made a crinkling sound.

"It's alright, Frank. He's gone."

He looked at her. Angry. What was she talking about? Gone?

"Let it go, Frank. You can't hold onto him anymore."

There were tears in her eyes. Can't hold on? Had she any idea what he was holding onto these days? The chaos at headquarters he had just left behind.

Then he stopped. A whole year he had tried to hold onto him, held him tight as he could before they buried the body.

"Frank?"

She stopped, realizing that the shaking coming from her husband were big silent sobs. He angrily pushed his glasses aside to rub at the tears. She held his hand tight.

"He's gone, Frank," she repeated.

Then he was holding her. Sorry. Sorry. Sorry. For all the ones they had lost. For leaving her alone because he couldn't take the empty house. For not being able to change the huge city or the men of it. For letting it beat him. Sorry.

"Frank! Frank," she pleaded. "You don't have to beat anything. Let's go. Why don't you really retire? Retire from the force. You've given enough to this city. Jesus! We haven't had a proper holiday in twelve years."

He took a big heave of a breath, looking at her with the eyes of a repentant child.

"You're right," he said. "I'll tell this new mayor to go hang. Then let's go. Let's go back to Ireland. We can afford it."

"Yes," she agreed; eyes bright. "Visit my people in Feakle and yours in Cork. I'll finally get to see Tralibane. We'll take a ship…"

"You know they've invited me to judge a *Feis* in Cork, because of the book. And I could research…"

Their voices overlapped, both thinking aloud.

"Oh, Francis," she smiled, wiping her eyes. "You and your music."

He looked away from her, out the carriage window, not yet able to smile back. They must be around 83rd Street. A tramp was at the street corner. He did a double-take at the sorry figure outside. That couldn't be *him*?

Was it? The rim of red hair on the balding head. The ravaged pale face. The rags. He opened his mouth to ask Anna if she also recognized the specter from their past. If it were really him? But she was looking out the other window now, lost in planning their trip. Should he stop the carriage? Go back? What would the rest of the cortège say?

Then it hit him. The tune. The name of the tune. How could he have forgotten it? When he was a boy, that red-haired woman in the water sang it. He looked ahead, straightening his spectacles.

Finally, he had it.

Tralibane Bridge

Daniel Francis O'Neill (1848-1936)

O'Neill's Music of Ireland (1903)

The Dance Music of Ireland, 1001 Gems (1907)

O'Neill's Irish Music: 250 Choice Selections Arranged for Piano and Violin (1908)

Irish Folk Music, A Fascinating Hobby (1910)

Irish Minstrels and Musicians (1913)

O'Neill's Irish Music: 400 Choice Selections Arranged for Piano and Violin (1915)

Waifs and Strays of Gaelic Melody (1st ed: 1922, 2nd ed: 1924)

Author's Note

The main characters and events of *Chief O'Neill* are based on historical accounts, many related by Francis O'Neill himself in his memoirs: *Chief O'Neill's Sketchy Recollections of an Eventful Life in Chicago* [Skerrett & Lesch]. In the interest of story-telling, I have added certain embellishments. There never was a Zakiyah, although Francis did aid the Jewish anarchist Emma Goldman. Hubert Murdoch is also fictional but the person who called in his assassination, revealing to Chicago their police chief's obsession with Irish music, was never found. There are some other smaller historical fibs which I hope the reader will forgive. Historical facts are black notes on a white page, the starting point for the tune to be played.

Special thanks to: Michelle Jackson, I would never have got here without your encouragement. Stephen Kennedy, for showing me the importance of editing. Mary Lesch and Ellen Skerrett, thank you both for sharing the incredible scholarship that went into *Sketchy Recollections* and showing me around the chief's old haunts in Chicago. Particular thanks to Mary for access to heirlooms from O'Neill himself, including his private note-books. David Corrigan, for the use of his cottage in Prince Edward Island to finish the first draft. Breege Murphy, for hosting me in Chicago while I did research that involved going to a lot of pubs. Ernie Hadley, as good an editor as James was to Francis. Patrick O'Donnell of *The Celtic Junction Arts Review*, for publishing early excerpts of the manuscript. Richie Piggot, for turning my Dad into a literary agent. Finally, thank you to Andrew Russell of Somerville Press for taking a chance on my first novel.

Thanks also to: Cecelia Wilcox, Aedín Ní Broíthe-Clements of the Hesburgh Library at the University of Notre Dame, David Havelin, David Ross, Tom O'Neill, Bert Hornback, Sean Cleland, Dr. Aileen Dillane, Liam Ronayne, Maura Mulligan, Gillian O'Brien, Emily McEwan, Emily MacKinnon, Bill Driscoll and Gerard Collins.

Made in United States
Orlando, FL
26 June 2022

19171683R00178